James Evans

Trojan Submarine

 New Generation Publishing

Chapter One

Admiralty London. Early Spring 1942

Recently Promoted Commodore Douglas Warwick stubbed out his cigarette stood up and moved over to a huge map of the Atlantic pasted onto the wall. Picking up a broken Billiard cue he tapped it hard onto America,

'The biggest Convoy yet is to leave New York at the end of this Month bound for.' He moved the Cue and tapped again, 'here in London.' He paused for a second or two, 'and Gentlemen I don't think I need to remind you how desperate we are for just about everything since the Germans stepped up their attacks in the Gap. If we can't hit back before the Convoy reaches them,' he paused again 'I dread to think what would happen.'

Captain Brian Wells who'd been listening intently to the Commodore and somewhat amused by his Boss feeling the need to point out New York and London unfolded his arms, 'Commodore' he started, 'you and I have had this conversation many times before and we both agreed that sending the few ships we have available into those areas would be a disaster'

'And that of course Sir was before the latest report that most of their U-Boats have been congregating there' Commander William Briggs added,

'So who said anything about surface ships?'

'You're thinking of sending a Submarine?' Wells asked in astonishment.

The Commodore grinned, 'Three actually'

'To do what exactly Sir?'

'Find and destroy their supply ship'

'Wasn't that done a year or so ago?'

'It was indeed Brian by one Commander John Tremain on Point Ness which proved so effective by dispersing their major Wolf Pack as they were forced to make their way back to St Nazaire with hardly any fuel or Torpedoes.

1

It really ruined Hitler's day apparently and I'm hoping we can do the same'

'Which boats are you thinking of sending Sir?'

'Ursula, Umpire and Undaunted I think will fit the bill.'

'Forgive me for being a bit dumb Sir but weren't Coastal Command supposed to be taking delivery of long range aircraft to finally put this mid-Atlantic gap out of business?'

'Not for a few months yet I'm afraid'

'And I heard tell of a super Submarine being constructed at Portsmouth'

'Again not in time for this. So we need to get these boats back to Plymouth as soon as possible'

'Undaunted is already there, Umpire should be back in a couple of days, Ursula isn't due back for a week or two so will have to be signalled.'

With that the meeting ended, Captain still not convinced that three Submarines operating at just about their maximum range would be able to make much of an impact and at worst hiding amongst many dozens of U-Boats easily located and destroyed.

'So what did you think of that William?'

'I'm a bit bothered about his choice of boats Brian'

'In what way?'

'Well all of them are short hull versions, Undaunted has still got the two external tubes, Ursula has had her gun removed to give a greater submerged speed which incidentally Pitman assured me that it made so little difference he'd rather have it replaced'

'Feels a bit naked without it?'

'I guess so but what they really did desperately need was direct access to the gun platform rather than having to use the conning tower hatch'

'I don't think their Lordships are likely to sanction major design changes'

'Possibly not'

'What about Umpire?'

'She's a Group two so no external tubes to have her

accidently bobbing up to the surface from Periscope depth'

'Seriously William what do you think of their chances?'

'Knowing those three Skippers as I do' he paused, exhaled loudly and smiled, 'let's put it this way I wouldn't want to be a German Sailor aboard that Tender.'

Somewhere in the Atlantic

Lieutenant Oliver Pitman completed an all round sweep and gave the order for Ursula to Surface. The weather was fine the blue sky turning crimson as the sun dipped towards the horizon. The normal Atlantic swell brought water boiling over the casing the spray displaying a myriad of colours as it was whipped away by the strong breeze.

Oliver had been in the Navy for just under six years, the last four in Submarines. At 22 his promotion up from Midshipman had been swift, due some said because only idiots take command of Subs. In some ways he had to agree with them as he'd lost so many good friends, Jack Robinson, Peter Stone, Albert Johnson, Freddy Garson all entombed with their crews somewhere in the unforgiving cold dark depths of the Atlantic.

Able Seaman Fred Sumner struggled through the conning tower hatch with his pride and joy; a Mk 2 Bren gun which he and his close Oppo AB Michael "Ginger" Rogers, the pair branded by the crew as Fred and Ginger had lovingly stripped down and religiously rebuilt. Where they'd managed to get the ammunition from was still a closely guarded secret. He snapped it down on a mount that Ginger had expertly welded to the bulkhead.

'Sumner I'll remind you once again that if we have to crash dive that thing stays there ok?'

'Yes Sir' Sumner replied drearily having heard the same old story over and over again.

'Small boat starboard quarter Sir.'

Oliver swung his binoculars around, 'Looks like a

Spanish fishing boat'

'They seem to be waving their arms and shouting Sir'

'You speak Spanish Roger?'

'Me Sir?' The First Lieutenant answered laughing, 'not a chance.'

'I think Ginger Rogers does Sir' Sumner suggested, 'shall I go get him?'

Able Seaman Rogers cupped his hands around his mouth and bellowed at the top of his voice, 'What iz zee matter Signor?'

'Very funny Rogers' the First Lieutenant said sarcastically trying to stifle a laugh.

'Only joking Sir.' Again he cupped his hands and shouted, 'Cuál es el problema?'

The reply was shouted over almost immediately, Rogers turned to Oliver looking concerned, 'My Spanish isn't too good Sir but theirs is worse.'

Oliver reacted instantly, 'Full ahead starboard ten.'

As they turned away the forward gunwale of the fishing boat dropped down to reveal a large gun, its crew struggling to load and train it as the boat was broadside to the swell.

Everyone on Ursula's Bridge jumped as Sumner unexpectedly opened fire with his Bren gun. Small spurts snaked over the water as he found the range; wooden splinters flew high into the air as he raked the deck toppling the gun crew. He then turned his attention to the Bridge as Ginger quickly supplied more ammunition. Shards of glass flew skyward as bullets continued to slam through the flimsy structure. Flames followed by a large explosion brought the onslaught to a close. Ursula's bridge crew, ears still ringing watched as the fishing boat turned turtle and with hardly a ripple bow first slowly slip below the waves.

Sumner was grinning like an idiot; rubbing his hands together in glee he turned to Oliver who held his hand up, 'Ok Sumner well done'

'Bloody good shooting' the First Lieutenant added, 'also well done Rogers for the warning'

'No medals I'm afraid' Oliver said winking, 'but an extra tot perhaps.'

A head appeared above the hatch 'Signal for you Sir.'

Oliver bent down and took it from him, 'Well I'll be dammed'

'Problem Sir?'

'Not at all Number One we've been ordered back to Plymouth'

'Does it say why?'

'No so it can't possibly be anything good' he replied moving to the hatch, 'I'm going below to write up the log.'

The First Lieutenant called after him as he descended into the red lit control room, 'Lovely stuff Sir, bath and soft bed.'

After making the latest entry into the Log he wondered if he should've omitted Sumner's Bren gun incident, but there again who bothers to read it?

Putting his hands behind his head and shutting his eyes he leant back against the Bulkhead allowing the vibration of the two Diesels pounding away to recall distant memories.

His Sister Clara, ten years his senior married a Cornish fisherman. At twelve years of age Oliver used every opportunity to go out with him on his boat Lilly Anne always reluctantly confined to the cabin when the nets were hauled in. He smiled as above the vibration he was sure he could still hear his Brother-in-Law bellowing at the crew.

Just after his fifteenth Birthday with exams looming he was banned from taking the time out from his studies, 'Far more important than fishing,' his Sister had said dragging him off the Quay for the umpteenth time. The following Month during a terrible storm the Lilly Anne failed to return.

Clara totally consumed with grief had sat on a bridge waiting for a train, any train. That day the London to Penzance express was held up at Exeter so was running late. Was it only by chance or Heaven sent that a young Curate rode over the bridge on his bike, stopped, chatted and helped her to walk back home? He's now a Rector in a small Cotswold village with Clara as his Wife.

A tap on the door frame woke him from his thoughts, 'Yes what is it?'

The curtain was pulled aside, 'Another signal Sir they want our ETA at Plymouth'

'Ok I'll be along in a minute.' He stood up and caught sight of himself in the small mirror, 'surely that's not me' he thought as this pale grim face with ten days of stubble and sunken tired eyes stared back at him. Where on earth had that strapping nineteen year-old Midshipman gone, the one with neatly cut light brown hair, green eyes, aquiline nose constantly smiling mouth and the best Mediterranean all over tan in the fleet? He sighed pushed the curtain aside and swung through the hatch into the control room.

'Just on two hundred and forty miles Sir'

'For a bit of leeway give them twenty four hours'

'We could do it in twenty Sir' the First Lieutenant suggested

'Longer days and shorter nights Roger so best we calculate at a maximum of ten Knots.'

As the First Lieutenant predicted Ursula docked in Plymouth twenty hours later, her bedraggled crew moved into Drake for unrestricted showers, more space to move around in and good food. The down side was that with a copious water supply came Grog not the "Neaters" they were used to so "up spirits" was a bit of a disappointment for many.

Drake Barracks Plymouth

'Charlie lovely to see you again, how are things?'

'Mustn't complain Oliver but I'm bloody well going to'

'Good for you. Any idea why we're here?'

'Not a clue. You?'

'Nope.'

'Hello chaps I'm Peter Sturdy Umpire, and please' he added quickly as he shook hands, 'don't ask what we're playing it's all been said before and I'm bored with it.'

'Hello Peter this reprobate here is Oliver Pitman Ursula and I'm Charles Smith Undaunted and' he said smiling, 'I often get the same kind of remarks as you. Any idea why we've been dragged here?'

'None' Peter replied, 'was hoping you may have had a clue'

'Well I'm afraid we haven't.'

'Gentlemen thank you for your attendance' Commander Briggs bellowed as he stormed into the room closely followed by a weedy looking man in civilian clothes, 'this is Doctor Julian Short from Naval Intelligence.'

The man smiled, 'Lovely to meet you chaps. Now there is just a few things to tell you' he screwed his eyes up and scratched the back of his neck, 'um let me think, ah yes um, I guess you all know of the mid-Atlantic gap' he paused as if waiting for confirmation as none arrived he continued, 'we require you chaps to enter the area, search for the Tender and what do you call it?'

'Sink the bloody thing' the Commander interrupted shaking his head in frustration,

'Quite so, quite so. Not how I would've described it but that will do.' He looked at his watch and huffed, 'Intelligence that we've received suggests that all the German Submarines patrol with the minimum of fuel, water, food and rarely more than four torpedoes each.' He rubbed his hands together and raised his eyebrows, 'so if as the Commander said you manage to sink the bloody thing they'll be forced to make their way back to Port as soon as possible where we intend to have the Fifth Destroyer flotilla skulking about plus of course Coastal Command will be able to have a field day. He looked at his watch again and shook his head, 'now on no account must you mount any attacks before engaging the Tender, not even' he continued wagging his finger, 'if Adolf Hitler himself is drifting by on a life raft.' He checked his watch yet again, 'Elizabeth should've been here by now to explain about some new kit just developed so in the meantime are there any questions?'

'Have you a rough idea where the Tender will be?'

'And you are?'

'Charles Smith'

'Well Charles we believe it moves to a new position each day so…'

'You have no idea at the moment' Charles interrupted to complete his reply

'Yes I'm afraid that's true'

'It's a huge area for us to search Julian'

'No problem to you Smith you're undaunted' the Commander chipped in grinning broadly as though it'd never been thought of before, 'then you Sturdy can umpire the whole thing to make sure it's fair' he added laughing loudly.'

Fortunately before he could think of any further puns the door opened and a middle aged woman entered carrying a small suitcase, 'So sorry I'm late Julian but we've had a slight problem with Ursula'

'Problem?'

'I assume you're Lieutenant Pitman' she said holding out her hand, 'Doctor Elizabeth Hardy Naval Communications.'

Shaking it briefly 'I am, so what kind of problem?' He asked again

'We're fitting small devices to the conning towers but found some kind of welded structure in the way. We've removed it now so everything is fine.'

'*Sumner isn't going to be too pleased about that*' Oliver thought to himself as Elizabeth opened the suitcase.

She was very smartly dressed, greying hair tied back beneath a fawn cloche hat with a huge bow. Her frilly white blouse with suit jacket pinched into the waist and the skirt just below her knees showed off a fine figure for a Lady of her age.

'This device is an experimental underwater communication system' she said removing a grey box 'It should allow you to keep in touch during the search. This control turns up the power to give greater ranges'

'Up to what?' Peter asked,

She smiled, 'I'd love to say a hundred miles but our tests proved about ten at best'

'Surely the German hydrophones would pick it up'

She smiled again, 'You know, Charles isn't it?' He nodded, 'we do try to think of everything. Yes of course it'll be picked up but only producing short hisses and unintelligible squawks. One warning however and this is important' she stressed as she replaced the box into the case, 'at maximum range it needs masses of power.'

'What's masses?'

'Around twenty Kilowatts Peter'

'Could we be fitted with a couple more batteries to run it?'

'No time I'm afraid' the Commander cut in 'you sail tomorrow and I've decided' he paused to light a cigarette, 'that you Lieutenant Pitman will plan and lead your little band of merry men.' He blew out a long stream of smoke, 'in fact I think we shall call it Operation Robin Hood.'

The three Commanding Officers were still chatting about the Operation as they walked along the Jetty, 'The thing is its all well and good....' Peter stopped dead pointing up to Ursula's Conning Tower, 'What on earth is that?'

At first Oliver could only see a mop of ginger hair so laughed and was just about to announce it was only Able Seaman Rogers when he noticed a pole at least six foot high with what looked like a football perched on the top.

'I thought that Elizabeth said a small device'

'Well Oliver the Woman obviously has a strange idea of small.'

They all went aboard and climbed up onto the Bridge, Sumner and Rogers were still there sorting out where their Bren gun support would be able to be reattached, 'What is this thing Sir?'

'Some sort of underwater communication device Sumner'

'Well I don't like it much Sir they just drilled through the deck here' he pointed, 'and passed the cable through then bolted it down.'

Oliver inspected the base of the pole, 'I don't like it much either looks as though it's been sealed with some sort of rubber compound'

'Well one thing's for certain' Peter said firmly, 'I'm not taking Umpire out until this is sorted'

'Time I think to have another chat with Briggs.'

'So what you three are saying is that you refuse to take your Boats to sea yes?'

'Until these new fittings have been installed properly Sir that's correct'

'So Lieutenant Pitman what exactly do you think is wrong with it?'

'It'll leak like a sieve Sir'

'And you all agree?'

They nodded, 'Right I'll get Elizabeth back and then hopefully we'll be able to sort it out.'

'There is no reason at all that it will produce any leaks'

'Have you any idea of the pressure..'

'Of course I have' she interrupted crossly, 'it's all been tested'

'Where?'

'To be honest Oliver I'm not sure but I have assurance

that it'll be fine'

'May be you have but I think for the moment we're the experts and we all agree that it'll leak.' Oliver turned to the Commander 'will you give permission for a static dive?'

'Best you go out into the sound and dive to around a hundred feet and' he added turning to Elizabeth 'you can go with them'

'But...'

'No buts.'

Elizabeth feeling extremely claustrophobic in the cramped Control Room looked nervously at the two depth gauges where one read fifteen feet the other zero.

The First Lieutenant noticing her dilemma smiled reassuringly, 'That one Ma'am is the depth of the keel and the other our depth in feet.'

'She nodded wishing desperately that she'd refused to make this trip. Suddenly everyone piled down from the Bridge, the outer hatch clamped shut.

'Leave the lower hatch open Chief.'

Chief Petty Officer Malcolm Snow, a Submarine Veteran of some thirty years exhaled loudly, 'Are you sure Sir?'

'We need to know immediately if that fitting leaks.'

The Chief nodded and climbed down the lower ladder reluctantly leaving the hatch wide open.

Ursula with planes at thirty degrees gradually descended into the depths. Ninety feet was about the limit in this part of the sound but as they passed seventy-five feet there was an ear deafening pop and water started to pour into the conning tower and down into the Control Room.

Elizabeth looked sheepish as Oliver gave the order to surface. Once on the Bridge it became clear where the weak point was, not as they'd imagined at the base of the support pole but the football shaped dome had flattened and split allowing the water to break through. Elizabeth, her modesty now protected by a pair of oversized trousers climbed the steep ladder to the bridge to witness the damage, 'I'm shocked' she said shaking her head, 'I can only apologise but I was told that extensive tests had been carried out. So Gentlemen can any of you suggest a solution?'

'Perhaps not in the time left' Oliver said, 'We're supposed to be sailing tomorrow but I guess something will have to be done before then.'

Sumner who'd been listening came forward, 'Could the dome thing be made as a diamond shape?'

Elizabeth pondered on it for a second or two, 'You know I think that could work and easily be completed over night'

'So what about like a golf ball with dimples?' Rodger suggested,

'Both hopefully could reduce the pressure on it. I'll report back and see what the Boffins say about it.'

She returned within the hour to inform them that the design would be altered and the work carried out overnight, also the support pole would be filled to stop any water getting through if the dome failed.

Chapter Two

Dorfhaven Germany

Otto Steiner was in his favourite Bier Keller waiting for his Fiancée Helga to arrive. They met here each Month when their time off from shift work matched. He was a Naval Petty Officer Radio Operator and was working at a wireless station situated on the cliffs above the local Submarine Pens, she at a communication relay station in Fort Kruger a few Kilometres away. Both were fluent in English having met at a language school in Berlin just before the war.

She was late, their normal time was eleven-thirty and it was now twelve-fifteen. The door opened, he stood up but it was only his friend and work colleague Dieter, 'At last' he shouted, 'the lovely Helga has seen sense and jilted you.'

Otto sat back down and waved, 'Don't look so worried Otto I'm only joking.'

Otto had cause to worry as Helga and he had a closely guarded secret, a secret that neither would dare divulge to any living soul, she was half Jewish, fortunately on her Mother's side so her solid German family name of Gerber had been overlooked but recently even the merest of hints was enough for the authorities to investigate.

He uttered a sigh of relief as the door opened and she came in. Immediately Dieter jumped up, went down on one knee in front of her and put his hands together as if praying, 'Dearest Helga please Marry me'

'Oh dear Sir' she replied sweetly, 'I cannot for I am betrothed to another'

'Then I shall away and put myself to death.' He whined scuttling back to his table feigning great misery, 'After I've drunk my beer of course' he added mournfully.

Helga was beautiful, twenty one years old, five foot six

13

tall, shoulder length auburn hair that seem to glow at any hint of sunshine, strikingly pale blue eyes, luscious lips, pale complexion with a natural blush to her cheeks and a superb slender figure and a full bust. Simply everything a man could dream of. His friends like Dieter were insanely jealous and always said that he must've hypnotised her to fall in love with him although he was no slouch having maintained his muscular build from many torturous hours of compulsory exercise as a young Navy recruit. With cropped blonde hair, blue eyes quite tall at six foot his round clean shaven fresh face, small nose generous mouth and a dimple chin made him look more youthful than his twenty two years.

She bent forward and kissed him, 'Sorry I'm a bit late but the Tram's are all running behind schedule because of last night's bombing'

'I was worried'

'Why?'

'You know why'

'Oh Otto' she whispered, 'there won't be a problem with that I promise'

'All the same' he replied as the door burst open and a young SS Officers obviously drunk staggered in. He immediately approached their table then fumbling in his pocket produced a couple of notes and a few coins. Slamming them down on the table he pointed to Helga, 'I'll have her first you'll have to wait.'

Otto stood up 'She is not a Prostitute you fool. Now go away'

'Of course she is' he slurred 'All of them are around this shithole of a place.'

As he made a grab at her Otto quickly moved round the table, the Officer pushed him aside hard enough for him to lose his footing. Helga stood up and stepped back as he weaved towards her grabbing at her shoulders ripping the seam of her dress which dropped down revealing much of her breast. He pounced trying to pull the remainder down. Otto leapt to his feet but before he could wade in, he along with the half dozen other men in the room rushing over to help winced as she swept her leg up deep into his groin. He squealed like a pig, dropped to his knees clutched his groin and threw up.

Otto took hold of him and helped by Dieter dragged him to the door and threw him out into the street caring little that he landed on his head and was in mortal danger of being run over by the constant movement of Vehicles.

When they returned Helga was being led behind the bar by a rotund Woman who called back over her shoulder, 'Dress fixing time and stiff drink for the Lady.'

Otto sat down still shaken from the experience. Dieter plonked himself down next to him after retrieving his beer when suddenly the door burst open and two SS Officers staggered in holding up the third still doubled up in pain, 'Where's the whore who crippled our friend?' the taller one shouted, 'tell us or you'll be in trouble'

'Whore?' Dieter questioned, 'sorry no whores here. Have you tried the Windmill Rooms along the street there's plenty there?'

'Very funny you little shit. Bring the Whore out or suffer the consequences'

'They being?' Dieter demanded standing up

'You?' The Officer snarled dropping his comrade who still moaning fell to the floor with a thump, 'I shall take pleasure in smashing your ugly face to pulp'

'Mine too?' Otto asked standing,

'Ah another little squirt wanting a sound beating. Anyone else?'

A figure moved from behind the bar, 'Yes me' he shouted squeezing his huge bulk through the bar flap. Johann the Bar owner was immense, well over six feet tall and nearly as wide. He'd thrown beer barrels around for all of his working life so had arms and chest like tree trunks. He faced them, leant forward grabbed their collars and hoisted both up in each hand as if they were children, 'So you think it's ok to molest Ladies do you?' He growled as they began choking, 'I've a good mind to strangle the pair of you.' He lifted them even higher then released his grip letting them drop in a heap to the floor. Purple faced and gasping for air they jumped to their feet rubbing their bruised necks, 'So pick up your disgusting friend and bugger off before I grind your ugly faces into dust. But first you can clean that lot up' he said pointing to the vomit by the bar.' They both looked at each other unsure how to react, 'Hilda fetch a mop and bucket please' he called loudly then facing the two Officers again snarled 'You're lucky I don't make you eat it like the pigs you are.'

Their grim task completed they picked up their friend who was still mumbling and holding his groin and started to leave. The taller one turned as they reached the door, 'We'll find out who the whore is and everything about her don't you worry.'

Johann stepped forward; they quickly left slamming the door behind them.

'Well that'll teach those bastards a lesson' Dieter said gleefully, 'at last the boot's on the other foot. About time they were on the receiving end'

'Do you know them then?'

'No of course not but did you see their arm flashes'

'Not really no'

'SS Security from our place you know those grubby little bastards who poke their noses into everybody else's business. They're the ones who had Karl and Reiner taken away God knows where they ended up poor sods, nobody's laid eyes on them since'

'What were they supposed to have done?'

'Not sure but the word was that Karl's wife had a Jewish relative and he'd not reported it. No idea about Reiner.'

Otto felt a cold shiver go down his spine; they'd threatened to find out everything about Helga. She'd always said that after her Mother died her Father who worked in the records department of the Dorfhaven

Rathaus had managed to locate and destroy all references to her Mother's family. Perhaps they'll give up when they get to a dead end.

'What are you looking so worried about' Dieter asked noticing the look on Otto's face

'Nothing really'

'Good, Ah here's Helga back again looking as beautiful as ever. I'll leave you alone now I'm sure you've plenty to say to each other.'

Helga looked pale as she sat down and he'd noticed a little unsteady on her feet as she'd made her way over to the table,

'Are you feeling ok?'

'Not really no'

'I'm not surprised with that bastard all over you'

'Oh that? No I'm fine it's all the drink that Hilda gave me. She made a fine job with my dress though look.' She leant forward so he could inspect her needlework. As her dress dropped down slightly he noticed a rather nasty bruise on her shoulder,

'Is that painful?'

'What?'

'The bruise on your shoulder.'

She sat up and pulled the top of her dress out and peered down, 'Oh I see. No it isn't.'

Hilda came waddling over and put a jug down on the table, 'Get that down you' she said smiling broadly, 'it'll do you a world of good. My own recipe you see'

'Thank you you're most kind' Helga replied hoping against hope that it didn't contain any more alcohol, it did and plenty of it. She poured a small amount into a glass and took a couple of sips, 'I think you'd better have a glass as well Otto'

'Best we sort out the codes first.'

They had worked out a method of keeping in touch when away from each other on their shifts, highly illegal and would result in severe penalties if discovered. They wrote down a random series of letters and numbers for each day followed by frequencies between eight and thirteen Megacycles. At an arranged time they would take turns in transmitting their set, the other would return the transmission with the corresponding ones. This way they always knew each were safe and well especially after bombing raids.

'That bitch of a supervisor nearly caught me last week'

'The fat one who looks a bit like a heavy weight boxer?'

'Yes that's her Oda Hahn. If anyone needs a man it's her'

'I always thought she preferred Ladies'

'I think it's a bit of both to be honest, she tried it on once with my friend Klara'

'What did she say?'

'Klara?'

'No! Oda when she nearly caught you'

'Just demanded to know why I was searching out of my band'

'What did you say?'

'Said I was daydreaming and put on a few tears'

'That works with her?'

'Good Lord no, she still hurls abuse threatens you with all sorts of horrid things and then with luck wanders off'

'Well you'd better take a bit more care'

'I will I promise.'

'Now are you sure that your Father got rid of all your Mums family details?'

'Yes I'm sure as I've said every time you've asked so why again now?'

He pondered on whether or not he should say but decided that it would be best so that at least she could be on her guard.

'So?' She said giving him a sideways glance,

'The chap you kneed in the balls'

'What about him?'

'He's from the area SS security department'

She giggled, 'Well I don't think things feel too secure for him at the moment do you?'

'His friends threatened to find out everything about you.'

She leant forward and kissed him, 'You worry too much Otto. They won't find anything.'

Chapter Three

Plymouth Dockyard

Oliver stood on the Bridge inspecting the redesigned mount and dome; it was now as his First Lieutenant had suggested, like a golf ball. Able Seaman Sumner was close by cursing over and over again,

'What seems to be the problem Sumner?'

'Our Bren gun mount Sir. Twice we've welded the bloody thing but both times it's failed'

'Okay as it's seems to be so important to you Sumner I'm prepared to call in a Docky to give it a go'

'Well it did get us out of a hole last time Sir'

'It did indeed Sumner and you'll be pleased to know that we're going to get our three inch gun back as soon as we return.'

Just before nightfall the three Submarines slipped their moorings and moved out into the sound. They were to proceed on the surface at full speed for as long as possible. Ursula and Umpire could make just over twelve knots, Undaunted a little more but submerged all three could only manage around nine.

In discussions with Commander Briggs Oliver, Peter and Charles had put forward concerns about maintaining maximum speed whilst submerged as the noise and disturbance it causes would be picked up at some distance by hydrophone. To their amazement he'd brushed it aside stressing how little time there was remaining before the Convoy sailed.

The weather was perfect, a cloudy sky, small swell and very little wind. By morning they had covered 150 miles and continued on the Surface until a little after 1300 when ships were sighted on the horizon.

'Time to give this new kit a try' Oliver said picking up

the microphone, 'Charlie can you hear me over?' Silence. He tried again, still nothing,

'Try turning the power up Sir'

'Guess it's worth a try Number One.'

He turned the dial up slightly, 'Charlie can you hear me over?'

They all waited quietly, the silence was broken by a tinny voice coming out of the speaker, 'Just about Oliver' Charles responded

'I can as well but then we aren't too far apart are we?' Peter said.

Almost immediately they heard the unmistakeable and dreaded pinging sound from an asdic sweeping for them from above.

'So much for only producing hisses and squawks. Thirty degrees down bubble, three hundred feet.'

Ursula slid quietly down, 'Stop engines level off' Oliver whispered.

They heard the distant sound of depth charges hoping that the other two boats hadn't been detected.

An hour passed before Oliver felt confident to come up to periscope depth. He completed an all-round search, seeing nothing he decided to risk surfacing. As they reached the Bridge the water started to boil both to port and starboard then as if in unison Umpire and Undaunted surfaced. An Aldis lamp flickered from Umpire's Bridge, 'He asks whether we think our transmissions were detected' the Signalman announced plugging his lamp in, 'reply Sir?'

'Say that it could've been a coincidence but best we only use it when essential.'

They proceeded at full speed for the remainder of the day and through the night.

On day three they had to crash dive to avoid a flotilla of Destroyers. Back up to Periscope depth still completely undetected Oliver felt the enormous frustration of having an Enemy Destroyer in his sights but strict orders to avoid any attacks before locating the Tender. He slammed the handles shut and lowered the scope, 'Like fish in a barrel and we have to sail on' he complained, 'it's going to be at least another two to three days before we can start searching'

'Well Sir it'll save one more torpedo we can slam into the Tender'

'Providing we can find the damn thing Number One'

'I'm pretty sure we'll be able to do that Sir. I'm certain that the Tender will be transmitting to their boats so with three of us we should be able to get a pretty accurate DF bearing'

'Well I hope you're right.'

The First Lieutenant was correct as the following day they managed to get a fix on the Tenders current position. She lay about ninety miles south west of them, around ten hours sailing.

'That'll mean we'll be within range around dusk' Oliver said checking his watch, 'just light enough to see what we're up against. Chief get on that box thing and let the others know that we'll surface at 2300 and mount a combined attack at 2315.'

The message sent and responded to Oliver relaxed in his cabin thinking how best to mount the attack when a shout from the Hydrophone operator disturbed him.

'At least three screws Sir'

'How many ships'

'Not sure Sir could be one'

'Heavy?'

'Yes Sir and fast.'

'Three hundred feet please Number One.'

The thrashing of the screws were clearly audible in the deathly silence, each man looking upwards as though they could see their enemy passing overhead,

'No Asdic yet' Oliver whispered, 'I think they're listening.'

The screws faded but then returned over and over

again.

'It's that bloody box Sir every time we use it Jerry arrives' the Chief muttered quietly.

Oliver nodded, 'Certainly looks that way although I think they would've been a bit more aggressive.'

The search lasted for forty-five minutes keeping them deep and almost motionless. Returning to periscope depth Oliver completed an all-round search sighting the Destroyer steaming away from them but in the direction they needed to make. They'd been dived most of the day, the air was foul but it was far too light to surface safely. Should they dare use the now dubbed squawk box? Oliver took the decision that they must.

At twenty miles to the target Oliver ordered periscope depth. He looked, took his eyes away shook his head and looked again. Doubting what he'd seen totally against convention he invited the First Lieutenant to look, 'Bloody hell talk about confidence. They must be mad.'

He moved away and Oliver looked again, increasing the magnification to maximum. A pool of bright lights were visible on the horizon, 'If they keep those on I think it's going to be a pushover.' He snapped the handles shut and sent the periscope back down into the well, 'Time we got back onto the squawk box and planned the attack.'

Aboard the Tender, the ex-German Luxury Liner Beatrix Korst Captain Rayner Wendorf was extremely unhappy. His orders had yet again been countermanded by Standartenfuhrer Gunther Henkel, the SS Colonel foisted upon him who had decided to hold a massive celebration for Hitler's Birthday. He'd ordered coloured lights to be strung from the mast, searchlights to be shone into the air and all deck and loading lights kept on. When the Captain objected he was immediately chastised and accused of being unpatriotic. Reluctantly he stood aside and despite his misgivings didn't feel able to prevent it taking place.

Henkel even ordered all the U-boats within the area to dock for the grand occasion.

Oliver couldn't believe their luck, the Tender with ten U-boats moored each side against a makeshift wooden jetty was lit up like a Christmas tree, every detail stood out. Their presence away from the lights even on the surface remained undetected. Their plan was simple, they would lay off at one thousand yards, Ursula on the Starboard side, Undaunted and Umpire at the Port bow and stern, synchronized firing firstly at a running depth of twenty-five feet to go beneath the U-boats would be made via the squawk box, then independent firing at a running depth of ten feet to destroy any U-boats not damaged by the first attack.

They dived and moved into position, everything was ready; Oliver held up his hand, the Chief manned the squawk box, 'Fire one, Fire two.'

The fish sped through the water, twenty seconds later despite its huge size the Beatrix Korst appeared to leap out of the water as six torpedoes slammed into her hull; minutes later the next six blew the outer moored U-boats to scrap. Umpire and Undaunted surfaced and opened fire with their guns adding to the destruction. With an enormous explosion the Beatrex Korst finally split in half and sank within minutes dragging the remaining docked U-boats down with her leaving only a sea of burning oil.

An Aldis lamp flashed from Umpires Bridge, 'He asks if we can go home now Sir' the Signalman read out.

John nodded, 'Yes I think we can, and signal both well done and we'll dive at first light.'

He flipped open the voice pipe cover, 'Get a signal off to Flag. Operation Robin Hood successfully completed. All three Submarines returning to base.'

With an ear shattering crump four plumes of water shot high into the air between Ursula and Undaunted.

'Where the hell did that come from' Oliver shouted' as

they scrambled through the hatch, 'Diving stations. Three-hundred feet.'

His well-trained crew leapt into action and with planes to maximum down position, all vents closed off, bow tanks flooded and motors full ahead they plummeted into the depths, 'Stern tanks flooding now Sir.'

Oliver nodded just before to save precious power even the red lights of the Control Room were momentarily switched off before the less energy hungry emergency lights cut in, 'Stop engines' Oliver whispered. The silence was broken only by a distant ping of Asdic, sweeping and searching them out, 'Approaching fast Sir.' The report from the hydrophone operator was unnecessary as the Asdic volume increased second by second finally a crescendo as it found them.

Oliver knew he only had seconds to react, 'Full ahead, Port thirty.'

The depth charges exploded just clear of them this time but the cat and mouse chase carried on throughout the night and into the dawn forcing all three of the Boats to remain submerged preventing them from recharging their Batteries.

The German Destroyers Captain Werner Kuffel was an old hand at this. When questioned by his Officers as to why he'd deployed no more depth charges even when each of the targets had been confirmed he smiled, 'Watch and learn' he told them, 'keep the bastards submerged and eventually they'll have no choice but to surface. Even the English need to breath and their batteries have to be recharged, and when they do.' He clapped his hands together, 'that's when we strike.'

Oliver called for periscope depth hoping to get a shot at the Destroyer but immediately ordered a crash dive to avoid a collision.

'We can't stay down much longer Sir' the First Lieutenant stated the obvious, 'only ten percent remaining'

'So let's use some of that ten percent with the squawk box to plan an attack with the Undaunted and Umpire'

'How Sir?'

'If you notice as soon as we blow ballast the Destroyer is on us within minutes'

Roger nodded, 'so' Oliver continued, 'if we all blow the tanks at the same time he's got to choose one of us. When he does the other two should be able to loose off at least two fish each'

'No time for plotting him accurately Sir?' the First Lieutenant asked picking up the is/was range finder,

'None at all it'll be a quick and rough estimate then pray and fire'

'Worth a try Sir'

'Right let's get to it.'

'All three submarines are coming to the surface Kapitan' the hydrophone operator shouted excitedly,

'Good' Werner replied 'now let battle commence.'

The German gun crews knew their job well; as soon as the Boats surfaced they picked a target each. Shells screamed over sending plumes of water high into the sky and peppering the Submarines with large chunks of shrapnel.

Oliver took a quick sighting, manoeuvred the bow towards his target passed on his best guess to his Torpedo Officer, 'Fire one, Fire two.'

Twenty seconds passed with no explosion but seconds later one of the fish fired by Undaunted exploded beneath the Destroyer damaging the rudder and one of the screws.

Submerged again Oliver swung the periscope around and saw the Destroyer swing away to Port. Undeterred by the torpedo strike the gunners were still sending shell after shell at their quarry. Horrified he saw Umpire floundering on the surface with planes still in the vertical position take two direct hits, one on the conning tower the other just forward of the gun which blew large chunks of the casing into the air. She slew sideways, listed wildly to Port then bow first slipped below the surface.

The last thing they heard from Peter was on the squawk box 'Oh damn' was all he said above the horrendous nightmare sound of water cascaded in. With no chance of escape they plummeted down to a certain death beneath the unforgiving green depths of the Atlantic.

Oliver franticly launched his last two torpedoes but both passed harmlessly beneath the Destroyers hull.

Werner furious at having to accept he'd lost the advantage and with the earlier damage causing massive problems in steering he reluctantly withdrew and limped away.

Initial Jubilation was forgotten as Ursula and Undaunted batteries fully charged dived and set course for home. Each man silent, lost in their own thoughts mourning their fellow Submariners all mindful that it could well have been them entombed hundreds of feet below.

'Do you think they'd be able to escape Sir?'

Oliver shook his head, 'Highly unlikely I'm afraid Collins.'

With no prompting the entire crew started to sing Eternal Father, men hardened to witnessing death and destruction singing at the top of their voices with a tear or two carving a trail down their oil-stained faces. Then with great reverence recited the Lord's Prayer.

'I hope that Kraut Bastard rots in hell'

'The thing is Taff' the Chief said quietly, 'Eternal Father is for all Seafarers and includes all those blokes we sent to the bottom on the U-boat tender'

'That's bollocks Chief. God hates them Nazi Bastards'

'They're not all Nazi's Mathews' Oliver interrupted, 'most are men just like you'

'No Sir I can't believe that. They killed my missus in Portsmouth she hadn't done anything to them. I hate them, all of them, the more of the bastards we kill the better.'

Oliver had no answer to such conviction so ended the conversation.

Chapter Four

An RAF Airfield North Yorkshire

The Briefing room was thick with tobacco smoke as seven young Airmen, three Pilots and four Navigators all in their twenties waited patiently for their commanding officer to make an appearance. The door opened and Wing Commander Robert Thorpe DFC breezed in. A true Yorkshire man, short and stocky with a neatly trimmed moustache his curly brown hair a little longer than regulations. A man of few words but what he did say mostly counted for many.

'You must've been early' he said, his manner of an apology. Making his way to the front of the room he threw his briefcase onto the desk leant over and pushed a window open then turned to the men and grinned.

Flying Officer John Wright turned to his Flight Sergeant and whispered in his ear, 'I don't like it when he grins it always means trouble.'

'Right down to business. Dorfhaven.' There was an audible groan from the aircrews, 'I know each of us have been over there a few times but this visit we'll be packing bombs not cameras so at long last our opportunity to give Jerry a pasting that's well over due.'

'Haven't the big boys had a good few goes at those Pens?'

'They have Sergeant but our Lord and Master thinks that our nice shiny new Mosquitoes are faster and able to fly much lower so we should be able to pop our bombs straight down Jerry's chimney'

'Has our Lord and Master ever flown over Fort Kruger?'

'That's highly unlikely John but if we go in early, fast and low we may just catch them on the hop'

'I understand that they've increased the number of Anti-Aircraft weapons there Sir'

'So Flight Sergeant Parker who have you been talking to get that information?'

He knew fully well as he'd recently seen him walking out with a rather good looking WAAF Sergeant from Reconnaissance. The men jeered as Parker refused to reveal his source.

'But is it true Sir?'

'To be honest I don't know. Perhaps we should invite Flight Sergeant Parkers Belle to the briefing. What do you think Sergeant?' Parker mumbled something intelligible as Thorpe carried on above the light well intentioned banter, 'All four aircraft will be involved. Take off tomorrow at 0530 so we should arrive over our target, providing of course Milner there doesn't get us lost.' He waited until the laughter died down, 'around 0645. I shall lead with the rest of you in strict order following at twenty second intervals'

'That's bloody close Sir. Aren't we likely to get clobbered by the blasts?'

'Ah that's the thing I've not mentioned yet.' The room smog had cleared a little so he leant over and closed the window, 'our bombs will have one minute delay fuses. Tight but achievable as hopefully we shall prove this afternoon.

He removed a set of photographs from his briefcase and laid them onto the desk. The men gathered round, 'Once these doors are shut even the largest bombs seem to make little impact'

'So what bombs are we to carry Sir?'

'Nothing fancy because we're pretty sure that the doors are wide open first thing each morning to let boats in and out. Once the alarms are sounded it's estimated that it must take at least four minutes before they shut completely. Our job is to fly in low and fast to jettison our bombs deep inside the pens.'

There was a long pause as the men digested this information. Finally Pilot Officer Albert Milner said what they were all thinking, 'There's a bloody great cliff there

Sir'

'That's true but with the climb rate we can achieve it shouldn't be too much of a problem because the boffins have done all the sums and calculated that at an altitude of one hundred feet and speed of three-hundred we should be able to release the bombs at one thousand yards'

'So all we've got to do Sir is release the bomb and then less than a second later climb over the remainder of the cliff?'

'Pretty much yes'

'Can I stay at home please Sir?'

'I'm excused boots with bunions Sir'

'And I've got a bad cold'

'Good so it sounds as if we're all raring to go. Twelve-thirty take off for a practice run on Scarborough. Dismissed.'

A little after 1230 the four Mosquitoes lifted into the air and headed for Scarborough. Flying line astern in the order they'd been allocated Thorpe ordered them down to fifty feet and kept close to four hundred Knots.

With sweat pouring from his brow John Wright struggled to maintain position as number two and more than once came perilously close to the sea. His Flight Sergeant constantly read off the height, speed and course as all of Johns concentration was fixed on keeping Thorpe in view, difficult in the changing light and virtually impossible with the two mile gap between them.

The whole exercise was a total disaster as none of the trailing three Mosquitoes managed to keep anywhere near their allocated position. The tail-ender would've certainly been blown out of the sky by any blast from the previous three.

Back in the Briefing room they were all expecting a sound Yorkshire bollocking from their boss. He stormed in slamming the door behind him.

'That was one God almighty cock up.' John went to

speak but Robert raised his hand to silence him, 'I don't want excuses Gentlemen just ideas because that just 'aint going to work.'

'What if we go in slower, higher and in pairs Sir?'

'And?'

'Well for what I've seen Sir they have a dozen or more new aerial arrays on the top of the cliff above the Pens'

Robert huffed loudly, 'Despite not having Girlfriends in Reconnaissance Sergeant we've all seen that for ourselves but carry on'

'Well obviously we aren't going to have time to climb over it at that speed are we?'

'From this afternoons performance clearly not. But firstly Gentlemen do we agree to bomb in pairs?'

They all nodded, 'Seems a better and safer idea than line astern Sir'

'Good that's settled, and what height and speed do we think is possible?'

'Without another practice Sir not entirely sure.'

'Right then we've just enough time to give Scarborough another fright.'

After three attempts they settled on one hundred and ninety five miles per hour at one hundred and twenty five feet. The bombs would still have a delay fuse but all at ninety seconds. It was also agreed that Robert would illuminate a flashing tail light to help the two trailing to keep him in view.

This was quickly passed to the boffins who agreed that the bombs should still have enough momentum to get beyond the doors.

At 0515 the four Mosquitoes with one engine fired up taxied away from the apron and line astern waited at the end of the runway.

Smoke billowing from the exhaust in the chilly air of the morning the second engines were started. At exactly 0530 they climbed into the air taking up their pairs as they headed out over the North Sea.

In Dorfhaven dawn was breaking and life was very much as it was every morning. A light mist was forming over the Elbe. The Town was slowly waking as Bakers were busy completing the nights baking for their boys to cycle round with baskets full delivering to the larger more prestigious properties. Stray dogs roamed the streets sniffing around for a meal as gulls squawked their delight as the shrimp boats pulled into the harbour.

The Anti-aircraft gun crews at the Fort were relaxing as their long uneventful night watch was nearing completion. Breakfast call took half of them away.

Major Friedrich Merkel tucked his serviette into his collar as the Steward placed the bread, cold meat and a selection of cheeses onto the table, 'No boiled eggs?' he complained,

'Sorry Sir we have none today.'

His disgust was muted by the alarm sounding, men tumbled out from their Breakfast and slumbers too late to catch the four Mosquitoes, throttles wide open almost at sea level shooting by well before they could man their guns. The Submarine pens now alerted started to close the enormous doors.

The Mosquitoes swung to starboard and started their run, 'Close up you're too far back' Thorpe shouted over the radio, 'that's better. Releasing bomb now.' The first two bombs dropped away as the pair climbed steeply to clear the cliff.

John Wright lined himself up, 'Bomb gone' his flight Sergeant shouted. Thrusting the throttle to maximum and pulling hard back on the yoke the nose rose but then the starboard engine emitted a cloud of oily smoke and lost power. John with a mere second to spare threw the aircraft into an extremely tight turn as the engine picked up. They cleared the cliff face with inches to spare and climbed to join the others as the bombs exploded throwing masonry high into the sky.

The gunners at the fort now wide awake put up a massive barrage. John grimaced as chunks of shrapnel slammed through the wood and fabric, his flight Sergeant cried out in pain as a small lump imbedded into his thigh.

From a small airfield in Norden a lone ME109 lifted into the sky, its mission was to intercept the Mosquitoes. The Pilot Helmut Keller was happy as he like other German Pilots were aware that the only defence the Mosquitoes had was their speed. His 109 had been extensively and secretly tweaked to increase the maximum speed from 380 to 410 MPH, now well fast enough to match them.

A sigh of relief from everyone as they cleared the flack and sped out over the North Sea.

'109 on your arse John.' Robert warned over the radio, 'break away.'

John immediately pulled back on the yoke putting the aircraft into a steep climb breathing a sigh of relief as both engines responded under full power.

Cannon shells hissed past as he threw the aircraft into a tight left turn then a right,

'I can't shake the bastard off' he shouted over the radio.

Thorp swooped in behind the 109; Keller briefly saw him in the mirror but kept his focus on the weaving Mosquito in front of him cursing as yet another short burst missed.

'Dive when I say' Thorp bellowed over the radio. 'Now.'

John pushed the yoke forward and throttled back forcing Keller to make a rapid manoeuvre to avoid a collision. Surprise turned to terror as 20mm cannon shells ripped into the 109 setting the engine ablaze. Keller just managed to slide open the cockpit cover and throw himself clear before the 109 exploded now with the blunt realisation that at least some of the Mosquitoes have a whole lot more defence than speed.

All four Mosquitoes landed safely and their weary crews, except Parker who was whisked away by the medics made their way over for a debrief with the Station Commander,

'All four bombs exploded beyond the doors'

'You're sure?' They all nodded 'excellent that should've made quite a mess.'

'One other thing Sir is that it looks as though Jerry has beefed up his 109's'

'Really Robert how so?'

'Speed Sir. John couldn't shake him off.' He grinned 'I bet the poor sod had the fright of his life when I managed to ruin his day'

'So you're claiming a kill?'

'Never really thought about it Sir but yes I guess I am'

'Enter all the details into your log and then report it to Nigel he'll do the rest'

'I think that all the Mosquitoes should be fitted with cannons Sir'

'I agree Robert and it'll happen soon.'

Dorfhaven

Helga had been told of the bombing at the Submarine pens and was worried about Otto. It seemed an eternity before the clock finally reached time for their pre-arranged communication. She checked the frequency and code then after ensuring that the Supervisor was well out of the way swung her dial round to ten point four kilocycles, trimmed the aerial tuning and quickly sent the code then waited for a reply. A bit of a panic set in as the minutes ticked by with only the buzz of static coming through her earphones. She quickly checked the frequency again fearing she'd misread it but then in his normal faultless Morse code came the answer she'd been waiting for.

Happily she swung back to her allotted frequency humming a tune to herself dreaming of the next time they could meet up,

'What are you so happy about Gerber?'

'Nothing really Mam'

'Good. Remember happiness is laziness Gerber' her supervisor Oda snarled throwing a heap of paper onto her desk 'so get busy and send all of these off and be quick about it.'

Chapter Five

Whitehall London

Commodore Douglas Warwick, Air Commodore Hamish Dewar and Brigadier Thomas Belton-Perkins were leant over the table examining reconnaissance photographs from the raid on Dorfhaven.

'It certainly doesn't look as though we put them out of business Hamish'

'That's true Douglas but so far we've completed three sorties of high level bombing now this latest low level where there's clear evidence that all bombs exploded inside'

'Torpedoes?'

'No chance of that Thomas they've installed two strings of nets all the way across'

'Well they must lower them for the U-boats in and out'

'Obviously but I definitely wouldn't want to be at periscope depth anywhere near the damn place.' Thomas looked surprised, 'this time of the year' Douglas explained, 'the water can be as clear as the Mediterranean so from the cliffs spotted in an instant.'

Hamish exhaled and rubbed his chin thoughtfully, 'You know' he paused to pull a cigarette from a fine silver case, he offered them round Douglas accepted Thomas shook his head, 'photographs are all well and good but we lack the intelligence we need to decide what if anything we can use to permanently stop their operations'

Douglas drew deeply on the cigarette sending a spiral of smoke to the ceiling, 'So what you're suggesting is someone on the ground?'

'I think it's the only way.'

Thomas with his head down seemed deep in thought for a moment, 'I think I have someone who could fit the bill, Guy Robins still one of your lot Douglas, well a Royal Marine Major actually, he's Polish'

'Strange name for a Pole'

'Not his real name Hamish he's a Polish Jew, came over here in the early thirties fluent in English and German lost all his family except one brother so hates them enough to do just about anything. He led four of his men through fifty miles of occupied France, stole three German kayaks in Calais and paddled back to Dover.'

'Sounds like just the Chap we need so do you know where he is?'

'Ah that's the rub I don't know but I'll find out.'

'Well Thomas if you can locate the man I'll provide his transport, I've got a couple of Boats due back at Plymouth in a day or so.'

Somewhere in the Atlantic

Ursula and Undaunted had both been submerged for hours, it appeared that every German ship in the Atlantic were after their blood. Time and time again they'd had to crash dive with batteries still depleted to avoid Destroyers, Cruisers and a couple of U-boats. With no remaining torpedoes it was a case of hiding away as best they could.

Having watched Umpire being sunk Charles on Undaunted had no intention of waging a gun battle with a superior armed opponent.

Oliver ordered periscope depth as the hydrophone operator reported no activity. A quick all round search proved otherwise as two Destroyers were stationary at about 2000 yards. An eagle eye German had obviously seen the periscope as two shells exploded in the water above them almost deafening the hydrophone operator who throwing his earphones down spouted a torrent of profanities aimed at just about everyone. His hearing temporarily impaired the Chief had him replaced.

'They're on the move Sir closing at one-two-zero'

'Thirty degrees bubble three hundred feet.'

As Ursula sank down the squawk box hissed and fizzed

for a second or two before Charles's strained voice came through, 'Can't last out much longer before we'll have to surface. This'll use up a lot of the Battery but I think the air will run out first. Over'

Oliver looked over at the Engineer; he just shrugged his shoulders and turned back to his work.

Taking this as "at your peril" he picked up the Microphone, 'Same situation here. It'll be dark soon we'll surface and make a run for it. Over'

'Not sure if we can wait that long. Over'

'Use your DSEA sets as a last resort. Over'

'We may as well because the escape hatches have been bolted down. Over'

Oliver shook his head, 'Ok let me know of any changes. Out.'

All eyes in the Control Room were fixed on him. Sumner was first to speak, 'Have our hatches been bolted Sir?'

'No Sumner despite strict orders from above they most definitely have not.' The men returned their attention to their duties.

The Chief came up close to Oliver, 'I hope that wasn't....'

'No it wasn't Chief' Oliver interrupted, 'Look I'd rather risk them being blown open by depth charges than be trapped like a rat. But for Christ sake don't let our esteemed leaders know or I'll certainly be for the high jump.'

As the Sun sank into the horizon casting dark shadows over the water the squawk box hissed into life, 'It's now or never Oliver I'm surfacing. Out'

'Periscope depth Number One. We may as well join him.'

Oliver completed an all-round search, Undaunted was already on the surface but apart from her silhouette against the setting sun he could see nothing else. He slammed the handles shut, 'Surface.'

By the time they clambered up to the Bridge an Aldis lamp was already flashing from Undaunted. The Signalman read it word by word:

Think. Safer. We. Disperse. See. You. In. Plymouth.

Oliver acknowledged and altered course for home, 'Should be tucked up in the Wardroom by this time tomorrow Sir' the First Lieutenant said dreaming of a hot bath and soft bed.

Oliver rubbed the stubble on his chin now more of a scruffy beard, 'Certainly be good to get a shave at last. I can't help thinking I look more like a U-Boat Skipper than a Naval Officer'

'Do you know many U-Boat Skippers then Sir?'

'Come to think of it' he paused, 'no but I've seen pictures.'

Morale amongst the rest of the crew was just as high, one more day cooped up in this stifling diesel stinking metal box then freedom to roam amongst the pubs of Plymouth then for some no doubt ignoring the sick bay pill rollers advise end up in Union Street.

Sumner had once professed, much to the amusement of his pals that he only frequented Union Street because all the red lights reminded him of the Control room during a night attack.

The night was particularly dark the moon and stars obscured by low cloud. It was quite warm for the middle of April but then it started to drizzle made worse by a keen wind that drove it at them like irritating midges.

Visibility was almost non-existent but the lookouts binoculars clamped to their eyes still scanned the darkness for any movement. Every few minutes they had to wipe away the spots of water that accumulated on the lenses giving even less chance of spotting anything.

'I think I'll take the opportunity to go below and write up the log'

'Don't worry about us Sir' the First Lieutenant joked, 'we'll just stay here and get soaked.'

Oliver slapped him on the back, 'Good for you.'

Ginger Rogers wiped the lenses for the hundredth time and scanned into the blackness, 'I think I saw something Sir Starboard bow.'

The very moment the First Lieutenant swung his binoculars round the moon finally broke through the clouds revealing a German S-Boat bearing down on them.

'Diving stations. Flood Q' he bellowed as they tumbled through the hatch and down into the Control room.

Water flooded into the forward tanks as Oliver swung through the hatch, 'What….' Is all he managed to utter before with a massive crunch they were rolled almost on their side spilling men over like skittles. The lights flashed but stayed on as Ursula rolled back still bows down. As they got to their feet men came scrambling through the hatch followed closely by tons of water. They managed with difficulty to secure it against the flow but fortunately helped to a large extent by the bow down angle.

'Blow all tanks stand by to surface' John shouted watching the depth gauge. Compressed air screeching like a steam train thundered into the tanks. Now all eyes locked onto the depth gauge. Slowly, very slowly it hovered on seventy five feet for a few seconds then gradually with a sigh of relief from the crew started their climb up to the surface.

'Strange noises from up top Sir' the hydrophone operator called out the stress still sounding in his voice, 'lots of banging and creaking.'

Oliver acknowledged but kept his eye glued to the gauge now at sixty-five feet. An ominous clang sounded on the casing quickly followed by a massive explosion. The lights went out as water poured into the Control room within seconds' ankle deep, 'Engine Room' Oliver bellowed above the terrifying roar of the cascade.

In the pitch dark they frantically swung through the engine room hatch one by one and managed to close it tight but within minutes they could hear the hiss of water squirting through the rubber seals as the pressure from the flooded control room increased.

With his heart in his mouth Oliver knew that this part of the Atlantic could be well over a mile deep and now forced out of the control room had no way of pumping or blowing the tanks. Ursula under the enormous weight of water plunged down but then with a horrendous squeal of tortured metal smashed into the sea bed. The impact woke up the emergency lighting throwing an eerie glow over the men.

Oliver looked over at the small engine room depth gauge it read ninety-five feet but in the past had proved notoriously inaccurate.

The Chief busied himself opening the locker and handing out the DSEA sets. Squeezing through the narrow gangway between the engines he approached Oliver concern all over his face, 'You were serious about the hatch Sir?'

Oliver nodded, 'Yes Chief I was. Have you done a head count?'

'Yes Sir.' He replied grimly 'nineteen.' Oliver's expression prompted him to add, 'I guess they were trapped in the forward Mess Sir.'

His blood ran cold. If those thirteen men hadn't been drowned they would've certainly suffocated by now in the cramped space.

He pushed this to the back of his mind to concentrate on getting the remaining men out and up to the surface. Not a mean feat as he knew that most had never been to Blockhouse in Gosport for underwater escape training and even those few like himself who had were only trained in their current fifteen foot tank.

'Shall I start to flood up Sir?' The Chief asked as he released the Twill Trunk.

'In a minute Chief wait until the First Lieutenant has checked that all of them have the DSEA's correctly adjusted and know what to do. We can't lose anymore we really can't.'

'All the men are ready Sir'

'Ok Chief Flood up.'

As the water depth increased so did the pressure and the unmistakable yellow green haze of the chlorine gas dense enough to be seen under the dull emergency lanterns.

Once up at waist level the Chief ducked under the trunk, climbed the ladder and turned the wheel to release the hatch. It flew open with a crash shooting him through like a cork out of a bottle, the air in his buoyancy bag propelling him towards the surface. Within seconds water in the engine room now with a thick coat of Diesel reached chest level. AB Rogers waded his way past the line of men. He took a deep breath then removed the mouthpiece, 'I'll man the ladder and push them through Sir' he croaked his voice fighting against the enormous pressure making it more and more difficult to speak. After another deep breath, 'Fred will push them along from the back.' He then ducked under the trunk climbed the ladder and anchored himself just below the hatch. His goggles were pushed so tight against his face it felt as though his eyes were in danger of being sucked out, the pain in his ears excruciating. He sensed rather than saw the first man ascend the ladder followed closely by the next. Within a minute Fred Sumner made his way up and he and Ginger struck out for the surface.

Oliver indicated to the First Lieutenant to leave. The water in the engine room was now at neck level; He was just about to duck under the trunk when he heard loud tapping. He stood up again and listened. The tapping now sounded more like scraping, the men trapped in the bow he wondered?

Ursula with hundreds of tons of water flooding in could no longer sit at the cliff edge they'd been fortunate enough to ground on, so with steel plates squealing in protest started, slowly at first to grind her way towards the abyss.

Oliver his mind turning over and over in a desperate

attempt to find a way of reaching his trapped men finally grasped where the noise was coming from. With just seconds to spare he climbed the ladder and it was more the case that Ursula left him rather than the other way round as She and thirteen of her crew plummeted down to the Ocean floor a mile below.

It was light as he popped to the surface; he spat out the mouthpiece, removed his goggles which were smeared with oil and the nose clip that had painfully made deep depressions. He looked about him, the sun was up and apart from a light morning mist it was already quite warm but the water felt ice cold.

'Over here Sir'

He swivelled around and saw a small raft with the Chief leaning out with Rogers holding on to him as he beckoned him over.

'Up you come Sir' the Chief shouted dragging him inboard,

'Where did this come from?' Oliver asked starting to shiver

'From the S-Boat Sir' he said pointing.

A little way off the remainder of his crew were precariously balanced on the upturned S-Boats hull, 'It must've flipped over as soon as it collided with us Sir'

'So they didn't drop the depth charge it must've fallen off when they turned over'

'Guess so.'

Oliver started to count his men, 'Sixteen'

'Seventeen Sir' Sumner said as he hauled himself over the side, 'it was Midshipman Creswell and Sub Peterson that never made it up Sir.' He threw two DSEA's onto the raft, 'I've released them Sir. Said a few words for them and that. No point in dragging them onto here Sir.'

Oliver nodded in acknowledgement struggling with the fact that he had now lost fifteen men and they weren't out of the woods yet not by a long chalk.

The day dragged on with a watery sun shining down. Gradually the raft had drifted away from the upturned hull which was now just a dot on the horizon. Fortunately the swell wasn't as high as normal so the small raft was pretty stable.

'Any idea whereabouts we are Sir?'

'Last plot put us around a hundred miles west of the Channel Isles'

'Do you think they'll be looking for us Sir?'

'Not for a day or so Sumner no. Not expected to report until this evening. Or was that yesterday evening? To be honest I don't really know.'

As evening fell they heard the sound of powerful engines. As it drew closer Oliver's heart sank as he realised that it was a German S-Boat.

It drew alongside and they were pulled up onto the deck and made to sit down leant against the guard rail. Not a word was spoken as they surged ahead. After about four hours they slowed and made their way into an empty harbour and tied up against a small jetty. One member of the crew indicated for them to get off then once they were all on the Jetty with engines fire up they sped off into the dark.

'Where the hell is this place?'

'I would guess that as they came in with no problem it must be France or the Channel Isles'

'So' the Chief added 'I guess they'll radio for their troops to pick us up in the morning'

'Then the best thing to do is to hide ourselves away and plan an escape.'

They moved as silently as they could through the darkness. Sand turned to gravel then Tarmac. After twenty minute against the early morning sun struggling above the eastern sky they saw an old rickety wooden barn, 'That should do nicely for a while' Oliver whispered moving forward.

Sumner and Ginger stopped both sniffing the air, 'So

what do you two think you are, Blood hounds?'

'No Chief but I can smell those Girly Cigarettes that Knobby Clarke smokes'

'He would've lost those in the water'

'No Sir he always kept them in a tin with his precious zippo.'

As they drew closer they could hear the sound of muffled laughter. Sumner moved ahead, 'Knobby is that you?'

The laughter immediately stopped. Sumner called again, 'Knobby I can smell your poofy fags.'

A figure emerged from the Barn 'Is that you Fred?'

'Who the bloody hell do you think it is?'

They went into the barn and found the remainder of the Crew. The First Lieutenant came over to Oliver and shook hands, 'We thought you chaps hadn't made it. A Jerry S-Boat picked us up and dropped us off here'

'Same as us. Any idea where we are?'

'It was still light when we got dropped off. Duval was born in Guernsey and said he didn't recognise anything at all so we thought it could be France but earlier on we sent a couple of chaps out for a look round and they saw a telephone box beside a cottage so we reckon we must have been dumped on one of the Channel Islands Alderney or Sark perhaps.'

Oliver shrugged his shoulders, 'Good enough guess but how the hell do we get out?'

'Well there was one boat in the harbour when we were dumped so I guess we could take it over and make a break for it.'

They discussed their escape throughout the day and late into the night eventually having to spread out heaps of hay to sleep on.

The following morning they were rudely awoken by a loud shout from outside, 'Kommen sie die hände hoch.'

The men fell into silence looking to Oliver, 'Schnell.'

The voice bellowed again.

'I think we've been rumbled Sir.'

Oliver resigned to being a Prisoner of war with hands on head as ordered led his men out of the Barn and into the sunlight to be faced with a dozen old men brandishing a wide assortment of weapons.

'Fritz is even wearing British uniforms' one man clutching a pitch fork whispered but loud enough for Oliver to hear,

'Fritz?' He shouted back loudly, 'We're not German we're British Sailors from HM Submarine Ursula'

'So what the devil are you hiding for?' A portly red faced Gent dressed in a deer stalker hat, tweed jacket and armed with a double barrelled shotgun asked,

'We thought we were in the Channel Islands.'

The Gent doubled up with laughter, 'Channel Islands? Good God man you're bloody miles out. This is St Agnes' He chortled and lowered his shotgun 'Isle of Scilly' He turned to his neighbour who was armed with a scythe, 'guess we'd better find these lost jolly jack tars a boat back to the mainland don't you think?'

'What about your pet German S-Boat couldn't he give us a lift again?'

There was silence for a moment, 'Don't know what you're on about old chap. We certainly don't keep pet Germans here.'

'Well be that as it may but the fact remains that we were picked out of the sea and dropped off in your harbour by an enemy craft.'

The old gent shouldered his shotgun as they were led back towards the harbour, 'Well it'll be by our one and only fishing boat this time. And' he added lowering his voice, 'I think it'll be wise for you all to forget about how you got here'

'I thought you said you didn't know anything about it' Oliver retorted

'And so I don't' he replied quietly.

Within two and a half hours they were in Penzance a sorry bunch of foul smelling oil stained unshaven individuals waiting for the requested transport to take them to Plymouth. The local populous could be forgiven for thinking that a band of cut-throat Pirates had suddenly been dumped upon their shores.

A mobile NAAFI canteen had been parked up to serve the local "Ack Ack" crews so was immediately besieged by the starving men who'd not eaten anything for many hours. They gratefully gulped down the huge mugs of tea and chomped on the doorstep sandwiches with little regard to their dubious fillings.

'What do you think that old chap knew about that Jerry S-Boat?'

'I really don't know Roger and I doubt we'll ever find out.'

A Royal Navy lorry bounced over the cobbles and came to a halt by the Harbour wall. The driver jumped down from the cab approached Oliver and saluted smartly, 'Transport for Drake Sir.'

'Thank you Petty Officer I'll get them rounded up as soon as they finish their tea.'

Chapter Six

Drake Barracks Plymouth

Commodore Douglas Warwick had travelled down from Whitehall to get first-hand accounts of Operation Robin Hood from Oliver. He'd already had some information from Lieutenant Charles Smith who'd arrived back in Plymouth on Undaunted badly damaged but still serviceable. Another reason he had for travelling down was to suggest a new posting for Oliver.

'I can't leave you for a minute before you run into trouble Oliver' Charles shouted as he caught sight of him making his way to the Wardroom,

'Charlie' he said shaking hands warmly, 'glad to see you made it home'

'What happened to you?'

'Collision with an S-Boat then depth charged. Lost fifteen men, bloody disgrace really'

'Ooh don't go blaming yourself Oliver I'm pretty sure it would've been a lot worse without you. Drink?'

'Not now no I'm on my way for interrogation by Commodore Warwick'

'Good luck although I don't think you'll need it he seemed pretty pleased with our performance.'

'So what do you think Lieutenant?'

'A new Submarine you say Sir?'

'Yes completely new just nearing completion in Portsmouth'

'Promotion?'

Douglas drew in his breath and smiled, 'One thing at a time young man. We'll see about that later'

'Then I'd like to accept the command Sir'

'Excellent. You'll have to stay in Portsmouth Wardroom for a while until Troy is ready for sea'

'Yes Sir looking forward to it'

'Good. I'll give you lift to London then arrange transport to Portsmouth. I've got a meeting with Captain Wells but should be ready to leave at around 1500 shall we say.'

Oliver waited impatiently alongside the Commodores car; the sun had shone for the best part of the day so had warmed things up nicely. A perfect day to lounge in a deckchair on the Wardroom Lawn having a Gin or two rather than stand on the concrete kicking your heels waiting for a Commodore to grace you with his presence.

The Civilian driver got out of the car stretched his arms up and yawned, 'I've no idea when he'll be back, any later and we won't make London much before Morning. My Missus isn't going to be too pleased' he took a cigarette out of a pack and offered it to Oliver who shook his head. After lighting it and taking a few drags he continued, 'it's the Air-raids you see, worries her sick so likes me to be around. I've told her there isn't much I could do about it but I guess it makes her feel better.'

'Tell me what do you and the Commodore chat about on the longer journeys?'

'Chat?' he said laughing, 'He sleeps most of the time. You wait and see.'

The Commodore eventually put in an appearance at 1830 and true to the Drivers word was fast asleep snoring quietly long before Exeter.

The Driver pulled over and leant back, 'You may as well sit in the front Sir at least we can have a chin wag.'

The journey even with little traffic was long and difficult. As soon as it got dark it was almost impossible to make more than twenty miles per hour with slits in the headlights which only produced a glow on the road just a few feet ahead.

A snort from the rear seat indicated that the Commodore was awake, 'Where are we Harold?' He asked yawning 'must be close by now. Did I say I want to be dropped off at my club?'

'You did indeed Sir it'll be about another fifteen minutes or so.'

He'd hardly stopped talking when a Warden jumped in front of the car waving frantically with a torch. Screeching to a halt the Driver leapt out, 'What's your game mate? You'll get yourself killed if you carry on like that.'

'Yes so will you pal if you keep going. There's an unexploded bomb in Wandsworth High Street. You can wait or follow the signs we've put out'

'That's ok mate I know the way' Harold replied climbing back into the driving seat and reversing back along the road.

It was just on six in the morning that the Commodore was dropped off at his club in Chelsea. He leant through the window, 'Your transport is arranged for 0800 from Admiralty Arch don't be late.'

Oliver shook his head as they drove away. Harold said aloud what he'd been thinking, 'Bloody cheek coming from him Sir if you don't mind me saying.'

'Is he often late?'

'Always. One time I had a puncture so popped into the Garage to get it fixed. Arrived about half an hour late, even saw him walking out of the building as I drew up. Gave me a right fizzer he did. Got my own back though Sir'

'How?' Oliver asked politely by now far too exhausted to care.

They arrived at Admiralty Arch before Harold had chance to continue, 'Do you want me to wait Sir?'

'No I'll be fine thank you.'

Oliver hadn't visited London since before the War. He looked about him in disbelief, huge areas lay derelict with blackened masonry scattered everywhere. An unpleasant pungent smell like burnt wet timber hung heavy in the morning air.

Two Nuns were walking along the pavement comforting a distraught woman who despite their best efforts was sobbing uncontrollably. As they drew level one smiled and nodded a greeting as the other still attempted to pacify the woman, 'It was only a house my dear' she said holding her closer, 'no one was hurt that's the main thing.' The poor woman tears rolling down her cheeks burbled between sobs, 'It's all me clobber, it's gawn all gawn I 'aint got nuffing now.'

Quite saddened by the event and with the best part of an hour to kill he decided to walk the short distance to St James's Park. An elderly man was walking towards him. As he reached him he doffed his cap, 'Morning Governor you 'aint the one waiting for transport to Portsmouth are ya?'

'Yes I am actually. How on earth did you know?' Oliver replied quite taken aback.

The old man laughed, 'Not too difficult really, a Navy Lieutenant wandering around here at this time of the Morning. I'm William by the way, most call me Bill.' He held out his hand, 'pleased to meet you Sir, and you are?'

'Oliver.'

'Right Oliver we're a bit early but we might as well get a move on then we can stop at Guildford for a cuppa and a pee. You wait here and I'll fetch the waggon, it should be loaded up by now. Is that all the luggage you have?' He asked pointing at the small travel case,

'Yes that's it'

'Okey doke I'll be back in a tick.'

While he was waiting his thoughts went back to the poor woman who'd obviously lost her home and everything in it which reminded him a bit of his own situation. His suitcase now contained just about everything he owned in the World and that was only thanks to shore lockers Submariners were allowed to have in Drake to keep personal items safe. He'd kept a spare uniform which he was now wearing, photographs of his parents and sister and a few bits and bobs from his past plus the dreaded Will left for others to find in the event of death. The rest of his case had a few underclothes, shirts, collars and pyjamas all gratis replacements from Naval Stores.

A rather elderly Lorry shuddered to a halt, Bill struggling to keep the engine running hung out of the window, 'Better hop in quick before the bloody thing packs up altogether.'

Oliver went to climb up into the cab, 'You'd better chuck your case in the back we've got another passenger for Portsmouth.'

As Oliver climbed up Bob kept revving the engine, 'It's a real blighter this one, ok once it warms up but the gearbox is a bit buggered.'

An extremely good looking young woman walked through the Arch. Bill nudged Oliver, 'Gawd blimey if my old gal knew what I was thinking she'd do me in right and proper.'

She came up to the Lorry, 'Portsmouth?'

'Yes Miss hop in.'

Oliver opened the door and held his arm out to help her up. Her hand was soft and delicate as she grasped hold of him tightly as he hoisted her in. Leaning over to close the door her perfume wafted up at him, 'Thank you kind Sir' she mocked, 'you may let me go now.'

He realised that he was still holding on to her hand, 'I'm so sorry' he apologised feeling a little stupid, 'I'm Oliver this is William'

'How do you do Miss everybody calls me Bill'

'Hello I'm Pamela, Pam to most.'

'No luggage Pam?' Bill asked still revving the engine

'Daddy's taking it down this evening'

'Daddy?' Oliver asked

'Yes sorry I'm Pam Warwick' she said smiling to reveal pearly white teeth,

'Commodore Warwick's Daughter?'

'The very same' she giggled sweetly 'this is cosy isn't it?'

Bill now satisfied that the engine was warmed up enough

crunched it into first gear and surged forward then nearly stalled. Pam grabbed Oliver's arm as they were thrown back and forth. Oliver couldn't help noticing how warm and soft her body was against him and was pleased that she continued holding onto him.

The sun was up and the cab was getting a little hot so Bill rolled down the window.

'Can you help me take off my cardigan please Oliver?' Pam asked quickly adding, 'it's a bit squashed in here'

'My pleasure' he said not failing to notice her slim figure as she wriggled about in the seat to free the other arm.

She smiled her thanks as she folded the cardigan and laid it in her lap Oliver returned the smile then looking forward but in truth swivelling his eyes as far left as he could to study her. She was wearing an apple printed dress with thin shoulder straps; her bare arms were fair and silky smooth, her hair a light brown colour swept back behind her ears. As she spent much of the time looking out of the side window he only caught glimpses of her face but the little he had seen proved she was a very attractive and desirable young Lady.

'We'll take a break here' Bill said screeching to a halt just a few inches short of hitting the NAAFI waggon. Pam grabbed hold of Oliver to save ending up on the dashboard. Unperturbed Bill turned the engine off, 'We can have a cuppa and a jimmy riddle here' he said swinging down from the Cab and slamming the door.

Pam looked at Oliver 'Help' she whispered and started to laugh, 'I don't think I'm dressed to jump in and out of Lorries'

'Hang on a mo' he said sliding over into the driving seat, 'I'll come round and lift you down.'

She leant forward and swivelled round; as he put his hands onto her waist she slid off the seat and into his arms.

'Thank you Oliver. You can put me down now'

'So I can' he replied reluctantly releasing her.

Now briefly able to look at her properly he could see

that she was slim, had blue eyes, a soft face with rounded cheek bones, slim nose, soft pink lips, small chin and a gorgeous smile that produced shallow dimples on each cheek.

'Shall we have Tea Oliver?' She asked sensing his mind was somewhere else,

'Yes, yes of course sorry I was miles away.'

He took great pleasure in pulling her back up into the cab; it was no accident that she almost ended up on his lap before sliding back onto her seat.

In no time at all they were approaching Portsmouth, 'Will you be able to drop me off at the house Bill? It's quite near here'

'No problem Pam if you give me directions.'

After a few lefts and rights she pointed to a large house, 'In here please Bob.'

He carefully manoeuvred the Lorry into the gravelled front garden rounded a huge Oak tree and stopped opposite an ornate porch. She looked at Oliver pointed to the ground and smiled, the dimples showing up even more in the sunlight, her eyes twinkling as if looking for mischief,

'Bob I need to help Pam down so....'

He got the drift straight away, opened the door and jumped down.

Again she dropped into his arms but this time her lips brushed his cheek, 'Thank you Oliver I hope to meet you again' she said politely, 'Bye Bob thanks for the lift.'

Victory Barracks Wardroom Portsmouth

'Lieutenant Pitman I'm Commander Paul Harvey welcome to Portsmouth.'

Paul was fifty-five years old immaculately dressed and although only five-foot-eight very erect in stature. A stern almost poker faced man with combed back black hair his staring green eyes rarely blinked so appeared to look through people instead of at them. His fair skin tone suggested he'd not been to sea for some time. Even his full lips seemed reluctant to break into a smile in all a quite grumpy looking man.

He looked down at Oliver's case, 'I trust that's not all your luggage'

'I'm afraid it is Sir'

'So you've not brought your Mess Dress?'

'No Sir I've not found any need for one since Dartmouth'

'Not even in Drake Wardroom?'

'No Sir it's quite relaxed'

'Good Lord obviously everything must've gone to pot there. Well you'll need to find one before Dinner which is at 1800 on the dot or go hungry. Your choice.' He went to walk away but turned, 'there are two Naval Outfitters just down the road almost opposite the Brewery they may be able to help. If not then as I said don't bother to come you'll have to eat elsewhere.'

A Lieutenant who'd been reading a notice board close by came over and extended his hand, 'Hello I'm Steven Boniface' they shook hands, 'I heard you've met grumpy'

'Is he always like that?'

'No, sometimes he's a bloody sight worse. Anyway I think you look about the same size as me and I've got a spare tunic and trousers, you'll need to pop down the Outfitters for a shirt though.'

Fully suited and booted Oliver entered the Dining Room at exactly 1800. 'When I say 1800 on the dot Pitman I mean five minutes before. I hope you remember that in future now sit down.' Oliver went to sit, 'Not there man over there with Boniface. Yes that's right. Good God man if you don't know your place then things really have fallen apart in Drake.'

Oliver was taking an instant dislike to this rude arrogant pompous individual and was thankful that his stay here was most probably quite brief.

Oliver was amazed at not just the amount but variety of

food on offer. They'd felt lucky to have two courses at Drake but here food kept coming. Hard to accept when he was pretty sure that not far down the road Housewives were scuttling round worried that they'd not be able to eke out their ever decreasing rations which they'd most likely queued up for hours to buy.

'What's the matter Pitman not good enough for you?'

'On the contrary Sir it's more than adequate.'

Harvey grunted then turned to the Petty Officer Steward, 'Phillips make sure everything is locked away and bring the keys back to me.' As he moved towards the door, 'and remember if I catch anyone pilfering anything they'll be for the high jump. You understand?'

The PO Steward nodded and left the room.

Oliver was extremely tired, 'Excuse me Gentlemen' he apologised standing up, 'I've had a long day so I'd like to retire to my cabin.'

The Commander shot up his face contorted with rage, 'You certainly have no manners Pitman' he almost spat his name out, 'perhaps they're good enough for Submariners but here' he thumped his fist down, 'you'll leave the table when I damn well say you can and not before. You understand?' Oliver said nothing and sat down again as the tirade continued, 'and as for going to your cabin' he scoffed, 'I'll wager you'll need someone to show you where it is.' He paused looking around at all the blank faces. Oliver like the others was at a loss to understand what on earth he was on about. 'Well' he continued smirking, 'aren't you the chap who hid yourself away in the Scilly Isles for a day or so thinking you were in France or something?'

Peals of laughter erupted from the Senior Officers who banged the table in applause.

Oliver eyes shut and hands grasped tightly together listened to the voice screaming at him from within his head, "Just shut up Oliver ignore him and stay in your seat." But the Genie was out of the bottle and he had no way of putting it back. He stood up and stared directly at the Commander, 'Yes Sir that was after we were sunk and drifted around the Atlantic for a day following an operation where we sank twenty U-Boats, their supply tender and crippled a Destroyer. We lost forty-seven men so that the Convoy from New York could find safe passage, a Convoy with tons of supplies apparently' he swept his arm over the table, 'so you and your Barrack Stanchion pals can stuff yourselves.'

There was absolute silence from around the table. Then the Commander spoke, 'Have you quite finished Pitman?'

'Yes Sir I have'

'Then I suggest you leave the room right now'

'That Sir is exactly what I wanted in the first place.'

He threw his napkin onto the table turned, bowed sarcastically and strode out.

As he climbed the staircase the voice in his head returned, "You bloody clot why didn't you just shut up?"

A frantic knocking on his door woke him from his much needed sleep. Bleary eyed he opened it, 'What do you want?'

'The Sirens gone off Sir you need to get to the shelter now'

'I'm too bloody tired I'll take the risk and stay here. You get yourself down there'

'I can't do that Sir. Please hurry or I'll be in real trouble.'

Oliver grabbed the dressing gown that seemed to come with the cabin and followed the Steward rushing along the corridor.

The crump of bombs got louder until with a series of deafening thumps a stick landed close by along the street rattling windows and bringing lumps of plaster down on their heads, 'What's in here?' Oliver shouted above the din,

'Brooms and things Sir.'

Oliver pulled the door open and they both squeezed

into the confines of the cupboard pulling the door shut behind them.

As the raid continued bomb after bomb rained down shaking the very foundations of the building the constant shattering of glass almost drowning out the sound of Anti-Aircraft guns blasting their high explosives into the air and bells ringing as Fire Engines rushed to deal with the hundreds of fires breaking out throughout the City.

At last the all-clear sounded. Oliver and the Steward freed themselves from the cupboard, 'Better get downstairs Sir they'll want a cup of tea. Would you like me to have one sent up Sir?'

'No thank you. And what did you mean when you said you'd be in trouble?'

'Haven't got time Sir must get down now' he replied breathlessly as if close to panic.

As he rushed away the Commanders voice boomed from the bottom of the stairs, 'Where the bloody hell have you got to boy? Ah there you are about time too. Now get the tea and chop chop about it.'

Oliver shook his head in disbelief at the sheer arrogance of this despicable man who it appeared revelled in a game of humiliating people with his archaic idea of Leadership.

Yawning he returned to his cabin and dropped off to sleep until a knock at the door disturbed him, 'Sorry to bother you Sir' the steward muttered holding up a tray, 'but I was ordered to bring Breakfast up to you.'

Oliver took the tray placed it on the small table and went out into the corridor, 'Your name?'

'Harrison Sir'

'Ok Harrison it looks to me that we both seem to be in trouble so what's your story?'

'Well Sir' he looked around to check that nobody was within earshot, 'when the siren sounds we have to make sure that all Officers get to the shelter'

'And I wasn't there'

'Yes Sir'

'Well I'm sorry Harrison I'll have a word with someone if it helps?'

'No need Sir at least I'm all in one piece' noticing Oliver's puzzled look, 'oh you haven't heard Sir Petty Officer Steward Phillips and Leading Steward Clegg were badly injured in the raid' he smiled, 'I would've been with them Sir but I was stuck up here with you'

'So where were they?'

'Crossing the road to the Barracks Sir'

'Why?'

'We're not allowed in the Wardroom shelter Sir it's Officers only.'

Oliver's Genie was bashing at the top of the bottle but he managed to keep it corked and hold his tongue professional enough not to make derogatory remarks about any Officer in front of a Rating,

'I see. Right Harrison I guess you'd better be back to your duties'

'Thank you Sir.'

Oliver removed the plate cover, it was a sort of rubbery scrambled egg on a soggy piece of toast, a note accompanied it. He exhaled loudly in exasperation as he read it, "This Lieutenant is probably more like you're used to in your grubby little submarine so enjoy. As of today due to your insolence you are barred from the Wardroom so will need to arrange your own accommodation."

'Is there no end to this man's disgusting behaviour?' he muttered to himself placing the cover back over the plate.

With a quick tap on the door Lieutenant Boniface put his head round, 'Hello Oliver who's been a naughty boy then?'

'Ah Steven I guess you've come to collect your Monkey suit?'

'Well if the rumours are correct my dear sir you won't have need of it anymore.'

Oliver picked up the note and held it above his head,

'You are indeed correct as I have here a letter from Mein Fuhrer banning me from his Fiefdom.'

'Yes Harrison?' Oliver asked as he saw the Steward standing in the open doorway, 'I assume you've come to take the tray away?'

'No Sir I've orders to collect you and your luggage then direct you to Commodore Warwick's Office over the road.'

Commodore Warwick lit a cigarette and blew a spiral of smoke into the air, 'Well Lieutenant you have certainly created havoc'

'The man's a bloody Tyrant Sir'

'Tyrant or not he's a Commander and you're a Lieutenant which I'm led to believe you seem to have completely forgotten'

'So am I expected to be humiliated, have the brave exploits of my crew laughed at and my reputation ripped up without redress?'

The Commodore took another puff on his cigarette held it in his lungs for a second or two then exhaled slowly, 'Absolutely not. If you'd just shut up then made an official complaint of his behaviour I can assure you that he would be the one sat here not you. As it is Commander Harvey is demanding that you be Court Marshalled for Insubordination and behaviour contrary to Naval Discipline.' Oliver shrugged his shoulders, 'damn it man you don't seem to realise the extent of the problems you've caused. With this hanging over your head I will not be able to put you in command of the Gosport Ferry let alone Troy. It's as simple as that. Now to save any danger of a repeat performance you'd better make yourself scarce as Commander Harvey's on his way over and for the moment I suggest you get yourself booked in at what used to be the Officers club along the road here. I don't know what it's called now but I'm sure you'll find it.'

'The man is a peasant Sir, insolent and with absolutely no

manners, he didn't own a Mess Dress and had no idea of protocol he didn't even know where to sit at Dinner, believe it or not he actually went to a seat on the Senior Officers side of the table. Not cut out to be an Officer Sir obviously from working class and time we put him back down where he belongs. He referred to us as Barrack Stanchions for goodness sake'

'Tell me Commander when was the last time you went to sea?'

He thought for a minute, '1932 Sir why do you ask?' The Commodore remained silent, folded his arms and looked directly at him raising his eyes, 'oh yes I see but that's no excuse Sir'

'So you're still hell bent on a Court Marshall?'

'Of course Sir what else?'

'Well obviously I'll call for one to be convened at your request but just a friendly warning before I go ahead'

'A warning Sir?'

'There are four Junior and one Senior Officer who have indicated that they will testify on behalf of Lieutenant Pitman'

'Give me their names Sir and I'll soon sort that out'

'That is not how it works Commander' he snapped crossly,

'So what would you suggest Sir? We can't just let him off scot free surely?'

'As you know I have no sway over what happens in the Wardroom but I understand that you've barred him so I think that'll be punishment enough in this instance'

'He'll have to apologise to me in front of the Officers Sir'

'That Commander is something you and I know is not likely to happen'

'It will if you order it Sir.'

The Commodore lit another cigarette and coughed repeatedly, 'God I really must pack these things up they'll be the death of me. Now where were we?'

'You ordering Pitman to apologise to me Sir'

The Commodore folded his arms then with a determined face and steady voice, 'I understand you were pretty rude to Lieutenant Pitman from almost the second he arrived'

'He was late Sir I said 1800'

'No I'm advised that you said 1800 on the dot and I believe that on the dot he was. Now as for him not having a Mess Dress and being unsure where to sit at Dinner.' He paused for a last puff before stubbing his cigarette out in an overflowing ash tray, 'he's a Submariner, as I was in the early days. To be honest I'm surprised he even had a cap to wear and furthermore he would normally be used to taking his meals from a table a little bigger than the chair you're sitting on. And as for' he became more serious, 'your cutting and may I say rather unwarranted remarks about him hiding in the Scillies'

'Well it was true Sir' the Commander interrupted,

'Yes it was but were you aware that he and his crew were plucked out of the water by what for all intents and purposes they believed to be an enemy craft and dropped off during the night in a harbour they didn't recognise?'

'No Sir I wasn't'

'You see my point Commander?'

'Yes Sir I think I do'

'Good. Now I know that I'm not at liberty to influence any procedures in the Wardroom but this nonsense of Ratings not being allowed into the Officers air-raid shelter is to stop.' The Commander shifted awkwardly in his seat, 'you were damn lucky those two Stewards weren't killed else I think you'd be the one being Court Marshalled. Even so they could still be advised to put in a formal complaint against you. Something for you to seriously consider Commander don't you think?'

'Yes Sir' he replied sheepishly, 'I guess that means Pitman is off the hook?'

''Yes I do believe he is.'

Oliver left the Barracks and picked his way along rubble

strewn Queens Street. Remarkably all the shops, even quite badly damaged ones were open for business. The Barbers shop with a queue of Soldiers lined up outside, some leaning against the remaining wall of the Naval Tailors next door it's once decorative sign now set over bricks to make a handy seat for the Housewives to rest their weary legs as they queued for their rations at the Butchers.

'Greetings Oliver where are you off to in such a hurry?'

'Hi Steven. The ex-Officers Club to beg a room'

'That'll be expensive. Do you mind if I accompany you?'

'Not at all but you're sure you'll not be reprimanded for association with the enemy?'

'I'll risk it.'

They continued to chat together moving aside to let a coal lorry squeeze past the driver unaware of a scruffy looking kid on the back throwing lumps of coal down to his young mate below who was struggling along dragging a quite heavy sack behind him. As the Lorry cleared the obstructions and speeded up the Lad jumped down to join his mate, 'Morning Guv' he said standing to attention and saluting smartly. Oliver smiled and returned the salute.

'You're lucky Sir we have a room that's just become vacant it's ten and six per night in advance no meals included and' he droned on 'I'm obliged by law to point out that our shelter is over the road behind the pub.' He noticed Oliver's look, 'most Officers can claim the expense back'

'Unfortunately I don't think I'm most but I'll take it'

'How long?'

Oliver thought for a couple of minutes, 'Just a couple of nights'

'Is that two nights three nights or what?'

Steven leant over, 'I can stump up a few bob if you need it Oliver'

'Thanks but I reckon I can manage four nights'

'So it's four nights then?'

'Yes four nights' Oliver replied begrudgingly digging out the two guineas

'Do you want a receipt?'

At first he was going to decline but it would be worth a try to get it refunded, 'Yes if you will and the key please.'

'No keys' he said bluntly 'none of the locks work anymore so no point.'

The room was horrid, it reeked of tobacco smoke, the sink was dreadfully stained, half the bed springs were missing, the windows were filthy and there were huge holes in the Lino revealing bare badly discoloured floor boards.

'God this is bloody awful Oliver you can't stay in this dump'

'No choice old chap, won't be for long though because…'

A knock at the door interrupted their conversation, 'Just had a telephone message from a Commodore Warwick you're to meet him at dry dock number four.'

'Did he say when?'

'No.'

'Guess that means now then' Oliver said waving the receipt above his head, 'perhaps I'll be able to convince him to sign this off.'

Oliver was unusually lost for words. Even in the gloom under the camouflaged tent structure Troy even though all vessels look much bigger in dry dock was huge, much wider than normal with a beam of 38 feet due to having internal saddle tanks and shaped like a cigar at a length of 390 feet with all the pressure hull panels welded not riveted. The conning tower was much further forward than was normal.

Finally finding his voice, 'So am I to command this giant Sir?'

'Unless you're unwise enough to cross swords with Commander Harvey again then yes'

'Can we go on board Sir?'

Oliver was surprised as they climbed down through the hatch and into the control room. It certainly seemed no larger than his short hull U Class. Looking round everything seemed quite normal and in the usual place except the steering position that had a yoke and column similar to an aeroplane.

'Single man control' the Commodore said demonstrating by moving it back and forth screwing his face up as a swift rebuke was bellowed from the next compartment, 'For God sake leave the bloody thing alone you'll have me bleedin fingers off.'

'Operates the planes and rudder' he whispered stepping back as a head popped around the hatch, 'Oh it's you Commodore, sorry for me cussing and that.'

'I didn't realise sorry.'

With the thump of sturdy boots on ladders and loud voices more workers swarmed into the Control room, some carrying large coils of wire, others lugging heavy tool boxes as they noisily made their way through to other parts of the Boat.

'Think we'd better call it a day' the Commodore shouted above the din now filling every space.

Back out on the Caisson Oliver was again surprised by the Boats size compared to its equally cramped interior of a conventional Submarine, 'What makes this so special Sir?'

'It's no good me trying to explain so I'll arrange a visit to the boffins who designed it. Even then I'm not sure we'll fully understand but worth giving it a go, not until tomorrow though let's say we meet here about ten hundred and then afterwards they can give you the full tour. Changing the subject Lieutenant what's your accommodation like?'

'Really awful Sir and expensive which reminds me could you sign it off for me?'

The Commodore gave him a hard long look, 'No Lieutenant I can't then perhaps you'll learn to keep your

65

mouth firmly shut in future.'

As Oliver walked past the Victory towards the main gate he looked up at the famous Warship and wondered humorously if Commander Harvey would've fitted in. He smiled as he visualised him gloating on the Quarter deck overseeing a poor Midshipman being flogged half to death for the heinous crime of sitting in the wrong chair at Dinner.

'You're looking happy Oliver'

He turned 'Pamela how lovely to see you again' he said surprised to see her dressed as a WRNS Second Officer, 'I didn't realise..'

'That I was a Wren or managed to be an Officer?' She interrupted him with a mischievous smile,

'You know exactly what I meant'

'I did yes. Anyway Daddy gave me a choice a Land Girl or the Navy' she grinned as he gave her an old fashioned look, 'Mummy said she couldn't stand having to wash muddy clothes so it had to be the Navy.'

The sun was low in the sky shining directly on to her highlighting her beautiful features. The uniform was obviously tailored so fitted her exquisite figure exactly. He'd never felt this way about a Woman. Although he'd only been with her for a few hours in the Lorry then once more today he was sure that he wanted to see her again. "*If only, if only she felt the same way*" he wished "*But me a Lieutenant and her a Commodores daughter?*"

'Are you on your way back to the Wardroom?'

'Sorry?'

'The Wardroom?'

'No I have a room at the old Officers club'

'Yuk how horrid for you, a no room at the Inn situation?'

'Umm something like that yes. Do you stay in the Wardroom at all?'

'A Woman in the Wardroom?' she mocked, 'Good Lord man are you mad? The Senior Officers would throw a fit at the mere thought of it; I'd be evicted within minutes'

'Believe me Pam I know the feeling. Can I see you again?' He asked boldly.

She thought for a second or two which seemed an eternity to Oliver, 'Yes I'd like that. In fact Oliver I'd like that a lot.' She leant forward and kissed him on the cheek, 'Bye for now.'

He walked the short distance back to the old Officers club jubilant that she'd agreed to see him again. The smell of hot food made him realise how hungry he was,

'It's a Bob Sir just twelve little pence for a bowl of ecstasy' the building owner crowed rubbing his hands together, 'knocked up by one of Portsmouth's finest Chefs'

'So what is it?' Oliver asked.

A very large Woman dressed in a tabard and a turban waddled through the door brandishing a huge serving spoon as if it were a weapon, 'Bunny Rabbit stew' she said loudly, 'just like yesterday and probably again tomorrow.' Oliver nodded. 'Good sit yourself down Sir and wait to be amazed.'

She returned a few minutes later with a bowl filled to the brim with stew and a thick slice of bread, 'You enjoy that Sir it'll put hairs on your chest. As good as the finest steak it is.'

Oliver finished every scrap. It was one of the best meals he'd tasted for ages, sweet succulent and as the woman had said as good as the finest steak.

Back in his room as dusk fell it was no surprise to find that the light didn't work. Still dressed he laid on the bed which creaked at every move. In the dark and stuffiness of the small room he started to snooze until rudely awakened by the whine of the air-raid siren. He put his jacket on and left the room. 'At least the corridor's lit' he thought as he made his way through,

'Make sure you take all your stuff with you Pal. I lost

my watch yesterday. They say its kids but I wouldn't be surprised if it wasn't that Bastard down stairs.' Oliver quickly went back into the room and picked up his bag and joined the chap who'd given the warning, 'Guy Robins' he shouted as they made their way out of the building, 'Major Royal Marines'

'No room in the Wardroom Sir' he panted as they ran over the road searchlights already waving back and forth punching beams into the sky seeking out their prey, the distant drone of aero engines clearly audible,

'No chance I'd most probably thump someone. Can't handle all that crap. You?'

'Barred because of my bad behaviour Sir'

'Good for you' he said laughing as they found the shelter and made their way down.

Guy was thirty eight just less than six feet tall with a muscular military upright stature, his dark hair cropped to a quarter of an inch small close set eyes craggy weathered face and chiselled chin gave him the looks of a career criminal.

Once the heavy steel doors were shut it was difficult to make out much at all in the gloom. Oliver found a space and sat down on the long wooden bench that stretched from one end to the other. An old woman was standing in front of him; he stood up and indicated for her to take his space. Now standing he felt a persistent tug on his trousers, 'Mister why 'aint you in the big 'ouse along the road?'

'Ronald!' a voice squawked out of the gloom, 'stop bothering the Gentleman. Sorry Sir he's always asking questions this one. Bit of a nuisance sometimes.' She dragged him away only to be replaced by a rather shabbily dressed woman who didn't smell too good.

Bombs fell thick and fast. Some close others far away but then the whole shelter shook violently as a massive explosion sounded almost on top of them. The lights went out,

'Oye let me go ya bitch. Ouch that hurts. What you up to you bloody cow. Let me go.' The lights flickered then came back on. The large Woman who'd served the stew was holding tight to the woman standing beside Oliver, 'Your bag Sir' she said holding it out,

'I want doin nuffing' the scruffy woman protested pulling her arm away, 'nuffing.'

'Of course you weren't love.' Now released she skulked off still protesting her innocence, 'Her and both her youngans are tea leaves the lot of them. Milk Coal Bread and anything else the little buggers can get their thieving hands on. If the lights go off again Sir keep the bag close to your chest, hug it like it's your favourite woman then you should still have it when we get out of here.'

Oliver smiled and thanked her; she just nodded and moved further along.

Wave after wave of bombers came over the City that night spewing out their packages of death and destruction so it was long after dawn before the welcome wail of the all clear sounded releasing them from the confines of the shelter.

The sight that met them was one of complete and utter devastation, most of the Pub had gone and the Side Street of small terraced houses had collapsed onto each other like dominoes. A huge water filled crater extended over the road and onto where the old Officers club once stood, now a heap of smoking rubble.

Cries of despair filled the air as more people emerged from their underground sanctuary. One woman passed with an arm around another, 'Well let's just 'ope that the Spitfires got em and they all burned up and drowned in the sea.'

An old man leant on a walking stick stood alone silently weeping as he gazed along his battered and broken street. A young girl, around ten years of age took his arm,

69

'Come on Grandad don't cry we can always go to Aunty Violets.'

He smiled weakly bent down and kissed her tenderly on the forehead.

A line of men started to form along what remained of the street, 'Well that's torn it' a voice said behind him, he turned to see Guy, 'guess we'll have to look for alternative accommodation.' A young man approached him and spoke quietly but loud enough for Oliver to deduce that it certainly wasn't English. Guy whispered a reply, satisfied the Lad moved on calling others to join him. 'Polish Dockyard Workers' he explained, 'He asked if I knew of anywhere else they could stay.' A wicked grin spread over his face, 'I told him to try the posh house opposite the Barrack gates'

'The Wardroom Sir'

'Exactly that'll stir up Commander what's his name. And for pity sake stop calling me Sir my name's Guy, yours?'

'Oliver.'

'How much did you have to pay for your room?' he asked quite out of the blue

'Two guineas why?'

He didn't answer but dashed off back towards the shelter.

'Hello Guv do ya fancy buying this watch? Works an all it does. Here listen.'

Oliver looked down at the scruffy little lad he'd previously seen on the coal lorry, 'Where did you get it from?'

'Found it Guv honest I did, you can have it for half a crown.'

Oliver took it from him and flipped the back open. "To Guy with thanks from Tom Harry Jock & Bill July 1940"

'Yes I'll take it but I'm not going to pay'

The Lad made a grab for it but Oliver held it up 'Oye you can't do that mister it's pinching that is. I'll report you to the Coppers I will you mark my words.'

'Now hop it before I call a Constable. You stole it from the Hotel over there the night before last'

'I didn't Guv honest I didn't so give it back'

'Well here comes the Gentleman you stole it from.'

The Lad was on his toes and away within seconds as Guy walked over holding something in his hand.

'Your Two guineas my good man. I don't see why you should pay for something you don't use'

'Thank you Guy. And here's your pocket watch'

'How on earth did you get that?'

'The scruffy little bugger who stole it tried to sell it to me'

'You didn't pay for it did you?'

'Of course not, although I was tempted at half a crown'

'Half a crown? It's eighteen carat gold' he paused and chuckled, 'although knowing those reprobates it's probably brass. But thank you for that. So what are we to do now?'

'Well at least you have the opportunity to go to the Wardroom'

He huffed, 'There's no chance of that. I'd rather shoot myself than associate with that bunch of stuck up twits.'

Oliver checked for the time on his watch, 'The little sod' he said holding up a bare wrist, 'no wonder he legged it so quick.'

As he spoke a Constable came round the corner dragging the lad along by the scruff of his neck, 'Which Gentleman?' He demanded loudly, 'speak up or you'll feel the back of me 'and.'

The Lad pointed to Oliver, 'It fell off his wrist it did honest.'

'Your watch I believe Sir' he handed it over, 'we have to go round searching for this little tyke after every raid just in case he'd been up to his usual little tricks. Come on you I'll get you back home'

'Ouch your 'urting me' the lad protested as the Constable carted him away

'You're lucky I don't tan your hide Lad.'

'Good Lord it's nine forty-five I'm supposed to meet the Commodore at ten'

'Well Oliver you'd better get a move on' Guy said shaking hands, 'and thanks for rescuing my watch.'

The Commodore was already waiting as Oliver made his way over the Caisson towards him,

'My God man' he shouted noticing Oliver's bag, 'don't tell me you've been kicked out of that flea pit as well'

'No Sir' he replied still a little out of breath from hurrying, 'not kicked out Sir but more like bombed out'

'I see. Right we'd better get a move on he's only in the semaphore tower.'

"I wish you'd told me that before" Oliver thought to himself having had to rush right past the damn place to meet up with him.

The Commodore set off at quite a pace but in his fifties, quite unfit and more than a little overweight he soon slowed then stopped, 'Must have a smoke before we go in' he muttered breathlessly then persistently coughed at just about every puff, 'that's better' he croaked, 'I'm ready for him now.'

Professor Victor Landor Chief Naval Scientist was quite irritated at the prospect of having to demonstrate the workings of this craft. He had plenty of other things he should be attending to rather than pandering to a couple of Officers who he was sure wouldn't understand anything he'd try to explain.

Victor was in his late fifties, bald except for a shock of grey hair above each ear, the furrows across his brow made worse by him constantly squinting over the top of a tiny pair of metal rimmed glasses perched precariously on his nose. His pasty appearance proved he didn't get out into the fresh air very much and painfully thin body that food wasn't his first priority.

Constantly muttering to himself he scrabbled around in

his brief case for a minute or two then placed a small metal box on the table in front of him before shuffling over to a blackboard. Quickly scribbling down an equation he turned to face Oliver and Douglas, 'Do you know what that is?' He asked pointing to it.

The temptation to say it was a blackboard was strong but resisted so Oliver answered, 'Basic stuff really it's Newtons law of gravity.'

Victor nodded, 'So do you think we can play around with it?' With no reply he carried on, 'if a gravitational pull can be applied in front of an object it will move forward. Correct?'

'I guess so' Douglas replied drearily hoping this wasn't going to take for ever.

Victor hobbled back to the desk, 'Bit unsteady on my pins' he explained, 'fell down one of your stupid ladders. Why the hell you can't have stairs I'll never know.'

Douglas without a word stood up took the chalk from him and wrote down a formula, 'Do you know what that is Professor?'

'Of course I do' he snapped irritated at the interruption, 'it's the volume of a cylinder'

'Exactly, so to answer your query we only have an infinite space to pack things in hence ladders being vertical.' He passed the chalk back to him,

'My query as you call it was rhetorical. Now can we get on please?' He moved the box to the end of the table and pushed a button. The box moved slowly forward but still too fast for him to catch so as it reached the end of the table it tumbled to the floor, 'oops' is all he could say as he bent down and retrieved it.

Douglas had completely lost interest and was looking out of the window but Oliver was intrigued, 'So you put the gravitational pull in front of the object and it falls into it?'

'Until it drops off the table' Douglas said yawning still looking out of the window.

'I'm sorry if you're bored Commodore but remember

you're the one who asked for me to give up my valuable time to explain how the Submarine will be driven so thank you and good day'

'Whoa there Professor I'm sorry but honestly it's not a case of being bored, we're not used to magic electronic devices, engines are what we understand.

'And young man what do you think?'

'Fascinating Professor and I do have some questions'

'Fire away' he said perching on the side of the table

'How do you control the velocity of the object?'

'More power the greater the velocity'

'And how do you stop'

'Put a field behind the object'

'And I won't have to surface to charge any batteries?'

'You're to command this vessel?' He asked with surprise

'Yes'

'Goodness me talk about old heads on young shoulders. Look I've got to be somewhere else but I'll send one of my team over to show you around the ship and he'll be able to answer any more questions you have but to answer this one, yes you do need a recharge but only after an average one hundred and twenty hours of operation. There are three propellers on the stern of the ship that rotate as it moves through the water. Two outer ones drive generators to give a constant charge the middle larger one to power the compressor and there's a diesel generator complete with a snorkel so you could keep the ship submerged for ages'

'Boat' Douglas corrected him, 'submarines are boats'

'Quite so quite so boat it is.'

Leaving the semaphore tower they made their way back to the dry dock but were intercepted by a signalman riding a Pussers red devil, he carefully propped the bone shaker up against a post and handed the Commodore a message. He muttered something under his breath then after dismissing the Signalman announced, 'I've been called to London for an important powwow you take your tour round Troy and I'll get hold of my Daughter to meet you later. I guess you'll have to stay at our place as it appears that you've been kicked out of one and bombed out of another.'

Oliver couldn't believe his luck *"Thank you Luftwaffe for bombing the flea pit"* he thought grinning with joy as he made his way back to Troy, *"staying with Pam. Fantastic."*

A short chubby chap with a flushed face dressed in overalls was waiting for Oliver on the dockside. He shook hands, 'Hello old chap I'm Rupert Longhurst here to give you the Royal tour'

'Hello Rupert. I'm a bit surprised that she looks pretty big on the outside but not much difference to a normal boat inside'

'Ah yes that's because the drive unit takes up loads of space.' He replied as they clambered down through the forward hatch into quite a large flat with twenty-four bunks in threes, four fixed against the port and four to the starboard bulkheads, 'This is the only ratings mess except for a small four berth for Senior Rates which is just aft of the drive unit.'

'Crew?'

'Same as your U-Class thirty two. Four Officers, four senior rates and twenty four ratings.'

'No hot bunking then?'

'Not unless you intend to take passengers.'

He led Oliver through a very narrow passageway, 'Wardroom to the left, your cabin to the right.' Oliver poked his head through the curtain, 'Looks rather posh' he commented quite pleased as it looked slightly larger than he'd been used to with a good sized table plenty of storage space under the bunk and most unusually for a Submarine panelled bulkheads. The Wardroom was to the same high standard and again panelled bulkheads. Oliver queried it, 'Weight isn't a problem Oliver, in fact it helps with the performance'

'So what is its performance as you call it?'

'On the surface around thirty knots, submerged possibly forty maybe forty-five.' He smiled and held his hands up as Oliver gave him a confused look, 'yes I know it sounds the wrong way round but it's been dynamically designed explicitly for being submerged' he paused for a second, 'to be really honest Oliver we believe it'll be a real pig on the surface.'

'Weapons?'

'Not my field really but what I can say is that there's four forward tubes and two aft all twenty-one inch but no idea of the type of Torpedoes you'll carry'

'Maximum depth?'

'Test depth seven-hundred feet collapse depth twelve hundred'

'And the what did you call it?'

'The drive unit?'

'Yes'

'It's known as a Graviton Generator, I'd show you but there really isn't much to see apart from miles of wire. I know how it works and how to operate it but as for maintenance that I'm afraid is way beyond me'

'So what if it goes wrong while we're out at sea?'

'At least two of your Engineers have been working with our team for months so they should be able to cope with most situations.'

The tour continued for the best part of an hour, much of it conducted amongst Dockyard workers frantically finishing off bits and pieces before as Rupert announced that D lock was to be flooded the following morning.

'Where will she be moved to?'

'Most likely Fountain Lake jetty but that's not really up to us'

'Last question I promise'

'Fire away that's what I'm here for'

'Is Troy the only one of its type?'

'No we have one other in Belfast but not yet fitted with the drive unit.' He chuckled, 'got to see how you chaps bugger about with it before our Lord and Masters will commit to the cost'

'Expensive?'

'I think mind blowing is closer to the mark I once overheard Windy complaining that the cost had reached nearly a million'

'Windy?'

'Sorry it's Admiral Bernard Beaufort hence the nickname'

'I don't think I've ever come across him'

'I'm sure you will at some time especially if any Politicians show up'

'You're not too keen on the chap then?'

'On the contrary he's a real Gent always fights our corner and most importantly for us can't stand Politicians. As I say you're bound to come across him.'

Oliver thanked Rupert for his time and made his way towards the main Dockyard gate where the Policeman called out from the Guardhouse, 'Excuse me are you Lieutenant Pitman by any chance?'

'I am yes but how…'

'Quite easily really' he interrupted his metal studded boots clunking as he walked across the cobbles, 'we were told to look out for a Lieutenant carrying a small brown bag and to give him this note.'

The note was from the Commodore telling that he'd arranged for him to meet up with Pamela outside the Main gate at 1800. He looked at his watch 1600, *"Guess I'd better get over to the Outfitters and buy some clobber"* he thought knowing that his complete wardrobe only amounted to his Uniform a couple of white shirts, a few underclothes, some socks and a spare handkerchief. Not exactly what he assumed would be required lodging at the Commodores house.

'Can I help you Sir?' The Tailor enquired rubbing his hands together

'You may yes I need quite a few bits and pieces'

'Is it to be cash or account Sir?' He asked waving his hand over a large ledger.

Oliver was a past master at reading text upside down so noticed that the page was open against Commander Harvey's account. A wicked thought crossed his mind, revenge perhaps, 'Account' he replied loudly,

'And the name Sir?'

'Uncle Douglas'

The Tailor just stared at him, 'Oh sorry' Oliver apologised, 'Commander Douglas Harvey'

'And you are?'

'His nephew Paul Harvey' Oliver replied trying to keep a straight face.

'Just one moment please' he replied going out to the back of the shop.

"What a stupid childish thing to do" he thought regretting that he'd even considered it. He'd been paid so could well afford the few bits he needed.

The Tailor returned, 'I'm sorry Sir but my assistant has just reminded me that the account has been temporarily frozen. Perhaps you'd be kind enough when you see him next to remind your Uncle that payment is well overdue.'

'Yes of course I will. That's no problem it'll be cash then' he replied somewhat relieved

'Very well Sir. What do you need?'

Pretty near broke but with new casual shirts, trousers, socks, shoes and plenty of underwear he made his way back to meet Pamela.

'You're late Oliver' she complained, 'we've missed the Bus'

'Hello to you as well Pam how are you?' he replied glancing at his watch, 'it's nowhere near 1800.'

She smiled sweetly, 'Well I thought you'd be here by now so that makes you late'

'You've not been taking a leaf out of Commander Harvey's book have you?'

'Yuk perish the thought' she replied thrusting her arm through his and leading him to the bus stop.

Admiralty London

The meeting hadn't gone too well, Captain William Briggs and Commander Brian Wells had been seriously delayed just outside Exeter and again as they entered London leaving frustrated Commodore Douglas Warwick, Air Commodore Hamish Dewar and Brigadier Thomas Belton-Perkins kicking their heels in Whitehall.

'Is your man going to join us today Thomas?'

'Guy Robins? Yes I found him lurking about Portsmouth so he should be around here somewhere'

'Not a good time keeper then?'

'No less so than your Captain and Commander Douglas'

'Touché Thomas. Does he know what we want him for?'

'One of my men briefed him so he's aware it's to be Germany and an intelligence gathering exercise'

'But not exactly where?'

'No not yet but you can rest assured that he's already made a specific list of requirements.'

All three finally arrived at the same time only to be met by the wail of the siren grimly announcing the approach of even more death and suffering to a City already close to breaking point from night after night of bombing'

'Would you Gentlemen proceed to the shelter please' a Steward asked politely holding the door open for them then added quietly, 'quickly Sirs the Bastards 'll be here soon.'

The raid only lasted for just over an hour so they decided even at the late hour to move the arranged meeting to a private room at the Commodores club in Chelsea.

Guy was uncomfortable with the opulence of the plush

surroundings and availability of the variety of alcohol that had long since disappeared from the British pub.

'So Gentlemen' He announced after much discussion, 'in a nut shell you want me after landing close to Dorfhaven to find any weak points in their defences'

'That's about it Major yes. So tell us what will you need?'

'My Sergeant Harry Langford for a start' he paused for a moment, 'one complete and authentic Standartenfuhrer uniform with a' he rubbed his chin, 'and umm a Wehrmacht Sergeants uniform, ID papers, I've got the names here.' He passed them to Thomas, 'money and plenty of it, a Kayak, rubber dinghy and explosives'

'Is that all Major?' Brian asked somewhat sarcastically

'Probably not Captain but I'll let you know' he replied just as sarcastically then warned, 'but one thing is certain, no Sergeant no go.'

The Brigadier chuckled, 'I know you well enough by now Major so that's already been arranged he's waiting for you in Plymouth'

'Plymouth?'

'Yes Brian is that a problem?'

'It is rather I've sent Undaunted to dock at Haslar Lake tomorrow. Well' he added checking his watch, 'today really'

'You can recall her?'

'Bit difficult now I've arranged for the specialist teams to meet her to take off all Torpedoes, Shells and any Cypher equipment plus of course the accommodation for the sixteen crew not required'

'And you're sure Brian that Undaunted can operate with the remaining sixteen crew?'

'Lieutenant Smith assured me they can.'

The Brigadier stood and scooped up his cap from the table 'Ok I'll leave word for Langford to get himself down to Gosport as soon as possible. We finished?'

The Commodore shrugged his shoulders and looked around at the others who nodded, 'Then I guess we have.'

Dorfhaven Germany

'I've got the Bitch' SS-Hauptsturmführer Gerhard Altmaier shouted jubilantly as he rushed into the Security Office, 'I've found a woman who knew her mother and she was pretty sure that her family name was, wait for it, was Joachim'

'So what?' his friend and subordinate SS-Untersturmführer Heiko Muller asked drearily looking up from his work,

'So what? So what? That means my dear Heiko' he shouted rubbing his hands together 'she's a stinking Jew so we can bring the whore in for questioning'

'Look Gerhard all she did was knee you in the balls so why make life so bloody difficult? Just leave it'

'No bloody fear that bitch is going to pay'

'So do you know who she is and where she works?'

'I know her name is Helga Gerber but I'm not sure where she is but I'll find out that's something you can bet on Heiko and when I do.'

Haslar Lake Blockhouse Gosport

Charles despite the outgoing tide brought Undaunted alongside with absolute precision. Within minutes a group of men swarmed over the casing, the loading hatch was opened and a crane brought up as they struggled to unload their six torpedoes.

Sub Lieutenant Archie Clark, the First Lieutenant climbed up to the Bridge to join Charles, 'So remind me again Sir why we've got to lose all our armaments and half the crew?'

'Our Torpedoes are new types so their Lordships don't want Jerry to get a look at them if we get captured'

'Fine but our shells aren't exactly secret are they?'

'No I guess they're not but ours is not to reason why'

'Pity their Lordships aren't the ones to face the enemy with nothing to chuck at them. I suppose we could use potatoes but that's only if we're allowed to keep them onboard'

'I think just having sixteen crew is more of a worry Number One'

'Weren't you consulted Sir?'

'I was yes; well sort of I think it was more like you'll agree of course Lieutenant?'

'When is the off Sir?'

'We've got to wait for some Commando types to get here and then I guess we can go.'

Dorfhaven Germany

Otto ordered a beer and sat himself down to wait for Helga. The weather was warm with a soft breeze and with the bar doors wide open he could hear the Birds singing amongst the trees. Johann came over to him and whispered into his ear, 'Those SS Bastards have been sniffing around again I think they mean trouble'

'They always mean trouble but thank you I'll keep it in mind.'

Dieter walked into the Bar closely followed by Klara Engel a close friend of Helga's. Immediately Dieter was on to her, 'My lovely Klara'

'Get lost Dieter I'm not in the mood.'

Klara was quite plump with large melon shaped breasts, her full face, small close set eyes, slightly protruding teeth and double chin done little for her looks but she had a strange allure, her inner beauty and warm nature captivated many men and she was rarely without an admirer.

She walked over to Otto her face set, a tear forming in her eye, 'Sorry Otto but they've taken Helga away.' She burst into tears.

'Who have?'

'Some SS men' she blubbered, 'earlier today'

'Why on earth would they want her?'

She blew her nose on a lace handkerchief, 'We don't

know Otto we really don't.'

'Do you know where they took her?'

'To the Base here I guess.'

'Right' he growled standing up

'Whoa there Otto' Dieter said jumping up from his seat, 'don't do anything stupid it won't do any good for you or Helga'

'But…'Otto protested

'No buts. Look all they've got on her is that she kneed one of them in the balls. They'll let her go by tonight trust me you'll see that I'm right.'

Worried sick that they'd somehow discovered that her Mother was Jewish he returned to his room desperately wondering what on earth he could do to help her.'

Chapter Seven

Blockhouse Gosport

'And what the hell am I supposed to do with that lot?' Charles muttered getting more and more irate at the amount of bags being manhandled down the torpedo loading hatch, 'Is the man going on holiday or what?'

'No' a stern voice came from behind them, 'the man isn't going on holiday he's just trying to survive if that's alright with the Navy.'

Charles turned and saluted, 'Sorry Major but it does seem quite a lot of kit'

'No need for all that saluting malaki Lieutenant' he extended his hand, 'the names Guy and this reprobate is Harry my Sergeant.' Charles nodded, 'to be honest we may not need all of it but we've always found that if we haven't got it we're bound to need it.'

Undaunted slipped and slowly wound her way out into the Solent packed with ships of all types, the whoop whoop of Corvettes wending their way around mixed with the deep resonating horns of the numerous Merchant Ships on the move.

Once clear of the Isle of Wight remaining on the surface they set course to the east hugging the relative safety of the coast.

When asked all of the crew had immediately volunteered so it'd been a little difficult to select the sixteen. Charles had intentionally left out the married men except for the Chief then due to the required long hours with hardly any chance of rest concentrated on the younger members of the crew. After forty-eight hours this proved to be the right choice as every man, despite only brief spells of rest remained upbeat and focused on their work.

As they approached the German coast constant ship

movements kept them deep for much of the day. At a little before midnight Charles ordered periscope depth then after completing an all-round search surfaced,

'Is that close enough for you?' Charles asked as Guy joined him on the Bridge,

'Would be helpful if you could manage another few hundred yards.'

Charles carefully navigated as close as he dare without grounding as Guy and Harry pulled their Kayak through the hatch and laid it on the casing followed by a couple of waterproof bags which they carefully stowed in the Kayak.

Charles climbed down onto the casing to hurry them along as the moon was highlighting them against the dark water and the tide was ebbing far too quickly for comfort.

'Yes we're ready to go. Now the day after tomorrow Charles if you can move into the same place, let's say midnight, yes?'

'Well don't be late Cinderella or the tide will certainly leave your pumpkin coach well and truly stranded.'

Guy chuckled, 'And it won't be the fairy queen coming to visit that's for sure.'

They shook hands. 'Good luck Guy we'll see you the day after tomorrow.'

He nodded and turned to Harry, 'Come on then Buttons it's time to go.'

Charles climbed back up onto the Bridge and stared out into the blackness muttering a short prayer for their safe return.

'Three fathoms Sir' a voice called urgently through the hatch

'Course two-seven-zero half ahead.'

Guy and Harry beached in a small cove that he'd chosen from postcards sent in to the Ministry by pre-war Tourists. It was an ideal spot as there was a small cave which they could use to hide the Kayak and change into their uniforms plus there was a steep but easily negotiable path that led up to the cliff top.

A little before dawn fully suited and booted they made their way up the path to a narrow dusty road that led to a small air base. As they approached the gate they were challenged by a young Soldier obviously extremely nervous at impeding such an important Officer. Guy passed him his papers, 'Well done Soldier I'm glad to see that someone is taking things seriously.' The lad puffed himself up and saluted smartly. 'Where is your motor depot?'

'Follow this road Sir and it's just to your left.'

Guy nodded and both set off arriving at the depot just minutes later confronting a very flustered mechanic dressed in filthy overalls, 'Everyone wants a bloody car' he muttered, 'they don't grow on trees you know'

'I know they don't' Guy snapped, 'if they did I'd get my driver to pick me one wouldn't I? Now what about it? Am I to get one or should I ask your Commandant if he's quite happy to allow a senior SS Officer to walk to Dorfhaven?'

'May I ask what happened to your own car Sir?'

'Broken down a mile or so up the road'

'I can get it towed and fix it for you'

'Look I'm growing increasingly tired of standing here arguing with you I'm taking that car over there'

'But…'

'No argument.' He turned to Harry and pointed, 'Schmidt we're using that car.'

Harry walked over slid into the driving seat and gunned the engine into life. Completely ignoring the mechanics continued protests Guy sauntered over and waited by the rear door. Harry leapt out and opened it for him, 'Sorry Sir I wasn't thinking'

'I'll let it go this time Schmidt but it's not to happen again.'

They sped away kicking up a cloud of dust which hung in the calm early morning air seemingly reluctant to drop back to the ground. The mechanic exhaled loudly wiped his hands on a cloth that was nearly as filthy as his overalls, 'But' he said sardonically, 'you won't get far.'

The Sentry sprang to attention and saluted as they passed through the barrier, 'Do you know the way to Dorfhaven Boss?' Harry asked over his shoulder

'No but it must be somewhere in this direction so just keep the water to your left and it should be fine.'

After about a mile the road turned away from the coast and joined a wider tarmacked main route, 'Well Boss?'

'Go left Harry.'

The road curved and dropped down steeply into a wooded valley, they drove on over stone bridges that spanned streams and rivers. The air was still, not a hint of a breeze to move the trees some laden with blossom. Guy pushed back into the plush leather seat feeling more than a little warm as the morning sun was beating down from a cloudless sky.

'Do you want me to fold the top down Boss?'

'No best leave it as it is.'

Suddenly the engine coughed a few times, picked up for a minute then died completely'

'Oh shit it sounds as if we've run out of fuel' Harry said thumping the gauge with his fist which still registered a quarter of a tank, 'I don't think it's going to be our day Boss.'

'I guess the only thing we can do is wait and see if anybody comes this way'

'Do you think that's likely?'

'Seems a major route to somewhere so fingers crossed'

Harry smacked his lips 'Don't know about you Boss but I'm bloody starving'

'Me too so we might as well break out the rations.'

They scoffed down their meagre meal and finished with a small bottle of German wine.

'Do you hear that?'

A sound of an engine reached them and within minutes a vehicle appeared slowing down as it approached. An extremely elegant immaculately dressed woman stepped out and walked over to them, 'My My Standartenfuhrer have you broken down?'

'Run out of fuel'

'Oh dear. I'm Eva Maas by the way'

'Hermann Kestler'

'And where are you off to my dear Hermann?'

'Dorfhaven'

'Well at least you nearly made it it's not far from here. I have a spare can of fuel that you may use I'll get my man to dig it out. Peter' she shouted, 'fetch the fuel can.'

An old man clambered out of the car and with some difficulty shambled to the back all the time muttering under his breath. Harry walked over to him, 'I'll take it for you if you like.'

The old man smiled, 'Thank you I don't think I'd make it' then in a whisper, 'not without dousing that bitch and setting her alight anyway.'

'Let me pay you for the fuel Eva'

'No need Hermann I get it for free'

'Well thank you so much Eva you've saved my life'

'Perhaps we shall meet again and you can thank me properly' she said smiling whilst seductively running her perfectly manicured nails down Guy's cheek. 'Door Peter!'

Her car trundled off and soon disappeared into the distance.

It took a while to get the car started again but eventually it roared into life and after twenty minutes arrived in Dorfhaven firstly parking alongside the old jetty from where they could view the comings and goings from the pens.

'Do you think we'll get a better view from up there Boss?'

'Probably not but we'll need to get into the base anyway so may as well go up now.'

Security seemed to be extremely lax when not being challenged at the barrier which had remained raised or again as they got out of the car wandered around some of the buildings for a while before standing on a platform to look out over the crystal clear water.

Charles had brought Undaunted in closer to shore to avoid the increasing number of ship movement further out but since then had struggled maintaining depth to counter the rush of fresh water streaming out of the Elbe. Fortunately the tide was turning providing a welcome rest for the planes operator.

'Ten fathoms Sir.'

Charles studied the Chart looking for some deeper water that they could sink into until nightfall. The First Lieutenant looked over his shoulder, 'More hills than Cumbria Sir' he remarked laughing,

'But unfortunately without the fells'

'What if we wait in deeper water around there' he pointed,

'That I think is the route the U-boats must use.'

'Torpedo Sir!' the hydrophone operator yelled in a panic

'Starboard thirty full…..' Is all Charles managed to get out before a massive explosion shook the boat from stem to stern. Bow first Undaunted crunched into the seabed throwing up tons of sand and silt. Miraculously the lights remained on and the forward hatch held tight only squirting small amounts of water around the rubber seals.

Charles's only concern was to get his men out to safety. He ordered that they all don their DSEA's and charge the bag to act as a life jacket 'Stand by to Surface. Take us up Number One.'

With the scream of compressed air thundering into the tanks Undaunted stern first started her agonisingly slow ascent to the surface, 'Listen up men' Charles shouted above the din, 'we'll make our escape through the Conning tower. Now I don't think she'll manage to stay afloat for long so we'll need to get a move on.'

The second the tower broke the surface the hatch was

opened and the men streamed out and jumped into the water. Charles was last quickly on the heels of the First Lieutenant who lost his footing on the wet ladder and in a hear stopping moment tumbled down on top of him but they both managed to keep hold as with the water just starting to pour down the hatch leapt over the side together.

Without a murmur Undaunted slipped below the surface to the seabed a mere fifty feet below.

All eighteen men were quickly scooped up by a Tug and ordered to sit in silence along the deck as it made its way back to shore. A U-boat kept pace its Skipper looking through binoculars at the men he'd managed to pluck from the safety of their Submarine. He counted them, 'Eighteen Klaus, just eighteen. How many do they carry?'

'Over thirty normally'

'God what a waste.'

'Something's stirred the buggers up Boss. Perhaps it's Sauerkraut for Lunch' Harry whispered as troops were being called out of their huts and marched off. An officer rushed by still buttoning his tunic, 'You there what seems to be the panic?'

Guys' heart sank at the reply, 'English Submarine crew taken Prisoner we're to bring them up here now.'

Guy shook his head, 'Shit that's really torn it'

'So what the fuck are we supposed to do now?'

'Guy who abhorred that kind of very strong language gave him a sideways glance'

'Sorry Boss but you know what I mean?'

As if to answer his question a Naval Officer walked up to them and saluted, 'Lieutenant Becker Sir.

Guy returned the salute, 'So what's going on?'

We've captured some English sailors but our Commanding Officer is away in Berlin so as you're the Senior Officer here would you be able to deal with them?'

'Yes of course but I must send a message to my superiors'

'Of course Sir I'll take you to the Communications Office.'

'I will need to take them to my base in Bremerhaven have you any transport I can use?'

'We have two small Lorries Sir but I don't think they're big enough for your needs.'

Guy remembered seeing a large motor yacht in the harbour, 'Who owns the motor yacht?'

'Our Commanding Officer Sir'

'And he is?'

'Admiral Oskar Schröder'

'Well Lieutenant I shall be taking possession of it.'

'But Miss Eva uses the Meerjungfrau almost every day'

'Well Miss Eva won't be able to will she?' He snapped, 'So where is the Communications Office?'

'This way Sir.'

Otto was slouched in the chair his hands locked behind his head and earphones casually draped around his neck the buzz of static quite audible. He was worried sick about Helga but still didn't know what he could do about it.

The door burst open as Guy and the Lieutenant breezed in, 'Steiner the Colonel will need to send a message to Bremerhaven so I suggest you sit up and take note.'

Otto sat up straight and put his earphones on properly but still kept an eye on the Colonel whom he feared had come to take Helga away. He could still hear the conversation so breathed a sigh of relief when he heard that it wasn't Helga he was after but a bunch of captured English sailors.

The Colonel sat down close to Otto and started to type on an old typewriter. Otto couldn't help noticing that he had his fingers on the row of keys above the normal position and was typing very slowly. When he'd finished he thrust it onto Otto's desk, 'Eight point nine Megacycles and be quick about it. They should reply' with that he left and started talking to the Lieutenant.

Otto looked at the message which the Colonel had

arranged into five character groups. He selected the frequency and transmitted the message which was responded to immediately. Otto noticing that the Lieutenant was busy on the phone with the Colonel alongside him bitterly complaining about something to do with security decided to decipher the message so looking at the keys on the typewriter and transcribing them he was shocked to find it was in English.

NEED RESCUE TWENTY SOULS ON YACHT
HUNDRED MILES
DUE WEST DORFHAVEN ZERO SIX HUNDRED
TOMORROW

He stood up unsure what he should do as the Colonel shouted at the Lieutenant, 'What the hell is wrong with your security department are they asleep or what?' The Lieutenant mumbled some kind of apology, 'I suppose I'll have to go there myself. So where is it?'

The Lieutenant was just about at the end of his tether, 'Steiner show the Colonel to security.'

Otto's brain was working overtime, should he report this man or could he use it to his advantage. He decided that the risk would be worth it so stopped and turned to face Guy,

'I want you to help me'

Guy was taken aback, 'What on earth makes you think that I should help you Lad?'

Otto breathed out nervously his throat dry and sweat forming on his forehead, 'Because' he stammered, 'I can speak English'

'So?'

'So you know and I know that you're not German and are planning your escape'

'What are you intending to do about it then?' Guy answered quietly releasing the strap on his holster

'As I said I need your help'

'Doing what?'

'My Fiancée is being held in the cells and I want you to get her out'

'And if I won't help?'

'Then I'd ask to borrow your Luger and shoot the SS Bastards myself'

'What is she being held for?'

'They think she's Jewish'

'And is she?' Otto didn't reply, 'I'll take that as yes. What's her name?'

'Helga Gerber'

'And yours?'

'Otto Steiner'

'And you're going to keep your mouth shut'

'Yes definitely.'

Guy's first instinct was to silence Otto but the fact that Helga could well be Jewish and that it'd always weighed heavy on his mind that he'd not been able to help his own family escape he felt he should at least try plus he could almost taste the Lad's desperation, 'Alright I'll see what I can do but be warned any word from you..'

'There won't be I promise' Otto interrupted, 'all I want is Helga to be safe that's all.'

SS-Hauptsturmführer Gerhard Altmaier strutted around swishing a long cane. Helga was bent face down across the table with SS-Untersturmführer Heiko Muller holding her down by her shoulders. Gerhard lifted the end of her dress with the tip of the cane then reached down and flung it over her back, 'I think a good thrashing will be in order' he snarled, 'but not with these on' he added ripping off her silk knickers. She struggled but was held firm as Gerhard swished the cane a few more times then kicked out between her ankles forcing her legs apart.

The phone rang; 'Ignore it' Gerhard said his voice an octave above normal, 'it won't be important.'

He stood back and viewed her bare silky smooth buttocks his breath became laboured his heart raced as he realised he was at liberty to do just about anything he desired to this Woman.

The phone rang again then a minute later once more but ignored.

Gerhard threw the cane down on the chair, 'It's no good Heiko' he spluttered unbuttoning his trousers, 'I've got to take the bitch now.'

A scream of agony echoed from the walls as the cane bit so deep into Gerhard's bare backside it drew blood. He whirled around, 'She's a stinking Jew Sir so why do you care?'

'I don't but when I phone I expect you indolent fools to answer. I've eighteen prisoners that need escorting to Bremerhaven so put that disgusting thing away and get you and that idiot out there.'

Gerhard pulled his trousers up wincing as the course material rubbed against the enormous welt forming over his backside.

Helga now released rushed to the sanctuary of the corner still terrified shaking uncontrollably cowered down sobbing and sucking her thumb like a child.

Against his better judgement Guy went over to her and gently lifted her to her feet then kissing her lightly on the forehead he whispered, 'Be patient Helga Otto will be along shortly to collect you'

She immediately broke down and hugged Guy tightly tears streaming down her face,

'Who are you?' She sobbed.

Guy carefully extracted himself from her embrace and smiled, 'You should be safe now.'

'Thank you. Thank you so much how can I repay you?'

'You already have Helga. Now I really must go.'

As he left he noticed a diagram of the communication system for the base just left lying on the desk. He picked it up and stuffed it into his jacket.

He slammed the security office building door shut and nodded to Otto who was standing a little to the side. He casually wandered over, 'What'll happen when those two bastards come back?' He whispered his voice still full of concern

Guy looked straight into his eyes, 'That won't be a problem if you keep your word. Now go and collect Helga.'

It only took about fifteen minutes to march the Prisoners down to the harbour. Gerhard constantly took his frustration and pain out on them by shouting and punching if he thought they were not moving fast enough or out of line. Guy dare not interfere so allowed it to continue. Harry sidled up to him, 'I managed to collect the bag from the car Boss'

'Good just keep it safe and for god sake don't drop the bloody thing.'

A car screeched to a halt as the last of the prisoners were being hurried up the gangway and straight down into the small saloon now packed to capacity.

The elegant woman they'd met earlier in the day got out of the car incandescent with rage. She stormed up to Guy, 'So this is how you repay me Standartenfuhrer by running off with my boat'

'I understood it belongs to Admiral Oskar Schröder'

'What is his is mine' she snapped, 'now will you get these people off immediately?'

'I'm afraid I can't do that Eva. These men are prisoners and I'm obliged to take them to Bremerhaven'

'English' she screamed, 'they're English? Then make them walk or shoot them either way I don't care just get them off my boat'

'Eva my love' Guy said affectionately 'I promise faithfully to bring it back tomorrow then I can show you my complete gratitude for all the help you've given'

'Well don't you dare damage it' she warned 'or you'll have me to answer to'

'No Eva it won't even suffer as much as a scratch' he promised

'Until tomorrow then. Peter door!'

'Do you know how to drive this thing?'

'No Harry I don't but one of these sailor types must'

'I don't know what these two SS goons will think of that'

'Just keep them out of the way and they'll never know'

'When are we going to?' He drew his hand over his throat

Guy smiled and tapped his nose, 'Just wait and see.'

The Solent Hampshire

Troy had been out on trials for twenty four hours her new crew drawn from Blockhouse and Plymouth. Oliver had requested his First Lieutenant from Ursula but was pleased to hear that he'd now got a command of his own however his Wardroom saviour Lieutenant Steven Boniface an ex Submariner totally fed up with life under Commander Harvey jumped at the opportunity and much to the disgust of his fellow Officers brought their beleaguered Steward Harrison with him.

Rupert Longhurst despite his strong protests had been ordered to accompany Troy's Engineers to help master control of this revolutionary drive system. He'd argued that it was so simple, push this to go forward, this to go faster and this to stop or go backwards. In truth he'd been terrified at the prospect of being submerged but then felt a little calmer as he threw himself into his work content that it would only be for the day which was almost over as they approached Portsmouth Harbour.

'Signal from Flag Sir'

Oliver read it through and shook his head, 'Obviously something of ours has been sunk'

'It doesn't say who it is then Sir?'

'No only that we've to take up position one hundred miles due west of Dorfhaven to pick up twenty survivors from a yacht at 0600 tomorrow.' He scratched his head, 'Sparks are you sure it said yacht?'

'Yes Sir we deciphered it twice just to make sure.'

'We only need twenty five knots to be in the area in plenty of time'

'Thank you Navi but I think we'd better drop our passenger off first'

'If we're to wind this thing up don't you think we may need him?'

'I think our Engineers can cope now Navi.'

One very relieved Rupert Longhurst was dropped off on Southsea beach by dingy and escorted over the stones to the esplanade by the Wardens whilst Troy clear of the Isle of Wight dived and set course for her rendezvous.

Dorfhaven Germany

Undaunted's Coxswain had been detailed off to take the helm of the Motor Yacht and expertly navigated along the Elbe soon passing the Fort and out into the North Sea. He had strict orders not to speak to Guy unless he was first spoken to. Noticing a lot of activity where Undaunted had been torpedoed he left the helm walked over to Guy and gently nudged him with his elbow then indicated for him to follow.

The site was crammed with small boats, a tug with search lights and an enormous floating crane with Divers in the water handling the cable. It was clear that attempts were underway to salvage Undaunted for the purpose he could only guess would be to uncover confidential documents analyse equipment or even attempt to refurbish it for their own use. "They'll be very disappointed' he muttered to himself aware that everything of importance had been removed before they sailed.

Otto almost ran to the cells Helga threw her arms around him tears streaming down her face, 'How did you manage to do it?' She sobbed, 'you can't bribe these SS filth so what did you promise?'

'Nothing that'll bother you' he assured her, 'so let's get you back to work before Oda blows a gasket'

'She was furious with them when they took me' she replied starting to feel a lot calmer but then in a panic, 'what'll happen when they find I've gone?'

Otto smiled reassuringly, 'You needn't worry about that either'

'Otto you must've done something'

'I said don't worry about it besides it's all over and done with and that's the end of it. Now let's go.'

'So Gerber why did they arrest you?' Oda shouted as Helga walked through the door,

'They never said why' she replied clamping her hand over her mouth and welling up.

In a rare show of compassion Oda came up beside her and put her arm around her shoulder, 'They're wicked people all of them' she whispered 'and looking at the state of your dress I can guess they didn't treat you too well so what you need to do now is go home and take the week off.'

As Helga left Oda immediately returned to her normal self, 'What are you gawping at Girl get on with your work and be quick about it or else.'

Guy had ordered the two SS men to stand guard on the Saloon door whilst he and Harry remained on the Bridge.

'Those two SS goons are getting pretty edgy Boss they've been trying to work out how far it is to Bremerhaven'

'Right you go down into the Saloon brief the men then bellow for assistance when they tumble in I think they'll be outnumbered don't you?'

Harry chuckled, 'I guess they might be. We just truss them up then?'

'For now yes and you as well remember. Then I want their Skipper up here as though they're taking the boat over ok?' Harry looked confused, 'I don't know what's coming to our rescue but I think it'll be best if you and I are taken off as prisoners and our two SS chumps can stay on here to baby sit our package'

'Fine with me Boss I'll get it all on the move.'

With the men in position Harry yelled out for help, the two SS men crashed through the door Lugers in hand both quickly overpowered.

'Fletcher find something we can tie them up with' Charles shouted keeping the Luger trained.

Fresh faced Able Seaman John Fletcher was just eighteen a farmer's son from Somerset. He forced open the door of a tall locker, 'Bloody hell Sir' he shouted, 'they must use this old tub to torture people look at this Chief' he said pulling some of the contents out and holding them up, 'Handcuffs, whips, bamboo canes and this rubber mask thing the cruel bastards'

'Oh the innocence of youth' the Chief replied chuckling 'just put them back Fletcher.'

'There's a small cabin we can lock them in' Charles said waving the Luger to indicate where they should move to.

The Chief winked and pointed to Harry who was being restrained by two of the crew, 'And what about this one Sir?'

'He'll come with me to the Bridge.'

Gerhard and Heiko were bundled into the cramped confines of the cabin and the door firmly locked. 'There must be a light in here somewhere Heiko.'

They both searched around in the dark for the switch running their hands over the bulkheads, 'Got it' Heiko whispered as they were both blinded for a second as the cabin was bathed in a bright light.

'I always knew the English were idiots Heiko and no doubt lose this war. Look where the fools have locked us up.' He removed a jacket that was hanging from a deck head hook to reveal the boats Radio. He slid into the chair put the earphones on and powered up the set. After a few minutes he'd managed to make voice contact with Dorfhaven causing a bit of a stir.

Otto's heart missed a beat as his Supervisor announced that the Meerjungfrau had been taken over by the Prisoners and had headed out to sea. He swung his dial to match Dieters frequency and listened intently to every word,

"What is your position?"
"We don't know"
"What course did you steer?"
There was a long pause. *"We think it was Westerly."*

'God help us' the Supervisor yelled raising his arms to the ceiling, 'that's bloody obvious if they're going out to sea. Steiner man the DF set and see if you can get a fix on them.'

Reluctantly Otto moved seats and rotated the aerial until the dial reached a dip,

'Along the line due West Sir'

'So she sailed what? Six hours or so ago which would make them somewhere between sixty and seventy miles out.'

Otto recalled the signal that had been sent stating one hundred miles due West at 0600. He looked at the clock 0245.

'What are you looking so nervous about Steiner?'

'Nothing Sir.' But that was far from the truth as his stomach was turning over and over and he felt sick. *"If those Bastards get back here they'll grab Helga again for sure"* he thought to himself.

'Wake up Steiner what the hell's wrong with you Boy? Take another bearing.'

He rotated the aerial many more times than necessary hoping to use up as much time as he could,

'Is it possible Steiner that you might manage it before Christmas?'

'Still on a line due West Sir no deviation.'

'That's definite then their heading is due west.' He walked over to a Map of the North Sea, 'That's where I think they must be. Braun check what ships we have in that area.'

Dieter checked through the reports that each ship sent in twice daily, 'We have two Boats S-130 within sixty miles and S-128 just over a hundred'

'Excellent. I think they must be making their way to Hull so both of ours will reach them long before they arrive there. Get a signal off to them then let the SS guys on Meerjungfrau know what's going on.'

A bleary eyed unshaven Lieutenant Becker wandered in, 'What's the situation?'

'All in hand Sir we've got two S-Boats on their way to intercept'

'One Sir' Dieter interrupted, 'S-130 has just reported an engine problem'

Everyone jumped as Becker slammed his fist on a desk, 'All three engines? No chance'

'A fire in the Engine room apparently Sir' Dieter called out.

'S-128 should be in position in three hours Sir'

'Well I guess that'll have to do.'

The door suddenly burst open with a mighty crash almost knocking Otto off his chair. Eva Maas stormed in bare footed wearing a fur coat over a white cotton nightdress. Her face devoid of makeup was like thunder, she pushed back her dishevelled hair stared around until she spied Becker, 'What the hell have you done with my boat?' She demanded prodding him repeatedly in the chest. Then screamed at the top of her voice 'it's your fault you idiot and you'll pay. I'll have your head for this. When I've finished with you you'll be lucky if you end up cleaning the Latrines.'

Becker remained completely calm and composed, 'Madame' he started, 'because you bed the General gives you no rights to demand anything. And' he continued bending towards her, 'absolutely no authority over me. Now this is a restricted area so unless you wish me to call a guard to escort you out I suggest you leave immediately.'

Peter her driver and long suffering Lackey waiting at the doorway started to laugh. She turned on him determined to rescue something from this humiliating situation, 'Go and get my shoes and bring the car round now this minute. What are you hanging about for you idiot?'

'Madame' he said bowing and tugging his forelock, 'I have had to put up with your childish rants ever since the General brought you out of the Windmill Rooms but no more so piss off and get the car yourself.' With that he turned and left.

Eva eyes shut head bowed and hands clasped together stood completely stunned unable to move. Her mouth was opening and closing but nothing came out. A pitiful and rather foolish looking figure.

'Steiner' the Lieutenant said quietly, 'escort Miss Eva back to the house.'

Otto still worried sick would've rather stayed put to keep up with developments but reluctantly took her arm and almost dragged the poor distraught woman the couple of hundred yards to the Generals residence virtually shoving her through the door into the arms of one of the Staff then rushed back in fear of missing anything.

Becker was on the phone arguing with the local air field to supply an aircraft to fly out and confirm the position of Meerjungfrau but by his tone wasn't getting too far. He slammed the phone down, 'Bloody Luftwaffe waste of space obviously they're frightened of getting lost in the dark because they've said they can only send one out in the morning.'

North Sea

Troy was making twenty-five knots quite comfortably but completely blind as the turbulence created by her rapid movement through the water completely eliminated any hope of the hydrophone operator detecting any activity. The Coxswain was also having a struggle as even the slightest touch on the yoke caused such erratic direction and depth variations that on more than one occasion they were very nearly toppled off their feet.

'Can we slow down a bit Sir?' The First Lieutenant asked grabbing the Periscope guard rail as they suddenly lurched to Port then to Starboard as the Coxswain tried to compensate.

'Navi?'

'Not if we need to rendezvous at 0600 Sir no'

'It's still dark so we could surface Sir then 'swain only needs to keep us straight.'

Oliver considered this but remembered the warning that Rupert had given about it being a pig to handle on the surface, 'Ten percent power, periscope depth let's have a look around.'

As they slowed the Hydrophone operator reported a lot of heavy and light propeller noise.

Oliver completed his all-round search, 'Well we seem to be in the middle of one of our Convoys so...'

'Ship approaching fast Port Quarter Sir' the Hydrophone operator called out urgently.

Oliver swung the scope round to see a Destroyer bearing down on them, 'Flood Q three hundred feet fifty percent power' he shouted slamming the scope handles shut sending it sliding silently back into the well.

Troy plummeted down the Coxswain still struggling with the controls as multiple thumps heralded depth charges being dropped fortunately some way off.

'That would take the biscuit if we were clobbered by our own chaps Sir'

'It would indeed Navi. Increase to fifty-five percent power then we'll try surfacing in a couple of hours.'

A little before 0300 they came to periscope depth, 'Two

U-Boats stationary on the surface. Target one bearing. Range' he pulled the trigger and swung the scope round 'Target two bearing. Range' another pull on the trigger. He lowered the scope and waited for the data,

'It's wrong Sir' The Torpedo Officer stated, 'completely wrong.'

Oliver stared at him waiting for an explanation. The First Lieutenant stepped in, 'Sub Lieutenant Jordan was on the Truncheon with me Sir and was never wrong. Never'

'Right do it your way.'

Sub Jordan his slide rule almost a blur called out his settings then, 'Fire one. Fire two.'

The seconds ticked away then one explosion was quickly followed by the second.

'Up scope.' A quick glance showed both U-Boats listing and crews pouring out of every hatch. Within minutes both disappeared below the surface. Oliver slammed the handles shut, 'that'll be two less waiting for the convoy. And Troy's first blood well done everybody. And as for you Sub Jordan why is this magnificent straight from America Torpedo data computer thing no good?'

'I'm not saying it's no good Sir just not always right'

'So what do the Americans say about it?'

'They don't like it either Sir it takes two men to operate it properly and theirs are fitted in the conning tower so it's a bit of a squeeze. I've been told that a new type's around now so perhaps you can ask about it when we get back.'

Oliver chuckled, 'Not much need for one while you're around but I'll bear it in mind'

'Bletchley Park' the First Lieutenant whispered after Jordan had moved away, 'they were rounding up Maths Graduates so tried to nab him but the Skipper on Truncheon kicked up such a stink they gave up'

'Good job they did. Right I'll be in my cabin to write up the log. Harrison tea if you please.'

Oliver sat down at the table pen in hand with the log open in front of him. A knock on the door frame startled him. A splotch of ink on the log and cold mug of tea showed he'd been asleep, 'First Lieutenants compliments Sir but its 0545 and we're just entering the search area'

'Thank you Harrison I'll be along in a moment' he replied stretching his cramped body wondering how the hell he'd allowed himself to drop off to sleep so quickly.

'Looks like our lift's on its way Harry' Guy said sighting a fast approaching craft, 'better get the men ready and prime our package.'

Harry went below into the Saloon; lifted one of the wooden boards opened the bag and set the clock for forty five minutes. Arriving back on the Bridge in time for Guy to admit his error, 'Not our lift Harry it's an S-Boat'

'Oh shit I've just set the fu...' he coughed and corrected himself, 'flipping timer for forty five minutes Boss.'

They both knew that once set it couldn't be changed. The clock so to speak really was ticking for all of them.

The S-Boat performed a sweeping circle around Meerjungfrau then laid off at a hundred yards keeping pace, 'Who is in charge?' a voice boomed through a loudhailer 'you must surrender now or I have rules to sink you.' There was a short pause, 'This is your last warning make all German Officers on deck.'

'What's the plan Boss?'

'Get Charles up here with the two SS types but keep a bloody good eye on them.'

'You must stop and prepare for boarding from us' the voice continued.

Guy cupped his hands to his mouth and shouted across in German, 'I am Standartenfuhrer Hermann Kestler and I forbid you to sink this Vessel'

'I have my orders Standartenfuhrer'

'Well you better damn well change them'

'You will have to get the English to surrender then I can change my orders'

'Then you will have to give me a few minutes to explain.'

Charles brought up the two SS Officers with Harry, 'Sprechen sie Englisch' he asked,

'A little' Harry replied as the other two shook their heads,

Guy nodded 'I speak it well.'

Charles turned to him now content that the two SS Officers wouldn't understand waved his arms about as if negotiating 'I'd accidently locked these two in the Radio Room hence the visitors I assume. So do we surrender or what?'

Guy looked at his watch, 'Well in about twenty minutes it isn't going to make much of a difference either way.

Oliver peered through the scope, 'Well we've found the Yacht but there's an S-Boat close by'

'How close Sir?'

'One hundred yards' he replied checking the scale again, 'yes one hundred yards. A bit close to target'

'Not at all Sir.'

'Ok Sub here we go then. Target. Bearing. Range. Speed. Have you got all that?'

'I have Sir. Do we know the draught of an S-Boat?'

'A little under five feet.'

Within a few seconds with all calculations made the Torpedo was launched.

Running just below the surface it was clearly visible but its speed gave no time for the S-Boat skipper to react. With a huge explosion and ball of scorching hot flame it disintegrated throwing huge lumps over and onto Meerjungfrau.

'Stand by to surface' Oliver shouted slamming the scope handles shut.

The men were patiently lined up along the deck as a small Dinghy was launched from Troy. Guy looked at his watch and went along to Charles and whispered, 'All those than can swim should dive in now and make their way over to the Sub as fast as they can. I only want non swimmers in the Dinghy.'

Charles issued the orders and one after the other the crew dived in leaving two who leapt into the Dinghy. Harry Charles and Guy were the only ones left on deck with the SS Officers. Gerhard nudged Heiko and cocked his head to one side. Heiko nodded and both made a break for it and dashed into the saloon locking the door behind them.

'Time to go Gentlemen I think' Guy said jumping down into the Dinghy quickly followed by the others,

'Right let's get a move on' Guy said checking his watch

'I don't take orders from Krauts' the Crewman rowing the Dinghy replied indignantly

'Then take them from me Lad get a bloody move on'

'What's the rush Sir?'

Guy answered 'About thirty-five pounds of plastic and I'm not a bloody Kraut'

'Plastic?'

'Explosives.'

He needed no further urging and rowed as though competing in the Olympics. As they clambered up onto Troy's casing Meerjungfrau exploded and was reduced to matchwood within seconds.

Dorfhaven

'Still no reply from S-128 Sir.' Dieter called out

'What about Meerjungfrau?'

'Nothing there either Sir.'

A messenger rushed into the room and handed Becker a single sheet of paper. He read it and with a grave face and faltering voice called over to Dieter, 'No need to try anymore Braun the Aircraft has confirmed two large areas of Debris. No survivors.'

Otto felt sad at the loss of life but jubilant that the two SS Men would not be returning and Helga was safe.

Chapter Eight

Portsmouth

Troy lay off the outer spit buoy waiting for permission to enter harbour. The weather for early May was appalling, dismal wet and cold. The persistent drizzle cast a fine mist over the Solent almost obscuring the nearby forts and narrow Harbour entrance. A head appeared through the hatch, 'Kings stairs Jetty Sir.'

Oliver called for twenty percent power and navigated their way through the heavy Solent traffic but as he approached the Harbour increased to thirty percent to counter the ebbing tide making the narrow entrance a virtual maelstrom their deep twenty-two foot draught being constantly pushed back by the strong current. Once through the entrance he was able to reduce to twenty-five percent but still had the unenviable task of coming about to dock Port side on and what made it ten times worse was they could see a welcoming party lined up along the jetty.

'One cock-up and I think I'll be out of a job' Oliver joked nervously, 'I wonder if there's an admin job available.'

Despite his reservations he brought Troy alongside without even the slightest murmur from the fenders.

'Are we there yet Sir?' Steven asked his eyes tightly shut, 'I've not heard your usual crunch'

'You'll hear a crunch in a minute Number One. Your bones'

'Blimey Sir' Steven whispered looking down at the jetty, 'there's more gold down there than in the Bank of England'

'So I see. Do you think you and I could hide?'

'Doubtful Sir they look a right sombre lot. Perhaps they've come along to give us a chest full of Gongs'

'Now that'd be nice but somehow I don't think that's

the case do you?'

The eighteen crew of Undaunted along with Guy and Harry were quickly loaded into a lorry and whisked away to the Barracks and a well-deserved ten days survivor's leave.

As Oliver came over the Gangway the Commodore walked across. 'Lieutenant Pitman I'd like to introduce you to Admiral Beaufort.'

He looked old his grey thinning hair craggy wrinkled face and stooped stature gave the impression of someone who should've retired some years ago. He stepped forward and shook Olivers hand with a surprisingly firm grip, 'Well done me boy' he said warmly, 'excellent job. Now I'll be kicking around here for a couple of days so would rather enjoy a tour round this beast of a thing.' He chuckled 'got to make sure we're getting our monies worth you see' then smiling broadly and lowering his voice, 'so I can prove it to those idiots in the War department. Again Lieutenant well done and please pass my congratulations on to your crew, job well done. Come on Warwick I'm gasping for a drink.'

Admiralty London

Commodore Warwick looked grim. He lit a cigarette took a long drag and coughed a good dozen times before being able to speak, 'I'm not happy that there's to be an enquiry Bernard and even less that it's to be chaired by Captain Harvey'

'Nor I' Admiral Beaufort replied, 'but despite what we feel the Geneva Convention must be observed and Lieutenant Smith is shown to be in breach'

'I really don't see he has a case to answer'

'Well I'm afraid the fact remains that he had two Prisoners of War and failed to keep them safe.' The Commodore stubbed his cigarette out and reached for another, 'I think Douglas it'll be a good idea if you cut

109

down on those a bit'

'I've tried Bernard but there's always something like this that keeps cropping up'

'Well I don't think we've too much to worry about with the enquiry do you?'

'With Harvey in charge yes. He hates Junior Officers and hasn't an inkling of the stresses in modern warfare. He even called for a Courts Martial for an Officer who basically sat in the wrong chair at Dinner'

The Admiral chuckled, 'I believe it was for a bit more than that Douglas but I understand your concern so just keep me up to date with the proceedings.'

The Commodore rushed along the corridor stopping briefly to light a cigarette then doubled up coughing before moving on, 'So sorry I'm a bit late' he croaked breathlessly, 'but I've just had a meeting with Beaufort.'

Brian Wells, William Briggs, Hamish Dewar and Thomas Belton-Perkins nodded dutifully as Douglas slid into his seat at the head of the table, 'So what have we learned?'

'Not much at all I'm afraid' Thomas said laying the communication diagram onto the table, 'I think most of the effort was to get the men out safely'

'Well that diagram may be useful at some stage. Anything else?'

'One other thing the Major reported was that the Germans were attempting to raise Undaunted'

'Did they succeed?'

The Brigadier shrugged his shoulders, 'Who knows? They only observed it as they passed by.'

'So' the Commodore started deep in thought, 'do you think they would try to salvage anything left for them?'

'What are you thinking Douglas?'

'Well Hamish if we dumped a load of bait on a beach would they be tempted to take it in to the pens?'

'Depends on the bait I guess'

'I'm sure it does so let me think about it for a while and

we'll meet again when I come up with some details.'

Portsmouth Barracks

Commander Harvey sat behind the desk with documents strewn all over it. Second Officer Pamela Warwick sat alongside him trying to put the papers in order.

'Send them in' he shouted to a rather uninterested Lieutenant Commander who preferred to be anywhere but here.

Lieutenant Smith and Major Robins trooped in, 'Sit.' Harvey commanded, 'you first Lieutenant what have you got to say for yourself?'

'Nothing more than I put in my report Sir'

'I assume you do realise that you could be charged with war crimes?'

Guy shot up, 'Don't be so bloody stupid Sir the Lieutenant here acted admirably'

'Sit down Major I'll be coming to you later. Now Lieutenant an answer please'

'We were torpedoed close to shore and all managed to escape but were taken prisoner...'

'Yes yes yes I know all of that from your report' the Captain interrupted, 'what I need to know is what happened on the yacht?'

'We overpowered the SS Officers and locked them in what we thought was a cupboard'

'Thought?'

'It turned out to be the Radio room so they were able to summon help'

'So why did you allow them to be killed?'

Again the Major chipped in, 'He didn't allow anyone to be killed he didn't know anything about the explosives we'd laid.'

'Alright Major as you insist on taking the blame for everything why don't you tell me what happened.'

Guy glared at him for a second or two, 'There isn't any blame we happen to be at war with Germany. Is the

Lieutenant here going to be charged with sinking an S-Boat....'

'They' the Captain interrupted loudly, 'were not Prisoners. Do you understand that Major?'

'Yes I most certainly do and when they died...'

'Killed Major killed'

'When they died' Guy persevered, 'they were not Prisoners'

'So what were they?' The Captain scoffed, 'guests?'

'If Captain you refuse to listen and at the very least try to understand what I have to say then may I suggest we stop this charade now and bring someone else in who may be more acquainted with military action'

Captain Harvey leant over the desk and thumped the ribbons on his chest, 'What the bloody hell do you think these medals were for Major? I know exactly what military action is all about'

Guy kept completely cool calm and collected, 'So Commander you've experienced how dangerous it is operating behind enemy lines. The decisions that have to be taken in an instant. The constant dread of being discovered...'

'Ok you've made your point Major. Carry on'

'Both SS officers made a dash for it when they felt that there were insufficient numbers left to prevent it. We had no time to stop or warn them. So as I say technically they were not prisoners at the time of their deaths.'

'One final question I do have is why you found it necessary to blow the yacht up?'

'It was an enemy vessel Sir isn't that what we're supposed to do?'

Harvey ignored his reply and turned to Pam, 'Have you got all of that Warwick?'

'I have Sir yes.'

'You two are dismissed. Send Pitman in.'

Oliver stood eyeing the Commander with hatred. He couldn't stand to be in the same room as him and it showed.

'Sit'

'Is it this chair I should use Sir? I wouldn't like to get it wrong'

'Don't push your luck Pitman just sit down. Now tell me what you saw.'

After Oliver had finished the Commander spoke quite softly, 'So you are sure that you saw the two SS Officers run along the deck and disappear below?'

'Yes Sir that is correct.'

'Fine you're dismissed.' As Oliver reached the door, 'Lieutenant.' Oliver turned, 'never mind it's not important.'

Admiralty London

Brian Wells, William Briggs, Hamish Dewar and Thomas Belton-Perkins had been summoned to an urgent meeting in London. They heard the rasping cough of the Commodore as he walked along the corridor, 'Thank you for giving me your time' he said sliding into his seat and carefully laying his cigarette case on the table, 'but I think we've come up with the makings of a plan' he opened his cigarette case, shook his head and snapped it shut without removing one, 'It's been suggested that we use T102 the sister ship to Troy pack her full of explosives and beach her at Dorfhaven. They'll certainly want to get her into the Pens and pull her apart'

'How will they be detonated, on a timer?'

'No daren't risk that as we can't be sure how long it'll be before they take her in. So we're working on a way to do it remotely.'

'Have you decided which beach?'

'We'll need to make use of your Major to survey the area and recommend one he thinks will serve our purpose'

'Well Douglas I will ask him but to put him in the same area so soon could be extremely risky'

'What I've seen of the chap Thomas I'm positive that he'll come up with exactly what we require'

'I'm sure he will but remember he's a Royal Marine commando so not particularly au fait with those kinds of maritime matters like dumping boats on beaches'

'Granted so what do you suggest?'

'Your Lieutenant Pitman goes with him.'

There was a stunned silence around the table. Douglas was first to respond, 'But he's a Sailor and certainly not au fait with operating behind enemy lines'

'My men will be there to keep him safe'

'That's all well and good but how are they to get to this beach' William asked, 'Using a Submarine is certainly out of the question going on the outcome of the last operation'

'Brian I think you have something to say about that?'

'Do I?' He thought for a moment, 'Ah yes you mean the S-Boat we captured?' The Commodore nodded, 'but we'll have to sneak it up from the Isles of Scilly'

'It can be arranged though?'

'Of course.'

William folded his arms and exhaled, 'So exactly how long have you had that hidden under your belt?'

'A little while now'

'So that's what Lieutenant Pitman and his crew were gabbling about after operation Robin Hood'

'Yes'

'And you dismissed them as though they'd imagined it?'

'Actually I ignored it rather than that but we'd only just managed to get hold of it so weren't sure of our ground'

'Surely the Germans have guessed that one's missing or sunk'

'Not for a while William we know it operated out of Sark so we're pretty sure it's a bit of a grey area for their Navy as they'll have little idea where it should or shouldn't be'

'The crew?'

'All fluent German speakers'

'Right I'll get on to the Major and we'll take it from there.'

Portsmouth

The Commodore briefly outlined the plans to tow T102 and beach her around Dorfhaven then after pausing to light another cigarette quietly mentioned Oliver's pre-operation role.

'You must be Joking Sir. What the hell do I know about surveying on any beach let alone a German one?'

'It's your decision of course Lieutenant but your expertise would be appreciated and required to determine if the beaching operation is viable or not.'

Oliver considered the request for a few moments, 'And you say that Major Robins will be looking after me?'

'Yes and his Sergeant of course'

'When's it scheduled?'

'That's very much up to the Major but quite soon I would think. So what do you say?'

Even the mere thought of being in Germany surrounded by the enemy horrified him let alone to actually go ahead and do it for real.

For Guy it would be water off a ducks back so he tried to convince himself that he'd be kept safe and of course he did get all of Undaunted's crew out after all.

In his head he was screaming an emphatic no but none the less heard himself say 'Alright Sir I'll go'

'Excellent. And when you get back there's a half ring waiting for you.' The Commodore stood up and leant over his desk, 'Congratulations Lieutenant-Commander.' As Oliver went to leave the Commodore called after him, 'Will you let Pam and my Wife know that I'll not be home tonight I'm off to London again.'

Oliver decided to walk by the longest route he could find through the Dockyard back to Troy. Now with more time to think about it bitterly regretting his agreement to go over to Germany with Guy. *'Why the hell did I say yes?'* he muttered to himself, *'what a clot.'*

'A letter for you Sir just arrived' the First Lieutenant smiling broadly announced as Oliver came across the Gangway, 'Stamped Admiral Beaufort's Office looks pretty official Sir and' he warned as Oliver walked towards the hatch letter in hand, 'I wouldn't bother going down to your Cabin everything's upside down panels off and deck plates up. They're trying to rectify the erratic steering the Fitter muttered something about Dampers'

'Well I may as well push off for the day then'

'Aren't you going to open your letter Sir?'

'Not yet I think I know what it is'

'So do I Sir'

'You do how?'

'I got one too Sir. Lieutenant Commander and a place on the Perishers course later next year'

'Well done Steven congratulations. You know it's a bugger of a course?'

'I do yes Sir but I've got over a year with you to hone my skills'

'I'm not sure you'll need to call me Sir now'

'You're still the CO Sir'

'Well you'll be in charge for a while I'm off to Germany apparently.'

Steven was speechless for a moment, 'When?'

'Not sure but soon. I'm going with Guy Robins'

'Rather you than me Sir'

'Quite so. I'll see you in the morning.'

Oliver and Pam had become extremely close; they thoroughly enjoyed each other's company had so much in common and both were positive that things would blossom further in the very near future.

'Why you Oliver?' She asked holding both his hands tightly 'it isn't fair you're a sailor not a soldier. Who said you've got to go?'

'I think I can guess' the Commodores wife Margaret said as she placed a tea tray onto a small table, 'the Commodore right?' Oliver nodded, 'thought so'

'I wasn't made to go' Oliver explained quickly.

Margaret huffed, 'Of course you weren't my dear but knowing him as I do he wasn't going to take no for an answer.'

Margaret at fifty years of age was an older version of her daughter Pam. Her skin was smooth with hardly a wrinkle the same colour blue eyes soft face with rounded cheek bones small chin and that gorgeous warming smile but no dimples and a little broader in body.

'Well it really isn't fair and I'm going to tell Daddy that'

'You can tell him what you like Pam all he'll do is shrug his shoulders insist he's taken it onboard walk off and forget all about it'

'I know you're right Mummy but can you talk to him?'

'There's no point darling and anyway I'm sure daddy will make sure he's kept safe isn't that so Oliver?'

'Well I'm going with the best the Commodore can offer a Royal Marine Major whose done this kind of thing over and over again so yes I should be quite safe'

'Who are you trying to convince Oliver you or me?' Pam said putting her arms around his neck and pulling him close.

He kissed her tenderly on the forehead, you silly.'

They all went to bed around ten-thirty frequently disturbed by the distant sound of bombs falling on Portsmouth.

Oliver heard his door open then quietly close followed by the sound of silk gliding over skin. She slipped into bed her soft warm body rubbing against him. Again and again they made love each better than the last until exhausted they fell asleep locked in each other's arms until a huge explosion rocked the house followed by the sound of shattering glass and toppling masonry. Oliver leapt out of bed and pulled on his trousers, 'Stay put and I'll go and see what's happened. He dashed out onto the Landing. Margaret was already there outside Pam's open bedroom door with her hands clasped over her mouth, 'She, she won't answer me' she stammered her eyes full of tears, 'look.'

The room was a complete mess, bricks covered the floor and huge branches from the oak tree completely obscured the bed. Oliver pulled Margaret back as part of the wall collapsed inwards throwing rubble out onto the Landing. She held onto him sobbing, 'My baby, I've lost my baby, oh my God please help please help. Oliver do something do something please.'

Pam poked her head out from Oliver's room, closed the door quietly and rushed to her Mother throwing her arms around her , 'Mummy I'm alright I went down to get a glass of milk'

'Thank God you did darling look at your room. I think we'll all need something a little stronger than milk don't you?' She said still shaking from the shock.

The Kitchen was in the same state as Pam's room, rubble over the floor and branches poking through the window frame. The larder door had been blown wide open and the valuable food rations spread out over the rubble like a mad man's picnic.

Margaret poured out huge measures of Brandy and passed a glass to each, 'At least you're safe darling the house we can deal with'

'But what about Daddy's oak tree?'

'I'm sure he won't give a hoot when he knows we're all safe and well.'

They dozed in the chairs for the remainder of the night. Douglas arrived at seven-thirty and immediately rushed in relieved that everyone was unhurt then went upstairs to see the damage to Pam's room, 'So you'd gone down to get a glass of milk?'

'Yes Daddy'

'Then it was most fortunate that you'd not reached the kitchen wasn't it?'

'It was yes. Really shook me up.'

He smiled bent forward and kissed her on the forehead

'I'm sure it did Darling' he said, 'as long as you're safe and well. So Lieutenant-Commander I assume your room was untouched?' He asked giving Oliver a sideways glance showing more than a little suspicion 'Lieutenant-Commander?' Pam and Margaret voiced together as they all went back down to the Lounge,

'You obviously didn't tell them Oliver?'

'No Sir.'

'He did tell us that he's got to go to Germany which I think is really horrid of you Daddy'

'I was going to send you darling but you'd probably get lost before you reached Southampton'

'No I wouldn't because…' A sharp knock on the door interrupted pam's rebuttal.

'Morning Sir everybody accounted for?'

'Yes thank you Constable'

'We've alerted the clear up Team Sir they should be along shortly'

'Much obliged Constable thank you.'

Douglas came back into the room, 'Right Oliver we'd best get back to work. You can be excused for the day Pam' he said kissing her on the cheek then embracing Margaret, 'you'll be able to cope with the clear up?' She nodded, 'Of course you will no need to ask really.'

Both remained silent for most of the journey to the Dockyard but then quite out of the blue the Commodore spoke, 'I feel I must ask you a question.'

Oliver stiffened up fearing it must be about Pam's whereabouts last night, 'Yes Sir' he answered quietly

'Are you absolutely sure about going over to Germany?'

Oliver breathed a huge sigh of relief, 'I said yes so I'll honour that Sir'

'Good.' He then lowered his voice to a whisper, 'Pam was rather lucky last night don't you think?'

'I do yes Sir' Oliver replied now positive what was coming next.

'Oliver I can't pretend to condone what obviously went on but Pam is only alive because of it.' Oliver tried to reply but the Commodore held his hand up and continued, 'we shall leave it at that and say no more.'

Steven was standing on the casing arguing with one of the Dockyard fitters who was gesticulating wildly, 'What seems to be the problem?' Oliver demanded as he crossed the gangway

'There isn't one as far as I'm concerned but this chap thinks there is' the fitter responded quite aggressively

'This chap as you call him is the First Lieutenant so if he isn't happy then nor am I. So I'll ask again what's the problem?'

'These dampers Sir….'

'I keep telling you there's nothing wrong with the bloody things they work fine'

'Work fine, work fine' Steven shouted

'Calm down both of you and explain what's wrong'

'Nothing' the fitter insisted, 'the dampers do the job they're designed to do'

'Ok you've had your say now Steven?'

'There's a twenty second delay before they operate'

'Um I see what you mean. Can't it be reduced to a couple of seconds?'

'Sure it can if you don't want them to work at all. Look you're the ones who moaned about it in the first place then when we put it right you still bloody moan. Never satisfied you lot'

'What's your name?'

'Burt'

'The thing is Burt twenty seconds would be enough delay for an enemy torpedo to sink us.' Oliver quickly bounced a few figures around in his head, 'At our operating speed we'd cover nearly five hundred yards before she would respond to any manoeuvre so now do you see our problem? All we're asking Burt is if there's anything you can do to significantly reduce that?'

'I'll look into it but I'm not promising anything' he muttered then giving Steven a filthy look wandered off.

A crash and a stream of profanities had them looking round to see a messenger lying on the ground with his Pussers Red Devil laid alongside him. He climbed to his feet picked up the bike looked up at Oliver and Steven, 'Sorry Sir but it's the bloody train lines I'm always getting the wheels stuck in the bleeding things.' He slammed the bike up against a bollard retrieved his cap and climbed the gangway, 'message for Lieutenant-Commander Pitman Sir.'

Oliver took it from him, 'I think it'll be safer for you to walk'

'That's what the Chief Yeoman says Sir but it's a fair old trek down here from the main signal office so what's a few bruises I says. Good day Sir.'

'Looks as though my holiday to Germany has been booked for the fourteenth of July'

'That's this Saturday Sir'

'I've to meet Guy at number two boathouse at 1900.' He rubbed his chin, 'why the boathouse do you think?'

Steven chuckled 'Perhaps you're going to have to row all the way Sir'

'Good Lord you may be right. On a serious note Steven whilst I'm away keep on to them about these damper things'

'How long will it be?'

'You know Steven I don't think I ever asked but I don't think it should be more than a couple of days.'

Pam threw her arms around Oliver's neck 'You will be alright won't you? You'll do what you're told you promise?'

'I'll be fine. Back before you know it'

'I still think it's beastly for Daddy to send you away'

'Well I can't be in Port all the time can I?'

'Daddy is and he isn't sent to dangerous places.'

Oliver chuckled and held her close to him her warm soft body a pleasant reminder of their wonderful night together. Not much chance of a repeat just yet as Pam had been moved into a Guest room right next door to her Parents whilst the repairs were made to the house.

Oliver was convinced that the Commodore had done something to her door as it squeaked alarmingly when opened or closed and now inexplicably the floor boards on the landing creaked. But talk was of both Douglas and Margaret paying a long overdue visit to Cousin Peggy in Northampton for a few days.

A little before 1900 Oliver entered the boat house it's smell of sawn wood and fish glue still heavy in the air despite work having finished a couple of hours before.

'Oliver lovely to see you again. You've met my Sergeant Harry?'

'I have yes but only briefly' Oliver replied shaking hands.

Guy handed him a bundle of clothes, 'First things first get dressed into this clobber then we'll talk about the mission.'

The trousers felt quite rough against his legs, the boots a little too small but not enough to cause pain the shirt and jacket fitted comfortably except the sleeves were a little short.

Guy and Harry were dressed in similar outfits but Guy had a Nazi party armband in his hand, 'I think I'll put this on later. Now we're being taken to Horseshoe Bay on the Isle of Wight to meet our transport to Dorfhaven. I believe you've been on it before Oliver?'

'I have?'

'Does S-148 mean anything to you?'

'I believe the Germans would call it a Schnellboot' he stopped for a moment as the penny dropped, 'you don't mean that one that picked us up after Ursula sank?'

'The very same'

'Well I'll be damned we were always told we'd been

mistaken so forget it'

'I guess they had their reasons but anyway we should be in the Dorfhaven area between 0900 and 1000 tomorrow morning. I've picked a beach that we believe not to be mined'

'Lovely that makes me feel a whole lot better' Oliver said sarcastically,

'In the unlikely event that the Germans take an interest in what we're doing you Oliver must play deaf and dumb so apart from shaking your head or shrugging shoulders just completely ignore anything they say to you ok?' Oliver shrugged his shoulders turned away and ignored him, 'good that's fine.'

Harry handed dog tags to Oliver, 'You must tie these around your neck so if we get taken...'

'Very unlikely but carry on Harry' Guy assured him,

'You'll still be treated as a combatant not a spy'

'You mean beaten not shot?'

Harry laughed, 'Pretty much Oliver but it isn't going to happen'

'Just a bit of insurance that's all' Guy added, 'right let's get going.'

The Phone rang waking a now very irritated bleary eyed Commodore, 'Yes' he snapped, 'why?' He growled then following a further unintelligible response slammed the phone down.

Margaret stirred as he got out of bed, 'What's the matter dear?'

'I'm needed at the Barracks'

'Must be urgent' she said sitting up, 'time for a cup of tea?'

'No I'd better get a move on' he replied disappearing into the en-suite popping back seconds later, 'will you ring for my car?'

As he left the room Pam was standing on the landing, 'It's Oliver isn't it? Something's happened to him I knew it would I just knew it' she wailed bursting into floods of tears.

'For God's sake Girl' he bellowed, 'it's nothing to do with Oliver now go back to bed.'

His car sped through the dark empty streets of Portsmouth swept through the Barracks main gate and screeched to a stop outside his Office block.

'So what's so bloody urgent' he demanded flopping down into his chair, 'it better be good'

'We have to tow T102 from Belfast today and Lieutenant-Commander Boniface here says that Troy is not fit for sea'

'Is that so?'

'Yes Sir they've fitted dampers to stop the erratic movement we experienced previously but it gives a twenty second delay before it responds.'

Godfrey Lister a red-faced larger than life Dockyard Manager coughed loudly, 'I don't think that's completely true Commodore it's nowhere near that'

'So exactly how long is it then?'

'Just a few seconds'

'How many Bloody seconds is a few for God sake'

'Fifteen perhaps a little less'

'Fifteen?' the Commodore shouted, 'It may as well be fifteen bloody minutes. Not good enough man get your men onto it now and report back to me at 0800 with the news that it's no more than a second.'

Godfrey sloped away muttering under his breath almost convinced they'd not got a chance in hell of completing the job by then.

'So why have we got to tow today?'

'Weather predictions are perfect for a surface or submerged tow throughout the Irish Sea and the Chanel also bombing has become a major problem. They say they can no longer hide it like we can here Sir'

'And Troy is the only submarine we have that's capable of towing it?'

'It is yes Sir'

'Get back to Troy Lieutenant-Commander and kick their backsides to get it done'

'And if they don't Sir?'

'We'll have to worry about that if it happens.

Somewhere in the North Sea

S-148 was ploughing through the water at an average thirty-eight knots. In the small cabin below it was almost impossible to communicate with the deafening roar of the three engines belting away at almost full throttle.

Guy leant close to Oliver and shouted in his ear, 'We should arrive a little after dawn at this speed.'

Oliver nodded then immediately returned his thoughts to his beloved Pam and the fantastic night they'd spent together dreaming that she was here with him her radiant smile creating the dimples he so loved. She leant forward to kiss him; he could smell her perfume and feel the heat of her body as her lips met his. A huge crump woke him, 'Getting a bit bumpy I guess the Skipper will have to slow down a bit.' As Guy had correctly predicted the roar of the engines dropped as S-148 slowed to a more moderate twenty-five knots, 'We should still be there in plenty of time' he added checking his watch which reminded him of something he'd possibly overlooked, 'Are you wearing a watch Oliver?'

'Yes'

'What make?'

'Smiths why?'

'You'll need to leave it behind when we go ashore.'

'I'll take it off now' Oliver replied removing it and putting it on a shelf behind him, 'what type is yours?'

'Helios good old German Army issue'

'Mine's a Moeris' Harry said holding his wrist aloft, 'both probably Swiss made but Smiths' he drew in his breath, 'a bit of a giveaway really and for now not exactly a German favourite'

'Especially when they salvage our crashed aircraft and

see that name stamped all over the instruments' Guy added thankful that he'd remembered to check but annoyed with himself that he'd been stupid enough to overlook something so basic.

They arrived off the German coast just after 0900 just in time for the high tide. Guy gave Oliver his identity and travel papers, 'Stow these in your top pocket and remember you're deaf and dumb' Oliver nodded, 'Right let's get to it then' he said helping Harry to lower the Dinghy into the water.

Portsmouth Dockyard

The Commodore was tired so even more irritable than normal and worst of all had run out of cigarettes, 'Well Mister Lister we've given you an extra hour so what have you to report?'

Godfrey was exhausted; he had a thumping headache and still a full day's work ahead of him so was in no mood for a dressing down from this Navy type who would most probably push off home in an hour or so, 'We've done the best we can and short of removing the Dampers we can do no more'

'That' the Commodore thundered, 'is not what I asked. I want to know how long the delay is now and' he thumped his fist on the desk, 'it'd better be just a second or less.' Godfrey muttered something, 'speak up man'

'Five seconds'

'Good God almighty what good is that?'

'Look' Godfrey shouted angrily, 'I've told you it's the best we can achieve without a complete re-design which would probably take a couple of months at least or we can completely remove the damn things in a couple of days so your bloody choice.'

The Commodore was livid, 'Have you any idea what even a five second delay would mean? Just imagine you're driving through the Dockyard towards an empty dry dock at forty miles an hour. Turn right here driver you shout…'

126

'I get the idea thank you Commodore' Godfrey interrupted sarcastically

'I really don't think you do so I ask again would you be happy that it would take well over a hundred yards for your car to turn?'

'Obviously I wouldn't but what you seem completely unable to grasp Commodore is there's absolutely bugger all I can do about it at the moment so if you'll excuse me I'll get on with the rest of my work and you can let me know your decision on what you want me to do.'

The Commodore incandescent with rage jumped up so quickly his chair toppled backwards and crashed to the floor, 'What I want you to do Mister Lister' he bellowed, 'is to fix it and that is my decision. I'll give you another two hours but that's all. Troy must sail by midday at the latest so you'd best get on with it.'

Godfrey shook his head and stormed out slamming the door hard behind him.

'And somebody please get me a packet of bloody cigarettes' the Commodore shouted retrieving his chair from the floor and slumping into it.

A beach near Dorfhaven

The Dinghy bumped ashore onto a completely deserted beach mostly of sand but there were a few areas that had boulders just showing above. As they walked forward a click sounded beneath Oliver's foot. 'Stand completely still Oliver' Guy whispered as he and Harry dropped to their knees delicately clearing the sand away, 'well I've never seen one like that have you Harry?'

'No Boss never. How do you think we should deal with it?'

'Well it may be best if you and I walk to the other end of the beach and he could make a dash for it'

'Yes that should do it Boss it would only be one leg lost then'

'And his marriage tackle of course'

'When you two have finished buggering about just get me off the bloody thing' Oliver sweating profusely and starting to shake uncontrollably whispered as loud as he dare

'I thought he was supposed to be deaf and dumb Boss'

'You're right Harry so we'd better get him off it before he squeals any louder.' They started to shovel sand around for a minute or so, 'Ok you can move now Oliver.'

He gratefully stepped back and flopped in a heap onto the sand as Guy held up a shell,

'A sea shell? You Bastards I near fouled myself' he said as the others were having a good laugh.

'We have to keep things a bit light Oliver it helps with the nerves' Guy explained between chuckles

'Well mine are shot to pieces now thanks to you two.'

'Fun over let's get to work. Oliver take this levelling pole and roughly pace out the beach and I'll look through the range finder to get the level. Harry you quickly plot where the rocks are then help Oliver to take some photographs.

They worked away for a few minutes when a shout came from the top of some wooden steps leading down to the beach. A German Naval Officer and two armed guards came down and approached Guy, 'And exactly what are you up to?'

'Surveying the Beach'

'I can see that but why?'

'Well I don't think I should say really'

'Papers.'

Whilst Guy was producing the paperwork one of the Guards made his way over the sand towards Oliver. Harry intercepted him, 'How you going mate?'

'Oh not so bad I suppose so what you up to?'

'Not really at liberty to say'

'Hope you're not going to shut the place off'

'Why? Do you swim here then?'

'No chance it's reserved for the Admiral and his mates. Your chum doesn't say much does he?'

'No he's deaf and dumb'

'So what good is he then?'

'Same as me just lifting and shifting and any other shit that comes our way'

'Huh rather like my job really. Anyway I need to check his papers.'

Harry turned to Oliver and tapped his top pocket who cottoned on immediately so pulled the documents out smiled and handed them over, 'That's fine thank you' the Guard mouthed handing them back. 'Does he understand anything?'

'Not a lot no but as I say useful for moving things.

The Guard turned to leave, 'Oh great it's the Admiral and his lot. Better get over there quick to worship the great leader and his whore' he snarled sarcastically, 'before the bitch starts bellowing about something or other that doesn't suit her.'

'Who's she then?'

'Eva Maas' he called over his shoulder as he left.

'Oh shit that's torn it' Harry whispered

'Problem?'

'Too bloody true Oliver she's met us before a few weeks ago.'

The Admiral approached Guy, 'So what are you doing on our beach?'

'We have to survey all the beaches in the area'

'For what reason?'

'I'm not able to say'

'What do you mean not able to say. I'm an Admiral for God sake so speak up my man'

'I can't say Admiral because I don't know. All we were told is to survey a list of beaches and hand it in to Berlin.'

Eva was staring closely at Guy, 'Have we met before?'

'I don't think so no'

'Well your face is very familiar'

'Then perhaps it's quite a common one'

'No we've definitely met and' she pointed to Harry, 'I also recognise him over there'

'Really? Now that is strange as we've not been anywhere near this area for months'

'It'll come to me I'm sure' she said gesturing to one of the stewards to erect her sunbed then suddenly blurted out, 'Standartenfuhrer and he was your driver.' She turned to face the Admiral, 'He's the one who took our Meerjungfrau him and that other one' she shouted Guard arrest him.'

The Admiral intervened, 'Hold fast both of you' he ordered. The Guards moved away, 'so who are you?'

As if in answer a voice bellowed from the top of the steps 'Well if isn't Doctor Emil Hess how on earth are you and what the hell are you doing in a dump like this?'

'General Milch' Guy shouted back, 'it's been a long time'

'Too long my friend' he said shaking hands enthusiastically, 'I would've thought you'd be enjoying the good life in Berlin not hanging about in this shit hole'

'Well General we all have to do our bit'

'You know this man then?'

'Of course I do Admiral. If life was fair my dear friend Emil Hess here would've been a Professor by now'

'Well Eva thinks he's a Standartenfuhrer she's met before'

'Rubbish he's a scientist and a bloody good one so I'm told. Is that your boat out there Emil?'

'It is yes'

'Where are you off to then?'

'Back to Sark I guess'

'Any chance of a lift?'

'You need one that badly?'

'Yes I need to get to Calais in a bit of a hurry if you don't mind dropping me off'

'Not at all.'

It was quite a squeeze in the Dinghy with the four of them. Oliver was quite anxious to have such a high ranking German Officer with them so kept up his deaf and dumb

130

act.

Once they were back in the S-Boats small cabin Guy embraced the General warmly, 'Edmund my dearest friend once again you've helped me out of a sticky situation'

'Thank god I did Jakub because things have been getting very difficult for me which is why I got myself down to this backwater to take the heat off'

'Gentlemen' Guy spoke loudly against the roar of the engines, 'may I introduce Edmund Branovic my dear Brother'

'Does that mean I may speak again?' Oliver shouted

'Only when you're spoken to' Guy replied laughing, 'Edmund do you really want Calais or England?'

'England I think will be best as there's a lot of suspicion about me doing the rounds in the Reichstag and I've amassed quite a lot of information that I'm pretty sure will be of interest to the Government.'

On passage Portsmouth to Belfast

Commodore Warwick had been most reluctant to allow Troy to sail without the problem being solved to his complete satisfaction but was forced to approve by operational demands from Belfast.

Despite the Damper delay reduced to three seconds Steven still narrowly avoided a collision with the tug and a Corvette waiting to enter Harbour, 'This is not going to be easy so thank God we're not needing full speed' he muttered to no one in general.

The Solent behind them and the Channel getting a little too choppy Steven ordered them to dive to two hundred feet and increase speed to fifty percent so that they could reach Belfast in just under twenty-four hours but then more confident in their renewed stability risked winding up to seventy-five percent cutting the time down to a little over fifteen hours.

Troy ploughed effortlessly through the water but unbeknown to her Officers or men left a long trail of turbulence behind her soon noticed by a flotilla of patrolling Destroyers.

Lieutenant-Commander Roger Creighton paced back and forth across the Bridge of HMS Zulu with Ashanti and Andromeda in line astern pondering what on earth could be pushing along at some thirty knots submerged, 'I guess it could be a Whale'

'I very much doubt it Sir' his First Lieutenant Winston Greggs replied, 'not around here surely.'

'Whatever it is Sir it's making one hell of a noise' the Hydrophone Operator reported, 'but nothing like I've heard before'

'Pipe it through to the Bridge.'

The noise was peculiar, rather like cascading water then accompanied by gurgling as if running down through a drain, 'Depth?'

'Two hundred feet Sir.'

Roger thought for a moment 'Ok signal line abreast and deploy the Hedgehogs on my command.'

Ashanti and Andromeda increased speed to come line abreast with Zulu.

Troy was running blind due to the speed but the Hydrophone operator was still listening intently. He shouted as he thought he'd detected some propeller cavitation from the surface.

'Stop Engines fifty percent astern' Steven ordered grabbing hold of the scope rail to prevent being thrown forward as Troy came to an abrupt halt, 'zero percent' he shouted urgently as they started to go astern.

'Six propellers at least Sir' the operator whispered, 'Ships passing overhead.'

Rather pointless report as the thrashing noise of the screws were quite audible.

'Ten percent ahead twenty degrees down bubble four hundred feet.' They drifted down in complete silence then levelled off. Steven's instinct was to stop engines stay put and remain silent but with Troy they should be able to creep away 'Five percent ahead.'

Zulu's Hydrophone operator searched for a few minutes, 'Whatever it was Sir it seems to have disappeared.' He made a few more turns of the wheel, 'A bit of noise now Sir but well astern'

'Depth?'

A few seconds past, 'Lost it again Sir.'

'Unless they're deaf they must know we're around so signal Ashanti and Andromeda to spread out and use Asdic. Prime depth charges for two, three and four hundred feet and report any contact.' He turned to the Lookouts, 'They're bound to mount an attack so keep your eyes peeled.'

The area around Troy was suddenly filled with the dreaded haunting sound of Asdic pings probing and searching the depths like fingers of death preceding a frightful cat and mouse game, 'I'd love to know what type they are and what weapons they carry' Steven said wondering if the best course of action was to call for one-hundred percent and speed away.

'British Destroyers Sir' the Chief whispered with great conviction, 'not only that but I'm positive that one of them is Ashanti'

'What on earth makes you think that Chief?'

'When I was on Torment Sir helping to calibrate her Asdic she ran over a half-submerged S-Boat hull and damaged her port screw I recognised the odd sound it makes when she went over'

'That's brilliant so if they don't clobber us with depth charges they can bomb us with their hedgehogs and we can't even outrun them, well by about two or three knots perhaps.' He shook his head, 'I'm beginning to realise what a U-Boat skipper faces. So what Gents will it be for us stay put or run?'

Portsmouth Dockyard

Commodore Warwick pushed back into his chair staring at the packet of Senior Service Cigarettes laid on his desk, 'Oh sod it' he decided pulling one out 'why not? Troy's on her way out and the Major and Oliver are on their way home. What can go wrong with that?' He lit the cigarette drew on it held his breath then sent smoke rings swirling up to his office ceiling. Then he sat bolt upright quickly stubbed out the partially smoked cigarette cursed loudly and grabbed the phone, 'Fort Southwark urgently.'

Following his desperate phone call a signal was sent out to all ships in areas Able Dog four to Fox George six that a new type of British Submarine was in transit.

Douglas cursed himself for forgetting such a vitally important thing. Obviously those areas were constantly patrolled and all ships tasked to attack any contacts made unless directed otherwise.

The signal quickly returned from Zulu was quite a shock when it explained the ease in which they'd discovered the Submarines position by the turbulence it left behind although Douglas was more relieved to know that despite his unforgivable failure to advise ships in the area no attack had been launched and Troy was able to continue to Belfast unmolested by British warships.

Lighting another cigarette he picked up the phone, 'Get me H and W Belfast please Janet.'

'Harland and Wolff yard management office Nigel Riley speaking

'Hello Mister Riley I'm Commodore Douglas Warwick would you be kind enough to contact me on Portsmouth 60048 as soon as our package arrives at your yard'

'Do you know what time its due Commodore?'

'Afraid not no'

'Not to worry I'll ensure it's passed on if my shift has ended before it's delivered'

'Much obliged thank you. Goodbye.'

Drawing on the very last bit of his cigarette before

stubbing it out in the overflowing ashtray he felt there was nothing further he could do to get Troy to Belfast safely so turned his thoughts to Guy, Oliver and Harry.

North Sea

S-148 was positioned fifty miles north of the English Channel motoring slowly in circles. To keep up the deception they were not offered any protection from attack by British Forces so had to wait for nightfall before making the mad dash through the straits of Dover. On board they were discussing the viability of a beaching.

Oliver looked over the soundings that had been taken, 'It's just deep enough at high tide'

'Am I right in thinking that this other boat hasn't any engines at all?'

'So I was told yes'

'How the hell can you ground it then?'

'The best I could think of is that I tow it at high speed, turn sharply and let it go'

'And hope you don't end up on this sandbank here' Guy said pointing to the chart they'd drawn up between them'

'Right.'

Guy sat back drew in his breath and exhaled loudly, 'Good luck on that one Oliver'

'You don't think it's possible then Guy?'

'Everything's possible' he chuckled, 'just a bloody sight more difficult that's all.'

Edmund who'd been sitting in silence throughout piped up, 'Changing the subject Gentlemen you don't happen to have a change of clothing handy do you? I feel a bit conspicuous in this clobber.'

Guy scrabbled about in a locker and found a seaman's Jacket, Jersey, Gabardine trousers and a Bretton cap.

Edmund struggled in the confines of the small cabin to get out of the uniform and into something a little more suitable for a clandestine landing in southern England.

'Saves me getting shot by some enthusiastic Home Guard chap' he chortled throwing the uniform under a seat, 'rum deal that'd be done in by your own side' He added carefully pushing something into the inside pocket of the Jacket

'Don't hold your breath Edmund we've still got to get through the straits in one piece' Guy warned as the three engines were wound up for full speed, 'in about an hour' he shouted above the roar.

Belfast

Troy had made good progress surfaced and waited for a Tug to escort her through the dark channel and into the Yard. Once tied up alongside Steven went to the Yard Office to collect the details of the tow.

'Your Commodore Warwick was on the phone a while ago wanting to know the moment you arrived'

'Ok I'll talk to him if you like'

'Fine but remember it's not a secure line so you're a package or item anything like that.'

The phone seemed to ring for ages before it was answered and not as expected by the Commodore but one of his junior staff, 'Sub Lieutenant Cattermole speaking can I help?'

'I wish to speak to the Commodore'

'Not here I'm afraid but I can take a message'

'Tell him that the package has arrived in Belfast'

'Is that all?'

'Yes'

'Who shall I say called?'

'The Postman'

'Righty hoe goodbye.'

Steven took a quick tour of the new boats control room and immediately noticed that the single man control was absent meaning when submerged it would take three men to manoeuvre but by far the biggest problem was that the requested underwater telephone had not been fitted so once dived no communication would be possible between them. The Yard fitters came up with various solutions but most if not all would take far too long but one would be a good substitute. A cable was attached along the tow line across the casings and plugged into the intercoms on the Bridge.

'I understand there's no drive at all' Steven asked

'None' The Yard Manager chuckled, 'unless it can run on ten thousand good old Irish Bricks'

'Bricks?'

'Without the weight Steven she'd bounce around like a beach ball.'

He returned to Troy his mind in a bit of a tangle trying to figure out how he could sort out the crew for the other boat. Originally he'd estimated it could be done with eight but now it looked as though he'd need to release one of the watches, 'Starboard watch' he said aloud, 'Sub Jordan you'll take command so round them up and we can get going.'

Slowly Troy took up the strain and with assistance from two Tugs moved out into the Irish Sea.

Steven felt confident to increase speed to twenty percent then as the night progressed to twenty-five. Troy was handling well so he decided that once submerged they should be able to maintain forty percent or more.

An Aldis lamp flashed from the bridge. 'They say everything's fine Sir.'

'Good. Tell them we'll dive at dawn.'

South Coast

S-148 with engines quietly idling lay off the entrance to Pagham Harbour. A single light flashed once from the shore, 'That's us' Guy whispered, 'time to go.'

They climbed into the dinghy and were landed onto the pebble beach. As they crunched their way up towards the road a voice called from the dark, 'I hope that's you Major Robins because…' The rest of his words were lost by the roar of S-148's engines as she sped away.

'I thought there were three of you not four' the man whispered crossly

'Why is that a problem?' Guy asked

'Not if three of you squeeze into the back seat no.'

It was a squeeze as Oliver, Harry and Edmund struggled into the Vauxhall 10 two-door saloon's tiny back seat. Guy climbed in and the driver who'd not once identified himself gunned the engine into life and slowly made his way along in the pitch dark with only a tiny pool of light from the shielded headlamps in front to guide him.

'So what's your name old chap?' Guy asked breaking the silence

'You can call me Jimmy' he answered in such a way that further conversation seemed unlikely.

An hour and a half later they were stopped at the Barrack Gates by two armed Guards, 'We were told to expect three people Sir not four'

'Quite so but if you'll allow me to speak to Commodore Warwick we can sort that out'

'I understand' the Guard said consulting a pad under the dim light of his torch, 'The Commodore left for the Dockyard about thirty minutes ago Sir'

'Can you contact him?'

'I shall try for you Sir' he replied returning to the guard hut.

'I knew it would be a problem' Jimmy squawked, 'now I'll be lucky to get home tonight'

'Well for some of us Jimmy we've not been home for years.'

The Guard returned, 'I've spoken with the Commodore and he says if you can vouch for the other Gentlemen Sir then to let you all through and he'll be back at his office in an hour.'

'Blimey' Edmund exclaimed as they went into the

Commodores office, 'smells like a Turkish Brothel in here stinks of fags but no decent women'

'You seem well acquainted with that fact Edmund I'm glad to hear that your visit to Turkey before the war wasn't wasted'

'Well one must try out the local customs Jakub it seemed rude not to'

'I think it'll be best if you call me Guy saves any confusion.'

Edmund nodded, 'Of course Guy as you wish.'

A lengthy bout of coughing announced the Commodores arrival. He strolled in completely out of breath from climbing the short flight of stairs flopped into his chair pulled open a drawer removed a packet of cigarettes pulled one out and lit it inhaling deeply before sending a spiral of smoke skywards, 'God that's better. I certainly needed it after conversations with that lot in the design office. Now who's this chap?'

Edmund stood up, 'Edmund Branovic Commodore'

'Branovic I've heard that name somewhere before'

'He's my older Brother Sir' Guy pitched in, 'We were recognised and as luck would have it Edmund turned up in his guise of General Milch'

'Heinrich Milch?' Edmund nodded, 'Good Lord I've heard a lot about you'

'All bad I hope Sir?'

'It certainly was, you've been a thorn in their side for months now almost every intercept we managed to get seemed to moan about you and your antics Goring hated you'

'He did indeed he'd hate me even more if he knew that I'd relieved him of this.' He pulled a black case from his Jacket inside pocket placed it on the desk flipped off the two gold clips and removed a beautiful presentation quarter sized Field Marshals Baton. The brilliance of the white blue and gold glistened like diamonds under the office lights, 'How on earth did you get that Edmund?'

'Invited to Dinner by his wife Emmy so when I was left

alone in the room I thought I'd help myself to it. Nice isn't it?' He popped it back into the case, 'The Dinner was pretty good too. Goring wasn't there of course'

'Please tell me you didn't Edmund' Guy said screwing his face up

'Of course not what do you take me for?'

'A common thief perhaps' Guy replied laughing.

Discussions then turned to the important matter of the beaching. Edmund was also able to contribute by providing detailed information of the area above and beyond the beach. No firm date could be set but it was decided that during a spring tide would be preferable as it could give a few feet more clearance for Troy to make the turn.

Oliver swept his finger over a curve they'd drawn on their chart 'It's going to be damn tight even then Sir.'

The commodore nodded, 'So I see and that's the only way you think it can be done?'

'Yes short of pushing it.'

'Have you finished with us two for the moment Sir as we'll need to find somewhere to bed down?'

'Of course Major I'll call for you if needed'

'Oh before I go Sir what was the outcome of that ridiculous enquiry against Lieutenant Smith?'

The Commodore rubbed the back of his neck and exhaled, 'To be honest I'd forgotten all about it what with you three in Germany and Troy off to Belfast but I'm pretty sure it's all over but I will find out'

'Thank you Sir. Come on Edmund we've a lot to catch up on.'

'Belfast Sir?' Oliver asked rather surprised

'Yes and I'm getting a bit worried I think they should've arrived ages ago. I did ask for them to let me know but I think I'd better ring again.'

As he reached for the phone it rang, 'Ah this must be it. Hello. Oh it's you Professor Landor. Yes I'll still be here. Ok see you in a minute or two' He hung up, 'Landor wants a word about the submerged wake Troy kicks up at speed'

'I think I'm missing something here Sir'

'I'm sure he'll explain everything he normally does' the Commodore replied reaching for his cigarettes, 'I need these to get through it' he said smiling, 'to be honest half the time I've no idea what he's on about.'

The Professor breezed in looked at Oliver then at the Commodore, 'I thought this chap was the driver'

'I am' Oliver replied drearily almost yawning acutely aware how tired he was, 'but I had something else to attend to.'

'Ok then Commander will you contact your man and let him know that the fitters in Belfast can alter the planes on the conning tower to this setting' he handed over a scruffy piece of paper, 'and that should do it for now and if you tell your man to replicate the speed and depth at least we can test the theory for stability on its way back'

'Oh I doubt they'll be able reach speeds like that while they're towing.'

There was a look of horror on the Professor's face. 'Towing?' he blurted out, 'you've never asked about towing we've never even discussed it'

'Professor I don't think we need your permission'

'Of course you don't Commodore' he almost shouted, 'but there are dire consequences'

'Like what?' He demanded stubbing out his cigarette, 'and don't try and baffle me with science'

'Do you recall when I explained what happens to make it stop or go astern?'

'Yes' Oliver replied, 'it puts a gravity field astern'

'Exactly so technically it falls backwards into it yes?'

'Get on with it Professor' the Commodore muttered folding his arms and exhaling

'So anything close behind will also fall into it' he leant forward and spoke quite sternly, 'therefor Commodore I would suggest that you postpone whatever you're up to and get the ship back here for some modifications.'

'Boat Professor it's a bloody boat.'

He merely smiled held his hands up in resignation shrugged his shoulders and left.

'Insufferable man' the Commodore said reaching for the phone, 'H and W urgently please.'

He put his hand over the mouthpiece, 'Oliver' he whispered, 'there's a bottle of Glenlivet in the filing cabinet it's been there for a few years crack it open will you there's some mugs in the Kitchenette. Hello Portsmouth here has my package arrived?'

There was a pause for a second or two, 'Yes and has been repacked and sent back'

'What? I asked to be informed…'

'You were informed' the voice interrupted 'a message was left for you in your absence'

'Well I never got it'

'Afraid that's not our concern if that's all Portsmouth goodbye.'

He slammed the phone down, 'Bloody cheek of the man' he bellowed, 'where's the whiskey?'

By dawn they'd consumed over half a bottle. Oliver was almost asleep when the door burst open and Pamela stormed in, 'Why didn't you tell me that you were home?' she demanded then not waiting for a reply, 'and you've been drinking I've been worried sick about you and…'

'My fault Pamela darling' the Commodore slurred, 'Oliver wanted to get home but I detained him'

'Yes of course Daddy. Aren't you supposed to be visiting cousin Peggy?'

'Oh bugger I'd forgotten. Anyway can't do that until Troy gets back'

'Mummy isn't going to be too happy about that'

'There's a bloody war on for God's sake'

'Is there Daddy? Goodness me I didn't know that' she answered sarcastically 'and as for you Oliver Pitman' she threw her arms around his neck and planted a long kiss on his lips, 'don't you dare worry me like that again.' Oliver stared at her trying to focus, 'I think it'll be a good idea if you both go home for some sleep.'

English Channel

Troy had been performing better than expected. Submerged they were managing twenty five knots and still remaining completely stable their tow thanks to expert steering and planes control keeping in line. Suddenly they started to veer to port quite violently. The intercom bleeped and Sub Lieutenant Jordan's voice sounded in a panic, 'The Conning Tower Hydroplanes aren't responding Sir we'll need to stop urgently.'

'Twenty-five percent astern' Steven ordered.

With an ear shattering crunch T102 ploughed into Troy's stern toppling men to the deck quickly regaining their feet as the sound of rushing water reached their ears. The damage reports came in painting a desperate situation,

'After torpedo space flooded and serious compressed air leak Sir'

'Propellers damaged and centre shaft broken Sir'

'Generators on forced shut down running on Batteries only Sir'

'Rudder not responding Sir.'

The intercom hissed into life, 'Forward Torpedo space and seamen's mess flooded Sir forward port and starboard hydroplanes unresponsive

'Stand by to surface' Steven commanded, 'Surface.'

They both struggled the two hundred feet up to the surface arriving in a very sorry state Troy's stern remained well down and T102's bows still submerged. He quickly checked their position before climbing to the bridge. They had less than an hour before first light and the closest port was Portland still some twenty miles to the east. Plymouth to the west would be a better bet but at more than twice the distance not feasible with the awful predicament they were in.

Chief Petty Officer Tommy Bird climbed to the bridge, 'It's a bit of a mess back there Sir but at least the drive's still working'

'May be it is Chief but we still can't steer the bloody

thing' he groaned then raised his arms and lifted his eyes to the heavens 'Oh dear God' he prayed 'please grant us real engines ahead on one astern on the other and always keep full control'

'I think we can still do it Sir' the Chief said calmly

'Fire away Chief I'm all ears'

'If T102 steers to port she should drag our stern round turning us to starboard and vice versa.'

Steven pondered on this for a moment or two, 'Well let's give it a try Chief.'

They proceeded very slowly at first but quickly increased to ten knots as it became clear that it worked well.

After a little more than two fraught hours they were met by the requested tugs and towed into Portland Naval Base.

Portsmouth

Shaken from his snooze Commodore Warwick opened one eye and groaned in protest. He was still dog tired and slightly hung-over from the whiskey,

'You've had a call from the Dockyard darling and you're needed there as soon as possible.'

He yawned, 'I'll need a Coffee first'

'We haven't any I'm afraid although we've still got that part bottle of Camp but I could only manage to get a quart of milk so it'd have to be mostly water'

'I'll have a cup of tea then' he said tiredly then added, 'if we have some of course'

'We do. Would you like me to tap on Oliver's door to get him up?'

He thought for a moment, 'No let him sleep he needs it'

'So do you' Margaret said crossly, 'you're getting too old to work day and night'

'I'll manage Love' he said with a weak smile.

A car horn sounded outside, 'No time for tea.' With a quick kiss he pulled on his Jacket grabbed his cap and climbed into the car, 'What's the panic Harold?'

'Troy's in Portland badly damaged from some kind of collision Sir'

'Oh God' he moaned rubbing his forehead, 'that insufferable Professor Landor is going to gloat for sure.' He raised the tone of his voice to mimic Landor, 'I told you so Commander but you never listen.'

Professor Landor looking equally bleary eyed and exhausted was waiting for him at his Office, 'You look as bad as I feel Professor'

'Long night as you know and please call me Victor'

'I'm Douglas. Well you were right Victor'

'I deliberated about it last night Douglas and I believe it's only reasonable that I should share some of the blame. It was remiss of us not to consider it. But at least we've come up with a solution.'

With a quick rap on the door Captain Harvey poked his head through, 'Busy Sir?'

Douglas shook his head 'Come in Paul. Have you met Professor Victor Landor?' They both shook hands, 'now what do I owe the pleasure?'

'Is it correct Sir that Troy has been in a collision?'

'It's true yes'

'So will I need to make arrangements for a Court Marshal for Lieutenant Pitman?'

'Certainly not'

'But Kings Regulations…'

'I know exactly what the Kings Regulations say thank you Captain but Lieutenant Commander Pitman was not the Commanding Officer he was in Germany'

'Germany? What on earth was he doing in Germany Sir?'

'Reconnaissance mission with Major Robins'

'A Lieutenant Commander you say Sir?' Douglas nodded, 'then who was in Command?'

'Lieutenant Commander Steven Boniface and before you start on about a Court Marshal as the Professor here can confirm there was a technical fault that we all overlooked.' The Captain replaced his cap saluted and was just about to leave, 'talking of Court Marshals what was the outcome for that enquiry you headed up?'

'Lieutenant Smith?' Douglas nodded, 'no case to answer Sir.'

Victor waited until the Captain had shut the door, 'If you don't mind me asking but does the Captain have a thing about Court Marshals?'

'Not particularly no but he certainly has about Pitman.'

They both jumped as the phone rang. Douglas made a grab for it but in his haste sent the whole thing crashing to the floor. Quickly retrieving it he was relieved to find it was still connected, 'Hello yes this is Commodore Warwick'

'Lieutenant Commander Boniface Sir. I'm sorry but Troy is very badly damaged as is T102.' He paused waiting for a rollicking but none came so he continued, 'I'm told that it will take at least three months to repair both. I don't know what caused the collision Sir we stopped and T102 didn't. Again I'm sorry and of course I shall take complete responsibility for it'

'We are aware of the problem so we know it wasn't anything you did wrong Boniface. Three months you say?'

'So they say Sir'

'Right I'll be down later today and having had no sleep last night am in a foul mood so that Lieutenant Commander' he chuckled, 'should knock a couple of months off the repair.'

As he replaced the Receiver he noticed a note that had obviously been tucked under the phone. He cursed as he read it, 'This Victor' he announced holding it up, 'is my bloody fault. It's to confirm that Troy had reached Belfast. I missed the damn thing'

'Well never mind Douglas it's happened and we'll have to deal with it. I guess I'd better go down to Portland with you don't you think?'

'I'd certainly welcome the support Victor thank you.'

The one hundred mile trip was a nightmare for Harry constantly being caught up behind convoys of army vehicles sometimes reduced to twenty miles per hour for what seemed an age before being able to pass. None of this bothered his two backseat passengers who'd been fast asleep well before they'd reached Southampton.

The Commodore was the first to stir, his stretching and yawning disturbed Victor, 'Goodness are we there already Douglas?'

'Looks like it' he replied still yawning as they approached the main gate.

Identity checks completed Harry dropped them off at the Jetty where both boats were moored.

'Good Lord' Douglas exclaimed as they stood surveying the damage, 'I'm surprised they didn't both sink.'

Victor shook his head in disbelief 'Obviously I knew they'd collided but never thought it could end up like this.'

Douglas equally stunned chipped in, 'No wonder they've estimated a three month repair.'

'Good Afternoon Sir' Lieutenant Commander Boniface said cheerily saluting smartly.

Douglas returned the salute, 'Looks a bit of a mess'

'You said that you'd identified the problem Sir'

'Not me I hardly understand any of it. Victor?'

'Quite simply when you switched into reverse your Tow fell into the field you'd created.' He pointed at the boats, 'and at quite a pace by the looks of things.'

Douglas smiled broadly, 'See what I mean?'

'Does Oliver know what's happened Sir? I assume he's back?'

'Yes he's back now but no he doesn't know you've bent his shiny new boat.'

Steven screwed his face up, 'Oh dear. Do you think he'll be cross Sir?'

'Furious' he joked, 'but not to worry I believe in Admiralty Regulations it states a limit of just one hundred lashes these days.'

Victor coughed, 'Putting all this aside what are we to do about it?'

'I think it will be best if Troy is towed to Portsmouth overnight and T102 left here to be repaired'

'That's if a Tug's available Sir.'

Douglas tapped the thick gold ring on his arm, 'Oh believe me a Tug will be available.'

'I'm afraid the answer is still no Commodore all the Tugs are required'

'Look' he replied angrily, 'they're all alongside doing absolutely nothing and I must have one.'

The equally irate Port Controller drew in his breath, 'For the last time Commodore all my Tugs will be stretched to breaking point when five Freighters and four Tankers arrive here later today'

'So what the hell am I supposed to do?'

'Call a Tug from Plymouth or Portsmouth your choice. Believe me Commodore I would love to have your Submarines moved out and free up the dock space they're using but I can't help you sorry.'

He turned and walked away but the Commodore called him back, 'Ok I'll accept there's no Tug but as you're so keen to be rid of our Boats can you get the Fitters to repair the Rudder on Troy then we may be able to move out ourselves?'

'I can't promise anything but I'll do my best.'

A few minutes later a grey haired old man in brown overalls wandered over and speaking very loudly introduced himself, 'I'm the Foreman Fitter Jimmy Duncan Sir.' The Commodore nodded an acknowledgement, 'I was told you need a job done in a hurry'

'That's right Jimmy I'd like Troy's Rudder fixed.'

He leant forward and cupped his hand to his ear, 'You'll have to speak up Sir I'm a bit Mutt 'n' Jeff you see' he grinned revealing numerous gaps in his teeth, 'too many hours with a windy hammer.'

The Commodore asked again and Jimmy went away to survey the damage returning later with a younger man who spoke with a London accent, 'It's one 'ell of a bleedin mess chum'

'But can you fix it up?'

'Jimmy says you want it done in an 'urry yeh?'

'Yes that's right we do. So?'

'Well' he paused to scratch his head, 'if we can fix it from the outside then I reckon we can do a bodge job to see you 'ome'

'That'll do fine. How long do you think it'll take?'

'Give us four hours and see 'ow it goes yeh?'

Steven Boniface was none too impressed with the Commodores plan but due to his mood a little reluctant to say but was obviously unable to hide it too well, 'So young Boniface what seems to be the matter?' He hesitated, 'come on Lieutenant Commander spit it out. If you've got a point then make it.'

Steven cleared his throat, 'The thing is Sir because of the flooding we just managed to get here. We were already running on reduced power and had a serious air leak. T102 wasn't in a much better condition and to be honest I'm a little bit bothered about it happening again'

'I see' the Commodore said quietly, 'the flooding and propeller damage we can't do anything about until dry dock but the Professor is going to fire up the diesel generator and make some adjustments to this field thing'

'And the air leak Sir?'

'Where is it?'

'Aft Torpedo space Sir'

'Um' the Commodore said stroking his chin horrified to feel almost two days of stubble, 'have a word with the Professor and ask if you can run up the electric compressor'

'It's extremely noisy Sir'

'I'm sure it is but I'm wondering if we can build up

enough pressure to expel the water or at least some of it'

'I'll get to it Sir'

'But Lieutenant Commander Boniface' the Commodore replied holding two fingers aloft, 'there are two things much more important to be dealt with first'

'Yes Sir?' he asked knowing fully well he was letting himself in for something

'Access to a shaving kit and' he lowered his fingers held his clenched fists up in front of him and grimaced, 'some bloody cigarettes I'm gasping.'

Having managed to blag a whole packet of cigarettes and happily puffing away on his fourth the Commodore sat in front of the steering yoke with a stern warning from the Dockyard Fitter still ringing in his ears not to touch, pull push or turn it. Steven had fled to the Bridge as he hated the smell of tobacco fumes and even at sea under normal operations when the order "One all round" was given would if possible escape to the Wardroom to avoid it.

'Can you shift please Sir we're just about ready to test it?'

The Commodore stood aside then decided to climb the steep ladder to the Bridge arriving completely out of breath. 'They're' he announced between puffs, 'just about to test the rudder.'

He'd hardly finished speaking when a huge bang sounded from the stern loud enough to echo from the dock buildings followed by a tirade of extremely rich language from the workers.

'Guess it didn't go too well Sir.'

'Well it certainly didn't sound like it but it's only been an hour or so.'

After another hour and a further four cigarettes the Commodore was informed by Jimmy that following a successful set of tests he was happy that it should hold out long enough for them to reach Portsmouth. 'But you mustn't dive' he said sternly as if to a child, 'or you'll really be in trouble. You see' he explained, 'what we've done is use the hydraulics from the Hydroplanes to power the rudder'

'Anything else?' Steven asked then repeated it much louder as Jimmy leant forward and cupped hand behind his ear.

He thought for a moment, 'I don't think so no. Your chap was poking about in the Engine room but I haven't a clue what he was up to.' He paused, 'I'm sure you're not going to say but' he paused again, 'where are the engines?'

'Below the boiler plate decking' the Commodore shouted, 'tucked well out of the way.'

Jimmy shook his head and grinned, 'I guess that's a sort of mind me own business thing then?'

The Commodore smiled and shook his hand, 'Thanks for your help Jimmy.'

To Steven's dismay the Commodore decided to stay on-board for the one hundred mile trip and volunteered the Professor to accompany him so the Bridge was pretty crowded as they released the Tugs and made their way slowly along the Dorset coast.

Steve was wary as he knew that the imminent arrival of the Merchant ships would bring out both U-Boats and S-Boats by the score.

They could only manage ten knots as even the slightest increase drove T102's bow down so both would be an easy target for a hungry German Skipper.

The moon was full; bright enough to see parts of the coast excellent for navigation but not so good for two Submarines wallowing around on the surface.

His worst fears were answered as with a tremendous roar an enormous pillar of water shot high into the sky followed seconds later with another close enough to have metal fragments rattling against the conning tower.

The intercom hissed, 'Sub Jordan Sir we've got the bearings on the gun flashes, green five zero, two thousand yards, speed and course unsure but I've done the calculations on what we've got.' Another shell erupted almost alongside T102 the shrapnel cutting deep into the casing, 'can they hear this at the Torpedo control panel?'

'Yes'

Sub Jordan relayed some figures to them then ordered complete silence as two acoustic torpedoes were fired. The moment they shot out of the tubes the Compressor decided to kick in. Steven grabbed the mike, 'For Christ sake kill that bloody motor.'

'Torpedo running and closing fast Sir' the Hydrophone operator whispered with panic in his voice, 'turning away now Sir.' Then with a huge sigh of relief 'passing by Sir.'

From the Bridge they could see the effervescent trail of their own fish streaking by as it sought out any noise it could lock onto.

'Looks like a miss' the Commodore said ducking as another plume of water shot skyward. Then in the distance an orange ball of flame followed by the boom of an explosion proved him wrong.

With hands shaking the Commodore lit a cigarette, 'Not a good idea on the Bridge at night Sir'

'Of course not rather stupid of me. I think I'll go below.'

'I reckon the Commodore's had a bit of a shock Chief'

'Well to be honest Sir when the Compressor started I was pretty sure we'd had it'

'Me too Chief' Steven replied laughing, 'that's for sure'

'A Destroyer do you think Sir?'

'With four or five inch shells it most probably was yes.'

The Commodore huffing and puffing squeezed his way through the hatch, 'How the hell did Jerry get a fix on us?'

'He's probably fitted with Radar Sir.'

'Something to starboard Sir, green four-five.'

As Steven swung his Binoculars around they could hear loud voices calling out from the dark,

'Jerry's Sir must be from the Ship we sank.'

Men had become hardened to passing by survivors

even ignoring their own in fear of becoming a victim of a patrolling U-Boat as they stopped to help.

'Cruel World now Sir no quarter given'

'By either side' the Commodore replied sadly, 'Radar you say?'

'Yes Sir'

'Well I'll look into it and see if we can get it into Troy.'

Steven had intentionally decided not to sail through the crowded Solent so keeping as close to the Isle of Wight as he dare made for the outer spit buoy arriving just as the sun was creeping above the horizon. Tugs were quickly despatched and with the minimum of ceremony manoeuvred both Boats into the Harbour.

Chapter Nine

Portsmouth

Captain Wells and Commander Briggs were waiting impatiently in Commodore Warwick's Office. They were tired and hungry following a long and arduous overnight Train journey from Plymouth and in no mood to be kept waiting without any reasonable explanation being offered by his Staff.

'Is the Commodore on his way yet?' The Captain demanded crossly

'I believe so Sir' one harassed Midshipman Horace Archer replied meekly not really knowing where he was or how long he'd be.

A bout of coughing from the ground floor announced his arrival. He walked in breathing heavily and flopped into his chair, 'Sorry' he gasped, 'had an appointment with the Doc. Got a touch of Bronchitis' he explained removing some papers stamped Secret from his briefcase laying them on his desk, 'We're intending to have Troy tow T102 loaded with explosives over to Dorfhaven and then beach her. Hopefully the Germans will tow her off and take her into the Pens and when they do we shall detonate the explosives remotely.'

Both somewhat stunned they remained silent for a moment the Captain was first to respond, 'You mean to say Sir we're going to give the Germans the chance to study our latest innovation at their leisure?'

'As I said Brian we shall detonate the explosives as soon as they take her into the Pens'

'And if they don't Sir?'

'We can still detonate them at any time we like Brian. Besides that she'll have nothing in her apart from the kit normally found in a standard boat'

'Then forgive me Sir but why would they bother to tow her off?'

'There will be no visible engines or motors William which we're convinced should get them a bit excited.' He paused and looked at their faces, 'you're obviously not convinced?'

They looked at each other before Brian spoke quietly, 'I'm just wondering how we would react if a U-Boat with no Crew and for no apparent reason suddenly popped up on one of our Beaches?'

'With great suspicion I would think'

'Exactly William enough to lob a few grenades around before taking a look.'

The Commodore was taking note of their comments, 'So how can we answer those concerns?' There was complete silence, 'Come on chaps you provided the flaws so now come up with some solutions'

'To be honest Sir we're both too tired and hungry to think right now so with your permission may we go to the Hotel we've booked?'

'Of course which one?'

'Queens'

'Then shall we reconvene tomorrow at ten hundred?'

The Commodore replaced the papers into his briefcase finding the bottle of medicine the Doctor had prescribed for him with strict orders to stop smoking. A tap on the door disturbed him so he replaced the bottle, 'Come in' he croaked,

'Sounds bad Sir'

'I'm sure it'll pass so Commander how can I help?'

Commander Harvey hesitated for a second, 'It's a rather personal matter Sir'

'Spit it out man'

'It's your Daughter Sir'

'Really? So what is it about my Daughter that seems to trouble you Commander?'

'Are you aware that she's seeing Lieutenant Commander Pitman Sir?'

'So what if she is?'

'Neither your Daughter or Pitman declared this at the Smith enquiry'

'And exactly what point are you trying to make Commander?'

'I think the enquiry should be held again Sir'

'Why on earth would you want that?'

'Your Daughter could've inadvertently passed information to Pitman to influence his evidence against the accused Sir'

'Enough Commander.' The Commodore bellowed slamming his fist down onto the desk, 'My Daughter doesn't discuss her work with anyone not even me.' With his craving for nicotine unfulfilled combined with the pain he was having just trying to breathe his dislike for this contemptuous man grew fourfold, 'I'm tired of this vendetta you have against Lieutenant Commander Pitman and now you have the audacity to include my Daughter in your warped World. It's to stop and stop now do you understand?'

'Pitman caused it in the first place by his impudence Sir'

'He sat in the wrong bloody chair for God's sake'

'Not forgetting that he referred to me as a Barrack Stanchion Sir. The man's a disgrace.'

'One I can do something about the other I don't agree with and now I suggest you leave to contemplate which way round I mean. Good day Commander.'

'Archer'

'Yes Sir?'

'Cigarettes'

'Do you think that's wise with your cough Sir?' The Commodore glared at him and growled menacingly, 'On my way Sir.'

The following morning Captain Wells and Commander Briggs arrived at the Commodores Office. He was already there an unlit cigarette in hand but still coughing continuously.

'We were aware that both Boats had been damaged Sir but never realised how badly'

'You've been along to take a peak then Brian?'

'Yes earlier this Morning'

'If you'd seen them when they arrived you'd see how quickly things are being fixed up.' He coughed several times before being able to continue, 'have you had chance to think about any solutions from our discussion yesterday?'

'We have Sir yes'

'Excellent fire away'

'Troy should be put on show as much as possible to make sure the Germans know we've got something special like a round trip to Gibraltar perhaps, we know damn well there are more Binoculars in La Linea than in the Ruka Factory in Germany so it would immediately get back to their high command.'

William pitched in, 'A few sightings at high speed and as many kills they can fit in will have them aching to get their hands on it'

'Aren't they more likely to want it destroyed?'

'Unlikely Sir'

'It's a gamble Sir but one we're sure to come up trumps' William added secretly crossing his fingers.

The Commodore rubbed his chin thoughtfully 'Sounds good but let me sleep on it.'

Troy and T102 were well on their way to being repaired with a guaranteed completion date now less than two months away.

Much to the dismay of the Yard Managers due to this strict deadline work had been ordered on a colossal scale day and night seven days a week tying up dozens of highly skilled workers so in their eyes disrupting essential work on other ships creating a backlog for their Lordships to moan about in the future.

Oliver and Steven were onboard each day to monitor progress and were pleased to see that Radar had been included in the schedule. Professor Landor visited frequently with his own team to make improvements to the drive unit.

A messenger arrived and handed Oliver a note from the Commodore requesting him to attend his Office, 'Seems a bit strange I only saw him this morning.'

Oliver's heart sank when he found Commander Harvey was also present in the Commodores Office. The Commodore indicated for Oliver to be seated, 'Right Gentlemen' he began solemnly, 'unfortunately Lieutenant-Commander Creighton CO of Zulu has been injured. Not badly' he added smiling, 'but bad enough to have him shipped over to Haslar so.' He reached for a cigarette but changed his mind and continued, 'There's a vacancy.'

'But Pitman is a Submariner Sir it's a different World on the surface'

'It is indeed Commander and that is why you will be taking Command as of Today.'

There was a pregnant pause for a moment as the Commander took it in, 'And Pitman's part in this Sir?' He eventually asked

'Lieutenant-Commander Pitman as you quite rightly said is a Submariner hence thoroughly experienced on last minute manoeuvres Skippers make to avoid detection and escape depth charge attacks so will be accompanying the flotilla on their next patrol'

'On Zulu Sir?' The Commander asked nearly choking on the words

'Obviously' came the terse reply, 'as Senior Officer you will be in total command of the whole shebang'

'But what about the Wardroom Sir?'

'Ooh I'm sure it'll still be there when you get back Commander it survived without your input for a good few years. Right' he added standing up, 'you'd both better gather up your kit and join your ship.' As they went to leave he called Oliver back, 'and as for you young man you are to be on your best behaviour' Oliver went to reply,

158

'even if provoked ok?' Oliver nodded, 'good because I really couldn't do with any extra grief.' He flopped back down into his chair, 'I'm already going to get a thorough ear bashing when Pamela finds out I've sent you off again.'

Five Commanding Officers squeezed into Commander Harvey's Wardroom Office chatting quietly amongst themselves. Edward Clements HMS Ashanti, Charles Monday HMS Dido, Rupert Lister HMS Amazon, John Collins HMS Harvester and James Jones HMS Andromeda. All were Senior Lieutenants hopeful that the meeting was to decide which one of them would be granted promotion to lead the flotilla and take command of Zulu until Lieutenant-Commander Creighton returned.

Within minutes of Commander Harvey entering their hopes were dashed and worst fears realised as he laid out his almost suicide engagement strategy towards any surface targets. All comments, questions or suggestions were rejected out of hand or redressed with flippant remarks. When Edward Clements reminded him that the flotilla's sole duty was to search out and destroy U-Boats it provoked a tirade of abuse with a firm commitment that he intended to sink everything. 'Including all of us' Rupert whispered to James.

'If you have anything to say Lister then do please let us all in to it.'

Rupert stood up, 'I have Sir. It is my firm belief that if we attempt to engage a capital ship using your method we will be smashed to bits within minutes'

'Nonsense man'

'Sir we have a combination of three and four inch guns with a range of ten to twelve thousand yards'

'So?'

'We could quite easily be up against ships with twice the range.'

'Then we shall have to try twice as hard won't we? Dismissed.'

James was the first to speak as they walked back to their ships, 'The man's going to get us all killed'

'He's bloody bonkers' Rupert said despairingly 'a line astern charge for God's sake'

'Do you think he organised the charge of the Light Brigade'

'Quite possibly John'

'Not a possibility Rupert a bloody reality'

'Seriously though chaps' Rupert said quietly, 'do you think I'd better have a quick word with the Commodore about it?'

'God no it'd be the end of your career'

'So would being at the bottom of the Atlantic'

'Well let's hope Jerry keeps all the big stuff at home and we don't need the famous charge of the seventh Destroyer Flotilla to go down in history.'

They all laughed but underneath still concerned at the apparent lack of expertise or understanding shown by the Commander.

Having held a serious discussion between themselves they came up with what they hoped would be acceptable as an alternative plan so later that evening Edward who had seniority over the other CO's was volunteered to visit Commander Harvey in a last ditch attempt to get him to see sense.

'Come' the Commander shouted abruptly

'May I take up some of your time Sir?'

'For what purpose?'

'We' he started nervously not really knowing why he should be so pulled himself together, 'are still very concerned about a line astern engagement Sir'

'Your objections?'

'With just the two leading ships firing we'll only be putting out about twelve or so rounds a minute each.'

The Commander remained silent with his eyes tightly closed. Edward waited his impatience growing, 'We have Quick Firing guns yes?'

'Yes Sir'

'Well that must be to our advantage I don't believe Nürnberg has so.' His voice trailed off as he realised he'd perhaps said too much in arguing his case.

Edward stared at him, 'Where the hell does Nürnberg fit in to this Sir?'

The Commander leant over opened a cupboard door brought out two glasses and a bottle of Brandy. He poured two good measures and handed one to Edward, 'We've had intelligence to say that she's been skulking about off the coast of Alderney over the last week or two so we're required to scare her off'

'Six Destroyers to scare off a light Cruiser Sir? I don't think so'

'Frankly neither do I.' He took a large gulp from his glass refilled it then held the bottle up. Edward who'd not yet eaten was already feeling quite woozy so declined, 'Look' he continued, 'it's obvious that you're unhappy about my plans so what have you and your Mutinous bunch come up with?'

Edward explained their ideas now more relevant than ever if they were expected to take on a light Cruiser. When he'd finished the Commander leant back in his seat polished off his drink and exhaled loudly, 'Yes I agree so let the others know'

Edward nodded, 'And about Nürnberg Sir?'

'Yes of course.'

'He agreed?' Charles asked in astonishment, 'just like that?'

'Well he'd had a drink so I guess he's a bit more amenable then'

'Smells to me like you had one with him'

'I did indeed John and I think you'll all need one'

'Uh Uh what's the catch?'

'Nürnberg is out and about and we're tasked with looking out for her'

'To do what?'

'Engage and destroy.'

The four looked at each other then back at Edward, 'Don't blame me' he said, 'I'm just the messenger.'

'The bloody thing's got two planes'

· 'And jolly big guns'

'Well' Edward chortled 'it's pretty large so we should be able to hit the damn thing if nothing else.'

Chapter Ten

At Sea

Commander Harvey had looked extremely nervous as the flotilla of six Destroyers now under his command picked their way through the crowded Solent and out into the English Channel.

Oliver was quietly standing at the back of the Bridge well out of the way of everyone so was quite surprised when the Commander swung round to face him, 'There's no need for you to be on the Bridge Pitman' then turning away added much louder than was required, 'I'll send for you when I think it's necessary, until then I'd prefer it if you would remain below.'

Oliver was furious as he went below to the Wardroom soon joined by Winston Greggs the First Lieutenant, 'Good God he hasn't chucked you off the Bridge as well?'

'Not yet no Sir'

'No need for the Sir especially in your own Wardroom. Oliver will do just fine.'

Winston plonked himself down in a chair, 'We'd heard a rumour that you and Commander Harvey didn't get along and after that display I guess it must be true.'

Oliver sighed, 'I upset him in the Victory Wardroom some time ago and it seems to have escalated from there'

'Well I don't think the men are going to like their Officers being spoken to in that manner..'

'The men aren't going to like what?' Commander Harvey bellowed as he stormed into the Wardroom, 'I think your place is on the Bridge Greggs rather than sloping off down here stirring up trouble with Pitman.'

Winston stood up his face contorted with rage, 'Commander' he started clenching his fists behind him, 'as First Lieutenant I am in sole charge of this Wardroom and as such am the only Officer who can invite you in here.' He paused for a second or two to control his breathing, 'I do not remember offering that invite so would you please leave Sir.'

The Commander remained silent the look on his face said it all. He stormed out into the Wardroom flat slamming the door behind him.

Oliver shook his head and chuckled, 'That Winston makes you enemy number two'

'I wouldn't imagine for one moment Oliver that he could only have two enemies. The man's insufferable'

'I think he's under pressure at the moment I doubt he's been at sea for years let alone in command of an entire flotilla'

'More bloody reason for him to get along with everybody.'

The tannoy sprang to life, 'First Lieutenant to the Bridge'

'Good luck Winston' Oliver called after him, 'behave yourself.'

Oliver smiled to himself holding the thought that it seemed like poetic justice that Harvey had been asked to leave the Wardroom by a Junior Officer.

He picked up a discarded Time Magazine and was about to read an article on Hitler's mental state when the Tannoy piped up again, 'Lieutenant-Commander Pitman to the Bridge.'

'We picked up a definite echo but it disappeared came back then disappeared again.' Winston quickly explained before the Commander chipped in,

'Time to earn your keep Pitman.'

Oliver ducked under the canvas screen and joined the Navigation Officer, 'What's the seabed like around here?' He asked himself checking the chart which showed numerous sand banks. He stamped his finger down on one particular deep trough, 'that's where he'll be.'

'Well?' The Commander asked abruptly, 'What's it to be?'

The Navi Sub Lieutenant Gerald Ford gave the course.

Oliver called for the depth charges to be set at three hundred feet. Line abreast the flotilla surged forward. The Signalmen working overtime passing orders between ships.

'Still no contact Sir' the Hydrophone Operator called out.

Harvey shot Oliver a filthy look, 'I do hope we're not wasting our time.'

Aldis lamps flashed the command sending twenty-four depth charges plummeting into the depths the explosions sending huge columns of water hurtling high into the air then tumbling back down into the boiling tumult. A loud cheer went up from the stern quickly passed along as a huge black oil slick formed with a very brief glimpse of a U-boats bow before it slipped beneath the surface leaving wreckage swirling around in the choppy water.

The Commander merely grunted an acknowledgement as he stared through his Binoculars at nothing in particular but inside he felt a little guilty at dismissing the idea of utilising the experience of Submarine Skippers so quickly.

Within the hour the Hydrophone Operator reported a ghost contact, 'It's somewhere then nowhere Sir.'

The Commander turned to Oliver, 'Does it make sense to you?'

He thought for a moment, 'Depth?'

'Hard to say at the moment Sir but my best guess around two-hundred and fifty feet.'

A quick glance at the chart confirmed his suspicions, 'He's sitting on the bottom blowing the tubes.' The Commander gave him a puzzled look, 'stirs all the sand up makes for a doubtful contact. What's the strongest you have?' The operator called out the best position followed by a rather weak 'I think.'

The Commander much to Oliver's surprise asked respectfully 'Charges or Hedgehog?'

'I think Hedgehog for this one Sir'

'Right leave it to us. Yeoman signal off our intentions the remainder lay off.'

The entire rack of Hedgehogs were fired then it was a waiting game as the bombs sank down towards the seabed. Two explosions were reported by the Hydrophone operator confirming a hit further proof came as oil and debris rose to the surface.

Oliver was just about to leave the Bridge, 'Stay put for a minute or two young Pitman I'm sure there's another one sloping around somewhere. And' he grinned 'if there is we'll nail him.'

Oliver wasn't sure what to think even the First Lieutenant looked confused and moved to the rear of the Bridge where Oliver was standing, 'What's the old bugger after? That's twice he's been civil to you'

'No idea' Oliver whispered, 'but it's a bit unnerving.'

'Your attention Number One. Now would be preferable' the Commander barked without once taking his eyes off the horizon,

'Thank God for that' Winston muttered, 'back to normal.'

The intercom crackled into life, 'Large contact red two-four-five range in and out of the fringe Sir so twenty-five miles plus.' Then a head popped up 'Disappeared again Sir.'

The Commander stood up and hung his Binoculars on the back of his chair, 'You have the Bridge Number One.'

He closed his cabin door selected a book from the shelf thumbed through it until he reached the page he was after then opened it flat on the table. 'Just as I'd hoped' he muttered to himself, 'Nürnberg still has a basic Radar installation and hasn't been refitted or updated since before the war.' He slammed the book shut then pressed the intercom,

'Yes Sir?'

'First Lieutenant to my Cabin.'

'Perhaps you're going to get the cane' Oliver joked as Winston squeezed past, 'better hurry or it could be more than six.'

'You wanted me Sir?'

'I've looked up Nürnberg and with her basic Radar I don't think she'll have much of a chance to pick us up until we're within ten miles of her'

'She'll definitely have at least one spotter plane Sir'

'Agreed but let me go through this with you and please say if you think…'

A knock on the door interrupted him, 'Yes?'

'The contact is at twenty miles now Sir and closing.'

'Have the flotilla come about and maintain at least a twenty mile range.'

The Bridge runner noisily clomped back up the ladder and passed the message to the Officer of the Watch, 'Right where was I?' The Commander asked grabbing hold of the table as the ship heeled over in a tight turn, 'ah yes if you feel something's wrong for God's sake say.' Winston nodded, 'We'll engage at zero five hundred using the formation already agreed with Zulu to Starboard and Ashanti to Port opening fire as soon as Nürnberg's in range then execute the Port and Starboard turn at five thousand yards launching two Torpedoes each before turning tail. Zulu and Ashanti will hoist and strike the pennant Victor to execute'

'Problem Sir'

'Go on'

'Dido and Harvester have early Mark Eight's with a maximum range of five thousand.'

The Commander thought for a moment, 'I'd prefer not to get any closer than that'

'So would we I think Sir but at full speed it'll only mean another half-minute at most'

'Right we'll peel off at four thousand five hundred yards. Have we got the weather report yet?'

'Not sure Sir I'll call in to the Wireless Office on my way back to the Bridge.'

'Have the Yeoman signal the flotilla with all we've discussed so far.'

'Did you get the cane then Winston?' Oliver asked chuckling, 'I forgot to mention that there's a Time Magazine in the Wardroom you could've bunged down your trousers'

'Didn't need it. He still seems to be in a conciliatory mood. Actually accepted my advice'

'Blimey things are on the up. Advice on what?'

'Engaging Nürnberg tomorrow.' Oliver just stared at him. 'Oh of course you wouldn't have known'

'I think I would've asked to get off if I had. It's a ruddy great Cruiser isn't it?'

'Yes but everything's in hand and nothing to say we can't do it.'

'Young Pitman having doubts of our capabilities?'

'Certainly not Sir but you must admit it's a tall order'

'It is but a question for you.' He walked over to Oliver and spoke quietly, 'do you think she'll be on her own?'

'From a Submarine point of view Sir?' He nodded, 'I think there'll be more than the two we've got rid of Sir'

'Agreed but I don't think it wise that we search for them yet I don't want to lob depth charges around to let them know we're close.'

'The weather report Sir'

The Commander looked at it, 'Excellent Gentlemen blue sky and bright sunshine.'

As forecast the morning dawned bright and clear. The normal Atlantic swell pitched them around as on the Commanders instruction they manoeuvred to engage from the East with the rising sun behind them making it more difficult for Nürnberg's gunners to train on them.

Happy they were closed up and ready he had the Pennant Victor hoisted looking astern to check his following two had it dipped in acknowledgement, 'Full ahead.'

They surged forward spray cascading over the bow and onto the gun crews sheltering behind the protection of their armour plating. The Gunnery Officer climbed up into the

Director calling off the range. The Torpedo tubes swung out in readiness calculations made, checked and made again.

The tension on the Bridge was immense. The Commander was in his chair hands clasped tightly together. The only sound above the thundering of the water as they dipped into each trough was the ticking of the range finder and update reports from the Radar operator.

'Contact now ten miles Sir.' At any moment they were expecting Nürnberg's nine six inch guns to open fire sending tons of explosives to rip them apart, 'twelve thousand yards Sir.'

Still Nürnberg's guns remained silent although she was now plainly visible bathed in the bright sunlight, 'ten thousand yards Sir.'

With the sound of express trains the shells rained in water columns shooting up between the charging Destroyers, 'Open fire' the Commander bellowed above the din his throat like others dry as a bone. The acrid smell of burned cordite wafted in waves back across the Bridge. An air burst sent shards of metal clattering through the mast puncturing the forward funnel.

''Six thousand yards Sir' the Radar operator called immediately drowned out by a huge explosion almost alongside Zulu cascading tons of water onto the Bridge toppling the men to the deck. They quickly regained their feet as the water poured back through the scuppers. Constant flashes proved that their salvos were hitting the target, the Commodores decision to engage with the Sun behind them was for the moment paying off.

'Five thousand yards Sir'

'Strike the Pennant Yeoman. Standby, standby Starboard thirty.'

Everyone grabbed anything they could find as still at full speed Zulu healed over as they made the turn. Two Torpedoes hissed out of the tubes, one appeared to break up as it hit the water but the other looked to be running true. With all twelve Torpedoes launched the Flotilla spread out and beat a hasty retreat their rear gun mountings silent until now sending shell after shell at the stricken vessel black oily smoke billowing out above her decks with flames clearly visible. Despite her predicament she continued to fire her six inch guns but only managed one close enough to Dido to cause damage.

The Commander had remained in his chair for the duration tightly clenching his fists. His heart even now out of range was still pounding. He felt nauseous and had a dreadful headache that seemed as though it would split open his skull. He looked down and saw that his hands were covered in blood. He opened his palms, 'Are you injured Sir?'

'No Number One' he replied rubbing his hands together, 'I think it's self-inflicted by my nails. Is everyone else ok?'

'Couple of cuts and bruises Sir but nothing serious. We're still getting damage and casualty reports in from the rest of the flotilla Sir.'

He wriggled in his chair to get more comfortable, difficult when soaked to the skin.

'Would you prefer to get changed Sir' Oliver asked noticing his discomfort,

'No I'll wait until all the reports are in.'

'Somebody's head is going to roll over this fiasco. It's a bloody disgrace' the Commander roared as he read through the reports, 'Twelve Torpedoes, three malfunctioned, four broke up and three never even reached the bloody target.' He got out of his chair screwed the reports up and handed them back to Greggs, 'we wouldn't have sunk the bloody thing with just two that's for sure'

'Would've caused quite a bit of damage though Sir'

'Granted but it won't take them long to fix it up and get it back out to sea. I'm going below. You have the Bridge Number One.'

'I don't think he's too happy Winston'

'I'm not surprised Oliver it was a bit of a disaster after all'

'Does it happen often?'

'The disaster?' Winston replied grinning mischievously, 'Seriously though' he continued the grin fading away, 'we've had a spate of it recently but not that bad.' He straightened out the reports 'eighty percent's bloody ridiculous'

'Thank God we all got out in one piece.'

Winston nodded then facing up to the sky held out his arms like a Cormorant, 'And thank God for the sunshine we should be able to dry out a bit.'

As Oliver joined in by holding his arms out the Commander clomped back onto the Bridge in his shirt sleeves still looking extremely grumpy, 'When you two have finished practicing semaphore are we going to continue looking for U-Boats or not?' he grumbled settling back into his chair

'Always on the ball Sir but no contacts yet.'

'Tell me Pitman do you get a lot of duff armaments?'

'We do sometimes Sir but not as bad as that.'

He grunted and settled back into his chair eyes tightly shut against the bright sun.

'Excuse me Sir'

The Commander opened one eye, 'Yes Doctor what is it?'

'I was wondering when we're due back in Port Sir'

Now both eyes were open, 'When I bloody well decide we've had enough that's when.'

The Ship's Doctor, twenty-three year old Lieutenant Bertram Russell persevered, 'The reason I ask Sir is that Able Seaman Cotton has a broken shoulder blade and Leading Seaman Warner a.....'

'Yes yes I get the picture' he replied irritably glaring at this fresh faced ginger haired youth wondering if he was old enough to shave let alone be the flotilla's Doctor, 'Perhaps tomorrow or the day after' he snapped then

171

waved his hand as if to dismiss him.

Oliver who was bursting to use the heads followed Bertram down, 'What on earth's eating the old chap?' he whispered, 'One thing's for sure if Roger was still in command he would've been down here in a trice to see how things were.'

'Oh I'm sure he cares Doc but I think he's feeling a bit upset about the attack on the Cruiser this morning' Oliver answered not really knowing why he was making excuses for the man. Perhaps he really doesn't care.

Oliver returned to the Bridge and took up his position at the rear well out of the way.

'Torpedoes port quarter' the lookout shouted.

Winston immediately swung Zulu to Port in a thirty degree turn as both fish fizzed just feet astern. Dido was still completing her turn when with a mighty explosion one Torpedo hit her stern slewing her round into the path of Amazon still struggling to make the turn. She avoided a collision by inches as Dido settled into the water motionless her crew valiantly attempting to fight the fire raging below.

The Commander rushed to the Bridge rail and leant over to get a better view, 'Yeoman signal Harvester to go alongside Dido and take off the crew. Pitman where the hell is that U-Boat? And why didn't we pick it up? Who's manning the ASDIC for Christ's sake?' He didn't wait for answers, 'Yeoman signal the rest of the flotilla to keep circling Dido and Harvester. And standby to drop depth charges to keep the bloody U-Boat at bay.'

'No Sir' Oliver shouted, 'no depth charges'

'No?' The Commander shouted back

'If we stir the water up it'll be ages before it'll settle enough for us to get any contacts'

'We didn't pick the bloody thing up anyway so what's the odds?'

'Today Sir is a perfect for different temperatures of water so he's found himself a layer to hide under. And to answer your question I think he'll be at least two-thousand yards away.'

Oliver was sure that the Commander wasn't really listening as he was still leaning over the rail watching Harvester now alongside Dido taking off the crew.

Winston came up alongside Oliver and whispered, 'He's taking one hell of a risk'

'Contact Sir' the ASDIC operator shouted over the intercom, 'seems to be moving away from us.'

'Why on earth would he withdraw Harvester's a sitting duck?'

'I reckon he's out of torpedoes' Oliver replied, 'lucky for us I think.'

By the time Harvester had rescued all the crew Dido was low in the water the fire still blazing out of control. A scream like an express train sounded as the water flooded her boiler room. Within minutes she capsized and stern first dipped below the waves.

'Signal from Harvester Sir'

After reading it he handed it over to Winston, 'Take care of this Number One. We'd better transfer our two wounded as well.'

Harvester had requested the Doctor be sent over as they had dozens of injured men from Dido including her Commanding Officer Charles Monday.

It was a daunting task to bring Amazon alongside Harvester. The Commander had rightly left it to the First Lieutenant to perform the manoeuvre as his experience was that much greater, but even so there was a horrendous squeal of tortured metal as the Bofors gun sponson grated hard against Harvester's davits slightly damaging their whaler.

The Doctor with his two patients were quickly pulled over and relieved the ships parted with no further damage.

The Commander returned to his chair, 'Yeoman have the Wireless Office signal Portsmouth that we are returning tomorrow, Dido sunk, injured crew on Harvester so will require medical services on arrival. ETA Navi?'

After a short delay as he checked their position, 'Mid morning Sir'

'Got that Yeoman?'

'Yes Sir.'

The Yeoman was back in minutes to hand the Commander a message still in its raw state from decryption making it a little difficult to read. He handed it to Winston, 'Am I correct Number One in understanding that we're to leave the flotilla proceed unaccompanied to' he pointed to the Message, 'those co-ordinates for a rendezvous with S-148 at twenty-one hundred tonight for a transfer of one?'

'I think that covers it all yes Sir'

'Except it gives reference to Pitman does it not?'

'Probably because it's a submarine Sir?'

He grunted then called Oliver over, 'What do you know about S-148?'

'It's a Schnellboot Sir'

'Don't be so bloody ridiculous Pitman we wouldn't be asked to rendezvous with the Germans for God sake' he shouted crossly

'We would if it was one of ours Sir'

'Well is it?'

'Yes Sir crewed entirely by German speaking volunteers'

'Well I'll be damned'

'How did you get to know Oliver?' The First Lieutenant whispered

'They plucked us out of the water when Ursula was sunk then took me to Germany with....'

'So that's why you thought you and your men were in the Channel Isles?' The Commander interrupted

'Yes Sir it was' Oliver replied a little too quickly as he embraced the warm feeling he'd managed to score a point.

'Well Navi I guess we'd better get a move on.'

The Yeoman was still hovering, 'Signal Ashanti to give Lieutenant Clements command of the flotilla'

'They'll ask where we're off to Sir'

'I'm sure they will Yeoman so just say we're tasked elsewhere. No more than that.'

After steaming at full speed they managed to reach the co-ordinates a little ahead of time. The Commander was pacing the Bridge concerned that even in this low level of light being barely twenty miles north of Alderney was not a safe place to be.

They heard the roar of S-148's engines as it approached at high speed completing a full circle before laying off at a hundred yards rocking violently in the dying remains of its own wake. A small dinghy was launched and rowed towards Zulu. A scramble net was lowered as it bumped alongside and a slight figure stepped onto it to start the short climb up. The dinghy immediately pulled away to re-join S-148 which with engines at full revs turned and sped away.

Harold Stratton a thirty-four year old larger than life three badge Able Seaman leant over the side, 'It's a woman Chief. Having a bit of trouble too'

'Well get your arse over and give her a hand then.'

He scampered down and grabbed her around the waist, she cried out in pain as he bundled her over the rail and onto the deck, 'Sorry Miss' he stammered, 'thought you were going to fall see.'

'It's a female Sir' the Chief announced as he jumped over the bridge coaming, 'in a lot of pain I think Sir. She yelled a bit when Stratton pulled her in.'

'Thank you Chief.' Then without turning called mockingly over his shoulder, 'Pitman you can look after her you seem to have a way with the Ladies.'

Stratton was stowing the scramble net with his mate, 'Light as a feather she was Taff' he said proudly, 'she didn't smell too good though and I'll tell you something else mate she isn't wearing anything under that dress either'

'Had a good feel then did you Harry?'

'Don't be so bloody disgusting Taff she's only a kid.'

In the light of the Wardroom Oliver looked in disbelief at the state of the Girl. She was bare foot wearing a simple thin cotton dress covered in stains ripped down the back almost to the waist revealing large angry welts still weeping from several severe beatings her short blonde hair matted with filth and blood, face and eyes swollen by countless bruises, split lips and lacerations to both ear lobes.

'What's your name my dear?' He asked feeling as stupid as the question.

'She didn't answer but moved forward, flung her bruised arms around his neck and burst into tears. The smell was overpowering, a mixture of manure sour milk and vomit with a hint of old fishing boat thrown in. It was all he could do to prevent himself from gagging, 'Mary' she said between sobs, 'Mary Matson. I'm sorry I know I stink but please hold me.'

With a quick tap on the door the Commander stood on the threshold, took one look at her battered back, 'Good God you poor poor Girl. Oliver' he said sternly 'use my cabin, there's a clean robe in the right hand drawer under my cot' He drew back a little from the smell, 'she can wash or even shower I'm sure there's enough water.' He lowered his voice, 'look Oliver I don't know how old she is but I'm sure you've been told where I keep the Brandy. Better have one yourself too.' He left but returned almost immediately, 'Bloody nuisance I let the Doctor go. Use the kit in my cabin. The young Snotty that's always in the way on the Bridge, what's his name?'

'Midshipman Weston Sir' Oliver prompted still completely phased by the Commander actually using his Christian name and more than once to boot.

'I reckon he's about the same size as the Girl I'll get him to leave some clothes in the flat.'

Oliver extricated himself from the embrace and found the

Commanders robe. Although reduced to ten knots Zulu was pitching and rolling in the heavy swell making it impossible to use the tiny shower. Oliver set up the tiny washstand located a small bar of Wrights soap, Shampoo, flannel and a clean towel,

'Mary I'll let you get on now' Oliver said quietly heading for the door.

She grabbed his arm, 'No please, please don't leave I don't want to be on my own.'

'But you need to wash'

'I don't care' she whispered dropping the remains of her tattered dress to the floor any modesty compromised by the recent appalling actions of the Gestapo, 'Please stay' she begged, 'please.'

Oliver was mortified as he saw her small breasts were covered in cigarette burns as was her stomach. Her buttocks had the same welts as her back from severe beatings.

'How old are you Mary?' he asked as she started to carefully wash herself down

'Nineteen' she replied drawing in her breath and screwing her eyes up with the searing pain of the rough flannel against her injured body.

A knock came at the door, 'Midshipman Weston Sir I've left some clothes in the flat here Sir.'

Oliver left it a minute or so then retrieved them. There was a shirt, trousers a seaman's jersey and a pair of thick sea boot stockings. Weston may be short but he's a great deal stockier than Mary but at least they were clean and would cover her body.

'No underclothes I'm afraid' he said laying them on the cot.

She grimaced, 'Have you anything for the burns. They're the most painful?'

As Oliver sorted through the Commanders first-aid kit the intercom crackled, 'How are things going young Pitman?'

'Can't find anything for burns Sir'

'Burns?'

'Cigarette burns all over her' he paused 'her um, top parts and stomach.' There was a stony silence, 'so she tells me Sir' he quickly added

'Go to my pantry I think you'll find there's an ounce or so of butter use that.'

Mary winced as she dabbed the butter on each of the burns the salt making them even more painful but after a few minutes the smarting stopped so she carried on until it was all used.

Oliver was amused at the expert way she'd magically turned the towel into a turban to soak up the water from her hair but still felt a little uncomfortable at her padding around the cabin completely naked. She noticed his embarrassment, 'I'm sorry Oliver but it's a lot more uncomfortable for me to have clothes rubbing against my skin for the moment'

'Then would it be better if you use the bunk?'

'I'll certainly give it a try. Can you help me up please?'

'What on earth would Pam think of me lifting a naked young lady into a bunk' he thought silently to himself as he gently took Mary by the waist. The Commander chose this very instant to order a course change which pitched Zulu violently to Port. Oliver leant against it but Mary fell back onto him then because of the butter on her stomach slipped through his arms, he tightened his grip a little but then horrified to discover his hands were now cupping both her breasts gently lowered her to the deck,

'I'm so sorry' he stammered red faced 'it was the butter.'

Zulu settled onto her new heading so Oliver was then able to help her up onto the Bunk with no further mishaps.

To his relief she pulled the sheet up to her neck, 'They promised I'd be looked after' she said her voice trembling, 'it wasn't true they lied to us all of us'

'Who promised you?'

'Lady Collins and a man Lord somebody but I can't remember his name. She said that as I was fluent in French

I could work for them and help us win the war'

'Doing what?' Oliver asked pretty sure of the answer as he opened the cupboard and removed the Brandy and glasses. He poured a small amount and passed the glass to her; she grinned and held it out to him. He took the hint and poured some more for her. She took a sip wincing as the alcohol burned her split lips, 'Getting information from the Germans'

'Was that why you were in Alderney?'

'No I was in Brest but only for a day before I was captured and taken to...' She stopped as her eyes filled with tears the trauma flooding back into her mind, the shouting, the screaming and the begging for it to stop. Ignoring the smarting on her lips she took a long swig of Brandy, 'it was horrible simply horribly.' She grabbed Oliver's arm, 'I don't care what they say I'm not going again'

'You were there for one day?'

'Yes'

'How did you get there?'

'Small plane dropped us off'

'Us?'

'Me and two other Girls, they were a bit older than me'

'Did you know them?'

'No I'd never met them before. Can I have some more?' She asked holding out the empty glass.

Oliver could tell that the Brandy was taking effect as her eyes were half shut and she'd started to slur her words but none the less he poured another good measure for her which she almost finished in one.

'This Lady Collins who does she work for?'

'SOE silly'

'Who?'

'Special Operations Executive' she replied over pronouncing each word

'Do you think you should get some sleep now?'

'Will you stay?'

'Until you're asleep yes' he replied taking the empty

glass from her, 'then I must get back to work but I'll look in as often as I can'

'You promise?' she said snuggling down falling asleep almost immediately.

The Commander turned in his chair as Oliver came onto the Bridge, 'Is that you sloping around in the dark Pitman how is the poor Girl?'

'Asleep Sir. Have you ever heard of SOE?'

'It's some spy type of thing hales out of Baker Street. Is that what she was?'

'Yes Sir'

The Commander shook his head in disgust, 'Sending our young Girls into war now are we? What on earth is it coming to?'

'You've not slept at all Sir'

'That's true Number One but I think my Billet is occupied at the moment'

'You would be most welcome to make use of the Wardroom Sir and' he chuckled, 'we have a cupboard just like yours Sir'

'Not a secret then?' He joked sliding out of his chair,

'Not at all Sir it seems that our Stewards talk to each other.'

The Commander was back almost immediately, 'The Girl's screaming her head off down here'

'On my way Sir.'

He'd hardly shut the cabin door before still stark naked she threw herself into his arms. Even through his shirt he could feel her heart thumping, her breath short and erratic, 'You' she gasped, 'promised to stay.' Her breathing started to slow down, 'they came for me I heard them I knew they would.' She pushed her face into his chest, 'I didn't tell them anything honestly I didn't. I told them I didn't know anything but they wouldn't believe me.'

'Who didn't believe you?'

'A big fat vile woman she ordered two men to keep beating me until I told them everything. She was the one who pulled my clothes off and burnt me with cigarettes.'

'How did you escape?'

She lifted her head and looked up at him, 'I'm not really sure. I remember a lot of noise and guns being fired then I was being dragged along it felt really cold. One man speaking in English said something about a boat; a woman was arguing with him demanding to know why he brought me out as well as Francis I think it was so he'd better move me on quickly because she wasn't going to risk being shot for harbouring some English whore. The next thing I properly remember was when one of your men grabbed me and carried me up.'

'Well' he said extricating himself from the embrace, 'you're safe now and they won't be coming for you so my Girl its back to bed'

'You will stay? Say you will please.'

The weather worsened throughout the night a summer storm surged through the English Channel forcing them to stay in the Atlantic to ride it out.

Oliver had slept in a chair woken on numerous occasions as the ship plummeted into a deep trough then with a boom like a bass drum smashed headlong into the next wave shuddering as with the weight of water pouring through the scuttles struggled its way up to reach the crest balancing for only seconds before plunging down again. He looked at his watch, five forty-five. Mary had uncovered herself during the night so he walked over and pulled the sheet back over her. She opened one eye and smiled.

'I've got to go to the heads I won't be long'

'Where?' She answered sleepily

'The Toilet'

'Alright I'll have to go too' she said turning over and dropping back off to sleep.

By late morning she'd washed and Oliver helped her into the clothes Weston had provided. She looked like a character from Oliver Twist and for the first time she laughed as she viewed herself in the mirror holding on for dear life as the ship rolled and pitched.

'Are you hungry?'

'What have you got to offer?'

'Well in this type of weather it's what's called Pot Mess'

She turned her nose up, 'Doesn't sound too good what is it?'

'A sort of stew that they add things to each day'

'I'd like to try some if I may'

'I won't be long then.'

Oliver was quite glad to be out of the confines of the cabin. He poked his head around the Galley door where the cook had roped himself to a bar on the range as he chopped some more vegetables to add to the huge pot anchored onto the stove.

'Anything ready yet?'

'About quarter of an hour Sir' he replied still chopping away, 'be a bit raw Sir but there 'aint no meat so it 'aint going to kill anyone.'

'Would you mash one up as small as you can when it's ready?'

'For the Lady Sir?' Oliver nodded, 'certainly Sir it'll be like puree.'

He returned to the cabin, 'It won't be ready for a little while so I'll have to get some work done.' She pulled a face, 'you'll be fine here.'

He dashed into the Wardroom grabbed his foul weather gear and made his way to the Bridge. The Commander was slumped in his chair cap pulled down arms folded face set to fed up. He turned as the hatch slammed shut after Oliver. He waved him over, 'How's the Girl?' He shouted above the screeching wind,

'Doing well Sir asking for food'

'Good. I sent a signal earlier to say we would put her ashore at Plymouth as it's nearer but got one back to say it's got to be Portsmouth'

182

'Did they say why Sir?' The Commander raised his eyebrows, 'Obviously not Sir.'

'Small contact bearing three-hundred degrees fifteen miles Sir' the Radar operator called over the intercom

'Course?' Winston asked a little irritated that he'd had to,

'Seems to be stationary Sir or moving very slowly'

'Close up both watches Number One let's go see what it is.'

'Always bloody dinner time' the port lookout complained loudly, 'I suppose Tot time's gone to the dogs an all'

'Well Catermole perhaps if you're lucky you'll be able to have two tomorrow' Winston shouted back

'And pigs might fly Sir.'

As Zulu increased speed the forward gun crews took refuge behind their armour plating now doubling as a wind break, the bridge crew ducking each time the bow ploughed deep into the swell sending sheets of spray cascading over them.

Oliver went below to check up on Mary. The Captains Steward was standing in the flat with a small bundle of clothes, 'We've dhobied her dress Sir and as Tommy Starkey was a Tailor in Civvy Street he stitched it up and made some other stuff.' He handed them over, 'oh and she may as well make use of the slippers Sir. I bought them for my Nans Birthday but' he shook his head 'the Blitz.'

'I'm sure she'll appreciate it from all of you. Chivers isn't it?'

'Chiverly Sir.'

The ship rolled as Oliver pushed the cabin door open so he entered somewhat quicker than he intended. Mary was cowering down on the deck leant against the bunk drawers her hands covering her mouth seemingly scared half to death.

'Are we sinking?' she squeaked trying to get up but falling back down as Zulu heeled over

'Of course not what ever gave you that idea?'

'The alarm sounded.'

Oliver chuckled, 'That was for Action Stations we've picked up a contact on Radar that's all.' He put the clothes on the chair and helped her up, 'the men have dhobied. Laundered' he explained as her face went blank, 'and repaired your dress' he held it up 'still badly stained but a lot fresher and also the resident Tailor has made you these.'

She unfolded them, 'Oh that really is sweet of them' she said laying out a vest made of an old white front and a pair of knickers from a pillow case, 'and some slippers too.'

'They would've had to guess your size so I hope everything fits'

Still completely uninhibited she stripped off and eagerly pulled on the underclothes. They were by no means perfect but based on a guess reasonable. The vest was a little large in the breast area; she smiled and pulled it out away from her,

'Wishful thinking on their part' Oliver said laughing, 'all heart though.'

The intercom hissed and buzzed for a second or two, 'Lieutenant Commander Pitman to the Bridge.'

'Got to go I'm afraid hope not to be long.'

He dashed into the Wardroom to retrieve his foul weather gear and then straight up to the Bridge quite expecting to be consulted on U-Boat tactics.

'What do you reckon to that?' The Commander asked handing him his Binoculars.

Steadying himself against the Bridge screen he peered through the spray at twenty foot of ships bow riding almost vertical with each wave.

'That's Sea Mist a US type C3' the First Lieutenant pitched in, 'sunk well over a week ago.'

Oliver handed the Binoculars back, 'Obviously enough air trapped to bring it back up'

'Quite so but the question is if the air is breathable

perhaps some of the crew could still be alive and trapped in the bow?'

'Nice thought Sir but unfortunately not possible. The air would've got so compressed their eardrums and lungs would've burst and they'd die within minutes.'

The Commander climbed back into his chair, 'Well we can't leave it there. Guns?'

'Yes Sir'

'Put a couple of rounds into her and let her rest.'

Two shells smashed into the bow the released air screeching like an express train then with a huge water spout she slowly rotated and slipped into the depths.

'I can't really put down that we sunk a US Cargo ship can I Sir?'

The Commander guffawed, 'I guess you can't Number One so just make something up.'

With the weather moderating and the outlook fair Zulu headed into the English Channel making for Portsmouth.

Oliver returned to the Cabin where Mary was now fully clothed. The bruises on her face were gradually getting lighter; the puffiness had completely gone revealing a very pretty girl. He daren't ask about the burns as he felt sure she would immediately show him. She'd managed to scramble up onto the bunk unaided and was sitting with her legs dangling over the side.

'Do you think I'll be in trouble?' She asked her face showing concern

'For what?'

'Being captured. But honestly I didn't tell them anything. I wouldn't do that.'

'You shouldn't be in trouble at all.'

'I went to the Café like they said to meet a man called Francois and give him the information I'd had to commit to memory before we left'

'And did you?'

'No he wasn't there. I waited then some soldiers came in and took me away.' Tears welled up in her eyes, 'Lady

Collins said that I mustn't tell anyone what I was doing or where I was going not even my Mum and Dad or I'd be put in Prison'

'What do your parents think you're doing?'

'Working on farm Accounts in Cumbria.'

'Why Cumbria?'

'That Lord somebody, I can't remember his name told me I had to tell them that because it was a long way from Dorchester where I live.' She put her head down and started to cry quietly, 'I know I'll be in trouble' she sobbed, 'I'm scared of her she'll shout at me like she did before.'

'How did she recruit you in the first place?'

She wiped the tears from her cheeks with her hand 'I went for an interview in London for an Accounts position in a Baker Street Office. After the Interview I was taken to see this Lady Collins who said I was perfect for the position and I was to start straight away.'

Oliver shook his head and exhaled loudly. The tail she was telling would be worthy of a West End Drama, 'When did you find out that it wasn't quite the position you were expecting?'

'I had to go with Lady Collins to see this Lord in Westminster and he told me that I was just the person to help shorten the war so would I agree to go to France for a couple of days to deliver information to someone then I'd be looked after until I was brought back home.'

It was a long shot but he thought he'd ask anyway, 'What information did you have to give?'

She shook her head, 'I mustn't say I really mustn't.'

Oliver put his hand on her shoulder; 'That's fine' he said assuring her she was right to refuse.

A tap on the door brought the conversation to a close, 'Sorry it's a bit late now Sir but grubs up so I've brought the Ladies over. Cook mashed it right down. Shall I bring yours here as well Sir?'

'Yes Chiverly if you will.'

Despite not having eaten properly for quite some time

she spooned the Pot Mess slowly into her mouth.

A further tap on the door delivered his food which for the extra boiling looked little different from the mashed down version along with a plate of not so fresh bread.

She stopped eating and looked over at him grinning mischievously; 'No' he said firmly, 'I think you've had enough.'

'Spoil sport' she moaned, 'it really helped with the pain'

'So would Morphine but you're not getting any of that either.'

She finished her bowl of Pot Mess along with most of the bread, 'Not even a little drop?' She persisted cocking her head to one side belching loudly, 'I'm so sorry' she apologised, 'but perhaps it would settle my stomach. Please just a drop'

'You do realise that I could be in trouble with your parents if they found out I'd plied you with Brandy?'

'Then I won't tell them if you don't'

'Then just to keep the peace young Lady you may have another small drop.'

Oliver remained totally amazed at this young slip of a girl who'd not too many hours ago been so savagely tortured and beaten now smiling and joking. He looked on as with both legs dangling over the side of the bunk she slowly sipped at the Brandy. He couldn't even begin to envisage the horror and pain she must have been through any more than he could understand the people who were prepared to do such things to other human beings.

'Who was it you said sent you over?'

'Lady Collins'

'And you still don't remember the name of that Lord chap?'

She thought for a while turning the empty glass round and round in her hand, 'Sutton' she shouted gleefully 'that was it Lord Sutton.'

Chapter Eleven

Portsmouth

Zulu moored at Fountain Lake Jetty in the early afternoon sunshine. From the Bridge they could smell and see the acrid smoke still hanging over the North of the City from the overnight raids the inshore breeze blowing it towards Portsdown hill where it slowly rose into tall wisps their tips toppling over once caught up in the breeze again.

An Ambulance with two nurses waited as the gangway was rigged. A hacking cough announced that the Commodore was around somewhere but out of sight.

'Better get below and take the Girl ashore. I guess the Ambulance is for her?'

Mary was physically shaking as Oliver escorted her off the ship, 'Are you sure I won't be in trouble?'

'There's no earthly reason why you should be' Oliver assured her as the Nurses stepped forward.

'We'll take it from here'

'Where are you taking her?'

The elder of the two Nurses who Oliver guessed was in charge gave him a scornful look, 'Well it's hardly going to be the flicks is it?' Oliver glared at her, 'up the hill probably hut seven but there's no visiting allowed yet.' With that they whisked her away.

Oliver suddenly felt a great sense of loss even after only being with her for such a short time she'd left quite an impression on him.

'Penny for them' the Commodore whispered tapping him on the shoulder

'Sorry Sir I was miles away'

'Saw you with the Girl how is she?'

Oliver shook his head, 'Mary? Beaten burnt and generally bashed about. I just can't understand these people Sir'

'Nor I but I'd hardly call them people. Anyway' he

lowered his voice, 'how did you get on with Commander Harvey?'

'Very frosty at first Sir but now we seem to get along just fine.'

'Good. I've got a bit of bad news for you' he paused 'Pam's away on a course for the week. Even I don't know where but she'll still blame me. She said she'd phone but I doubt she'll be able to. Ah Paul' he boomed as the Commander walked over, 'enjoy yourself?'

'Immensely Sir but as for the munitions we're being fobbed off with its disgusting.'

'So I read on the flotillas reports'

'I never did manage to find out Sir did we lose many men off Dido?' He asked grim faced.

The Commodore smiled, 'Not one. Forty seven wounded but even the most seriously injured are on the mend'

'Mainly thanks to you I would think Sir' Oliver said chuckling, 'with your madcap circle the waggons system.'

Unusually for the Commander he looked rather embarrassed, 'I understand that the U-Boat pushed off so a bit of luck really but thank you anyway.'

The Commodore smiled to himself content that his plan appeared to have been successful as both Paul and Oliver now seemed on the surface at least to be rubbing along quite well. 'Well Gentlemen as Pamela is away on a course and Margaret is visiting yet another one of her clan I thought we may as well have a jolly good chat about things back at my house. What do you think?'

'I'd better let the First Lieutenant know and collect a change of clothes Sir then I'll be straight with you.'

The journey to the Commodores residence took much longer than they'd expected. Gas and water mains had been ruptured causing deep flooded craters over the roads. Surrounding buildings still smouldering had exhausted fire crews scrambling all over the rubble still dampening the area down painfully aware that the whole episode would most likely be repeated tomorrow, the next day and the day after.

As they climbed out of the car the Commodores driver indicated for Oliver to hang back, 'The young Lady sends her love to you Sir' he whispered, 'and says she'll ring if she can'

'You've seen her?'

'Yes Sir dropped her off the day before yesterday'

'Where?'

'Baker Street in London Sir.'

An ice cold chill ran straight down Oliver's spine and he suddenly felt physically sick. Had Pam been drawn in to volunteering for SOE? In his panic all he could visualise was Mary's burnt and battered body.

'Good Lord Oliver you look as if you've seen a ghost what on earth's the matter?'

'Can Pam speak any foreign languages Sir?'

'What an odd thing to ask'

'But can she?' he asked his voice trembling

'She took French and Latin at school. Don't remember her being particularly interested in it she was more into history than anything else.' He handed Oliver a brandy and motioned for him to sit 'get this down you then perhaps you'll let us into what's obviously got you rattled.'

Oliver finished the drink in one gulp the strong spirit burning his throat, 'Your driver' he gasped swallowing repeatedly, 'dropped Pam off in Baker Street'

'What's so bad about that?'

'SOE' the Commander said quite loudly, 'Lady, what's her name?'

'Collins and Lord Sutton'

'Bertie Sutton? I've known the chap for years he's a member of my London club, works somewhere in Whitehall'

'He's the one who duped Mary into going to France promising faithfully she'd be looked after'

'Bertie Sutton? Surely not.'

The Commander leant forward in his chair, 'So you're

concerned he's recruited Pam?'

Oliver accepted another drink, 'Worried sick, why else would she go off to Baker Street?'

'There must be other organisations there surely' the Commodore chipped in now fairly concerned himself, 'besides I'm positive she'd have the sense to know what it was all about'

'Mary thought she was having an interview for an Accountancy position.'

The phone rang, the Commodore leapt up and headed for the hallway, 'this may be Pamela' he called over his shoulder, 'I hope so anyway.'

They could hear him talking but weren't able to piece the words together. It was obvious that it wasn't Pam as he started to raise his voice, 'Well you'd better damn well find out and quick' he shouted, 'so get hold of Lord Sutton and have him ring me at home.' There was a long pause, 'I don't care if he's busy just do it.' The phone was slammed back into the cradle, 'Not Pamela' he said crossly as he came back in 'but some minion from Whitehall who says that you two are to attend a meeting at ten hundred tomorrow at sixty-four Baker Street with the Admiralty research and development department. Which I guessed could be some fancy fictitious name for this SOE you were talking about so I asked to speak to Lord Sutton'

'I bet that went down well Sir'

'Actually Paul they didn't know what to say but eventually muttered something about him being very busy.'

The phone rang again the Commodore beckoned them to follow him to the hallway, 'Two-three-eight hello.' He smiled covered the mouthpiece and whispered, 'Bertie Sutton.' Removing his hand he spoke louder, 'Bertie how the devil are you. Good. Now I have a question for you. Yes it can be answered over the telephone. Have you seen or heard from my Daughter Pamela? You haven't? Now are you positive Bertie? What about the Lady?' He looked round at Oliver who quietly mouthed her name, 'Collins has she seen or heard from her? You're pretty certain she hasn't? Really? Well I'll be. Very strange. Anyway Bertie if you do come across her you're to send her home straight away. Excellent must catch up soon Goodbye.' He put the receiver back down, 'well Pamela certainly isn't with them and apparently this Lady Collins isn't a Lady.' He laughed at the two blank faces, 'apparently it's her Christian name and she's a Miss, Miss Lady Collins. Bertie hinted that's who you'll be meeting tomorrow.'

'Goodness only knows why they want to speak to us Sir'

'Plus having to travel to London' Oliver added, 'they certainly don't want to put themselves out at all do they?'

'You may as well bed down here Paul Pamela's old room has just been repaired. I'll ring Harold.' He paused then suddenly asked straight out of the blue, 'Do you fancy some fish and chips?' They both nodded, 'then I'll ask him to bring some in and then order a car for five-thirty to the Station. You'll be able to take the six-thirty-three to Waterloo that should get you there in plenty of time.'

Harold dropped them off at Portsmouth and Southsea station at six. Even at this early hour it was already packed solid with service personnel. The Commander went over to the ticket office returning a couple of minutes later looking a little perplexed, 'For some reason I couldn't get first class'

'All that was scrapped in thirty-nine Sir it's a case of buy a ticket get on and grab a seat if you can.'

A Porter came out of the waiting room and using a loud hailer bellowed across the platform to announce that the six-thirty-three express was now the seven-o-four slow train to Waterloo.

Luckily they managed to get a seat, the carriage compartment was filthy and had quite a large hole in the roof fortunate for ventilation as the window was stuck fast and wouldn't lower.

Paul checked his watch for the umpteenth time, 'I don't

think we'll make it for our meeting' he said as the train slowed then shuddered to a halt outside of Guildford. They waited for fifteen minutes before it finally pulled into the station. The Guard walked along the platform shouting into each compartment that the train would now because of damage to Waterloo station terminate at Clapham Junction.

'No chance now' Paul declared raising his voice above both the clatter of wares being piled up on the platform and the Station Master continuously bawling at the Porters to stow the goods in the correct loading areas.

It was a few minutes after nine-thirty before they eventually crawled out of Guildford station. A rather plump red-faced Gent with mutton chop sideburns wearing a tweed jacket and flat cap exhaled irritably, 'Quicker to bloody well walk these days' he moaned, 'you chaps got a meeting you say?'

'We have yes in' Paul checked his watch, 'twenty minutes'

'Should've set off yesterday' he replied sarcastically wriggling around on the seat to get comfortable, 'may well have made it on time then.'

'I travel this route often' a very slightly built elderly woman trilled, 'it's never been on time yet. I think they always use the war as an excuse.'

Everyone grunted an agreement then fell back into silent contemplation as the train moving at a snail's pace crawled towards London.

'You're late' a flustered Orderly complained, 'you should've been here at ten. We are busy you know'

'I'm sure you are' Paul replied, 'obviously too busy to travel anywhere by train.' The Orderly looked confused, 'they don't run on time and very often don't reach their destination'

'Well' he huffed 'I'm not sure that Miss Collins will have time to see you'

'Look' Paul replied very firmly, 'she asked to see us so

to be honest we couldn't give a fig whether she can or not.' He turned towards the door, 'come on Oliver we'll leave and let these very important people carry on with whatever they get up to'

'Wait' the Orderly said quickly, 'I'll see if she's available.'

Miss Lady Collins was a slim sixty-two year old with unkempt grey wiry hair swept back and tied into a bun behind her head. Her face and brow were quite wrinkled, small piercing grey eyes stared out below bushy grey eyebrows, thin straight lips and hooked nose presented her as a cold severe uncaring person. Her starched white blouse, military style khaki fitted jacket and matching skirt done little to dispel her apparent lack of femininity.

'You're late' she snapped in a well refined strong voice

'We've already been through this with one of your minions. So what do you want?' Lady glared at Paul with total contempt. No wonder Mary was scared stiff of her Oliver thought to himself as Paul continued, 'Well?' he demanded, 'like you we're busy people so can we get on please?'

'You're Pitman?' She asked staring at Oliver indicating for them to take a seat

'Lieutenant-Commander Oliver Pitman yes'

'You spent some time with Mary Matson?'

'Yes'

'Did she say much to you?'

'Like what?'

'Anything'

'She told me her name'

'That couldn't have been all she said so what else?' she demanded irritably

'She slept quite a bit'

'Of course but who else did she name?'

'I can't really remember'

'Did she name any other operatives?'

'No'

'You seem to remember that alright so I'll ask again was there anyone else she told you about?'

'She was scared stiff of you'

'If she'd done her job properly she'd have no need to be scared of me'

'So did she?' Paul asked

'Not really no' she muttered the reply so quietly that Oliver missed it but Paul was closer and cottoned on immediately,

'My God' he snarled, 'you informed on the poor kid and expected her to give over the information you'd fed her' he paused then looking straight into her eyes added sarcastically, 'but she didn't tell did she?'

Lady red with rage spat back, 'She would have done too had it not been for that irritating interfering Royal Marine Major poking his nose in where it wasn't needed.' Oliver chuckled, 'something amusing you Pitman?'

'You must be talking about Major Guy Robins surely?'

'You know him?'

'Yes very well.'

'Never mind all of that' Paul shouted getting to his feet, 'you don't seem too bothered about a nineteen year old kid being beaten burnt and bashed about just to pass on duff information.' He leant over the desk towards her, 'you knew bloody well that as soon as she had they would've dragged her outside and shot her. And you know what?' He said pointing an accusing finger at her, 'you wouldn't have given a fig. You're despicable no better than they are.'

The door swung open and a portly gentleman some six feet tall with thinning white hair a round face bulbous nose and hooded eyes hurried in. He was wearing an obviously very expensive three piece pin-striped suit with a white shirt and black bowtie, 'And what the hell's going on here to justify all that damn racket?' He demanded glaring at the two men as Paul sat down again.

'Well Sir Giles he' Lady explained pointing at Oliver 'I believe is withholding information and the other is making accusations of a very serious nature'

'Oh dear that won't do at all' he said as though talking to a child, 'so what are these accusations that you're making?'

Oliver could sense by his body language that Paul was getting extremely annoyed, 'Firstly who are you?'

'Sir Giles Hutchins'

'And your position here?'

'Classified I'm afraid. Your accusation?'

'Is it possible to discuss this with Lord Sutton?'

Sir Giles looked at Lady who shrugged her shoulders, 'I've heard of him in fact I believe I met him once but he has nothing to do with our department'

'That's rather strange as a telephone call to Commodore Warwick would prove otherwise.'

Sir Giles ignored this completely, 'If you wish to make accusations against us then just bloody well get on with it'

'Your department after notifying the enemy of her arrival in France duped a nineteen year old girl to go over with a head full of duff information knowing fully well that she would be tortured until telling them everything then without any doubt executed.'

Sir Giles drew in his breath then exhaled noisily, 'If either of you repeat these claims outside of this room.' He paused looking at each of them in turn, 'things could be made quite difficult for you.'

Paul leant forward in his seat, 'Really?' he replied angrily, 'And exactly how do you think you'll be able to do that?'

'Quite simple it'll be placed under the Official Secrets act.'

Oliver had been silent for some time but the thought of this despicable chap just hiding it away as if it were nothing annoyed him immensely, 'Is that what you do with all your grubby little mistakes just bury them under the Official Secrets Act?'

'Obviously' Paul cut in before Sir Giles had chance to answer, 'the information the girl was carrying wasn't much of a secret if you wanted her to give it up?'

'No it wasn't but none the less of vital importance to the war effort'

'So are we allowed to know about it or is it just for the Germans?'

'I'll ignore your pointless sarcasm but yes I see no reason why not. I would've preferred to discuss it with the Commanding Officer first but I was informed that he was otherwise engaged, doing something quite unimportant I would guess. Only a young chap I understand, far too young in my opinion to command such an experimental vessel.' Lady was desperately trying to catch his eye but failed as he carried on, 'but I guess somebody must think the lad's bright enough to pull it off. One hell of a risk I'd say.'

'A young lad you say?' Oliver asked enjoying the spectacle of Lady squirming around in her seat while her Boss was digging himself into a hole.

'Yes far too young' he replied smugly, 'and as you've asked we were requested to drop as many hints as possible to show that we've developed a fast almost undetectable new design of submarine.'

'And that's all she was to give up under torture and lose her life over? A load of baloney'

'We' he almost spat out, 'only tell them exactly what and only what we want them to know and nothing else do you understand?'

'Seems a bit excessive if you don't mind me saying?'

'I do mind actually. Look' he raised his voice angrily, 'I'll do my job and best if yours is left for you to sail your little ships around and leave the difficult stuff to us.'

Oliver furious at his remark shot up from his seat, 'What's so bloody difficult about sending young girls to their deaths? I doubt you have a conscience or lose any sleep over it'

'When you grow up' he replied sarcastically, 'and have occasion to make difficult decisions then perhaps you'll understand.'

Oliver remained standing and extended his arm. 'Lieutenant-Commander Oliver Pitman the lad who's far too young to be the Commanding Officer of this new design submarine the far too young man that you believe needs to grow up and learn to make difficult decisions. You know' he continued, 'I find it rather strange that at twenty-two you think I'm far too young but seem quite content to wave off a nineteen year old out into enemy territory without a chance in hell of surviving'

'Enough of that' he shouted roughly brushing Oliver's hand aside, 'once and for all let me assure both of you that we had people standing by to free Mary the moment we knew she'd passed the information over so she definitely would not have been executed'

'She had a lot more guts that you reckoned though didn't she?'

He nodded and then glared at Lady who he guessed had failed to advise him that Oliver was the Commanding Officer of Troy, 'Now I firmly recommend that you both heed what I've said, not a word to anyone about the incident outside of this room. You understand?'

As he closed the door behind him Paul stood up, 'Is that our meeting finished?'

'For now yes but we may need to talk to you again'

'Well goodbye Miss Collins I can't say it's been a pleasure. Oh and bye the way do please give my regards to Lord Sutton when he pops in.'

As they walked back down Oliver caught sight of Pam sitting in the lobby. He almost ran down the stairs, 'What on earth are you doing here?' he gasped, 'who are you waiting to see?'

'Waiting for you silly' she replied kissing him lightly, 'daddy said you were here so suggested I meet you to travel back together.' She acknowledged Paul, 'Commander' she said sweetly then turning back to Oliver, 'why were you so bothered about me being here?'

'I'll tell you later let's just get outside.'

'Have you got your train ticket Pamela?'

'Not yet Sir no.'

He fished around in his pocket, 'Take mine I've got some business to attend to'

'That warning we got in there was real Sir so I hope you're not going to......'

Paul laughed, 'Thank you for your concern Oliver but I'm meeting Admiral Beaufort to officially complain about those failed Torpedoes.' He crossed his fingers and held them up, 'he provided a slap up meal last time so with luck he may do the same again. Anyway I'm a bit worried about you'

'Me? What on earth for Sir?'

'You seemed to be as obnoxious as I was in that meeting and at twenty-two that's not good. Alright for me my careers almost over you've got a long way to go so yes you'd better heed their ridiculous warnings.'

They hailed Taxis and went their separate ways. Pamela snuggled into Oliver, 'The Commander's mellowed a bit hasn't he. Did I hear right that he called you Oliver?'

'I think we have a renewed respect for each other. Did you hear that despite a U-Boat sneaking about he actually had all the crew taken off Dido before she sank?'

'It was the talk of the Dockyard. Anyway' she said as they entered a now repaired but rubble strewn Waterloo Station, 'where did you go off to when the flotilla came back?'

'Had to pick someone up off the coast of Alderney. I can't say any more than that really.'

He was somewhat relieved that Pam accepted his answer without further question as he would've found it quite difficult to explain about Mary without mentioning her nasty injuries. Pam being her normal inquisitive self would've certainly grilled him for more. Quite how she would react if she became aware that for most of the time Mary was padding around the cabin completely naked and even worse where his hands accidently ended up as he attempted to help her into the bunk.

'Everything alright Oliver?' She asked with some concern in her voice, 'you look a bit, well serious and anxious about something.'

He smiled broadly; 'Sorry I was just mulling over the meeting we've just had' he lied.

They had to run for the train jumping on just as it pulled out much to the disgust of the Passengers in the Compartment as a huge cloud of dust billowed in before Oliver had chance to slam the door behind them, 'So sorry' he apologised to the glare of a huge woman, her double chin wobbling as she shook her head, 'Thank you very much young man' she muttered sarcastically as she dusted herself down, 'that's all we need a good coating of London filth.'

Others mumbled their agreement except a rather attractive young Lady dressed in a green jumper, brown Land Girls dungarees and felt hat who was squashed up against the door, 'I rather like it you know' she said in an obviously refined and very well-educated voice, 'it's the fresh air and cow shit that gets to me.'

Pam giggled at the comment but the others remained stony faced and silent until the Land Girl got out at Woking, 'More room for you to spread out now dear' she said grinning mischievously as she jumped down onto the platform.

'What an awfully rude girl' the fat woman moaned, 'if that's who we rely on then God help us.'

'They work bloody hard to keep us Townies fed' an old Gent remarked

'That doesn't give her an excuse to use foul language and be very rude to her elders' the fat woman complained.

The train pulled into Portsmouth and Southsea station just forty minutes late. Oliver called a cab over and they were soon back at the Commodores house. Both Douglas and Margaret were at home.

'Oliver' Douglas started, 'I don't think you've taken

much leave just lately'

'Not recently no Sir'

'You have a Sister I believe?'

'I have yes Sir Clara' he replied hesitantly with some suspicion in his voice

'Well perhaps it's high time you paid her a visit.'

Oliver's suspicions were well founded as there was certainly a lot more to this than just the opportunity of seeing his sister, 'As you know Sir I've just had a meeting with Miss Lady Collins and Sir Giles Hutchins they also seemed to be reluctant to come clean if you get my drift Sir.'

He roared with laughter, 'Ok Oliver but for God's sake look surprised when you're contacted'

'By who Sir?'

'Somebody from Military Intelligence'

'Why me particularly?'

'Quite close to where your sister lives is a Factory producing mainly aircraft instruments but also some other types of bespoke panels and dials. You've been invited to view a fictitious range of gear ready to be fitted into Troy then straight afterwards meet a chap in the local Pub to finalise a few bits and pieces. And that's about all really'

'Well that explains what I'm to do Sir but not exactly why'

'As I understand it Military Intelligence and the local Police have been keeping an eye on a cell with at least three enemy agents operating in the area, so I can only assume that as we're so keen to get the Germans interested in Troy the chap you'll meet in the Pub will somehow make sure the information gets back to them'

'Well I guess that's a better way than a nineteen year old girl being half beaten to death by a bunch of Nazi thugs'

'Umm' the Commodore said warily, 'I had an urgent call from Bertie Sutton earlier today ordering us to forget all about that. It never happened Oliver.'

'That's rather strange Sir when it was made abundantly

clear to the Commander and I that he had nothing to do with their department.'

He gave Oliver an old fashioned look, 'It didn't happen' he persisted 'now forget it.'

Pam had been sitting quietly on the sofa her slim legs tucked under her, something her Mother disapproved of but seemed to tolerate, 'So Daddy how long will Oliver be away this time?' she moaned, 'I'm beginning to think that you don't want us to spend any time together at all'

'Well you can think again young Lady because this time if Oliver's sister Carla agrees you can go with him.'

Their long train journey proved to be even more frustrating by a long delay on Salisbury Station causing a frantic mad dash platform change to make their connection the moment they finally arrived at Swindon, then another hour wait at Gloucester for the Cheltenham train.

'Olly' Carla shouted from behind the barrier, 'over here.'

He swept her up into his arms, 'Hello you. May I' he said plonking her back down, 'present the love of my life Pamela Warwick. Pamela this is my dear sister Carla.'

They embraced politely, 'You didn't tell me how gorgeous she was Olly'

'You would've only told me I wasn't good enough for her'

'That's true' she replied smiling sweetly, 'anyway I've borrowed Johns car so it won't take a tick to get home.'

Carla was thirty-two her natural blonde hair was cut short and flicked out at the end. She was just five foot two a little plump with a full face rosy cheeks small nose and azure blue almond eyes that glistened, her lips were full and she seemed to be always smiling, 'Now' she said, 'down to business I hope you've both brought your Military Personnel visiting ration cards with you'

'We have so what's on the menu for dinner?'

She missed then crunched a gear before calling over her shoulder, 'Rabbit stew potatoes carrots and whatever other veg we've got the staple diet around here. It's either that or Pidgeon pie. John and I belong to a Pig club and we keep chickens but it wasn't worth it because they cut our meat and egg ration and even then wanted half the pig'

'That seems a bit unfair'

'It is Pamela but' she chuckled, 'they don't know about the other pig.'

The Rectory was a large formidable looking building just a stone's throw from the village. All the rooms were big sparsely furnished almost empty spaces, 'John must be at the Church' she said closing the huge wooden front door, 'but he should be home soon. I'll show you to your rooms.' She took them up a rather ornate staircase and along an uncarpeted hallway, 'This is your room Pamela' she said pushing a door open. 'I hope it's comfortable for you. The Loo is just a few steps along there.'

A few feet on she stopped and turned to Oliver and whispered, 'Olly have you, umm are you. Oh for God's sake have you been intimate with Pamela?' Oliver a little stunned at his sisters candour didn't reply immediately, 'Don't look so shocked Ollie' she whispered, 'it's the forties not the twenties. Anyway I'll take your silence as a yes' she said pushing a key into his hand, 'but' she warned, 'make damn sure you're back where you should be by the time Mrs Redgrave comes round in the morning at eight with tea. Dinner will be at six-thirty.'

Oliver entered the room and saw a door that obviously connected the rooms. He pushed the key in and unlocked it. Pam was sat on the bed looking out of the window and showed little surprise as he came in, 'I heard' she said sweetly, 'I don't think Husband John the Rector would be quite so understanding though'

'You're quite happy about it?'

She grinned mischievously slid off the bed put her arms around his neck and kissed him on the lips, 'Does that answer your question?'

The Rector John McBride was a thirty-nine year old ginger haired Glaswegian, a giant of a man more akin to a Highland caber tossing champion than a man of God serving his Parish in a sleepy Cotswold village.

'Hello Oliver lovely to see you again and your lovely Lady Friend Pamela. Carla has been keeping me up to date with your exploits'

'That must've been a dreadful bore'

'Not at all' he said grinning politely then with a straight face, 'Do you know a chap called Samuel Knight?'

'No. Should I?'

'He came into the Vestry at Lunchtime and asked me to tell you that he would pick you up outside the Tithe Barn at ten tomorrow.'

'Oliver' Carla cried feigning hurt feelings, 'and there's me thinking that you'd come all this way just to visit us'

'Sorry but I shouldn't be long. And before you ask....'

'I know mums the word, walls have ears and all the other stuff we've heard about. Anyway I'll take Pamela into Town that's if you don't mind?'

'Not at all thank you' Pam replied 'I'd love that it sounds fun'

'Don't get too excited Pamela' John warned, 'it's not exactly the hustle and bustle you're used to'

'None the less John I'm sure I'll enjoy it.'

Dinner was excellent. The Rabbit stew was so rich and tasty as were the myriad of fresh vegetables served up with it, 'That Carla was smashing I never knew you were such a good cook.'

'Moi?' She said holding both hands to her chest in mock surprise, 'I must be honest Ollie Mrs Redgrave prepares it all I just chuck it onto the stove.'

'If you'll excuse me a minute please' Pam said looking a little concerned, 'back in a mo.'

'You've picked a good one there Olly'

'I think so too.'

'She's a Commodores daughter isn't she?' John asked

raising his eyebrows

'She is yes but I don't think that'll cut any ice on the promotion stakes'

'Pity' he replied smiling broadly, 'I was a good friend to the Bishop of Truro…'

'And a lot of good that did when he dumped you here' Carla interrupted

'Surely it's not that bad?'

'Of course it's not John I'm only teasing.'

Pam poked her head round the door, 'Can I have a quick word Carla.'

A lot of muttering went on in the hallway before they both disappeared upstairs returning five minutes later.

'Anyone for pudding?' Carla asked, 'stewed plums and real custard.'

Pudding over Oliver pushed back in his chair, 'Mrs Redgrave again?'

'No' Carla protested loudly, 'this time all my own work.' John coughed, 'well admittedly she bottled the plums last year'

'Last year?'

'You really have become a Townie Olly we've got bottled Gooseberries from two years ago still perfectly fresh.'

'What do you do about sugar?' Pam asked 'the custard was wonderfully sweet'

'There's a sugar beet plant at Stoke Orchard so we don't have too much of a problem really. We're probably a bit better off than you in the Cities as we can grow most of the fruit and veg we need and the countryside is awash with Pigeons and Rabbits.'

Oliver yawned, 'Sorry but I think I'll turn in now it's been a bit of a day.'

'Me too I think' Pam said stifling a yawn.

Carla walked up the stairs with them, 'no need for a chaperone Carla I'm a big boy now' he mocked putting his arm round her shoulder and squeezing her, 'no need for bedtime stories either.'

'Well' she whispered looking round to make sure that Pam was in her room, 'I've got one for you anyway'

'Go on'

'This is a small Village with the usual Village Gossip. Mrs Redgrave bless her is the local radio station with twenty-four hour broadcasting. One morning John and I had a few words about something quite trivial but later that day we had a frantic telephone call from the Bishop of Gloucester who'd heard we were discussing Divorce.'

'So where is all this leading to?'

'Like I said earlier make damn sure that you're back in your own rooms by the time she arrives with your tea. I dread to think what would get around the Village; we'd probably be accused of running a house of disrepute I shouldn't wonder. Pam's borrowed a long cotton nighty from me which is a little more in keeping with the situation'

'Don't worry Sister dear we'll behave I promise

She kissed him on the cheek, 'You'd better night night Olly.'

Exhausted they both fell asleep almost immediately and didn't wake until Mrs Redgrave chapped on the door, 'Good morning Oliver' she boomed, 'sleep well?'

As Oliver's eyes cleared a bit he was sure he recognised her face. She was a short slightly built jolly looking woman wearing a bright flowery tabard with a yellow scarf expertly folded into a Turban on her head with a huge clip on the back to keep it there.

'Have we met before?' he asked stretching his arms above his head

'I wouldn't think so Oliver, may I call you Oliver?' She didn't wait for a reply, 'not recently anyway or I'd remember.' She thought for a moment, 'you come from Portsmouth though don't you?' He nodded, 'it's unlikely but you may've met my twin sister Dolly, huge woman heart of gold. She worked in a Hotel by the dockyard gates but it was bombed out a little while ago.'

'She cooked a superb Rabbit stew as well I think.'

Her face lit up with a massive grin 'It was our Mum's Recipe' she said proudly, 'everyone seems to like it. Anyway I'd better get on got a lot to do today.' She closed the door but he could still hear her outside, 'Fancy that him knowing my sister Dolly. Small World it is for sure.'

Once he knew she was out of the way he used the key and went into Pam's room. She was sat up in bed sipping her tea, 'Nice nighty' he said chuckling

'Isn't it just?' she replied carefully pulling the covers back to reveal the rest, 'almost keeps my toes warm.'

A knock at her door had him scampering back to his room quietly closing the door behind him. It was Mrs Redgrave, 'If you have any laundry dear just bung it in the box over there and I'll get it done for you. Will you let Oliver know that he's got one in his room too? Don't want to disturb him again.' She grinned, 'he might be in the all together. Right I'll leave you in peace Breakfast is at nine.'

As Oliver and Pam walked down the stairs together the smell of fried bacon filled the air. Breakfast was superb, egg, bacon, pork sausage and black pudding, 'Certainly the best I've had for quite a while' Pam said putting her knife and fork down, 'very often we can't get bacon and have to get it replaced with some stuff called Spam. Have you ever heard of it Carla?'

'Can't say I have but as I said we're in a Pig club so it isn't often that we're without bacon.'

Just before ten Oliver crossed the road and waited outside the Tithe Barn. A young man clomped past wearing brown overalls and wellington boots. He nodded then went into the yard alongside the Barn picked up a pair of shears and started to clip away at the hedge. Now his back was towards him he noticed the chap had a large grey patch on his back.

A car drove slowly towards him and stopped. A lanky chap with dishevelled light brown hair wearing a beige suite and thick lensed glasses got out leaving the engine running. He smiled, 'Samuel Knight' nice to meet you. After shaking hands he leant over the dry stone wall, 'good' is all he said as he stood back up.

'What's good?' Oliver asked

Samuel lowered his voice to a whisper, 'Did you notice the chap working in the Yard?'

'Yes he walked past me and nodded'

'Did he say anything?'

'No just nodded'

'He's a German POW that's why he has the grey patch on his back. The Kids and a lot of the locals call him Herman the German, he's harmless enough to them but he's caused us a bit of concern. I doubt he's supposed to be in the yard but we let slip that I was meeting you so he's been instructed to make sure I do'

'Instructed by who?'

Samuel indicated for him to get into the car, 'We know there's a cell in Evesham, they've set themselves up as watch repairers lots of the Soldiers from the camp in Tewkesbury mail off watches to have them fixed and sometimes they're even delivered back by hand'

'So this POW chap is allowed to wander around where ever he likes without a guard?'

'Sounds odd I know but it isn't really. This is as far as he's permitted to go along the Cheltenham road. If he dares to go any further he'd be confined to the POW camp in Gotherington. And to be honest Oliver he's useful at the moment.' He put the car in gear, 'right let's go for a drive'

'No factory?'

'Good Lord no we only want them to think that we've had to visit a Factory the other side of Cheltenham. They've no idea where it is really and we'd like to keep it that way. A coffee in Cavendish House I think is in order. Do you drink Coffee Oliver?'

'Occasionally yes but it's mostly Camp Coffee now'

'Well you're in for a treat.'

As they drove through town Oliver was surprised to see

bomb damage, 'I didn't think Jerry would bother to bomb here'

'We think the Coach Station must've looked like a factory from the air or as some believe they just dumped excess bombs after they'd hit Coventry.'

Carla had parked in Pitville Street then with Pam in tow walked along the High Street into the prestigious Promenade just as Samuel parked outside Cavendish House, 'Isn't that Oliver getting out of that car?'

'It certainly is' Pam replied indignantly, 'what a cheek I thought he was supposed to be visiting some Factory or other.'

They were too far back to catch them before they disappeared into the store, 'Shall we go in to see what they're up to?'

'The only reason I've found for men to go in there Pam is to have a coffee'

'Then shall we?'

Carla laughed, 'Even a Rector's stipend certainly wouldn't cover such an extravagance. Best we go to Brunners Café it isn't far and won't break the bank.'

As they went to walk passed a young boy came out of the store, lifted the bonnet of Samuels car and removed the distributor,

'Damn and blast' Carla cursed, 'I forgot to disable the car'

'Will anyone notice?' Pam asked hopefully

'Probably not but the fine is huge so we'd better get back and do it.'

Samuel paid the Bill for the Coffee, 'We could almost get a meal thrown in for that in Portsmouth' Oliver commented

'Fantastic Coffee though aye?' He chuckled, 'worth every penny of Government money.' He gave a long sigh, 'I've good memories about Portsmouth'

'Did you live there then?'

'Ryde on the Isle of Wight. My Father had a boat so we'd often sail across the Solent and through the Dockyard to view all the Naval Ships.' They returned to the car, 'I think we've been long enough' Samuel continued starting the engine

'Long enough for what?'

'One of Herman the Germans job is to clean the Toilets in The Kings Head at lunch time. There's only two rooms neither with locks so I reckon by now he would've been in and photographed the documents I've left on the bed ready to pass on.' They drove slowly through the Town, 'You know Oliver' He said chortling, 'according to those documents your Submarine has more science fiction bits and pieces fitted than in one of Flash Gordon's space ships. The Germans are going to be desperate to get hold of it.'

They turned into the tiny Kings Head car park and found their way blocked by a Police car. A man approached, Samuel rolled the window down, 'Are you Samuel Knight Sir?'

'I am yes'

'And you are Sir?'

'Oliver Pitman'

'I'm DCI Henry Guilder Gloucester Constabulary we've had cause to detain Karl Scholer for attempted theft.' He frowned, 'from your room in fact. And I think it was rather remiss of you to leave documents stamped secret out on view. In fact' he continued in a hushed voice holding up his hand to silence Samuel, 'you could also be charged for such a serious offence.'

Samuel fished around in his inside pocket produced an ID card and held it up, 'Ah I see'

'Well actually DCI Guilder I don't think you do because we intentionally left the documents for him to find. Has he been searched?'

'Of course Sir'

'And?'

'Nothing at all Sir'

'Who caught him?'

'The Landlord Sir. So MI5 has an interest in this Karl fellow then?'

'Very much so. The Landlord?'

'Yes of course Sir I'll have our car moved out of your way'

'Don't take the Prisoner away until I say so and make doubly sure he hasn't anything concealed on him.'

The Landlord Geoffrey Moore was a short plump completely bald fifty-five year old bright red faced man with enormous ears and a brash manner, 'You caught him red-handed?'

'Well sort of.' He replied tersely. Samuel removed his glasses and just stared at him, 'I thought he was taking quite a time. He's normally pretty quick you see because he gets a Pint when he's finished. So I went up and he was standing by your open door'

'Was he on his way out of the room do you think?'

'Don't know. I asked him what the hell he was doing but he wouldn't say so I kept hold of him and had my daughter phone the Police'

'Did he have anything with him?'

'Like what?'

'A camera or anything that looked like one. It would've been very small'

'No nothing that I saw'

'Right thank you I may need to talk to you again.'

The Landlords Daughter Prudence wandered over, 'I don't know whether it's important or not' she croaked as if she had a sore throat, 'but he was wearing quite a posh watch. I noticed it when he came in.'

Samuel looked at the DCI, 'I'll check with the Lads.' He was back within a couple of minutes shaking his head, 'no luck I'm afraid none of them have seen it.'

'You're sure he was wearing it?'

'Yes I'm sure' she persisted, 'I thought it a bit strange it isn't something you'd want to wear if you had cleaning to do.'

'Have you seen him wearing it before?'

'I've not noticed it no.'

Samuel called the Landlord back over, 'The German was wearing a watch do you know what happened to it?'

'No' he replied a little too quickly, 'I don't.' Again Samuel didn't reply but just looked at him, 'I don't ok?' he shouted and went to walk away.

'DCI Guilder would you be so kind as to search Mr Moore please'

'You can't do that you'll need a warrant'

'Oh but I'm afraid we can Mr Guilder because it's a matter of National Security'

'Ok, Ok' He said removing the watch from his trouser pocket, 'it doesn't work anyway'

'Rather hypocritical of you to report the German for stealing whilst quite happy to steal from him'

'Do you want him charged Sir?' the DCI asked.

Samuel rubbed his chin thoughtfully, 'Your choice DCI but it would seem a shame to deprive the villagers of a Pub so we'll let it go for the moment. But' he warned, 'if there's anything else you've not told us about then…'

'He had a thick envelope' he said quickly interrupting Samuel

'And what happened to that?'

'I threw it in the bin'

'Then you'd better damn well go and fetch it and quick.'

He rushed off and returned with a rather bedraggled looking envelope. Samuel took it from him read the address which brought a smile to his lips, 'Bingo' he said jubilantly, 'that's all thank you and in future Mr Moore I would suggest that for your own sake you tell the truth. Believe me if you'd as much as held on to this envelope you could've quite easily been charged with assisting an enemy agent' he smiled and drew his hand over his throat, 'then this place would've definitely needed a new Landlord.'

'DCI Guilder you may take your Prisoner away now but we can't really charge him with anything but he won't know that so before you do perhaps you could persuade him to say if he managed to photograph the documents or not. You may be able to frighten him enough to come clean. Then of course ensure he's confined to the Camp.'

'Good Lord Oliver you still here?'

'I don't remember you dismissing me' he joked, 'anyway I'm keen to know what went on.'

Samuel held up the watch, 'A camera takes pictures onto microfilm' then the envelope, 'mailed off to our friends in Evesham who open it up process the film then mail it to the South Coast for a Trawler to deliver it to a U-Boat presumably'

'All sown up then?'

He shrugged his shoulders, 'Not exactly no. The Landlord didn't know if the German had been into my room or was just about to'

'So there may be nothing on the camera?'

'Exactly but at least we're be able to follow the trail and put a stop to them.'

A thought popped into Oliver's head, 'Do you know how to use the camera?'

'No but I don't think it'd take long why?'

'Well you could take some of your own and then send it off couldn't you?'

Samuel was quiet for a while cursing himself for not thinking of that, 'I must be losing my touch' he said laughing, 'can't see the wood for the trees sort of thing. Ah here comes the DCI. Well did you manage to get anything out of him?'

'He admitted that he'd taken all the photographs he needed but refused to say who gave him the camera or what he'd got to do with it now and categorically denies stealing anything. In fact he did say that if anything had been stolen talk to the Landlord who he says took ten and six from him which was over a month's money for the odd jobs he does round the village'

'And you're quite happy that's true?'

'I see no reason for him to lie. And even though it was from a German POW I'm certainly going to charge Mr Moore with theft.' He paused, 'Actually he stole from the enemy so I reckon I could call it looting. The Lad earned that money so should be able to keep it.'

'Good luck with that I hope the Judge is in the same frame of mind.' He shook hands, 'Goodbye Henry pity you had to cock up our plans but thankfully it turned out alright in the end.'

'Am I dismissed now?'

Samuel took Oliver's hand and shook it warmly, 'You are indeed. Thank you for your company and good luck with whatever operation they've got in mind for you. Take care'

'You off home now?'

He grinned, 'I think the Pub will be closed for a while so no room at the Inn so to speak but in truth once I've mailed this off my work here is done so I may as well get home'

'Where is home?'

'Leamington at the moment but after that who knows?'

Oliver turned and waved as he crossed the road for the short walk back to the Rectory.

Samuel popped the watch inside the envelope and walked to the Post Office. He handed it in and paid the fourpence postage, 'When will it be delivered?' He asked, 'it is rather urgent.'

The Postmaster groaned and picked up a printed sheet of paper, 'Should be tomorrow Sir around seven in the morning.'

He thanked him left the post office and noticed a public telephone box outside the Blacksmiths shop. Just before he reached it an old chap with a large handlebar moustache wearing a brown cap tweed shooting jacket and jodhpurs beat him to it. He waited patiently outside but could hear the conversation going on, 'Yes the damn Pub's shut you know. Herman the German has been taken away. I know that wouldn't shut the pub you fool they've taken Geoffrey away as well. Freda Redgrave says she's heard they had a fight over Prudence. I don't know but I expect the Kraut was up to no good with the girl and Geoffrey caught them at it. Yes I know we'll have to use the Royal Oak until he's back. Damn nuisance though. Goodbye.' He slammed the receiver down and pushed the door all the way open, 'There you go old chap all yours.'

Samuel's call was quite short just enough to organise surveillance on the watch repair shop in Evesham and vet all their outgoing mail then have it followed for its onward journey to the south coast. Satisfied he collected his luggage from the Pub and left the village.

'Did you enjoy your trip to the Factory?' Pam asked before Oliver had chance to sit down

'Didn't go to any Factory'

'So we saw.' Oliver's face was blank, 'going into umm, what was it called Carla?'

'Cavendish House' she replied still trying to get a small patch of grease off her dress left by carting the distributor cap around with her,

'Cavendish House' Pam repeated

'Had a coffee that's all. Dash expensive though'

'So what've you been up to since then?'

John breezed in throwing his mac over a chair, 'Valery Gleeson's been into the Church again still wanting me to officiate at her wedding to William. She says he's written and will definitely be coming home next month'

'Poor Girl do you want me to have another word with her?'

'It would be nice if you could yes'

'William Hopkins' Carla explained 'was a Leading Seaman on HMS Hood but even after a year she just won't believe he's gone. It's so sad.'

'Anyway' John said lightening the mood, 'There's been

215

a right old commotion in the Village Herman the German has been carted off by the Police so it looks as though we won't be getting the spouting cleaned for a wee while yet'

'Guttering' Carla translated for their benefit, 'so what's he been up to then?'

John laughed, 'It depends who you talk to. Mrs Redgrave says he was having a bit of a fling with Prudence and General Groves says the man was planning to plant a homemade bomb in the Pub. Either way he's not coming back so I'll have to find someone else who's willing to risk their lives up that ladder to do it'

'Talking of Mrs Redgrave Ollie I understand that you know her twin sister'

'I don't exactly know her but I met her at a Portsmouth Hotel I was staying in and again later in the local air-raid shelter. Actually you know she managed to stop my travel bag being stolen. A really huge woman but with an almost identical face and definitely the same skill in knocking up a real tasty Rabbit stew'

'Really? So why on earth weren't you staying in the Wardroom?'

'Long story'

'He was barred' Pam said giggling, 'upset the Commander. They're good friends now though. Isn't that right Oliver?'

He nodded, 'I guess that's about it yes.' Then to quickly change the subject. 'And to put the record straight from today's commotion in the Village Herman the German as you call him was not having a fling with anyone and certainly had no intentions of planting a bomb but was caught photographing secret documents about new equipment being fitted into my Submarine and what you may not know is that the Landlord was charged with theft'

'Geoffrey? For stealing what?' Carla asked as if she couldn't believe the man could do such a thing

'Money apparently. All the odd job payments the German had on him, ten and six I believe'

'That's awful but so is trying to steal our secrets' Carla

said severely, 'so serves him right.'

Oliver would dearly love to tell them what really happened but it was out of the question. Pam would be fine but with Carla she certainly couldn't keep it to herself so would definitely feel obliged to put people right about what went on whenever she waited in the meat queue or in the Church hall or in fact anywhere then rather pointlessly swear them to secrecy.

The telephone jangled. John went over to answer it, 'Yes. Yes of course one moment please.' He covered the mouthpiece, 'it's for you Oliver a Commodore Warwick.'

'Yes Sir?' He looked over at Pam and pulled a face, 'of course Sir Goodbye.'

'So what did Daddy want?'

'He wants me back in Portsmouth tomorrow for a meeting on Friday'

'That's not fair' Pam complained bitterly, 'no wonder he didn't want to talk to me. I bet he's planning to send you off somewhere'

'Well we'd better make it a special evening then' Carla said standing up, 'I'll see what's for Dinner.' She was back in seconds with a glum face, 'Rabbit stew would you believe left over from yesterday but never mind I'll break out a bottle of wine' she looked over at John who nodded enthusiastically, 'or two and heat up some gooseberries for pudding'

'Lovely' Oliver moaned, 'how old are they?'

'Younger than you and watch it or you'll go without.'

They all went to bed a little after ten-thirty. Oliver waited until eleven before letting himself into Pam's room. She was fast asleep; even a kiss on the cheek didn't make her stir. He crept back to his room shut and locked the door and slept soundly until woken at eight with a cup of tea.

Chapter Twelve

Portsmouth

'I'm sorry to drag you back from your sisters but I've arranged a demonstration with an explosives expert who specialises in remote detonation and today is the only time he has and I want you to be involved'

'I understand Sir'

'Good because the ear bashing I had from Pamela was enough for anyone to take.'

Oliver realised how important the demonstration was when Captain Wells and Commander Briggs turned up.

'If we still have a few minutes may I bring my First Lieutenant in on it Sir?'

'Already done so he should be here. Ah talk of the devil.'

Steven Boniface nodded an acknowledgement to the Commodore and sat down next to Oliver,

'How did your leave go?' He whispered

'I'll tell you later' he replied as a wiry skinny man wearing a grey badly fitted jacket and trousers marched in carrying a large black box which he dumped down on to the table. He was unshaven his hair quite long and unkempt with deep set eyes a stubby nose and thin straight lips giving the impression of a rather shifty untrustworthy individual. Not too far from the truth as forty-eight year old Aidan Riley cared little for whom he worked. A staunch Irish republican he hated the British but quite happily put it to one side if the money offered was good enough. He learned his skills with explosives as a member of the IRA then graduated from UCD with a degree in electronic engineering. He'd even worked for the Germans on numerous occasions but for all his faults he would never divulge any of the jobs to a third party. A strange kind of loyalty but loyalty none the less.

'Good morning Gentlemen I'm Aidan Riley and I deal

in explosives.' He started in a soft Irish brogue then paused to remove various items from the box, 'You've asked me to design a system that would remotely detonate explosives using codes sent by wireless transmissions and this' he swept his arm over the table, 'is the best I could come up with so without sounding too smug it must be the best.'

He placed a small cardboard box onto a metal tray at one end of the table. It was attached to a square grey metal box with a lamp on top. Moving to the back of the room he set up another metal box a little larger than the other one with a Morse key attached.

'Are we ready Gents? Then I suggest you cover your ears.'

'He tapped the key, the lamp flashed, then flashed again then with an almighty bang the cardboard box flew into pieces the toxic smell of burnt almonds filled the room. The Commodore leant over and opened a window as the door flew open and two MP's dashed in Pistols at the ready, 'Stand down' the Commodore shouted, 'it was a demonstration that's all.' They replaced their firearms saluted and left.

'Are there any questions Gentlemen?' Aidan asked as he collected up the boxes

'Do you set the code?' Captain Wells asked

'Your Commodore has already furnished me with them.'

"Them?" Oliver thought to himself, *"Why them."* He made a mental note to quiz the Commodore about it later, 'What's the distance to activate it?'

'As far as the Radio Signal will travel and remain strong enough'

'The lamp flashed twice'

'It did Commander because the code has to be repeated three times on a specific frequency, the first two prime it the third detonates. And you'll need to select a radio operator to train with the demo kit I'll leave behind for you because the Morse has to be perfect. Anything less and it'll fail.'

The Commodore stood, Thank you Aidan for sparing us your time. If you see the Sub-Lieutenant at the desk outside my Office he'll take care of everything for you'

'Much obliged and good luck' he replied making his way to the door closing it quietly behind him.

'Does he know what we intend to do with his design Sir?'

'Absolutely not Brian it's our own fitters that will install it'

'When Aidan talked about codes Sir he used the word "them", why "them" Sir? Do we need more than one code?'

'There is a good reason Oliver but I'd rather not discuss it here. You look very thoughtful Steven so spit it out man what's up?'

'If as intended we're to detonate the explosives once the decoy is inside the Pens.' He hesitated, 'I don't think Radio Waves travel through concrete too well'

'That's very true Steven that's why our Communications Boffins are working their socks off to find a solution.' He paused briefly, 'Anymore? No? Good'

All but Oliver and the Commodore wandered off, 'I guess you want to know why there are two codes'

'I would yes Sir.'

The Commodore seemed edgy and rubbed his hands together nervously, 'The thing is Oliver' he started hesitantly, 'we can't allow Troy to fall into the hands of the Germans so....'

'So you're thinking of stuffing Troy full of explosives Sir' Oliver interrupted anticipating the explanation, 'I don't think I like that too much and my crew aren't going to be too impressed either knowing that we're riding a massive bomb that can be detonated at a whim'

'Two things' the Commodore replied sternly, 'one, your crew are not to know anything about it and two, only I hold the code so detonated at a whim would never happen. Surely Oliver you must understand that if the

Germans really did get hold of Troy we would be in big trouble. Our convoys wouldn't stand a chance of getting through the Nation would starve to death in months'

'Will my First Lieutenant be made aware of it?'

'You can tell him. But as I said before the remainder of the crew including other Officers must not be told anything about it you understand?'

Oliver nodded, 'I do yes Sir but I'm still not entirely happy'

'Then answer me this. When you have a primed Torpedo in the tubes ready to launch do you worry about that?'

'No Sir'

'But you agree that it could explode before leaving the tube'

'It could do I suppose'

'Then' he added 'these explosives are no different really are they?'

Oliver although extremely unhappy reluctantly had to accept it so just shrugged his shoulders and nodded.

'Anyway changing the subject Oliver I understand your visit to your Sister ended in a bit of a stir in the village'

'It nearly scuppered the whole thing Sir'

'So I heard but we'll be getting a full report in the next few days and I'm pretty sure it'll be one hell of an interesting read.'

After Oliver had left the Commodore wondered if his choice of codes were adequate, 'Too late now' he muttered to himself 'it's set in stone.' When he'd asked how many characters that the codes would need Aidan said it was his choice but warned that too many could cause problems. Pushed for time to come up with anything credible he'd looked down at his desk for inspiration and quickly decided on PEN with Margaret's date of birth for the frequency 8/4 and INK with Pam's 12/6.

Aidan said that would do and specified that he would mark the letters "P" on one and "I" on the other, "*That*" he'd said with a large grin across his face "*is so you don't blow the wrong thing up.*" The Commodore decided there and then that "I" would be for Troy and "P" for T102.

Evesham

Sergeant Harry Bellringer watched from a small room above the undertakers as the Postman handed over the mail to a middle-aged man who he knew to be the eldest of the two watch repairers dubbed the Swiss Brothers because of their documented Nationality. They'd allegedly moved over from Cricklewood where they professed to have worked for a local watch and clock manufacturers for many years but further investigations had proved otherwise. Both had arrived in England a few months before the war and had lived in London above a small rented shop in wood green buying, repairing and selling second hand watches. Now identified as Hans and Klaus Gunst from Arbon on the shores of Lake Constance where many families had moved away from the area in fear of being so close to the German Border. The Brothers motives for moving however had turned out a little different. The only mystery remaining is why they chose a small place like Evesham for their latest operation.

After a brief conversation the Postman moved on then looked up at the window where Harry was sitting and waved to indicate that the identified envelope had been delivered.

A loud knock at the door made him jump. He stood up and limped to the door his leg even after twenty four years still painful from the shrapnel wound he'd suffered at Arras in the closing months of World war one, 'Ah Playdon' he said standing aside to allow the Constable to enter, 'the package has been delivered just keep your eyes open for anyone leaving the shop and taking anything to the Post Office. And for goodness sake Lad take your helmet off and your Tunic or you'll stand out like a sore thumb. I'll be back in a couple of hours.'

They didn't have to wait long as within a couple of hours Klaus, the younger Brother walked the short distance to the Post Office and handed a single envelope in for posting. He paid the postage and left returning directly to the shop.

Harry went into the Post Office and with permission into the back room. The Postmaster handed him the envelope, 'Good Lord!' he exclaimed as he read the address, 'Whitby? Now that's something we really weren't expecting. I'll need to take it back to the Station for closer inspection by one of our experts'

'Experts?' the Postmaster joked, 'who would that be then?'

'Young Freddy Stubbs'

'I thought you'd just nicked him for tampering with other people's mail'

'That's right I did' he replied waving the envelope, 'that's rather convenient don't you think?'

'What's in it for me then?' Freddy Stubbs demanded

'We may be able to arrange something' Harry replied pointing to the envelope

'Perhaps "may be" isn't good enough'

'Well what about a trip to the Theatre?'

'What Theatre?'

'The Operating Theatre when PC Playdon breaks bones'

'You can't do that' Freddy protested noisily, 'it isn't lawful'

'War Office memo number three-one-one says that we may beat our criminals as long as we don't actually kill them'

'You made that up'

'Playdon' Harry shouted out at the top of his voice

'Okay okay but I'll need some gear'

'Like what?'

'I assume you want it sealed up again?'

'Of course'

'Then I'll need a magnifying glass, tweezers, a scalpel and glue. Not the cheap brown smelly stuff either'

'You mean like all the gear we removed from your digs after you were arrested?' Freddy grunted, 'and you still maintain your innocence?' Another grunt, 'Playdon go along and fetch the evidence bag for our distinguished very innocent guest to use please.'

They watched in awe as Freddy skilfully sliced the bottom of the envelope then carefully removed the contents with the tweezers and passed them to Harry who satisfied it was microfilm passed it back to him, 'Ok put this back and seal it up again.'

When Freddy had finished even under the closest inspection using the magnifying glass it was impossible to tell that it had ever been tampered with.

Harry after copying the address returned the envelope to the Post Office, 'Tomorrow all being well but we've had a bit of delay through our centre at York but should be back to normal now.' The Postmaster droned in reply to Harry's question.

Leamington

Samuel Knight was just about to tuck into his sausage and mash when the phone rang. He was tempted to leave it unanswered but it went on and on, 'Hello. Sergeant Harry Bellringer. Yes of course I do how are you? It has been posted on good. To where? Whitby? Good Lord. Just a tick I'll get a pen. Ok fire away.' He scribbled down the address, 'Yes of course I shall. In the meantime I think it would be prudent to arrest both of them but best leave their phone open and monitored for now. Is your DCI around? Compassionate leave? Both his Sons? Poor chap. Just do what you can Harry and I'll get back to you from Whitby.'

He rang off as his housekeeper tapped on the door and came into the room, 'Oh Mr Knight you've let your Dinner get cold. Give it here I'll bung it back under the gas'

'No need for that Mrs Carter it'll be fine. And I'll be

away for a day or two'

'Again so soon? My goodness your boss is working you far too hard. When are you leaving?'

'Tonight straight after dinner I'm afraid it's a bit of a rush job.'

He finished his meal, packed a suitcase for a couple of days stay drove to his local Garage which was closed, knocked up a rather grumpy proprietor handed him the cash and his Motor Spirit Ration tickets filling the car up for his six hour almost two hundred mile trip to Whitby.

Whitby

Samuel arrived in the very early hours of the morning and drove straight to the local Police Station. He was met by a young Police Constable, 'We have a cell free if you'd like a couple of hours sleep Sir. You look as if you may need it.'

He did, so accepted the offer and despite the very thin mattress the Constable managed to dig up slept well until woken by the Sergeant armed with a huge mug of very strong tea,

'Good morning Sir I'm Sergeant Clegg. PC Battersby looked after you all right then?'

Samuel stood up yawned and stretched his aching muscles. He wasn't sure if it'd been the long drive or the thin mattress, 'He did yes thank you.' He looked at his watch but it'd stopped, 'what time is it Sergeant?'

'Six thirty two Sir.'

Samuel pulled a piece of paper from his pocket, 'Do you know this address?'

The Sergeant looked at it, 'Yes it's only just around the corner from here it's a small Hotel. Battersby get the Guest registration list for the Harbour Lights Hotel will you?'

'It was updated just two days ago Serge' PC Battersby said passing it to him.

They checked the six names. None matched with the Raymond Rutherford addressed on the envelope, 'So how does the Hotel owner know who it's for?'

'She wouldn't unless it was for her' the Sergeant replied, 'or it was to be passed on'

'That's more than likely so we'll have to have a word with this woman. What's her name?'

'Vera Shuttlesworth'

'I don't think she'd be up to much Serge her son's in the eighth army' Battersby said shaking his head, 'and she's lived here for years running that place'

'Stranger things have happened' Samuel replied, 'I've even had a Wife passing information whilst her own Husband was at sea on Convoy duties'

'Nothing as odd as folk' the Sergeant muttered.

The phone rang filling the place with noise as the extension bell clanged so loud it must've been heard streets away. Battersby dashed off to answer it. He came back with a long face, 'The Post Office Serge'

'And?'

'The envelope hasn't been delivered'

'Are they sure?'

'Positive. They've been through the mail a dozen times or more and it isn't amongst it.'

'What about the depot in York?' Samuel asked hopefully

The Sergeant shook his head, 'So short staffed these days I doubt we'd get anything there Sir they're sometimes so snowed under they can't get mail moved on quick enough but I'll telephone them anyway to check the situation today.' He was back within a few minutes, 'Everything for this part of Yorkshire was moved on successfully without exceptions Sir'

'Call me Samuel please Sergeant Sir sounds so bloody formal'

'Habit Sir, I mean Samuel'

'And your name Sergeant?'

Battersby laughed, 'Nobody here knows his name it's just Sergeant. Even our DCI doesn't know it'

'Oh yes he does' the Sergeant protested, 'but he daren't

ever use it.'

'Well aside from that Sergeant' Samuel chuckled, 'I think we'd better interview this Vera Shuttlesworth'

'Here or at the Hotel?'

'Hotel I think. It makes it less formal.'

Vera Shuttlesworth was a slightly built sixty-five year old woman with jet black dyed bouffant hair which made her head look enormous. She smelt of Lavender oil with a mix of carbolic soap. Her face was heavy with makeup which completely failed to mask her numerous wrinkles and thick bright red lipstick smudged at the corners of her mouth to complete the guise.

'I don't know anyone named Raymond Rutherford' she said defiantly

'So why do you think someone in Evesham would send a letter to him at this address?'

'I don't know and I don't know him. Furthermore I don't even know where Evesham is let alone anyone who lives there.'

'Have you ever had a guest here with that name?'

She shook her head, 'Not recently no'

'What about over the last couple of years?'

'How on earth do you expect me to remember that?' She snapped

'I don't so do you keep a guest book?'

'Of course I do but not every guest writes in it'

'May I see it?'

She opened a drawer and removed a large blue leather bound book, 'My pleasure' she said rudely thrusting it towards Samuel, 'as I said it probably won't do you any good'

'Well Mrs Shuttlesworth I think we'll be the judge of that. It'll be returned to you as soon as possible'

'You can keep it for all I care' she mumbled as they made their way to the door.

Back in the Station Battersby was left to leaf through the

Guest book. After fifteen-minutes, most of which wasted whilst arguing with a woman at the front desk about Seagulls eating all the food she puts out for her chickens he shouted through, 'Got it Serge. Raymond Rutherford twenty-eight Front Street Hastings'

'Damn and blast' Samuel cursed, 'it must've been re-addressed in York'

'Not Evesham?'

'No we tracked it out of there'

'I guess your be off to Hastings now Samuel?'

'No point it'll be long gone by now as I think Raymond bloody Rutherford will be as well'

'Not necessarily Sir' Battersby said, 'the envelope would've been sent overnight to London to be sorted'

'So' Samuel replied patting him on the back, 'earliest delivery would be tomorrow morning.'

Sergeant Clegg sniffed noisily as with brow furrowed he dug deep into the past, 'Battersby' he said finally, 'do you remember that Postman we had a year or so back? Transferred to York sorting office after he was bitten by some Dog or other. What the hell was his name?'

'I do remember him Serge Welsh bloke. Didn't we have to charge him with cruelty after he battered the thing to death with a pickaxe handle?'

'We did indeed so we'll have a charge sheet on him will we not?'

'Here he is Serge' Battersby shouted slamming the filing cabinet drawer shut 'Bryn Allen'

'Telephone York and find out if he's still there.'

Battersby replaced the receiver, 'He's a Supervisor now and declares that only two of his Staff were sorting this areas mail last night. One is in his sixties and worked there for years the other Alain Maurer a Swiss chap transferred from Evesham a few months back'

'Fancy a trip to York Sergeant?' Samuel asked picking up his hat.

York

With the local Police in tow they crashed into Maurer's rented rooms. Clothes and other personal effects were spread over the bed, 'Looks as though he left in one hell of a hurry' Clegg announced rifling through some folded freshly laundered shirts, 'I think he knew we were on to him.'

'He didn't even have time to pack his suitcase' a young Special Constable said pointing to it on top of the wardrobe

'Well get it down lad'

'Blimey it's right heavy Serge.'

He laid it down on the floor removed the catches and flipped the lid open revealing a Radio Transmitter.

'Telephone Evesham' Samuel ordered, 'talk to Sergeant Bellringer and ask him to search the Swiss Brothers shop from top to bottom. I'm pretty sure they must have a Transmitter hidden somewhere as well. And in the meantime send some of your men to the Train and Bus stations. They'll have a photograph of him at the Sorting Office so get that circulated as soon as possible. He may have gone to ground here in York.'

Samuel dropped Sergeant Clegg back in Whitby with instructions to telephone Hastings Police to bring them up-to-date with Maurer and to organise surveillance on the address they had for Rutherford.

He filled the car up with fuel and much to the disgust of the Garage owner both five gallon Jerry cans that he stored in the boot. This, the irate owner complained bitterly left his tanks almost dry so he wouldn't be able to service the Farmers who he insisted would turn up in droves the very next day. Samuel handed over the money and eight two-gallon Motor Spirit Ration tickets bade him a curt farewell and left for his eight hour three hundred mile trek along the Great North Road and beyond to Hastings.

Hastings

Samuel arrived a little before midnight. He managed to book into a Hotel close to the Harbour and asked for a call at seven.

'You won't need a call Sir' the night porter declared, 'Jerry will be along by then to strafe their way through the streets. So when it starts just keep your head down, stay away from the windows and fingers crossed for no bombs.'

At six-thirty Samuel was awakened by the haunting wail of the Siren closely followed by the scream of Aero-engines at full throttle and the rat-tat-tat of machine gun fire. Back and forth they pounced searching out those foolish enough to be on the street spitting death and destruction on each pass but quickly scuttling away over the horizon as soon as a squadron of Spitfires swept in from their base at Tangmere.

Over a sparse Breakfast he queried the Waiter about the raids, 'Almost daily Sir' he replied sadly, 'They've killed and injured hundreds of people. The RAF chase them off when they can but they're not always available.'

He made his way along the narrow streets towards the Police station. They were full of broken glass, masonry and other indistinguishable lumps of debris. Groups of people huddled together asking after friends and loved ones. The distant clanging of numerous Ambulance bells verified there had been casualties.

He introduced himself to the desk Sergeant and was shown into the DCI's Office, 'He should be along in a few minutes Sir' the Sergeant said, 'he's rarely late in.'

DCI Jack Hammond breezed into his office. He was a fifty year old tall but bulky man with dark brown hair greased and combed straight back emphasizing the receding patches each side of the centre. He had large round green eyes set into a big round jolly face; his double chin almost disappearing with his enormous wide grin. He extended his arm, 'Hello there its Samuel isn't it? Jack Hammond how do you do?' They shook hands, 'bit of a problem I'm afraid Samuel'

'Really Jack?'

'The Bloody Post Office decided to deliver the mail early to miss the raid. The PC who was on watch across the road obviously took shelter in an alleyway when the raid was on and when he checked afterwards through the shop window the item had gone'

'Shop?'

'Yes didn't you know? The address you gave us was an empty shop'

'No I didn't know so I guess this Raymond Rutherford chap wouldn't be living there'

'We're trawling through the registrations to find out exactly where he does live'

'Well we'd better get down to this shop and see what's what.'

Raymond Rutherford had slipped into the shop just as the raid had started. He'd meant to pick up the letter and leave immediately it finished but noticed the PC hanging around across the road so stayed put hoping he would move on.

Rutherford was a rather unimposing young man of average height and average build. Nothing much to distinguish him from any other man in the Town. He'd been brought up in Germany the son of a Bavarian Mother and an English Father who whilst serving with the British Army in the Great War although clearly suffering from shell shock was branded a coward so in the early months of 1919 along with his Wife who'd been an internee in Suffolk for the entire war had fled to Germany to escape the hatred and humiliation they'd continually suffered from the people of the Village. His father's forced exile from his home country and loathing from the whole Rutherford family forged his early beliefs. Fluent in German and English despite pleadings from his Mother he jumped at the chance to join the German Military intelligence organisation "Abwehr" and although still in his early twenties glad to have been shipped over to England to spy for his masters in Berlin.

He carefully peered round a dust covered tatty curtain and saw to his horror that the PC was still around so had no way of leaving without being seen. Now certain that they must be on to him he went to the back of the shop which used to be a Jewellers before finally closing down fourteen months ago. He'd accidently discovered where the safe had once stood in a head-height three foot by three foot cubbyhole hidden by a set of six shelves that could be swung out to give access. A perfect place to hide his radio, change of clothing and some tinned food.

Loud voices and a bang as the front door was being forced had his young mind in turmoil. He had no weapons to protect himself and was painfully aware of the treatment he would endure from guards and other inmates in Prison. In a Panic he squeezed into the cubbyhole and frantically pulled the shelves in behind him just as Samuel, Jack and four PC's rushed in.

Through a small crack in one of the shelves he could see them searching round, 'Looks pretty empty to me' Jack said loudly, 'our Bird has flown I think'

'Certainly looks that way Jack' Samuel answered with enormous relief as his whole intention was to discover who and how information was getting out and only to detain the perpetrators after this latest information had passed through safely. He dare not disclose this fact to Jack or any of the others as the fewer people who knew about it the better chance he had of pulling it off. 'He must have a boat or at least access to a boat so I'll get my men to keep watch on the Harbour.'

A PC rushed into the shop, 'DCI Hammond Sir' he said breathlessly, 'we've found his address it's only round the corner.'

Raymond was suffering badly in his tiny bolt hole. Cramp had set in on both legs his hands ached terribly from holding onto the shelving as tight as he could to stop it moving. He was certain that his heart was beating so loudly in his chest they must surely be able to hear it but worst of all the accumulated dust now disturbed was wafting up into his nostrils. He was in grave danger of sneezing.

'Should we leave someone here in case he comes back Sir' a PC asked.

Jack looked over at Samuel, 'I don't think that's necessary Jack I think he's long gone.'

'Right let's get round to his address and see what turns up there.'

A very relieved Raymond Rutherford extricated himself from the confines of the cubbyhole sneezing repeatedly to clear his nose and massaging his cramped legs and hands, 'Obviously' he muttered to himself, 'somebody has been captured and spilt the beans. But who?' He thought for a moment, 'It must've been Maurer he's the only one who knew about the shop.'

A hard rap on the door froze him to the spot, 'Hello Raymond' a voice called, 'are you in here?'

'Alain' Raymond shouted as he recognised the voice, 'I thought you'd been captured'

'I very nearly was. Did you get the letter?'

'Yes this morning'

'Why's the door broken?'

'Police'

'Looking for you?'

'Yes. I've no idea where they got the address from'

'I do' Alain replied, 'and I warned you about it at the time.' Raymond looked confused, 'That Guest house in Whitby. You left scathing remarks about it?'

'Oh God yes you're right I remember now putting this address down after that ugly old crone moaned at me for doing it.'

Alain nodded, 'So I think with both of us in trouble it may be time for us to go back home'

'True but with the harbour being watched I'm not sure how'

'Have you still got your radio set?'

'Yes in there'

'Can we summon up a U-Boat to send a dinghy into somewhere close by?'

'They're expecting to collect the envelope so I don't see why they shouldn't take us too.'

Raymond set up the radio and after a frustrating hours delay managed to get a message through. Arrangements were made to pick them both up at midnight in Sunlight Cove five miles east of Hastings, 'What the hell do we do until then?' Alain complained, 'we can't stay here any longer with the door off its hinges anyone can wander in'

'There's an old boathouse a couple of miles up the coast we should be ok there. I've got some food'

'You don't happen to have cigarettes do you?'

'Afraid not no' Raymond replied rather surprised that he would be worried about not having cigarettes when escape should be the major thing on his mind, 'I think it best if we concentrate on making a move while we can' He added sarcastically.

Deciding that taking the radio was out of the question they opened it up and destroyed as many components as they could.

'I do hope we don't need it again' Alain said smiling nervously, 'I don't think it'd work too well.'

The spare clothes he'd stored in the shop were divided up in an attempt to look as much like seamen as possible. Raymond was now dressed in a blue reefer jacket blue serge trousers and a Bretton cap. Alain a plain navy blue jacket, a little too big for him, his own faded blue trousers and a black knitted skull cap.

Raymond stowed the tin food and a torch in his discarded white shirt and slung it over his shoulder then after checking the coast was clear left the shop and made their way along the narrow streets. Within minutes they were confronted by a very smartly dressed man who politely doffed his Trilby, 'Good Afternoon Gentlemen' he said in a broad cockney accent 'this I must say is your lucky day 'cause I 'appen to 'ave some spare coupons available at a price you wouldn't Adam and Eve'

'No thank you I don't deal in black Market goods so good day to you' Raymond replied curtly.

Alain had different ideas, 'I suppose you don't have cigarettes do you?'

'I don't my friend but if you'd like to 'ang around 'ere for a mo I can get 'em for you.'

Raymond grabbed Alain's arm, 'We're late already'

'Can't we wait for a few minutes?'

'No we can't now come on.'

Begrudgingly Alain followed, 'If you change yer mind guv I'll still be around' the Spiv called after them as they rushed away.

'You know Alain I don't think you quite understand the danger we're in at the moment'

'Of course I do' he puffed, 'I'd just like a smoke that's all.'

They skirted the Harbour ducking into the shadows to avoid the Police patrols searching the area. As they rounded a corner they almost bumped into a PC coming the other way, 'Sorry Gents' he apologised stepping aside to let them pass, 'after you.'

'You know' Raymond said as the PC walked out of earshot, 'they're looking for one man not two so we're in with a chance'

'So we could've waited a few minutes for the cigarettes after all'

'For goodness sake Alain forget about the bloody cigarettes will you?'

'Okay keep your hair on. How far is this boathouse anyway?'

'Another mile or so but it'll only leave a couple of miles for us to travel in the dark tonight.'

They carefully approached the wooden boathouse but

retreated into the bushes above the beach when they heard loud voices and laughter coming from inside, 'I thought you said we'd be alright here' Alain whispered, 'God knows what you were thinking of'

'I'm thinking of escape not bloody cigarettes so you've not been much help have you?'

'So what do we do now?' He asked but before Raymond could answer he pointed, 'Look there' he whispered excitedly

'Where?'

'Against the boathouse.'

All Raymond could see was a crude wooden rack with four canoes neatly stowed in it, 'Canoes?'

'Why not? You said it was only a couple of miles, 'Once it's dark we could stick close to shore in the shallow water. Shouldn't take more than an hour or so. Now does that help?'

Raymond grinned, 'It does as long as you don't mention cigarettes'

'I won't' he replied clapping him on his back, 'I promise.'

An hour passed as they kept hidden amongst the bushes. The door of the Boathouse opened and four men came out walked to the side of the building and proceeded to remove the Canoes from the rack carry them to the water and paddle away.

'Now what?' Raymond asked in despair.

Alain shrugged his shoulders, 'God knows'

'Well it's obviously no bloody good asking him because he certainly isn't on our side'

'Perhaps they'll be back before dark' Alain said hopefully, 'I can't see them staying out too long.'

'I guess we can wait and see. If not we'll have to walk as planned.'

'Just a thought Raymond' Alain whispered with a grim expression on his face, 'I trust this cove isn't mined or covered with barbed wire'

'To be honest I've no idea'

'Oh well I guess we'll soon find out' Alain replied dryly as he laid back on the soft warm sand between the bushes, 'one way or another.'

The shadows started to lengthen and an inshore breeze began to slightly sway the bushes they were hidden in. Raymond checked his watch, 'Quarter to eight'

'No sign of them yet so....'

'Shush a minute' Raymond interrupted in a whisper, 'I think there's a waggon coming.'

With a crunch of tyres on the sandy road a solitary Van pulled in. A loud voice started to shout orders, 'Spread out men and stay low they must be along this way soon.'

Raymond looked at Alain and shook his head, 'Well' he whispered, 'it was a bloody good try.' He quickly removed the envelope from his pocket scooped a hole in the sand and buried it.

A man wearing waders slid in to where they were hiding, 'Blimey you really gave me a turn chaps. I guess you must be the Hastings contingent. Your DCI said he may not be able to commit any troops because of a bit of a rumpus in your Manor. But welcome I'm DI Arrowsmith, Dover. We've no idea how many men are involved in this smuggling racket but we've had some good information they'd be operating this evening.'

Raymond's heart was still thumping, 'Four' he said his voice a little squeaky,

'You saw them leave?'

'Yes'

'What kind of boat?'

'Canoes' he answered his voice now back to normal

'Good that means small stuff.'

A head poked through the bushes, 'They're on their way Sir just four canoes.'

'Thank you Sergeant get the men ready. Wait until they're well onto the beach I don't want any escapees.'

While Arrowsmith's attention was on the men approaching the beach Raymond dug the letter up and pushed it back into his pocket along with what seemed like a ton of sand.

On the blast of a whistle the men surged forward and overpowered the smugglers in seconds.

'Now what've we got 'ere then?' The Sergeant asked searching the first canoe removing quite a large package wrapped in a waterproof cover. Alain gasped as it was unwrapped to reveal packet after packet of cigarettes. The next exposed boxes of tea another sugar. The last canoe appeared to be empty but by probing around with a boat hook they discovered a cardboard box crammed with counterfeit clothes and food ration books. All four men remained silent when the charges were put to them and they were arrested.

'How did you chaps get here?' Arrowsmith enquired as the men were led away

'Dropped off' Raymond replied

'Are they collecting you?'

'No because we've got to move on to Sunlight Cove because of this business in Hastings'

'A bit of a squeeze but we can certainly give you a lift. You must be aware though that the cove is off limits.' He thought for a moment, 'We've got to pass the Wardens building so you can let him know you need access to the beach'

'Is it mined?' Alain asked

'No it's mostly pebbles but plenty of barbed wire.'

The Warden looked at both the men for quite some time before he spoke, 'You'll have to get back here before dark or you'll be stuck amongst the barbed wire maze until morning. So that gives you' he peered at a large Smiths clock on the wall, 'no more than an hour.'

Raymond spoke quietly and with some authority 'That shouldn't be a problem because we intend staying put until morning. Is there a safe area large enough for us to wait in?'

'Yes there's a lookout post on the end of the shingle spit but only accessible at low tide it won't be pleasant though especially dressed like that'

'Oh don't worry about that we're used to it'

'Hastings Police you say?'

'That's right yes'

'I can't remember the name of your DCI'

'Jack Hammond' Raymond replied immediately with complete confidence as he'd heard it used when confined to his bolthole

'Of course it is' the Warden replied, 'I remember now he's the skinny bloke with scruffy hair'

Raymond suspected the Warden was fishing and perhaps hoping to trip them up 'I think you must be thinking of the wrong man squire' he said thankful that he'd glimpsed the DCI through the tiny crack in the shelving, 'he's hardly what you could call skinny with a double chin and his hair's slicked straight back' then laughing added, 'we reckon he uses dripping to keep it down.'

The Warden joined the laughter, 'I guess that's why they say the dogs run after him. Anyway you'd better get a move on its pretty slippery along the spit and the tides on its way in'

'What time is high tide?'

The Warden consulted a chart, 'Eleven fifty-three.'

The spit poked out into the Channel for six hundred yards. The wet slippery weed made walking hazardous, 'I certainly wouldn't want to attempt this in the dark' Alain whispered then cursed loudly as he slipped almost up to his knees into a muddy pool left by the tide.

They made it safely to the stone built lookout post and climbed up to the top level, 'This should give us a pretty good view of the U-Boat surfacing' Raymond said hoping that the inshore wind picking up wouldn't get any stronger to push up waves and hide the disturbance that blowing the ballast tanks would make. He knew the U-Boat would only remain on the surface for a few minutes and would not signal their presence but look for the red light he would use to guide the dinghy in. Any delay in him signalling they would immediately dive again and not return. Alain lit a cigarette and drew on it deeply holding the smoke in his lungs for a while before blowing it out in a spiral, 'Where the hell? Oh of course' Raymond said shaking his head, 'you managed to steal a packet from the smugglers hoard'

'Two packs actually' Alain replied grinning widely, 'they were just hanging about doing nothing so I thought I'd help myself.'

Raymond checked his watch for the umpteenth time, 'Twelve thirty-five. Where the hell are they?'

'We couldn't have missed them' Alain said, 'not under the full moon anyway'

'Perhaps that's why they've not surfaced.'

It was just after one before the U-Boat finally came to the surface. Raymond switched on the torch and directed it out to sea. A few minutes later a small dinghy bumped up against the spit. They both gratefully scrambled down into it and were quickly rowed out to the U-Boat and safety.

Portsmouth

The Commodore had called Oliver to his Office whilst he pondered the report from Samuel,

'Good report I hope Sir' he said closing the door behind him

'Not so sure. Everything seemed to be going as planned but then they lost track of it when it reached Hastings'

'So we don't know if it got back to Germany?'

'No but Samuel. You know Samuel don't you?'

'Yes I do, nice chap'

'Well he reckons there's a very good chance that it has. He says in the report that two men had permission to go onto the spit at umm' He looked down at the paper, 'Sunlight Cove and weren't there in the morning'

'So it's more than hopeful then?'

'Yes. And Samuel's extremely pleased because they've managed to take out an enemy cell that operated from

Evesham, Whitby, York and Hastings plus of course that Cotswold Village your Sister lives in.' Then with sober face, 'Changing the subject Oliver have you mentioned this business of the explosives to your First Lieutenant?'

'Not yet Sir no. He's a first class Officer and I'm a bit concerned that he may put in for a transfer. I know I would'

'The chances of it being activated are millions to one' the Commodore snapped 'it'd only be necessary if we knew for sure that the Germans had captured Troy.' Oliver shrugged his shoulders, 'So the answer is to not get captured' he concluded grinning broadly.

Oliver looked at him thoughtfully, not a flicker of a smile 'If your First Lieutenant wants a transfer then he can bloody well have one with my blessing and you'll just have to lump it.'

He inhaled then exhaled noisily, 'I'm sorry Oliver I didn't mean that but I've packed up smoking' he announced, 'it's been a bit hard but at least I don't cough all the time.' Then smiling at last he joked, 'You'll need to watch it from now on' he warned wagging his finger, 'because I can sneak up on you lot now without announcing my arrival.'

'Well done Sir. I'll pass it on so in future we can mount sentries to keep a look out for you.'

'Shove off you cheeky pup' he replied laughing and pointing towards the door, 'and get back to work.'

Steven Boniface sat grim faced shocked into temporary silence. Finding his voice he mounted his displeasure, 'Explosives? Why the hell would they want to blow their own bloody Submarine up? What on earth are they thinking of? I reckon that most if not all the men will want a transfer as soon as they know and who could blame them?'

'The men are not, and I mean not to be told anything about it Steven and I've been assured that it would only be activated in the event of Troy being captured.'

Steven exhaled, 'And we're supposed to believe that are we?'

'No choice I'm afraid'

'So what are the chances of it going off accidently? One close depth charge and boom we're no more'

'I doubt it's that sensitive but I take your point. And for the record Steven I objected most strongly against it but was overruled. The Commodore believes that it's no more of a worry than having a primed fish in the tubes'

'No worry to him you mean?'

'You could always ask for a transfer'

'No bloody fear. Leave you on your own? You'd never cope with it.'

'So true Steven, so true.'

The curtain was swept aside, 'I thought I'd find you two loafing around here'

'Looks as though I failed to post the lookouts Sir' Oliver grinned, 'the Commodore' he explained to Steven, 'has stopped smoking so doesn't cough anymore to let us know he's on his way. Anyway how can we help you Sir?'

'Nothing special but I thought I'd have a look round to see how things are progressing'

'Just about completed Sir. Should be able to take her out for trials within a few days.'

'Good. You'll berth at Dolphin from now on but before the trials all the crew are to be billeted in the Barracks for two days to give time for the installation of' he tapped his nose, 'you know what. Once that's done and trials completed we'll need to hold a meeting to discuss the finer details of what's now officially named Operation Trojan Submarine'

'If I may Sir?' Steven spoke hesitantly, 'I would like noted my complete condemnation of any explosives being installed aboard Troy'

'You may and it's duly noted. But does that include Torpedoes or are they exempt?'

'Obviously they are Sir'

'Good then let's take a look around.'

Berlin Germany

Admirals Hans Klusmeyer, Manfred Tanenbaum, and Wolfgang Heidemann gathered around the table scrutinising this latest information collected by their operatives in England, 'I think it's a hoax' Hans said pointing to the set of developed photographs, 'I can't believe they have the ability to developed such a craft'

'But my dear Hans you still refuse to believe they could ever decrypt our codes'

'That's true Manfred because that's as unlikely as this heap of rubbish'

'Should we not inform the Führer? He can decide if it's true or not'

'Good God Wolfgang are you mad?' Manfred shouted 'He'd have us all swimming across the water to tow the damn thing back to Germany'

'If it exists' Hans said bluntly, 'has anyone seen it?' He looked at the other two, 'No because I think it's just like that Scottish Loch Ness monster of theirs. Make believe'

'I think that's believable with a few tots of their scotch whiskey Hans'

'Or' Hans cut in, 'with a proverbial pinch of salt.'

An orderly came into the room and passed an envelope to Hans, 'What are these?' He asked sarcastically, 'designs for a British space Rocket ready to go to the moon or perhaps a new Spitfire that can fly at one thousand kilometres an hour?'

'They're reconnaissance photographs taken over Portsmouth Dockyard Sir'

'Good so we can dispel this silly idea of super Submarines' he shouted tipping them out onto the table.

'So what do you think that is Hans?' Manfred asked holding his finger down onto the dark cigar shape of a very large Vessel

'Could be a dummy'

'Why on earth would they go to all that bother? And why did they chase our operatives all over England to stop this' he thumped his fist down onto the photographs Raymond had delivered, 'from reaching us?' He sat down before continuing, 'Look the fact is that from the original six operative's active in England we have just one left. She reports that after their latest mission one is back inside a POW camp, two from Evesham are in prison and we know that two despite overwhelming odds escaped to deliver this information'

'So you believe they do have a super Submarine'

'I do Hans. Look at the evidence here' he pointed to the dark image on the photograph, 'what size do you estimate?'

'They've measured it at around four hundred feet long and forty feet wide Sir' the orderly said loudly.

'I think' Manfred muttered quietly, 'that we need to get our hands on it one way or another and soon.'

Portsmouth

Troy had been moved to Dolphin much to the annoyance of many of the crew who had sweethearts, Wives or favourite pubs in Portsmouth as they had to rely on the Gosport Ferry which on many occasions didn't run to schedule and quite often not at all.

Oliver like the other Submarine Commanders had access to their own Launch which dropped them off at Kings Stairs Jetty inside the Dockyard.

Pam waved as Oliver reached the top step, 'Quick' she said smiling impishly, 'I've managed to purloin Daddies car to take us home. Harold said he could only wait another five minutes and that was ten minutes ago.'

They bundled into the back seat of the car, 'Thank you Harold' she said sweetly snuggling into Oliver, 'I've really missed you' she whispered, 'I guess there's no chance of us visiting your Sister Carla again?'

'I doubt it would be for a while but as soon as we can it'd be really nice.'

As they entered the house there was a strong smell of

tobacco smoke, 'Oh Daddy' Pam whined, 'you were doing so well too. Why didn't you carry on?'

'Don't blame him' Margaret said loudly, 'I bought them for him'

'Why Mummy?'

'Because he's grumpy enough at the best of times but without his cigarettes he was becoming intolerable so it was a case of him smoking or me leaving'

'Should've stuck it out then' Douglas replied ducking as Margaret feigned a punch

'At least he's a lot happier now.'

Twice during the night they were disturbed by the bombing raid on Portsmouth. From the hall window they could see a huge orange glow across the skyline evidence of countless fires burning throughout the city, and the brighter flashes as more and more bombs and incendiaries hurtled down from above.

During Breakfast the phone jangled. Margaret who was closest answered, 'It's for you dear' she said holding up the receiver, 'the Dockyard.'

Douglas with a grim face shook his head as he listened to the report, 'And you say it's all gone?' He asked quietly, 'And no survivors either?' He replaced the receiver, 'Professor Landor and his entire team have been killed and their Laboratory, workshops and drawing office completely burnt out'

'Why the hell didn't they go to the shelter?'

'Who knows? Tragic loss of life but without them or any surviving designs we're buggered'

'Douglas!'

'Sorry dear but it's a fact. Any problems and we're on our own'

'Didn't they submit any plans to be kept in secure storage?'

'Stupidly we ordered them not to so it's our own fault. At least it was with the full knowledge of Beaufort so they can't dump it at my door. But' he continued shrugging his shoulders, 'I'm none the less guilty. The sooner we get you to sea the better. Can't afford any damage to Troy'

'As long as you keep your fingers off the button Sir'

'I will'

'What button?' Pamela demanded

'Sorry Pamela it's classified information and nothing for you to be concerned about. Anyway Oliver we'd better get back to the Dockyard and you over to Gosport. Best you put to sea for trials this afternoon.'

'Good morning Sir' the First Lieutenant said saluting, 'we've had to take on two more crewmen to man the Radar and new Sonar equipment. They're waiting outside your cabin.'

Two beaming smiles met him as he reached his cabin, 'Sumner and Rogers. Both Leading Seamen now I see'

'And you a two and a half ringer Sir. Congratulations all round'

'I'm afraid we don't have a gun for you Sumner'

'So I see Sir but there's plenty of other stuff for us to play with'

'Pop up top and ask the First Lieutenant to join me in my cabin.'

Steven tapped on the door frame, 'You wanted to see me Sir?'

'Yes Steven we're to sail this afternoon for trials and' he added screwing his face up, 'am I dreaming or is Troy a different colour?'

'She is yes Sir. It's a very dark grey experimental coating the boffins thought up to stop rust and any crustaceans sticking to it'

'When did they put it on?'

'At the same time they installed the you know what'

'Did you hear that Landor and his team were killed in the raid last night?'

'No I didn't. That's awful poor sods. Who's in charge now then?'

'Us apparently' Oliver replied, 'we're on our own.'

Troy creamed her way out through the narrow harbour entrance and into the Solent. Once clear of the Nab Tower Oliver called down for fifty percent power. They surged forward at twenty-two knots but soon started to bounce alarmingly forcing him to reduce power, 'Take us down Number One'

'Standby to dive. Thirty degrees down bubble, two hundred feet, fifty percent power.'

Troy glided gracefully into the depths, 'Let's wind her up a bit' Oliver shouted out, 'seventy-five percent power.' At thirty-five knots Troy remained stable, 'One-hundred percent' Oliver ordered. He turned to Steven, 'Forty-two knots and as stable as....' He never finished his sentence before Troy started to vibrate dangerously, 'fifty-percent.' The vibrations stopped as quickly as they'd developed. An increase back to seventy-five percent gave no problem. Eighty then ninety percent kept stable but anything above that caused the vibration. Steven leant towards Oliver and whispered, 'I don't think it's wise to start any kind of vibration as we've no idea what it could set off if you get my drift?'

'I was thinking exactly the same thing so to be on the safe side I think eighty percent is the limit. Standby to surface. Surface.'

'Keep her at forty percent maximum Steven. Set course for home. In time for Tea' He added bracing against the swell pushed back by the southern coast of the Isle of Wight.

'Signal for you Sir.'

Oliver read it through, 'If we're happy with the trials we're to proceed to Gibraltar for a two day visit and have permission to engage the enemy at every opportunity. Are we happy with the trials?'

'I think so Sir'

'Good so plot our course to Gibraltar.'

'So no Tea Sir?'

'I think the cook should be able to knock something up for us. Diving stations please Number One.'

As Oliver dropped into the control room the Radio Operator handed him another signal, 'Countermands the last one Sir'

'It certainly does. Our orders now Number One are to proceed to Plymouth for further instruction.'

'Still no tea then Sir?'

'Afraid not. Thirty degrees down bubble - forty percent power - two hundred feet.'

Douglas Warwick was just about to pack up for the day when one of his staff Officers rushed in, 'Commander Harvey's been shot Sir'

'Good God I knew the man could be intolerable but that's going a bit too far. How is he?'

'Poorly but stable Sir. They say he'll make a good recovery'

'Do they know who and why?'

'The perpetrator actually stayed at the scene and was arrested by the Police. He's been identified as Colin Matson from Dorchester.'

'I've heard that name somewhere before.' He thought for a moment, 'Now where the hell was it?'

'Anyway Sir he was bawling something about his young Daughter being beaten, burnt and sexually abused by the Commander and his crew'

'Mary Matson' Douglas blurted out, 'the Kid they picked up off the Channel Isles. She'd been a guest of the Gestapo. Where on earth did this chap Matson get that information from? It certainly wasn't anything to do with Commander Warwick or his crew. Where is he now?'

'Police cells in Plymouth Sir'

'Does he have a Solicitor?'

'No idea Sir but I'll find out.'

Douglas was unable to get a connection to any of the Police stations in Plymouth but did manage to contact the Military Police in Drake, 'Yes Sir we were made aware that the Commander had been shot'

'Are you able to be involved in the interview with Mr Matson?'

'Afraid not Sir we've been warned off'

'By who?'

'I don't think I'm at liberty to give that information Sir'

'By who?' Douglas repeated more firmly

'Sir Giles Hutchins, Lady Collins and Lord Sutton. But you never heard that from me Sir'

'I understand. Go on'

'They apparently provided all the information to the Police then submitted an application for the whole thing to be dealt with under the Official Secrets act'

'Did they indeed? One other thing has Mr Matson got a Solicitor?'

'I heard tell that Smith Drew and Williams had been approached'

'Thank you for that. And of course I've forgotten your name already.'

He replaced the receiver pushed back into his chair and reached for his cigarettes.

An argument seemed to start outside, 'I don't give a damn if he's busy I want to see him now'

'Well you can't Major'

'I bloody well can.' Guy Robins shouted pushing the door open and barging in, 'What's this load of baloney against Commander Harvey'

'Calm down and sit down please Major. Believe it or not we're on the same side'

'I hope so Sir because I've heard that a warrant has been issued for Oliver Pitman'

'What on earth for?'

'Rape, conspiracy to rape, detaining a female against her will and quite possibly anything else they'd like thrown in just to save their evil backsides'

'Whose backside?'

'The truth is' Guy explained slowly, 'Mary Matson was barely sixteen when SOE sent her out. Just before she left they obviously found out so she was ordered to lie about her age and tell everyone who asked that she was nineteen.' Douglas indicated for Guy who was still standing leant over his desk to sit down. 'When her Father' he continued, 'almost had to break into the Hospital to visit her and saw her injuries he naturally kicked up one hell of a fuss about it demanding some answers. SOE immediately distanced themselves from any blame and had the story put round that she'd been forced aboard Zulu and, well you know the rest'

'But why would Mary go along with it?'

'My guess would be that she's been threatened with imprisonment or worse if she denies the story Sir'

'Good God who the bloody hell are we supposed to be fighting?'

'Well I don't know about you Sir but I'm not going to put up with it. A few bloody titles don't frighten me so I'm off to Plymouth to blow the whistle. I rescued that kid from the Gestapo and everybody's going to know who sent her there. Where's Oliver by the way?'

Douglas shook his head, 'On his way to Plymouth.'

Chapter Thirteen

Plymouth

'Lieutenant Commander Oliver Pitman?'

'Yes'

'I'm Detective Sergeant Minogue' He produced his warrant card, 'I'm arresting you on suspicion of rape, physical assault, imprisonment and sexual intercourse with one Mary Matson a minor.'

The assembled crew were shocked as a Police Officer read him his rights then securely handcuffed led him away to a waiting police car.

'There must be some kind of mistake Sir'

'I'm sure there is Sumner, I'm sure there is.'

At the first opportunity Steven Boniface put a call in to Commodore Warwick, 'Lieutenant Commander Pitman has been arrested Sir'

'Yes I was warned that it could happen'

'Is that why we were sent to Plymouth Sir?'

'Certainly not' Douglas snapped, 'If I'd known you would be miles away by now'

'So what's it all about Sir?'

'All you need to know is that Oliver is completely innocent. Have you ever come across a Major Guy Robins?'

'Yes Sir'

'Well he's on his way down to Plymouth and hell bent on kicking someone's backside and to be honest the mood he seems to be in I'm glad it's not mine.'

Oliver was booked in by the desk Sergeant and taken to the cells. He was dumbfounded his mind in turmoil, "How could Mary tell such a story?" he thought especially after the support and kindness shown by himself and so many of the crew. 'Good God' he muttered shaking his head in disbelief, 'they even dhobied her dress and made new underclothes for her. How could she be so mean and tell such awful lies?'

· The lock grated and handle squealed as the cell door was opened. Oliver was handcuffed and led to an interview room, 'Sit' the Police Officer ordered pointing to a wooden chair. The handcuffs were removed as two men in plain clothes entered the room and sat opposite Oliver.

'I'm DCI Brownlow and you've already met Detective Sergeant Minogue. Do you understand the charges against you?'

'No I don't because it never happened' Oliver replied abruptly 'and there are plenty of witnesses who'd testify on my behalf'

'So you deny that Mary Matson a sixteen year old was lured aboard HMS Zulu by Commander Paul Harvey and yourself abused, beaten and held prisoner until she was rescued by security officials in Portsmouth and taken to Hospital?'

'That's preposterous' Oliver shouted getting to his feet but immediately forced back down by the Police Constable, 'where the hell did you dream that up?'

'Well Sir please feel free to amuse us with your version'

'We were ordered to meet a boat off the coast of Alderney to pick up one person who'd been rescued from the Gestapo'

'Mary Matson?'

'Yes'

'A sixteen year old girl travelled all on her own into enemy held territory? A likely story'

'She was sent over to France by SOE'

'And who are they when they're at home?'

'Special Operations Executive'

'Never heard of them'

'I've never heard of you before today but you exist' Oliver replied crossly

'Very droll Sir. So this SOE had her beaten up as well I suppose'

'They may as well have done because they informed the Germans that she was there.'

Brownlow chortled, 'This is getting better and better don't you think Minogue?'

'It is indeed Sir. I'm taking notes in case I decide to write a novel'

'I reckon it'd have to be a fantasy.' He leant menacingly over the table, 'Just like this bloody story you've come up with' he bellowed, 'now let's get down to the truth shall we?'

'I've nothing further to add'

'Really? Well that's a shame. Charge him Minogue then take him back to his cell.'

On the way back to the cell Oliver noticed Mary sat on a seat with Lady Collins. He looked down and shook his head. Mary full of guilt leapt up rushed over flung her arms around him and with tears streaming down her face shouted, 'I'm so sorry Oliver they made me say those dreadful things I know they're not true and I didn't want to but they said I must or I'd be in trouble.'

Lady grabbed hold of her and dragged her away, 'Come along my dear I think we'd better leave now.'

DCI Brownlow who'd left his Office to see what all the noise was about took hold of Lady's arm, 'I don't think so Madame. Minogue take her to the interview room'

'Unhand me immediately or you'll be in serious trouble'

'And exactly how do you figure that out?'

'I'm Lady Collins I'm employed by Sir Giles Hutchins and Lord Sutton who I'm sure both know your Commissioner quite well so could make life very difficult for you.'

Brownlow looked at Oliver, 'SOE?'

Oliver nodded, 'She's Miss Lady Collins.'

'Miss Lady Collins' he said obviously enjoying the moment, 'I'm arresting you for perverting the course of Justice'

'You can't do that' she protested trying to pull her arm away from Brownlow, 'I work for the prime Minister'

'And Madame I work for the King. Book her in Minogue.' He turned to Mary, 'And as for you young Lady you'd better come into my Office and provide a full statement.'

Mary looked terrified, 'They told me that if I said anything else they would make sure I'd go to prison'

'Well they're wrong, you won't so come along and we're get things sorted. Constable take Pitman back to his cell then get him something to eat and a cup of tea. What the hell?' He bellowed as a mighty row erupted in the outer office.

With a Police Constable practically tucked under his arm Major Guy Robins barged through the door using the poor man's head as a battering ram and shouted, 'Who's in charge here?' Then clapping eyes on Oliver he let the unfortunate Constable loose who rubbing his sore head quickly scampered out of range, 'I'm Major Guy Robins and I've come to give evidence for Lieutenant Commander Pitman against the disgusting lies that SOE have been spreading around just to cover their backsides for sending a sixteen year old girl to be tortured by the Gestapo.'

Mary recognised his voice, 'You rescued me' she said beaming, 'and put me on that boat'

'I did yes and you look a lot better than the last time we met.'

Brownlow fearing he was losing control held his hand up, 'Right' He shouted above the din, 'you' he pointed to Mary, 'and you Major into my Office. You Lieutenant Commander Pitman are still under arrest so it's back to the cell for you but as I said the Constable will supply food and tea.'

'What about my Dad?' Mary asked her voice wavering with emotion, 'Will they hang him?'

'I don't think it'll come to that the Man he shot is making a good recovery'

'But he'll go to prison?'

'That's up to the Court to decide.'

Oliver who heard all of this asked, 'What Man?'

Guy answered cheerfully, 'Commander Harvey your favourite Senior Officer'

'Where?'

'In the Jaw' Brownlow replied

'No' Oliver said irritably, 'where was he?'

'Oh I see' Brownlow replied laughing at his mistake, 'Torquay visiting his Sister at Camberley Hall a convalescent place in Moon Lane'

'Good Lord. He and I went head to head with SOE he really tore them off a strip so I guess this was revenge on their part'

'My Dad wasn't working for them' Mary objected strongly

'But they would've told him exactly where Commander Harvey would be. Even I didn't know he had a Sister. I guess I was to be next.'

Brownlow rubbed his chin and with some thought said, 'A lot of questions for us to ask this Miss Lady Collins before her high powered friends get wind of it and have her released on some technicality or other.'

With all statements made Oliver was de-arrested and driven back to the Dockyard to join his Boat. The First Lieutenant was waiting on the gangway, 'They let you go then Sir?'

'They did yes thanks to Mary and Major Robins who gave evidence on my behalf'

'Well I'm glad to hear it because we're to shadow Bellerophon from here to Gibraltar and I have been threatened with a replacement for you and I didn't really fancy that'

'Who was it to be do you know?'

'One Captain Nigel Stockwell Sir'

'Never heard of him who arranged it?'

'All done through Drake Sir'

'I see. So what's so important about Bellerophon?'

'A load of Government bods having a conference before critical talks in Gibraltar. We've got a meeting with Captain Wells and Commander Briggs at zero eight hundred tomorrow morning to finalise the details.'

The meeting didn't last long as Captain Douglas Monkton the Master of Bellerophon refused to acknowledge that he would need any kind of escort and was sceptical that Troy could ever keep up with them anyway. He was quite a large man with blonde hair steel blue eyes and a square jaw with a film star dimple and although not shabby was dressed in a very old and dated almost Victorian merchant navy suit, the four gold rings on each sleeve had long since lost their brightness and two of the jacket buttons were hanging loose, 'I've sailed that route hundreds of times' he said resolutely, 'and we've always managed to get ourselves out of any kind of trouble. And believe me there's been plenty of it'

'Well Captain I'm afraid you're having an escort whether you like it or not and trust me' Captain Wells added peering over the top of his specs, 'Troy could quite easily outrun you.'

Monkton snorted, 'Of course it could' he replied sarcastically, 'You do realise that we make twenty four knots?'

'I do' Captain Wells said removing his glasses and laying them on the table then faced Oliver, 'tell me lieutenant Commander Pitman as Commanding Officer of Troy do you believe you'll be able to reduce your speed down to twenty-four knots?'

'I think I'll be able to do that Sir' Oliver replied, 'Fifty percent power should be good enough.'

Captain Wells passed a sheet of paper to Monkton, 'These are the frequency's you must have your Radio Officer manning twenty-four hours a day'

'The man has to sleep for God's sake'

'He does of course Captain but as with all experienced Radio Men the Callsign will wake him up.'

'And it has been decided that you'll take Route Baker four'

Monkton huffed, 'I don't like that route much' he replied turning his nose up 'it takes us into quite shallow water. We've not used it for ages'

'Exactly why we want you to use it now.'

Monkton took the paper folded it neatly in half then tucked it in his pocket and stood up, 'I still don't think you'll be required but of course I shall comply with all your requirements. I'm intending to set sail at dusk if that suits you?'

'Fine with me Captain' Oliver replied smiling 'we'll be well ahead of you sweeping the area'

'And if you find anything?'

'We hope it won't be there by the time you get there.'

Monkton just grunted grabbed his cap and left.

'I don't think our Captain Monkton is too pleased for our help Sir' Steven Boniface declared dryly, 'do you think he'll comply as he promised?'

'No doubt about it he's the most experienced and loyal Merchant Navy Captain we've got. He certainly won't let pride interfere with his duty especially with some top Civil Servants aboard'

'Do you know what they're going for Sir?'

'A meeting over the border in Algeciras but who with and about what I have no idea'

'But what we do know' Commander Briggs added, 'is that someone is hell bent on stopping it going ahead so what better way than to sink Bellerophon'

'You think we're going to run into a bit of trouble then Sir?'

'Pretty certain yes but you've got all the right kit now to deal with it.'

Wells pushed a few sheets of paper over to Oliver, 'These are the way points he'll be using. And be warned that Captain Monkton so I'm told is an advocate of zig-zagging. His first Officer isn't so it won't be all the time'

If at all' Briggs added, 'because I'm pretty sure he'll

want to reach Gibraltar within forty-eight hours'

'I would've thought twenty-four knots would outsmart most U-Boats Sir'

'True Oliver but just encountering one in the right position would be enough'

'Right Gentlemen that's all. Thank you and good luck. Hope you and your crew have fun on the Rock. Oh and before I forget Commodore Warwick wants you back at Portsmouth in seven days' time.'

Back aboard Troy Oliver was sitting in his cabin bringing the log up to date. With a quick rap on the frame Steven poked his head around the curtain, 'A DCI Brownlow to see you Sir'

'Send him in Steven.'

Brownlow muttering something about swinging a cat squeezed his bulk into the Cabin obviously uncomfortable with the cramped surroundings, 'Goodness knows how you chaps put up with this for weeks on end'

'This DCI is the luxury end of Submarines you want to try the old T class they're really cramped'

'No thank you I'd prefer not'

'Now how can I help you? I trust I'm not under arrest again?'

Brownlow laughed, 'No not this time I've just come along to let you know how things have progressed. No action is to be taken against the young Mary Matson. Her Father Colin Matson has pleaded guilty to causing actual body harm and we're happy with that but as expected I was ordered by telephone to release Miss Lady Collins immediately without charge'

'Who ordered you, Sir Giles or Lord Sutton?'

'Neither'

'Not your Commissioner surely?'

'Nope. Believe it or not it was from the Prime Minister's office'

'Blimey she must mean a lot to them'

'I think it's more of a case that they can't find anyone

else evil enough to do the job. One thing that we've not established though is where Colin Matson got the pistol from'

'He won't say then?'

'All he's said is that his Father brought it back from the Great War'

'Feasible explanation I suppose plenty of Soldiers did'

'Not when the serial number puts its manufacture in nineteen-twenty-nine it doesn't. But still we'll get to the bottom of it sometime or other'

'What's your gut feeling?'

Brownlow hesitated as if reluctant to answer but then in a hushed voice, 'I really believe that those people in SOE gave it to him with the express purpose of shooting Commander Harvey'

'But surely Matson would say something about it?' Brownlow cocked his head and raised his eyebrows, 'But then perhaps not' Oliver corrected.

'It's only speculation you understand' he continued still whispering, 'but I've been a Copper long enough to smell a rat and believe me this stinks. Anyway I'd better be on my way before Minogue thinks he's in charge'

'Well thank you for dropping by to let me know'

'You're welcome' he replied pretending to look around then joked, 'I'd say the classic, I'll show myself out Sir, but I haven't got a bloody clue which way to go.'

Oliver stood up, 'Okay I'd better show you.' He shook hands and smiled, 'I don't think you'd be too impressed if we put to sea with you still aboard.'

'I'd rather face the toughest most dangerous criminal gang in Plymouth on my own than be cooped up in a metal tube like this.'

Oliver returned to his cabin trying to make some kind of sense from the DCI's final comments. What secrets could SOE possibly have to make them desperate enough to arrange for Commander Harvey to be shot and himself arrested on trumped up charges?'

His thoughts were interrupted by Steven, 'Captain

Douglas Monkton to see you Sir'

'Send him in' Oliver replied wondering if he'd ever get the chance to bring the Log up to date,

'I'm sorry to bother you but I have a request'

'Fire away Captain'

'Is there any chance of borrowing a Radio Operator from you?'

Oliver drew a breath, 'That's a difficult one we only carry two ourselves. Your man unwell?'

'He went ashore yesterday and has failed to return'

'Is that like him?'

'I really can't say, he only joined the ship last week'

'Then leave it with me Captain I'm sure I'll be able to find one and possibly two for you from Drake. Just a thought though while we're on the subject I trust you do have a VHF Transmitter?'

'We do. Brand new fitted and tested the day before yesterday.'

Alone once more Oliver's head filled with even more questions. Did the Radio Officer go absent on purpose? Did he work for SOE? Did he know that something was planned to happen to Bellerophon? A sharp rap on the bulkhead made him jump,

'Deep in thought Sir?'

'No Steven just getting more and more paranoid that's all'

'The two Radio Operators you asked for have arrived' he grinned, 'in a right two and eight thinking they've got to come to sea with us'

'Put them out of their misery and have them escorted along to Bellerophon.' Steven went to leave, 'Oh and get them on a two watch system and make sure they have the frequency we're using and everything else they need and get our Sparkies to arrange a VHF test transmission with them before we sail.'

Chapter Fourteen

On Passage to Gibraltar

Troy slipped an hour before Bellerophon to maintain a fifteen to twenty mile gap between them, 'Signal from Bellerophon Sir they've a problem with one of their boilers so can only make twelve knots until it's fixed'

'Right we'll put in to Mounts Bay and wait for them.'

'This doesn't bode well Sir'

'It certainly doesn't Steven' Oliver replied leaning down the bridge hatch, 'Sumner?'

'Yes Sir?'

'I want to know as soon as you get a trace of Bellerophon on Radar.'

They waited for over two hours before they received confirmation that the boiler control was repaired and Bellerophon gave a trace on the Radar.

By first light Troy was eighty miles west of Brest with Bellerophon following five miles behind, 'Urgent signal from Bellerophon Sir they're coming under sustained air attack from four Messerschmitt fighter bombers'

'Brilliant' Oliver exclaimed, 'that's something we can't do much about but we'd better go back and take a look. We'll risk ninety five percent power Number One.'

At Periscope depth Oliver found it hard to believe what he was witnessing. Smoke was pouring out from almost the entire open deck space of Bellerophon, not from as he'd first feared the result of direct hits but the withering fire from her six quad forty millimetre Bofors guns filling the air with curtain of lead causing mayhem with the attacking aircraft.

As the four battered aircraft left for home, two belching black smoke from a damaged engine even Bellerophon's two inch gun joined in the melee belching smoke sending shells screaming after them.

'I can see what Monkton meant about getting themselves out of trouble' Oliver said stepping back as he sent the scope silently back down into the well, 'it's a virtual Battleship. They sent Jerry packing and it doesn't look as though they've sustained any damage but we'd better make sure. Philips' he shouted 'contact Bellerophon and get a damage report.'

None were reported so Oliver had Troy increase power to seventy-five percent to pull away. Every twenty minutes they slowed went to periscope depth and raised the Radar Aerial to perform a three-hundred and sixty degree sweep.

This went on for the rest of the forenoon and into the afternoon watch. Sumner who was squeezed into the small space in the conning tower manning the Radar looked; looked again and again, 'Three contacts red three-five-zero ten miles Sir. I think they're stationary.' Sub Lieutenant Jordan climbed the ladder and squeezed in beside him, 'Nicely grouped' is all he said before sliding back down, 'close to ten thousand yards please Sir.'

Through the periscope Oliver could identify two U-Boats and a surface vessel that he was unsure of,

'When you're ready Sir' Jordan prompted politely

'Red three-five-eight, ten thousand yards stationary with very little distance between them. No wait they're on the move, course zero-eight-zero, speed umm two knots at best'

'Still together Sir'

'Yes.'

'Close to five thousand yards same heading please Sir.'

Jordan called for three acoustic torpedoes to be loaded then as usual swiftly completed the calculations manually, 'Fire One, Two, Three' he ordered then pressed the button on his stopwatch, 'I've set them for thirty knots Sir' he whispered, 'no wake, no bubbles, no noise so they'll have no idea they're coming.'

The five minutes seemed like an eternity before three massive explosions resonated through the water the last even louder and more turbulent than the other two, 'That was the surface vessel' Jordan declared, 'she must've been carrying explosives'

'Or mines' Steven suggested.

After an all-round search Oliver brought Troy to the surface. The sea was littered with debris; wood mostly some still burning, the smoke wafting towards them reminded Oliver of the smell of an English Village during the winter months.

'Survivor Port Quarter Sir he's swimming towards us' the Lookout reported loudly

'Rogers get down on the casing and bring him aboard. Sumner you go with him.'

Obermaat Gunther Donitz swam as hard as he could his heavy uniform now soaked was pulling him down. He rolled onto his back and with great difficulty after swallowing a couple of mouth full of dirty sea water managed to remove his tunic and let it float away. Being a prisoner of war seemed a far better option than drowning in the Atlantic he thought as Sumner and Rogers grabbed his outstretched arms and dragged him onto the casing, 'Danke' he said raising a weak smile from his oil stained face, 'danke.'

'What the hell are we going to do with him Sir?'

'I think Steven it'll be the only way we can find out what they were doing out here' Oliver replied as he climbed down through the hatch and into the control room.

'Where shall we put him Sir?' Sumner asked still holding tightly to his prisoner.

Oliver thought for a minute, 'After torpedo space for now'

'But that means walking him past the umm, the umm, through the engine room Sir'

'Yes Sumner that's fine I don't think he'll take too much notice for now do you?'

'Sprechen Sie Englich?' Oliver asked hopefully

'Just piece little' came the reply.

'Keep watch on him Sumner I'll see if any of the crew speak German'

'Ginger Rogers might Sir'

'Oh I'm sure he does Sumner. What would it be this time, vos is das matter?'

Sumner laughed, 'Probably worse than that Sir.'

Oliver failed to find anyone who could utter more than a few words in German. Hande Hoch and Ubergabe seemed the favourite but both completely useless.

'So what can we do with him now Sir?'

'Well I guess we'll have to take him to Gibraltar with us. Can't exactly drop him over the side can we?'

'Excuse me Sir'

'Yes what is it Rogers?'

'Sumner says that the Jerry keeps saying Wir Legten Minen. Which we think means they've laid mines'

'Has he indicated where?'

'No Sir but he holds his hands up like a roof joins his thumbs to make a triangle then does the sound of an engine and shouts boom'

'Got it Sir' Jordan shouted, 'I reckon they've laid acoustic mines in a V shape then put a light gauge cable across the open end. As a ship goes through it snags the cable pulling each mine in turn off their moorings and close enough to explode, probably all together. Nasty'

'But why on earth would he be willing to tell us?'

'Probably Steven like us he doesn't want to die. Get him up here perhaps he'll indicate on the chart where they are. Rogers?'

'Yes Sir'

'Where's Bellerophon?'

'Ten miles astern Sir'

'Philips broadcast a warning over to Bellerophon we'll give the position as soon as we can.'

Gunther was more than willing to plot the exact position of the mines for them. Why should he get blown up he thought to himself? Rather a POW than dead.

'Damn' Oliver cursed as Gunther was led away, 'it had to be in an area too bloody shallow for us to stay submerged safely. Philips' He handed over the position of the mines, 'transmit this to Bellerophon.'

'Just a thought Sir' Steven said quietly, 'were these mines laid for us and Bellerophon or any ship that came this way?'

Oliver drew in a breath, 'Too much of a coincidence I think. Obviously Commander Briggs was right in his assumption that somebody really does want to stop this conference going ahead'

'But that would mean the route has been compromised Sir.'

Oliver nodded, 'It certainly looks like it.'

'What are we going to do about the mines Sir? We can't really leave them can we?' Jordan asked interrupting their conversation,

'Acoustic you say?'

'Yes Sir so we believe'

'Could we send a noisy fish through it?'

'I don't think so Sir but Asdic may set one or two off.'

Oliver gave it some thought before Rogers called out, 'Bellerophon is now in front of us Sir.'

Which brought him to his decision, 'Best we leave them. We can't risk Bellerophon being in front. Seventy-five percent power, two hundred feet, course one-eight-five.'

After Dinner and the completion of the all-important entries into the Log Oliver finally relaxed in his cabin,

'Excuse me Sir'

'Yes Steven what is it?'

'The men ask if they can have one all round.'

'Yes they may but I'd prefer if we could snorkel for a while straight after they've stubbed them out'

'Thank you Sir I'll let them know.'

Within minutes the boat was filled with the pungent smell of tobacco smoke, Oliver's curtain was no defence.

Relief came as the First Lieutenant took them up to periscope depth and deployed the snorkel sucking in the fresh night air.

Oliver's thoughts centred on the mines being laid on a course that would've been followed by Bellerophon which without their lucky intervention could've resulted in a disaster.

This only added to his suspicions over Commander Harvey being shot and he being roped in under trumped up charges, why? Are they connected in anyway? "It's obvious" he concluded "that someone must've briefed the enemy on the course Bellerophon was to take." How many people knew of it? Who were they?

'Sir' a voice sounded far away, 'Sir! You're required in the Control Room Sir'

'Right' Oliver replied realising he must've dozed off, 'on my way.'

'Bellerophon has stopped Sir' the First Lieutenant explained, 'we've asked why but got no reply'

'Standby to Surface we're go and find out. Jordan have two of your fish loaded ready to fire.'

They cautiously approached Bellerophon wallowing in the Atlantic swell. It was getting dark her outline stark against the setting sun, 'Redman?'

'Sir?'

'Signal her and ask what the problem is.'

The Aldis clicked away sending a beam of light streaking through the growing darkness; it seemed an age before a reply eventually flashed from Bellerophon's Bridge Wing.

'They have a total electrical failure Sir just running on emergency power'

'Fixable?'

'The Aldis lamp flashed again. A reply returned within seconds, 'They say the job should be completed within the hour Sir.'

'I'm surprised the Radio Room isn't on emergency power Sir'

'I was thinking the exact same thing Steven. Redman ask why they have no power to the radio room.'

Redman raised his eyebrows, fortunately too dark for Oliver to notice, it was quite a lot to ask using the stiff trigger of the Aldis. He clicked away for a couple of minutes then stood back to read the reply, 'Radio-room-working. VHF-not-connected. Boiler-electric-restarted.

Jordan poked his head through the hatch, 'Her screws are turning again Sir'

'Good. Standby to dive, Seventy-five percent power, thirty degree down bubble, two hundred feet. Oliver ordered sliding down into the control room.'

Troy surged forward and was soon someway ahead of Bellerophon. At periscope depth communication was re-established and Sumner reported no contacts on Radar.

At dawn and throughout the day they sailed unmolested along the Portuguese coast with Bellerophon only reporting sightings of fishing boats.

Despite the delays they arrived in Gibraltar as dusk fell. Troy was assigned a berth below the rock which even in the failing light could be seen towering above them. Bellerophon was astern of them where they could hear cranes working in almost complete darkness unloading stores. Both Oliver and Steven remained on the bridge taking in the fresh evening air.

'I would've expected the harbour to be crammed with ships Sir'

'I guess any intelligent skipper would put to sea each night to stay away from the bombing'

'But not us?'

'I've never been considered as being intelligent Steven'

'You said it Sir.'

'Message from the Communication Centre Sir.'

Oliver read it through then out loud, 'During the forenoon we've got to move out to the South Mole so that we can be better viewed from Spain but out of the way of saboteurs.'

There was an audible groan from the crew as the only

way ashore from there was by boat,

'That's worse than being at Dolphin Sir. All the action out of reach' one crewman complained bitterly, 'what do you think ginger?'

'Me? I think I'm going to get me head down I'm on the middle watch.'

Oliver returned to his cabin still troubled over the fact that someone must've informed about the route Bellerophon was to take. Should he make his suspicions known to the Commodore?

Best he slept on it, he thought, and then perhaps discuss it with Steven before committing to such action.

For the first time in many a night the Italians didn't launch a bombing raid on Gibraltar. Troy moved to the South Mole and took a few turns around the bay careful to remain outside of Spanish waters. Steven swore he could see the sun glinting off dozens of binocular lenses from Algeciras as they swept in tight turns leaving a wake of azure blue water behind them.

For a second night no Italian Bombers arrived.

Troy set sail for home at zero seven hundred. Oliver intended to remain submerged for the entire trip streaming the aerial at the pre-determined times for communication from Portsmouth.

Despite being submerged they fared well against the tidal surge running through the straits. At eighty percent power Oliver was hoping to Berth in Portsmouth within thirty three hours arriving at around sixteen-hundred.

Portsmouth

Commodore Warwick had hardly had time to sit down before the phone rang,

'Yes?'

'I have a Samuel Knight from Military Intelligence on the line Sir. He was asking for Lieutenant Commander Pitman but when I told him that he was unavailable until tomorrow evening he said he'd like to talk to you instead'

'Put him through. Hello Mister Knight how can I help you?'

'*Samuel please. Oliver told me a lot about you*'

'All good I hope Samuel'

'*Of course. Now Commodore we have obtained intelligence that Troy is under an immediate threat so we recommend that she be moored in Fareham creek and for security reasons I can't divulge for the moment Oliver must leave Troy and go to a room we've booked for him in the Red Lion in Fareham. I believe Troy's not back until tomorrow evening so best she moves there immediately she's in*'

'Fareham creek?'

'*Yes that's what we suggest*'

'You don't know much about Portsmouth harbour do you?'

'*Not at all I'm afraid. I live in Birmingham so rely on charts. Is that a problem?*'

'At low tide yes'

'*So where would you suggest Commodore?*'

'Dolphin as normal, it's pretty secure and we can camouflage her if necessary'

'*Then Dolphin it shall be. But please remember it is of vital importance that Oliver leaves Troy the moment she docks. Thank you for your help and please give my regards to Oliver.*'

Douglas hung up then after a minute or two of thought went out to his Secretary, 'Could you have that Number traced Doreen?'

'It was on a secure line Sir'

'Right I suppose that's okay then.'

He returned to his desk more at ease but still a little concerned over the Fareham creek issue, "Surely" he thought, 'he could see from the chart that the creek was far too shallow at low tide for Troy to sail in or out. Even at high tide it would be difficult."

Shrugging it off he got down to his days' work before arriving home at sixteen-thirty. Margaret was in the

Lounge with Pam, 'Hello dear good day?' He grunted, 'obviously not but you'll be pleased to know that the building inspector arrived from the Council today and' she said rather acidly, 'I wish you'd let me know when you've arranged these things.' Oliver shook his head, 'Didn't know anything about it'

'Well his name was Arnold Collingwood, married with two sons both in the Army. He'd worked for the Council for fifteen years the last ten in Planning. A really nice man we had a lovely chat. It was quite a relief to have someone to talk to'

'That's all very well dear but what did he want?'

'He came to check that the repairs we had done after the tree came through were up to standard and complied with their regulations'

'And did it?' Douglas asked quite bored with the whole thing

'Yes. He said it was a splendid job'

'Good. What's for Dinner?'

'And how was your day Pamela?' Margaret asked intentionally ignoring Douglas

'Boring Mummy. Really boring. When's Oliver back Daddy?'

'Tomorrow evening but I doubt he'll be here to stay for a day or so but I would think he'll at least pop in to see you.'

'Oh I do hope so'

'Do you miss him dear?'

'Yes Mummy I do. Quite a lot in fact.'

Overnight Douglas laid awake for hours turning things over in his mind. Surely if Troy and Oliver were in any kind of danger then the safest place for them to be was at sea so he made a decision that first thing in the morning he would signal Troy to berth at Dolphin as expected but then sail again. He was acutely aware that if things went wrong it could possibly land him in very serious trouble possibly ending his career and at the very least at home wouldn't sit comfortably with Pamela who was expecting Oliver back, but he had this nagging doubt in his head about the call from Samuel and was still finding difficulty in making any sense of it.

At Sea

'That's rather odd' Oliver declared, 'We're to enter Portsmouth Harbour during daylight then after dark put to sea until the following evening.' He handed the pad back to the signalman, 'Goodness only knows what's going on now'

'Bit of a nuisance really Sir. The crew never got a decent run ashore in Gib and now we're to miss out on Portsmouth as well'

'Only for a day I hope' Oliver replied equally disappointed that he'd not be able to see Pam, 'We may as well reduce power and just drift along.'

Troy swept into Portsmouth Harbour and tied up at Dolphin, then as ordered during darkness slipped secretly out to sea and spent the next twenty-four hours sailing up and down the Channel even venturing back into the Solent on a couple of occasions simulating attacks on the Ships passing through.

Portsmouth

'Douglas I need you at home now' Margaret shouted down the phone in obvious panic, 'there are Policemen all over the house searching everywhere'

'What are they after?'

'I don't know and I don't care just get home and please hurry.'

'You're Sergeant Phillip Cantle?'

'I am Sir'

'And exactly what are you doing in my house?'

'We are investigating a Murder Sir'

271

'Well forgive me for being a bit slow Sergeant but I think everyone is accounted for here'

'Quite so Sir but it is a Commander Paul Harvey that has been murdered Sir'

'As I understand it Sergeant the man who shot and wounded him is in custody'

'Maybe so Sir but he has been cruelly murdered in his Hospital bed and…'

'Up here Serge' a Police Constable interrupted from the top of the stairs.

The Sergeant returned a few minutes later, 'That's all Sir we have what we need. Good day to you.'

'What on earth do you think they found?' Margaret asked

'More to the point dear is that poor Paul Harvey has apparently been murdered'

'That's awful but why would the Police come here?'

'No idea but I'm going to find out before the end of the day that's for sure.'

'I don't think you quite understand Commodore we wish to take Lieutenant-Commander Pitman in for questioning so would you please tell us exactly where we can find him'

'But why do you wish to question him?'

'We believe he could've been involved in the death of Commander Paul Harvey'

'And when was this crime carried out?'

'Yesterday late evening Sir. It was reported at one-thirty this morning'

'Really. Well I can assure you DI?'

'Newman Sir'

'DI Newman that he was at sea as he still is at this moment.'

Newman pursed his lips and drew his breath, 'We understood that his ship entered harbour yesterday afternoon'

'It did for an hour or so then sailed again as soon as it was dark'

'And the Harbour Master would be quite willing to confirm this'

'I would've thought so yes. But why do you suspect Pitman?'

'He was the last person to visit the Commander in the Hospital last night and we have been made aware of the animosity between them'

'By who?'

'I can't say really Sir but if you're willing to sign a statement to say that Lieutenant-Commander Pitman was out at sea. And also at the same time be kind enough to explain this train ticket found in his room at your house. And' he continued removing a small glass tube from his pocket, 'this file of liquid that we now know to contain cyanide'

Douglas took the ticket from him. It was a return clipped as used from Portsmouth to Torquay for yesterday.

Something stirred in the back of Douglas's mind, 'The building inspector' he said quite loudly, 'what the hell was his name?' He thought for a moment, 'Arnold, that's what it was Arnold Collingwood.' Newman looked mystified, 'he came to my house this morning to check the bomb damage repairs. He told my wife he worked for the Council and it's entirely possible that he could have put them there'

'Well his credentials will be easy enough to check. However we'll still need to talk to Lieutenant Pitman as soon as he returns. Now about that statement Sir.'

Troy pulled in alongside the jetty and once secure the off duty watch piled ashore rushing along to catch the Ferry to Portsmouth.

'Oliver Pitman' a voice called from the jetty, 'a word please'

'DCI Brownlow what the hell are you doing here?'

'Bad news I'm afraid'

'Come aboard'

'I'd rather not I had nightmares for ages after the last

273

time'

'Okay give me a minute or two and we'll find an empty classroom.'

His face grim Brownlow explained quietly, 'I'm sorry to say that Commander Harvey has been murdered'

'What? How?'

'Injected with poison at the Hospital in Torquay'

'That's really awful, shot then poisoned who the hell do they think he is Rasputin?'

'Who do you think "they" are?' Oliver stared at him for a moment, 'your gut reaction would be helpful'

'He really upset that Miss Collins and Sir Giles Hutchins about Mary Matson being recruited at sixteen.'

Brownlow nodded, 'So you said before Oliver but I don't think that would provoke them enough to firstly have him shot, implicate you and he with rape and abduction then murder him and this Oliver is the bombshell, 'have you set up for it'

'What! I'm being framed for murder?' Oliver yelled, 'you're joking surely?'

'Not at all' he replied grinning, 'you certainly do seem to court trouble just lately young man but nothing to concern you this time because believe me the case against you is about as watertight as the Titanic.'

The door opened and a head poked round, 'God you're difficult to find. Hiding away are you?' The Commodore asked shutting the door quietly

'Not at all Sir. Did you know I was framed for Commander Riley's murder?'

'I suspected something wasn't right that's why I sent you back to sea'

'Good job you did Sir but what bothered you?'

'I had a call from Samuel Knight advising that you and Troy were in danger so suggested you anchor in Fareham creek then you were to stay in a room at the Red Lion in Fareham'

'He'd know that we couldn't anchor in the creek'

'How so?'

'He lived in Ryde and as a lad used to sail over the Solent with his father to view the ships in the dockyard'

'He lives in Birmingham?'

'No he lives in Leamington.'

'Well' Brownlow said with conviction, 'we can establish that it wasn't him that telephoned you'

'But it was on a secure line'

Oliver looked at Brownlow, 'Must be from SOE surely'

'I agree but why? I think it would be a good idea if we get this chap Knight down here. I said something stinks and it's just got a whole lot smellier.'

The Commodore, Oliver, DCI Brownlow, DI Newman and Samuel Knight crowded into Douglas's Office intent on solving the mystery of why Commander Harvey was murdered and the blame put on Oliver.

'Do we at least agree that the three from SOE are in the frame?' Brownlow asked

'For the moment yes' Samuel replied, 'but where's your evidence'

'We have none as yet but it's out there I know it is'

'Did any of you visit the Commander?'

'I did Samuel' Brownlow replied, 'but he wasn't able to speak because of the injury to his Jaw but I had the feeling he was trying to get something across'

'Well we've lost that avenue of enquiry. Anything else?'

The silence was broken by a knock on the door, Doreen came in, 'Sorry to disturb you Sir but this note was delivered for Lieutenant Pitman I've had it in my tray for a few days now.'

Oliver read it through, 'It's from Commander Harvey' He said with sadness in his voice, 'Well I'll be' he said smiling, 'He's really come up trumps. He may not have been able to speak but he could most certainly write. This' he announced holding the letter up is all the evidence we need'

'For goodness sake Oliver get on with it we can do

without the dramatics' the Commodore muttered irritably

'Well Sir Commander Harvey managed to unearth information that shows Sir Giles Hutchins and Miss Lady Collins were intending to have me replaced by one Captain Nigel Stockwell who was under orders to ensure that Troy was captured and delivered straight into German hands.' He shook his head, 'So after one failed attempt they eventually managed to kill him then went after me again'

'That's all well and good Oliver but have we got hard evidence?'

'Possibly yes as he's asked in this letter that I give his sister his love when I next see her. Which I guess means he's left something with her at the convalescence home'

'What brings you to that conclusion?'

'Because Samuel I didn't even know he had a sister let alone visit her'

'Surely' DI Newman said, 'we have enough to bring them in for questioning?'

'No chance of that' Brownlow replied, 'their high power friends would have them out again in minutes'

'So what can we do?'

'Firstly we can visit Colin Matson to persuade him to say who gave him the Pistol and information on where he could find the Commander that day'

'Where's Matson now?'

'Dorchester Nick. Then after that visit Harvey's Sister to get hold of whatever, if anything he's left with her'

'And then?'

'And then DCI Brownlow you can have the pleasure of accompanying me to Baker Street with a couple of burly London Coppers to well and truly ruin these three peoples day?'

'I would be delighted Samuel'

'What about Lord Bertie Sutton do you think he knew anything about this?' The Commodore asked

'He's not mentioned but we'll obviously be questioning him along with many others I would suspect.'

Oliver stood up and smiling broadly announced, 'I

think its poetic justice that a dead man may well have managed to solve his own murder.'

The others left leaving the Commodore and Oliver alone, 'Well that's possibly the end of that saga Sir.'

The Commodore looked concerned, 'I hope so'

'You seemed worried Sir'

'I'm hoping that they've not learned anything of our Operation Trojan Submarine that's all'

'Should they have Sir?'

'Bertie Sutton was involved in the very early discussions'

'Well let's hope he's kept his mouth shut Sir.'

Dorchester Prison

'I've already told you that my father brought it back from the Great War' Colin Matson said drearily, 'so why keep asking me?'

'Because Mister Matson we know you're lying'

'Really?'

'Yes really. The Pistol was manufactured in Nineteen-twenty-nine so as you can see that wouldn't have been possible. So who are you being threatened by?'

'Nobody' Colin retorted, 'now can I go back to my cell?'

'No you can't not until you've come up with some answers'

'Like what?'

'Like how did you know where Commander Harvey would be on that day?'

'Why are you dragging all this up again? I've already confessed so what else do you want?'

'Commander Harvey has been murdered and we believe it's the same people who you were involved with'

'Involved?' he shouted, 'I wasn't involved with them I just wanted revenge on the bastard who abducted and molested Mary that's all'

'But they didn't did they?'

'So it turned out no'

'Are you concerned about Mary's safety?' Colin didn't answer, 'By your silence I assume yes. So who do you believe could hurt her?' Colin shrugged his shoulders, 'Come on Mister Matson we're on your side. Mary will be much safer if you give us the information we're expecting'

'I don't know all their names'

'Well give us the ones you do know.'

'I daren't honestly I daren't they'll kill Mary' he choked up, 'they said they would and they will I know they will'

'Not if they're given the death sentence they won't'

'I shot him not them'

'Mister Matson we can't do anything for you unless you give us a name' Samuel said sternly, 'if you don't then Mary will be at risk for the rest of her life. Only you can stop that'

'A chap called Stockwell came to see me' he finally blurted out, 'he explained why Mary had been beaten and who'd done it to her'

'He gave you the Pistol?'

'No it was left in my Garden the following day. Then I had a telephone call at work to say that Harvey was to be visiting someone in Torquay. The address was put through my letter box later in the day'

'So who's threatening Mary?'

'A Lady visited me here and said that if I said anything they would have Mary tortured and killed'

'Did she give you her name?'

'No but Mary visited me straight afterwards and saw her leaving. She asked what Lady somebody or other wanted but I said I'd not seen anyone'

'Lady she said?'

'Yes Collins I think it was. Yes Lady Collins I remember now'

'Did this Lady Collins ever mention a Lord or a Knight whilst she was here?'

'No.'

Samuel stood up and shook Collins hand, 'Thank you Mister Matson you've been most helpful'

'Will it help Mary? That's all I'm bothered about'

Samuel smiled reassuringly, 'Yes it will.'

Camberley Hall Torquay

'I'm sorry Mister Knight you and the DCI have had a wasted journey Miss Moira Harvey left the day before yesterday. Her Brother had been murdered you know'

'Yes that's what we would like to have spoken to her about. Do you have her home address?'

'Yes of course I'll make a note of it for you.' As she removed a book from a wire tray on her desk Samuel saw a large envelope with Oliver Pitman's name scribbled on the front, 'That envelope' he said pointing to it, 'Is it something that Moira left behind on purpose?'

'Yes she said that her Brother had left it to be collected by this Oliver Pitman. Why? Is it important?'

'Very. May I have it?'

'I'm not sure that I should give it to you as Moira stressed that Oliver would come to collect it'

'It's actually Lieutenant-Commander Oliver Pitman and he was made aware by a note from Commander Harvey that something may have been left for him which is why we needed to speak to Moira in person'

'Well I suppose as it's so important and you're from the Police I can pass it on to you' she said handing it over

'Would you mind if the DCI and I sit in the lounge to read through it?'

'Not at all please feel free.'

It proved to be exactly the evidence they were looking for, 'No wonder they wanted Commander Harvey out of the way' DCI Brownlow said reading the last of three pages, 'they must've been desperate to get these back'

'Strangely enough' Samuel creased his brow, 'I have a feeling that Miss Collins and Sir Giles weren't aware that these still existed'

'So why murder him?'

'As soon as his Jaw healed they were convinced he would speak out'

'Have we enough to bring them in?'

'I think we'll pull Stockwell's chain first that'll ruffle a few feathers.'

Baker Street London

Lady's door burst open and Sir Giles obviously flustered stormed in, 'Stockwell's been arrested' he shouted his voice a little higher than normal

'So?'

'For God's sake Woman don't you see we'll be next?'

'Giles they have nothing on us at all. You worry too much. As long as Stockwell's destroyed everything we've told him to then we're in the clear'

'And if he hasn't?'

She smiled, 'They still have to prove it and I'm sure that our Ministers would pull them off of us pretty damn quick'

'But what about Stockwell?'

'Expendable I'm afraid so they can certainly put him in the frame for murder'

'Well I hope you're right Lady'

'I always am Giles, I always am.'

'DCI Brownlow how nice to see you again. Obviously you've not learned your lesson from last time. Who's this?' Lady asked glaring at Samuel

'I'm Samuel Knight Military Intelligence'

'So what do you want with me?'

'Miss Lady Collins' the DCI said loudly savouring every moment, 'I'm arresting you on suspicion of espionage, conspiracy to murder, perverting the course of justice and threatening behaviour'

'Really? Goodness that does seem a lot doesn't it?' She replied arrogantly confident in the belief that Ministers would immediately jump to her defence so she would be released within hours, 'I think we've been here before DCI Brownlow but this time' she threatened, 'you'll be directing traffic in some horrid poky little backwater village as a miserable lowly disgraced PC for tangling with me again. And as for you' she snarled at Samuel, 'I would've thought you'd have more intelligence.'

Samuel smiled, 'Oh believe me Miss Collins we don't need any more intelligence we have as much as we need.'

Crown Court London

Lady Collins was wrong. No Minister dared to support her with the espionage charge against her. The evidence was overwhelming; the three page document that Stockwell failed to destroy convinced a Jury of their guilt, the Judges black cap confirmed their sentence.

Oliver met up with Samuel outside the Court, 'I'm glad that Mary didn't have to take the stand'

'I don't think there was ever a need apart from the espionage charge against them'

'I'm still confused as to why they sent Mary to France. If they hadn't done that then perhaps none of this would've come to light and Paul would still be alive. Especially as she only had bogus information about Troy'

'Who told you that?'

'Lady Collins when they demanded an interview with Paul and me'

'Well Oliver I can assure you that was nowhere near the truth. Look let's go to the park it's quite near and I'd rather chat there.'

They discovered an old wooden bench almost lost amongst a huge out of control rhododendron and carefully sat down avoiding the end with a broken arm rest.

'Mary Matson' Samuel whispered despite them being out of earshot of people strolling in the late afternoon sun, 'has a phenomenal memory almost photographic. She absorbs information like a sponge. She was given and told to commit to memory the names and addresses of almost every resistance member running safe houses throughout France'

'So they informed on her so she'd get caught'

'Exactly'

'Why not just send it to the Germans surely that would've been easier?'

'They didn't want any link back to themselves. They believed that Mary would eventually give up the information then obviously be shot as a spy putting themselves well clear of any blame. Major Robins however inadvertently ruined their plans by rescuing her'

'Well it's a good job she didn't spill the beans'

'She couldn't have done even if she wanted to.' Oliver looked confused, 'Have you ever heard of Temporary Stress Amnesia?'

'Can't say I have no'

'Fortunately neither had Collins nor the fact that Mary suffered from it. You see with Mary any extreme pressure or acute pain triggers a reaction in her brain that causes her to temporarily forget just about everything apart from basic functions. Then as I understand from a Doctor chum of mine that when the stress goes and memories return she would have a tendency to act rather bizarrely and quite out of character'

'Hence why she was perfectly happy with me being present whilst she was padding round the cabin completely naked'

'I guess that proves the case. Anyway Oliver I must be away I've got a train to catch'

'No car?'

'Long story but safe to say it's in the Garage having the wing replaced'

'I'll walk to the Station with you'

'Walk? No chance of that I'll get a Taxi'

'Then I'll walk to the Rank with you.' They set off, 'Tell me Samuel how much did Lord Sutton know about it?'

'Nothing at all apparently until quite late on after the business with Mary in fact when he became rather unhappy and made his concerns known to Sir Giles'

'Bet that went down well'

'They seemed to successfully put his mind at rest for a while but I firmly believe that he would've been next on their list for murder'

'I guess that I must have been on that list somewhere'

'Quite possibly. Anyway take care of yourself Oliver' Samuel said shaking hands, 'perhaps we'll see each other again sometime.'

Chapter Fourteen

Portsmouth autumn 1942

Elizabeth Hardy was nervous. As head of the Naval Communications development department in Plymouth she now had the unenviable task of masterminding the clear reception of a radio signal through forty or fifty feet of earth and concrete. Her expertise and that of her team would be key to the success of Operation Trojan Submarine.

She'd travelled over night from Plymouth arriving tired and hungry early in the morning. Oliver and the Commander were already in his office, 'Elizabeth I'm so pleased to meet you. I believe you've already met Lieutenant-Commander Pitman?'

She smiled, 'You were a Lieutenant then I believe'

'I was and you installed a blessed great lump of a thing on top of my Submarine'

'So I did but I believe it worked beautifully'

'It did to a point yes so I can't complain'

'Did you manage to get Breakfast Elizabeth?' The Commodore asked

'No' she replied shaking her head, 'and to be honest I'm famished'

'Oliver will you escort Elizabeth over to the Wardroom and get the Chef to prepare something?'

Over Breakfast Oliver was able to quiz Elizabeth about the communication problem. She conceded that it was a tall order to find a solution but it had been solved but would require someone to install the required equipment in the base in Dorfhaven, 'I guess that would fall to Major Robins but he's already been there two or three times at least'

'I am aware of that Oliver but it's the only way we can get a signal down into the U-Boat pens and even then it's going to be a bit of a gamble'

'Where have you tested it?'

'Smeaton's Tower on the Hoe and Fort Picklecombe in the Sound, both reasonably successful but we've come across more technical information now so think we've come up with a fool proof solution' She chuckled, 'well by fool proof Oliver I think we mean a good chance of working.'

'Good morning Gentlemen and thank you for attending' Elizabeth began speaking to her esteemed audience of an Admiral, a Commodore, a Captain and Commander plus many other ranks down to Sub-Lieutenant. She took a sip of water before continuing, 'We believe that we've found a solution to getting a radio signal down into your target.' She cleared her throat, 'who's Major Robins?'

'I am' Guy called out from the back of the room

'Well Major I'm pleased to say that we've managed to get part of the solution from a communication diagram you brought back some months ago' she turned to a blackboard precariously balanced on two chairs and leant up against the wall, 'along the west side of the motor stores there's an outside telephone.' The chalk screeched as she drew an X on the board, 'This is serviced by connection twenty-eight on the main exchange.' Another screech as she drew an O. 'There is also a telephone down in the Pens which appears from the diagram not to be in use.' She took another sip of water and drew a letter Y on the board, 'But the wire is still in situ and connected to connection eighteen on the main exchange. What we need is the two points to be hard wired together to form a continuous connection.' She drew a line between all three points, 'Then a Radio Receiver and Amplifier installed on the motor store phone here.' She tapped the chalk against the X and a signal transmitter at point Y

'Oh I see' a loud voice called out from the back, 'I was beginning to wonder why I'd been invited along to such a prestigious meeting and now suddenly all has become a whole lot clearer'

'Major I have no say in who does what. I merely supply the equipment and a bit of expertise that is all.'

'And you're confident this will work Elizabeth?' Captain Wells asked

'It's been tested but I'd like something a little more challenging to be satisfied that it'll work first time'

'What about under Portsdown Hill?' Oliver suggested,

'You mean in the Communication Centre?'

'Yes Sir I think it'll be a fair enough test don't you?'

'Elizabeth?'

'It'll need an external wire running all the way down into this Communication Centre and something to prove the signal was strong enough'

'Well we still have the practice relay that Aidan Riley left for us'

'That'll do fine'

'Then I'll get the cable organised. Do you have the equipment with you?'

'No it's all a little too big and heavy for me to carry but I can get it shipped down for tomorrow.'

Guy shot up from his seat obviously unhappy, 'Elizabeth if this gear is too big and heavy for you to carry down here how on earth can you reasonably expect someone' he paused to poke his finger into his chest, 'obviously me, to trapes through the German countryside with it hidden. Where do you suggest Elizabeth? Under my shirt or perhaps down my trousers.'

Elizabeth didn't bat an eyelid and with a completely calm voice replied, 'Neither actually Major' she smiled sweetly, 'despite not being on the front line we're not completely stupid, well not all the time anyway. You see once the units have been tested and approved the final version will be fairly portable and quite possibly we might even manage to make them look like a German telephone junction box. So you see Major your shirt and trousers will be quite safe.'

The Commodore, Oliver, Steven and Guy remained behind

to discuss the towing and beaching of T102, 'One more to come' The Commodore said, 'he should be along shortly.'

A head poked round the door, 'Ah the right room at last. Oliver lovely to see you again'

'Well I never if it isn't Roger Collins himself how are you old chap?' Oliver shouted standing up to shake his hand, 'So how do you fit in to our little band?'

Roger took his seat as the Commodore introduced him, 'This gentleman for those who've not come across him is Lieutenant Roger Collins Commanding Officer of Taciturn ex First Lieutenant of Ursula. He Oliver to answer your question will be taking command of T102 during the tow.' He coughed which seem to remind him to light another cigarette.

'I thought you said he'd packed up' Steven whispered to Oliver

'He did but the wife bought him a packet because he was such a misery'

'Could she tell the difference then?' Steven joked

'Probably not'

'When you two have stopped muttering to each other I'll carry on' the Commodore said glaring at both of them, 'Operation Trojan Submarine will commence on the eighteenth of November.'

'There was a gasp from his audience, 'That's just six weeks away Sir'

'It is Oliver yes but that's the last of the highest tides of this year'

'Doesn't give much time for me to plant Elizabeth's gear Sir'

'I know that Major but as you've probably heard the U-Boat Pens at Brest have been put out of action so the Germans are relying on those at Dorfhaven to replace them. The pressure is on to put them out of action to stop the constant attacks on our Icelandic Convoys'

'Do we have time to practice towing Sir?'

'Your First Lieutenant has some experience with that Oliver'

'Not particularly successful though Sir' Steven replied

'Not entirely your fault. Bit of a cockup on the part of the design. You'll get a chance to test out one tow but not unfortunately a beaching'

'One thing has crossed my mind Sir'

'Just one Oliver?'

'Yes Sir for the moment. I was just wondering about a crew for T102. Won't the Germans be a bit suspicious when they discover nobody's aboard?'

The Commodore paused to light another cigarette, 'Regrettably something we're certainly not short of at the moment is' he drew deeply on the cigarette held his breath then blew the smoke up towards the ceiling in a long stream, 'a plentiful supply of corpses. We're currently holding thirty unnamed men in the local morgue'

Roger screwed up his face in disgust, 'I really don't feel happy about sailing with all those dead bodies laid about everywhere Sir' he moaned, 'it'll be bloody awful'

'Not to worry they'll be contained to one area until you're beached then put into position'

'Who will be on T102 with Roger during the tow Sir?'

'It'll be made up of some of your own crew Oliver, five possibly.'

'Nothing yet Sir' the Communication Centre's Petty Officer Telegraphist reported over the radio.

Oliver was getting frustrated as they'd been attempting to key the relay for most of the day. Steven came over to him, 'Do you think we'll do better if we move to Fountain Lake?'

'Not much closer though'

'But at least we won't have the Brewery and Power Station in the way.'

'Okay point taken Steven let them know at Southwick.'

Once Troy had moved the Telegraphist carefully tapped out the code then they all waited with baited breath for the response from the Communication Centre, 'Nothing's happened here Sir.'

'Can you push anymore power through?'

'No Sir it's tuned to the maximum.'

'So what the hell can we do about it?' Oliver shouted, 'If we can't reach it now then the whole thing will be a waste of time.'

The Telegraphist swung his chair around, 'The aerial Sir. I think that's the problem'

'So how can we prove that?'

'Zulu's just astern Sir I can go aboard and use their Transmitter'

'Worth a try so off you go.'

'The lamps come on and the relay's clicking Sir' the Petty Officer shouted, 'definitely working fine Sir.'

Oliver shook his head, 'That's all well and good but we've got to sort out our aerial somehow'

'Perhaps Elizabeth can come up with something Sir?'

Oliver laughed, 'I'm sure she could Steven but it'd probably the same size as the one on Alexandra Palace'

'What makes you say that Sir?'

'Something she had plonked onto Ursula. I'll tell you about it sometime but I think we'd better get over to see the Commodore and let him know we need a different aerial and fast.'

Elizabeth was delighted that her part of the system had eventually worked perfectly but was soon brought down once told that the transmission had not come from Troy, 'So what do you think was the problem Oliver?'

'Aerial not good enough'

'We can fit a whip aerial like that one on Zulu that shouldn't take long'

'We'd have to be able to tilt it when we're dived'

'Okay I'll have my team work on it'

'Please don't make it two hundred feet tall or thirty feet thick will you?'

Elizabeth chuckled, 'I'll try not to I promise'

'And you promise it won't leak?'

'I didn't say anything about that Oliver' she joked, 'I'll

be in touch.'

Major Guy Robins flipped the final versions of the equipment over in each hand. As promised they were much smaller than the prototype but they'd been unable to simulate a German telephone junction box. They looked identical each six inches long, four wide and two and a half thick painted grey marked with the number one and two in black paint 'So you say that they only have a sixty day life before the batteries die?'

The Engineer nodded, 'there about yes but no power will be drawn until they're fitted'

'Sixty days from installation?'

'Fifty eight days to be exact.'

'That doesn't give us much leeway for any kind of delay'

'Can't be any more than that because of the size we've had to shrink them to'

'Okay you'd better show me how I'm supposed to hitch them up'

'It's been made to be as quick as possible. Just cut and connect both ends of the wires into these screw connectors here then pull off these four strips on the back and stick them to the appropriate wall. Number one on the Motor store wall and number two down in the pens' He removed a sheet from his pocket, 'now although all of our main exchange connections are numbered it doesn't mean the Germans do the same but I would think that they'd follow convention by numbering from left to right on the top row then reverse for the next and so on. Are you familiar with telephone exchanges?'

'Not at all no'

'Well come along with me and I'll show you the workings of the Barracks one.'

The Engineer removed the back cover of the exchange Guy looked in dismay at the miles of tangled wire, 'Don't look so downhearted' the Engineer said chuckling, 'it isn't as difficult as it looks'

'I'll take your word on that' Guy replied shaking his head as he gazed at the twisted mass before him'

'As I said convention dictates that the connections are numbered from this point and then reversed for each bar. The German exchange is much smaller than this one so should be a lot easier to count across. All you need to do is locate number twenty-eight and wire it to number eighteen. You just have to loosen the connection push the bare end in then tighten it up again job done. Happy with that?'

'Fine with me' Guy replied hoping it would be as simple as that but knowing in his heart it never is.

'Good so I'll leave it with you and good luck. Oh and before I forget here is a tool bag and all the tools and wire you'll need.' Guy took it from him and looked inside, 'You'll find that Elizabeth is a stickler for details so you can rest assured that all the tools are German made and even the bag's marked with the German telephone company logo. There are also two sets of overalls that we were asked to provide with obviously the made in Germany markings and also with the logo on the front. Only one size I'm afraid but I'm sure they'll do'

'I'm sure they will.' Guy replied rather impressed with Elizabeth's preparations,

'Right-e-hoe I'll be off then' the Engineer said pushing the sheet of paper that he'd used earlier into the tool bag, 'the details of the connection numbers and instructions we've gone through.' He grinned, 'All in German of course.'

Chapter Fifteen

To Dorfhaven

Guy and his Sergeant Harry Langford stood on a jetty at a Hayling Island sailing club waiting for a boat to task them out into the Channel to meet up with S-148. Harry started to pace up and down, 'Nervous Harry?'

'I am a bit Boss we've never been back to the same place this often'

'True' Guy replied stroking his newly grown beard, 'at least we've got our new disguises'

'I still recognised you Boss even under the hair'

'Well let's hope we don't bump into anyone we know. At least we'll only be ashore for an hour or two so the chances of that happening are pretty slim' he replied hoping to convince himself as well as Harry.

A vehicle squealed to a halt at the gate. A man dressed in civilian clothes marched smartly over to where they were waiting, 'You Major Robins?'

'And you are?'

'Peter Hayes-Porter Military Intelligence'

'And your business with us Peter?'

'Your boat has been cancelled to pick you up in the Channel I'm afraid. To be honest Guy things have got extremely difficult for the chaps to get through the Straits of Dover so have had to stay north'

'So where are we to be picked up?'

'Crofton Head'

'Where the hell's Crofton Head?'

'A little north of Scarborough.'

Guy almost threw the tool bag to the ground in frustration, 'That's a bloody long walk'

'Then it's a bloody good job I brought the car isn't it?' Peter replied sarcastically

'It's still going to delay us'

'Actually I don't think it will Boss' Harry chipped in

'So how do you work that one out?'

'I reckon it'll be around six hours by car and not withstanding any course changes to avoid detection at least seven by boat even at thirty knots plus'

'Okay we'll see if your theory stands up Harry. Mind you it isn't going to matter much as we don't seem to have a choice in the matter do we?'

They climbed into the car, a rather posh Jaguar, 'Perhaps a little less than six hours then Harry. Anyway how come you know that's how long it would take?'

'Long story Boss?'

'Well we've got a few hours to kill isn't that right Peter?'

'It is indeed Guy'

'It's not really worth telling'

'Give it a go anyway' Guy asked settling down in his seat

Reluctantly Harry started his story, 'I was in the Barracks at Eastney before the war like and one day decided to take a run ashore with my Oppo Taff Jenkins. We met a couple of Girls in Southsea; they were twins on holiday from York.' He stopped to hang on for dear life as Peter with the Jags tyres squealing in protest took a very tight right-hand bend, 'anyway' he continued as they came to an even keel, 'we saw them a couple of times then Taff managed to get their address before they went home so the next long weekend's leave we had he borrowed a car and we drove up there'

'To York?'

'Yes'

'Well that's not exactly Scarborough is it?'

'No Boss but it can only be another hour or so to Scarborough and we made York in less than five'

'So you and this Taffy bloke had a good weekend then?'

'Ah not really Boss no. We never got as far as meeting up with them and I ended up getting the train back.' Again the story had to stop as Peter swerved around a bend causing Harry to slide across the leather seat and bash into the door, 'Bloody hell Peter are you trying to beat the time me and Taff took?'

'Certainly not but you're pick up has been scheduled for half eleven and for obvious reasons they can't hang about too long. So why the train?'

'The Cops were waiting for us because when Taff told me he'd borrowed the car he meant he'd stolen the bloody thing; not from just anyone mind but believe it or not from one of the Married Sergeants who kept his pride and joy outside his rented house in Tokar Street. Bloody stupid really because we always had to say where we were going and for how long in case we were needed back and somebody obviously must've seen us leave in the car. Hell to pay when I eventually got back God knows how many times I had to run up and down those bloody Wardroom steps with a Lee Enfield at the slope with the Sergeant bellowing his sodding mouth off. My shoulder was bruised for weeks'

'You were right Harry' Guy said pretending to yawn, 'it wasn't worth it after all'

'Finish it off though Harry what happened to Jenkins?'

'No idea Peter we never saw him again'

'Well that's wasted a good ten minutes or so what else have you got for us Harry?' Guy said looking at the clock on the dashboard, 'A few more hours to go yet'

'You've always been a sarcastic sod Boss. What about a story from you? Oh I forgot at your age the memory fails.'

Guy turned round and feigned a punch at Harry. Peter laughed as he shouted at them both, 'Now children play nicely please.'

Guy felt a great fondness towards Harry. He knew he could always rely on him to watch his back in all situations. They'd carried out many operations together and he honestly believed there was no one else he could trust with his life than him.

Like Harry he was very concerned about this one, "Too

many times to one place" he thought "Always a danger. A dreadful risk to both of them."

It started to get dark but Peter had no intention of reducing his speed. Quite a few times he ran up the sides and bumped over the grass for a while before getting back onto the carriageway. Guy was much happier when they got onto the Great North Road which was a good bit wider with many more straight stretches but this only encouraged Peter to push even harder.

Quite suddenly he swerved into the side of the road an switched the engine off, 'Fast but dash thirsty' he said getting out, 'would appreciate some help'

'Doing what?' Guy replied joining him

'Hold this torch for a moment.'

Peter opened the boot and struggled to remove one of three five gallon Jerry cans, 'Shine it on the filler please Guy.'

He inserted a funnel then with a grunt tipped the can up and sent the Petrol gurgling into the tank, 'All done that should do us for the rest of the journey' he said throwing the empty can back into the boot.

It was now pitch black but it still didn't deter Peter from speeding along with only a faint glow directly in front from beneath the headlight covers to guide him.

He slowed and squealed to a halt as a line of red lights shone at them across the entire width of the road. Peter felt down beside him and produced a Pistol, 'Can't be too careful these days' he said as a figure approached.

He rolled the window down, 'Hello chaps I'm Samuel Knight change of plan I'm afraid'

'Samuel its Peter I didn't recognise you in the dark how the dickens are you?'

'Peter lovely to see you again I'm dandy thank you. Now the change'

'Where the hell are we off to now?' Guy asked somewhat angrily, 'Glasgow?'

'You must be Major Guy Robins'

'I am so what's the change?'

'Nothing drastic Guy you'll be taken out into the North Sea by a Trawler from Hull. S-148 will be waiting for you just north of Owers Bank'

'How far is Hull from here?'

'Less than an hour I would say. We'll take them from here Peter thanks for your help and I hope we'll meet up again soon'

'So do I Samuel you owe me a drink'

'Do I indeed? Well I must repay that the very next time I see you.'

Samuel led them to their next transport. Guy took one look at it then winked at Harry under the dim lights of the army truck. 'Now my dear chap' he started in an extremely posh accent, 'this really won't do will it Chumley Warner?'

'No it won't Mister Graveson not at all' Harry played along, 'we my good fellow travel in Jaguars not scruffy old army waggons'

'Well it's either that or walk. Your choice.'

'Bleeding hell Guv this is nice 'aint it?' Harry said laughing.

Peter rather out of breath came rushing up to the truck, 'Your tools Guy you left them in the car.'

This gave Guy quite a jolt. Perhaps Harry was right perhaps his memory is failing. Forgetting the tools would've been a disaster. With this in mind he mentally started to go through the finer points of the exercise to make sure he'd covered everything.

'You're quiet Boss anything the matter?' Harry asked as they bowled along in the truck

'No not a thing Harry I'm just going through the bits we need to complete that's all.'

Within the hour they were in Hull where the lorry pulled in alongside a small Trawler moored at the jetty, 'This chaps is your transport out into the North Sea for transfer to S-148'

'What's with the motorbike?' Guy asked noticing one

strapped down on the upper deck

'You'll be dropped off in Dorfhaven in the early hours, possibly on the old jetty but your pickup will be much further along the coast so the bike, which incidentally is a genuine German Telephone Engineers model will I think come in quite handy'

'I guess it's still too risky for them to stay alongside in Dorfhaven to wait for us?'

'You guess right Guy they risk their necks every time they're just about anywhere. So good luck to you both and I hope to see you on your return.'

Guy and Harry settled down in the small cabin as the Trawler put to sea, 'So what are you really worried about boss?' Harry asked

'Nothing Harry honestly. If there were you'd be the first to know. Now I suggest we get some sleep.'

The transfer to S-148 and the crossing went without a hitch and they came alongside the Jetty in Dorfhaven at dawn. There was an autumn mist rolling across the silent Harbour causing a slight chill in the air. Dozens of cranes struggled aloft to continue their journey south for the winter. A dog barked for a few moments but then the Harbour was left in peace. The sun was shining brightly but the heat had gone, the clouds in the distance hinted that rain could be on the way.

Guy kick started the bike, the sudden noise disturbed more cranes to noisily struggle their way up into the sky heading south. A lone figure wandered along the quay towards them. He doffed his hat bade them good morning and passed by.

'Hop on Harry' Guy whispered just above the bikes engine noise, 'we should be able to get this done in an hour or so.'

They motored up the hill and after having their papers inspected drove onto the base. Guy parked the bike by the Motor Store wall, 'That's a good start' he muttered, 'no bloody phone.' A Soldier walked by, 'Have you any idea where the phones gone?'

He shrugged his shoulders, 'How the hell should I know do I look like a telephone operator?'

'I just thought I'd ask that's all'

'Well ask at the exchange they should know.'

Once he was out of earshot Harry came up close to Guy, 'What the hell we supposed to do now Boss?'

'The wires are still here so I guess it'll be alright to connect this number one thing onto it'

'We haven't got much choice have we?'

Guy pushed the wires into the connections and tightened them up then removed the tape and stuck it to the wall, 'Exchange next I think.' He looked at the crude map that had been sketched out for them, 'just around the corner in block E.'

The telephone exchange Operators were quite surprised of their visit, 'We've not reported problems so why are you here?' The Supervisor demanded rather aggressively

'So you obviously don't know about line twenty-eight then?'

'What about it?'

'The phone seems to have disappeared that's what' Guy explained quite abruptly

The Supervisor shrugged her shoulders, 'No idea where it's gone. It's so rarely used we'd not notice'

'That may be so but it's got to be terminated or it could cause a lot more trouble.'

The Supervisor nodded then wandered off. Guy removed the back panels. It was as he'd feared an untidy tangle of wires. Fortunately the connections were numbered but it was almost an impossibility to uncover and see them. After what seemed an age he managed to locate and wire together the required lines, 'We've not been here before so could you direct us to the way down to the Pens'

'What do you need to do down there?'

'Their phone only works now and again so we've been told to check it out to make sure it works every time'

She pulled a face of indifference, 'There's a lift down the corridor past that door, another outside on the other side of this building or if you're feeling very fit the stairs are beside each of the lifts'

'Thank you that's all we needed to know.'

A few minutes later after another identity check they stood in the enormous space of the Submarine Pens. Two U-Boats were being serviced, men crawling all over them with the sound of windy hammers clattering against metal hulls. They quickly found the phone and attached box number two then used the lift and thankfully out into the fresh air,

'So far so good Harry' Guy whispered confidently, 'all that's left to do is collect the motorcycle scoot along to the pickup zone and we're home and dry.'

As they rounded the corner a Naval Rating was pushing the motorcycle towards them,' I guess this belongs to you?' He said noticing the logo on their overalls,

'It does yes. So what are you doing with it?'

'Moving it out of the way so it doesn't get damaged'

'From what?' Guy retorted, 'it was only up against the bloody wall'

'It was yes but most of the wall's being taken down to make a doorway and this' he shoved it towards Harry who was closest, 'was in the way.'

They both heard the sound of a heavy vehicle whining to a stop, 'we'd better take a look Harry.'

It was their worst fear. The wall was being dismantled by a dozen brown overall clad men with hammers, chisels and bolsters overseen by a Petty Officer who was leant up against the Lorry smoking a cigarette shouting occasionally to have two other men wearing blue overalls moving faster to throw the bricks into the back of the lorry, 'And what do you two want?' He demanded throwing the stub down and grinding it into the tarmac with his foot

'We've just fitted a terminator box to that telephone point'

'Oh that grey thing you mean? I guess it'll be in the back of the truck somewhere'

'Won't be much good though' one of the blue overalls said as he threw an armful of bricks up onto the lorry, 'they had to bash it off with a chisel. I'll look for it if you like'

'If you would please otherwise we'll get charged for it.'

He hopped up onto the lorry climbing down a couple of minutes later with what looked like a flattened Spam tin, 'I told you it wouldn't be much use but you're welcome to it.'

Guys' heart sank. The mission was now a complete failure; surely it couldn't get any worse. He chucked it into his tool bag nodded to the Petty Officer then he and Harry walked back to their motorcycle, 'One thing's for sure Boss' Harry whispered, 'there's no bloody way I'm coming back here'

'Me neither Harry and that's definite.'

They were just about to leave when it started to rain, 'Hang on a minute Boss I saw some raincoats hung up behind the door we came out of. Won't be a tick.'

Harry's coat fitted perfectly, Guys a might too small but it would do.

The rain stopped so they pulled over and folded the coats up stuffing them into the tool bag.

'Well on track Boss' Harry said with relief as he saw S-148 speeding along towards the pickup, 'with luck I reckon we'll get there at the same time as they do.'

Suddenly the ground around them erupted up into hundreds of dusty spirals a Mosquito with guns still blazing skimmed overhead then turned sharply towards the sea sighting a far more attractive target. S-148 under full power swung wildly from port to starboard to throw off the attack. Guy and Harry watched in horror as a single bomb arched down striking amidships. S-148 seemed to lift clear of the water before being blown apart into thousands of pieces that scooted across the water like flat stones on a mill pond finally coming to rest in amongst the smoking debris. The Mosquito turned then at almost sea level sped off towards home.

Helmut Keller was leading a small wing of ME109's back to Norden from a North Sea patrol when he witnessed the Mosquito attack. Ordering the wing home he peeled off and swooped down towards the fleeing Mosquito easily catching up with his updated 109 now capable of four hundred and ten knots. The Mosquito was easy prey, shells slammed through the thin fabric shattering the instrument panel to shreds cutting off one of the engines leaving the other with oil and smoke belching out spluttering its last. Desperately short of fuel Helmut reluctantly swung away and returned to base without knowing the fate of his victim but content that at best they would have to ditch into the sea long before reaching England.

'So what do we do now Boss?' Harry asked completely dejected

'Well there's little point in going any further so I guess we may as well go back to Dorfhaven and have a long think about it'

'I noticed a Gasthaus in the village just before we took the road up to the base. Looked as though it had a pretty good Bier Keller attached'

'Typical of you to notice such things Harry'

'Well to be honest Boss it was only because of a very pretty young Fräulein sitting at one of the tables.'

'Well' Guy said laughing as he picked up the motorcycle and kick started it into life, 'let's hope she's still there.'

For a change Helga was waiting for Otto to turn up at the Bier Keller. There was a distinct chill in the air heralding winter would be all too soon upon them. She hated the winter months as snow would like every year frequently block the road between the Fort and the Base preventing her and Otto meeting up. January and February were normally the worst but last year it started in December.

Otto wandered over to her table, 'Sorry I'm late but there was an incident along the Norden road'

'What happened then?'

'English bomber sunk an S-Boat then one of our boys shot it down. Two beers please Johann' He shouted fearing that Johann was just about to disappear from behind the bar, 'anyway how are you?'

'I'd feel better if I'd got a kiss'

He leant forward and kissed her passionately 'Sorry'

'You two can pack that up' Johann joked thumping the glasses down on the table, 'anymore of that and I'll send you down to the Windmill Rooms.'

Otto casually looked up as two men in overalls entered. A flicker of recognition crossed his mind but he dismissed it until Helga leant forward and whispered, 'Don't you think that tall one has a remarkable resemblance to the Officer who rescued me from the cells?'

'I was just thinking the same thing but it can't be can it?'

'Probably not.'

Guy ordered a beer each and they sat down. He looked over at Otto and smiled, 'Getting cooler now'

'It is yes' Otto replied still not sure if he could be that Officer, 'have we met before?'

'I doubt it unless you've been to Bremerhaven recently. We're only here to sort out some telephone problems at the base.'

Dieter came dashing in, 'They've captured those English flyers that sunk the S-Boat. They'll be bringing them passed here in an hour or so on their way to Norden'

'Why Norden for God sake?'

Dieter smiled, 'Going to the Airbase for a surprise meeting with the Pilot who shot them down. Well that's what I was told anyway'

'Who by?' Otto asked always wary of Dieters information

'Lieutenant Berger'

'Then I guess it may be true'

'It bloody well should be he's head of security'

'Is he going with them?'

'No those two goons from security will be taking them. And best of all they're going to use Eva Maas's car'

'Bet she didn't like that'

'That's an understatement Otto she was still shouting and screaming at Berger when I left.'

A plan started to form in Guys head. A long shot, in fact a very long shot, 'Finish your beer Harry' he whispered, 'we've got a plane to catch'

'Ugh?' Guy nodded to Otto as they left, 'So does he know you Boss?'

'He suspects he does yes. He's Otto Steiner the guy who begged me to rescue his Fiancée from the cells'

'Oh shit will he say anything?'

'Very doubtful Harry I know too much about his Fiancée and her family's lineage'

'Okay' Harry replied hoping he was correct in his assumption, 'but what do you mean about catching a plane?'

Guy kick started the motorcycle, 'We're going to hijack that car release the Airmen borrow a plane and fly home'

'Oh is that all Boss? And there's me thinking it was something stupid.'

Flight Lieutenant Christopher Smith and Flight Sergeant Tom Lane were led out from the cells and ushered into the back seat of the car. Lieutenant Berger declined the offer of an armoured car escort in the belief that it was highly unlikely either the prisoners or anyone else would cause problems during the journey.

People came out onto the street to watch as they slowly passed through, some booed others threw small stones until one hit the driver who bellowed a host of obscenities before speeding off.

Guy and Harry were waiting some miles along the road

with their weapons of choice a hammer and a screwdriver from the tool bag.

They heard the car approaching as the driver crunched the gears changing down to make the hill. Harry stood in the middle of the road and flagged them down. This was the messy part of their job; a part neither of them had any taste for but war demanded it from them. With a single blow Harry's hammer smashed the guards' skull as Guy thrust the screwdriver deep into the drivers' throat. They dragged the lifeless bodies to the edge of the road and threw them into the scrub ensuring they were well hidden from view before returning to the car. Both Airmen were shocked at the speed and ferocity of the attack. They'd heard the rumour that bands of disgruntled Russians were operating in this part of Germany allegedly capturing both German and Allied personnel only agreeing to return them for money, 'So what do you want with us?' Christopher demanded defiantly, 'do you speak English?'

'Of course we speak bloody English' Harry shouted crossly, 'who the hell did you think we were'

'Russian Bandits'

'Russian what?' He shook his head and laughed, 'Bandits whatever next?'

Guy stepped forward, 'I'm Major Guy Robins Royal Marines and to answer your question what we need you for is to fly us home which we think is only fair since you shot at us on our motorcycle and then sunk our transport'

'That Boat?' Guy nodded, 'That was one of ours? How on earth could we know?'

'You couldn't and to be honest it was only a matter of time before something like that happened to them'

'But they were our own men we killed?' he said exhaling loudly, 'God forgive us.' He paused for a second to cross himself, 'I'm Flight Lieutenant Christopher Smith by the way and this is Flight Sergeant Tom Lane. Now you said that you needed us to fly you back home so' he looked around him, 'what in?'

Harry stepped into the car, 'I'm Sergeant Harry

Langford Royal Marines and that Flight Lieutenant is the problem. We've got to steal a plane from the Germans.'

'How the dickens are you going to do that?'

'Ah well fortunately I leave all the difficult bits to the Boss'

'Well Major?'

'Firstly we've got to get to the Airfield at Norden and see what's to be had.'

Guy dumped the car in a wood half a mile from the Airbase, 'Do you have a pen and paper Christopher?'

'A pencil yes and Tom has a flight note book'

'Excellent' Guy said, 'I only need one page.' He started to scribble a note. Harry looked a bit confused, 'Sorry but I really can't resist it' He said passing it to him.

My Dear Eva, It was most kind of you to lend us your beautiful motorcar. You will be glad to see that unlike your lovely boat Meerjungfrau it has suffered no damage at all.

'You're not going to sign it then Boss?'

'I think she'll guess don't you?' He replied smiling broadly,

'What have you written Guy?' Harry translated it for their benefit, 'So what happened to her boat?'

'We sort of blew it to bits' Harry replied, 'as you'd imagine she was none too pleased about it.'

'We'd better move on' Guy declared picking up the tool bag, 'we'll need to view the airfield in the light to see what we can borrow'

'Isn't the place well guarded?'

'It wasn't the last time we went in'

'We even managed to borrow a car that time' Harry added, 'ran out of bloody petrol though.'

From a small wood they could look across the airfield. It was getting dark but still light enough to see the aircraft. Christopher leant in towards Guy, 'That one next to the

ME109 is their new type Dornier fighter bomber'

'Can we all fit in?'

'I reckon so Guy'

'We need to be sure Christopher'

'When one like it was shot down over the North Sea four chaps were picked up by our Air Sea Rescue'

'Okay then that's the one we'll take. I assume you'll be able to fly the thing?'

Christopher smiled, 'Well there's only one way to find out.'

Tom wasn't quite so keen on the idea, 'The thing is that we accidently sunk one of our boats because it was dressed up as German'

'Your point Tom?'

'Even if we manage to get the thing airborne we'll be flying a German plane into England. I think the Spitfires will have other ideas don't you?'

'He does have a point Guy'

'Let me worry about that. As long as you can get the radio working I can deal with it'

'What's our plan Boss?'

'See that hut over there? We'll stay in there until about an hour before dawn then get these two into the aircraft to sort out the controls; you'd better stay with them to translate the switches. In the mean time I'll get up to the Tower and convince the night watch to let us go'

'I think I can give you better odds Boss. Have you still got that notebook Tom?' He handed it over, 'Before it gets too dark you tell me the controls you need and I'll translate it into German for you then I can help the Major to do the convincing'

'We'll only need the pre-flight stuff because hopefully' he gave the thumbs up 'you'll be back to help us with the rest.'

It was easy to scale the fence and make their way over to the small wooden building. Guy pulled the door open and fell backwards as a couple of dozen or more snow shovels toppled out onto him. He got back to his feet surprised that the crash hadn't alerted anyone,

'They seem pretty darn confident don't they?' Christopher whispered, 'not terribly well guarded at all.'

They quietly stacked the shovels behind the hut and squeezed in. With a bit of organisation they managed to sit down, 'You two better get a bit of sleep Harry and I will keep watch.'

Guy squinted at his watch; the luminous hands were still just visible showing six-thirty, 'Wake up chaps it's time for us to make our move.'

They crept as low to the ground as possible and made their way to the parked Dornier. Tom located the hatch and both he and Christopher climbed up and into the cockpit. Guy and Harry crossed the field and tiptoed up the metal steps waiting by the door for a second or two before bursting in shouting at the top of their voices. To their surprise there was only one man in the Tower who'd obviously been asleep as he was still stretched out between two chairs. Guy grabbed him and pulled him to his feet, 'What do you want?' He squeaked terrified for his life,

'There's a cupboard here Boss'

'What's in the cupboard?' Guy demanded, 'quickly Lad I've not got much time'

'Flight Logs, just Flight Logs' he replied still shaking violently,

'It's locked Boss'

'Where's the key?'

The Lad pointed to a box on the wall, 'In there number eight'

'If it fits it'll be your lucky number.'

Harry found the key and unlocked the door. Guy pushed the Lad inside, 'One peep out of you and you'll not be so lucky, do you understand?'

The Lad still terrified just nodded. Guy pulled the door shut and locked it then threw the key under a desk.

They ran as fast as they could over to the Dornier. Christopher and Tom had completed their checks,

307

'Moment of truth' he said starting the starboard engine. He let off the brake and started to taxi hoping he could remember where the runway started. Tom started up the port engine which took an agonisingly long time to fire up but responded to full power as they surged along. Christopher had to judge the takeoff speed then hope his conversion to kilometres per hour was about right. As the speed reached two-hundred he lifted the nose and under full throttle lumbered into the sky as the sun rose behind them, 'Tom's sorted the radio out Guy'

'Good' Guy said squeezing up beside them. He took the microphone 'tune to two one eight two for voice please?'

'Done'

'Will you write down our destination and where we'll approach the coast?'

Tom passed him the details he required,

'Peter this is Guy Over'

'Go ahead Guy Over' Guy breathed a huge sigh of relief at the instant reply,

'Harry is on his way home at' he looked at the Altimeter, *'four thousand three hundred feet towards Flamborough Head for Breighton Airfield. You'll see that Jerry, repeat Jerry is on his own and will require an immediate escort. Over*

'Received and hopefully understood Guy. Peter Out.'

The moment they were in sight of the coast a squadron of Spitfires surrounded them weaving back and forth inspecting every part of the Dornier.

Christopher prepared for the landing, 'Better hold on tight' he warned laughing nervously, 'it's likely to be a bit bumpy.'

For Harry who was sat in one of the two gun positions the ground seem to be coming up at a phenomenal rate but relaxed as it didn't appear to be bothering Tom or Christopher. They hit the runway hard, bounced hit again and again but this time sticking but slew round as they struggled with the brakes, 'Should we clap Boss?' a very relieved Harry asked

'I think it'll be better to get out' Christopher shouted releasing the hatch as black smoke started to pour out of the starboard engine.

All four men scrambled through and moved to a safe distance as with bells clanging loudly and men clinging on for dear life two trucks arrived and within minutes dealt with the overheated engine.

Another truck pulled up beside them, 'Our transport' Christopher announced smiling, 'after you.' They drove the short distance to a group of Nissan huts and came to a halt opposite one with a couple of easy chairs and a settee outside. The escort Spitfires had landed before Christopher so his chums were slumped into them clapping to welcome him home, 'Oh damn it's the Wing Commander' Christopher moaned, 'I'll be in for it now.'

'Welcome home Christopher where's my bloody aircraft?'

'Traded it in Sir'

'So I see and who have you brought with you? A couple of Germans I guess' the Wing Commander boomed noticing the German telephone company logo on Guy and Harry's overalls, 'get the guards to escort them away'

'I don't think so Wing Commander' Guy replied standing his ground, 'I'm Major Guy Robins Royal Marines and this is my Sergeant Harry Langford'

'We were taken Prisoner after we ditched Sir and these two rescued us' Christopher interrupted 'then they stole the Dornier and here we are. Oh and I must report that we bombed and sunk one of our own boats, the very one that Guy and Harry were supposed to use to get home'

'Before you blow a gasket' Guy intervened as the Wing Commander's face filled with displeasure, 'it was an S-Boat that we captured in Alderney still flying the German war ensign so neither of them can be blamed for that'

'It doesn't alter the fact that the only reason for being there was to take photographs. So how did you get brought down?'

'Jumped by a 109 Sir'

'While you were gloating over sinking the boat no doubt. Anyway both of you report to Rodger for your debriefing.' He turned to Guy, 'so where will you be off to?'

'I need to be back in Portsmouth as quick as possible to make my report'

'Is the training Spit still around Alistair?'

'Yes Sir'

'Right rustle up McGoogan tell her she's needed straight away.'

'I've got family in York Boss can I have a few days off to see them?'

'Of course Harry ring in again next week'

'We have a Lorry that goes there daily I'll arrange for them to give you a lift if you like?'

'Thank you Sir that'll be just the job.'

'McGoogan will fly you directly to Portsmouth Guy. I assume there's still some grass to bounce on? I'll phone through and let them know you're coming.'

Cecily McGoogan was twenty-six years old just five feet two the youngest Daughter of an Irish Father and Scottish mother so was well used to conflict long before the war. A cheerful individual with short curly ginger hair emerald green eyes and face full of freckles. Almost completely flat chested she'd been cursed with over large hips and legs for the rest of her slim body. An aunt used to often unkindly say that "She was a poor wee lassie who could easily have the bairns but no be able to feed them." Married for four years her husband Dougal was serving in the Far East. She'd heard nothing from him since January and hoped upon hope that he'd managed to escape before the Japanese took Singapore in February.

She smiled sweetly at Guy, 'I guess you're the chap who needs a lift to Portsmouth?' Guy nodded, 'and you've been on the end of a Parachute?'

'Too many times yes'

'The ground crew will strap you in the back seat.

310

They'll harp on about the life raft under the seat but as we're not going anywhere near water just grin and nod they seem to like that.' She giggled, 'I've never had the heart to tell them that there isn't one.'

Guy squeezed himself into the Spitfires rear seat, the ground crew ever attentive ensured that he was strapped in correctly with oxygen and communication mask plugged in, 'Can you hear me Guy?'

'I can Cecily yes'

'Good. Time for the off.'

With the Rolls Royce Merlin engine at full throttle the Spitfire climbed gracefully into the air. Through his bubble of a canopy Guy could just see the movement of Cecily's head as she constantly scanned the horizon for any threats, 'Would you like to take over Guy?'

'Rather' he replied knowing the opportunity would never come again,

'Right place your feet on the pedals and take the control column lightly into your hands. Are you Married Guy?'

'No'

'Girl Friend?'

'Yes her names Pamela'

'Okay Guy just treat the control column as if it's Pamela. Gently, gently does it. Now keep your eye on the Compass it's just in front of the column keep it on one-seven-seven and the Altimeter is on the front panel just to your left keep that at four-thousand feet.' Within minutes the Spitfire started to move off course and descend, 'Calm down Guy you're far too tense just relax. Pull back a little on the column and use the right pedal to bring us back on course. That's it you've got it.'

After what seemed to be just a few seconds her voice came through the earphones, 'I'm taking control back now Guy. If you look down you'll see we're just passing over Farnborough. Should only be a few minutes now.'

Cecily brought the Spitfire down for a perfect landing and taxied round to a gate at the side of the field where a lorry was waiting to take him to the Barracks.

She waved enthusiastically as she opened the throttles and taxied away increasing speed lifting effortlessly into the air. Guy watched until it was just a dot in the sky.

Portsmouth

Commodore Warwick sat grim faced as Guy outlined the failed mission, 'I think it best Major if you get some sleep now and I'll arrange a meeting for everybody who's involved in Trojan Submarine. Shall we say thirteen-hundred tomorrow?'

The Commodore's staff spent the remainder of the day sending urgent messages and making telephone calls gathering them in from Plymouth London and Portsmouth. Anyone lucky enough to be on leave was recalled including Oliver who'd managed to get away for a few precious days with Pamela, 'This happens every bloody time we get together' he complained bitterly, 'I'm sure your father does it on purpose. I sincerely hope it is really urgent'

'So what could you do if it wasn't?' Pam asked pushing the cork back into the Thermos.

Oliver exhaled, 'Not a lot really. But you could'

'Nobody's said I've got to go back' she said rolling away as he feigned a punch then added playfully, 'but at least we haven't got to leave until tomorrow morning have we?'

They walked arm in arm across the lawn to the Hotel determined to make the most of the time left together.

The meeting was deemed important enough to involve Admiral Beaufort and sensitive enough to have two armed Royal Marines on the door.

Guy stood out front more nervous of talking to these people than he'd like to admit.

'Lady and Gentlemen' he started hesitantly, 'the transfer to Dorfhaven apart from a last minute change of departure point went well. We docked at the pier and unloaded the motorcycle and drove up to the Base. We found that the telephone against the Motor Pool was missing but the wire remained so I connected box one to the wire'

'That would still be perfectly okay' Elizabeth called from the back of the room,

'The exchange wiring gave a bit of concern as the numbers were hidden by the myriad of wires but counting across as I'd been instructed enabled the correct connection to be made. We then managed to access the U-Boat pens to attach box two and got back out without any problems only to discover that our motorcycle was being moved because the wall, the one I'd attached box one to was being demolished to make a doorway into the motor pool'

'And box one?' Elizabeth asked her brow creased

'Destroyed when they hammered it off the wall, so we decided to make our way to the pickup point but were briefly machine gunned by an RAF Mosquito which then turned its attention on S-148 scoring a direct hit'

'So what you're saying Major without going any further is that we will be unable to detonate the explosives once the decoy is inside the pens' Steven Boniface asked

'In a nut shell Lieutenant yes.'

'I think' the Commodore announced gravely, 'we're going to have to postpone this operation until we find another way of detonation'

'Surely we could use a timer Sir'

'We've already discussed that but we have no idea how long it will take the Germans to remove T102 from the beach and tow her in.'

Oliver suddenly had a thought, 'I think we can use a timer Sir'

'Go On'

'Have you got a chart of the area Sir?'

The Commodore scrabbled around in the chart cabinet finally digging one out and pegged it up against the black board, 'Will that do?'

Oliver walked to the front and taking a pencil from his pocket drew a straight line from the entrance to the pens and almost out to the Fort, 'If we stay submerged anywhere along this line we can easily see when T102 is just about to reach the doors which I understand take around four minutes to close so if we can find a way to start the timer at this point she should be well inside before she goes up.'

The Commodore contemplated this for a minute or so, 'Elizabeth?'

She stood up, 'Possible Commodore but not easy'

'Got to be fool proof you know yes fool proof you see' Admiral Beaufort professed, 'only one chance you see. Once they've got her inside that's it' then dropped back into silence which some could call snoozing.

'So Elizabeth is there any way that we can confirm that the signal has been received and the timer set?'

'That's a pretty tall order Commodore but we'll look into it'

'I guess we won't need the whip aerial after all Elizabeth'

'Such a pity Oliver' she joked, 'I just found one too'

'Don't tell me Alexandra Palace?'

'Damn you guessed.'

The Commodore interrupted the banter, 'We'll wait on your design team Elizabeth. What time delay would you suggest Oliver?'

No more than ten minutes Sir'

'So there you are Elizabeth just a piece of kit that will let Oliver know that it's set the timer and then ten minutes later detonate'

Elizabeth chuckled, 'Sounds easy when you put it that way Commodore but we'll see.'

'Only four weeks to come up with something'

'Hopefully we'll be back to you well before then with at least a prototype.'

Captain Wells coughed and stood up, 'So basically we

are now hinging the whole operation on something that Elizabeth and her team can come up with in time?'

'I have complete confidence that they can do it'

'I do as well but I think it a little unfair to put so much pressure onto them'

'We relish pressure Captain' Elizabeth said, 'they all work so much better. Two weeks and we shall have a solution that I can almost guarantee'

'Then you won't mind us holding you to that?'

'Not at all Captain.'

A week later Oliver had the opportunity for the one and only towing practice. It had to be attempted at night so that T102 could be covertly towed out from her berth at Dolphin by a Dockyard Tug then attached to Troy once out in the Solent.

The first test was the communication between them which went well but the tow itself not so good. Each time, even at low speed Troy slowed or stopped T102 ran into their stern which deterred Oliver from attempting any high speed tests in fear of damaging Troy.

'At this speed Sir it'll take about forty-eight hours to get to Dorfhaven'

'Not too much of a problem with that Steven but what could be is the fact that we couldn't safely work up enough speed to beach her. They've estimated at least twenty-five knots to wedge her in'

'We could still achieve that Sir' Oliver shot him an inquisitive look, 'well you explained to me Sir that we're to turn away blow the cable loose and let her pass by under her own momentum'

'Very true Steven but we're not going to get the opportunity to see how she handles at that speed'

'So what's new Sir? We can't test that the cable will part either. Mind you I'll agree at around ten knots for the entire route will leave us pretty vulnerable for attack'

'Exactly Steven. If Jerry has a rowing boat and a couple of grenades we've had it.'

The Tug took T102 away from them and Oliver brought Troy alongside. The Commodore was on the jetty eager to know how it went,

'Bloody awful Sir the best we can do is ten knots because T102 bumps up against our backside every time we reduce speed or stop'

'Make your report as quick as you can and I'll get it over to the Dockyard Engineers to see what they can come up with'

'Such a shame we lost Professor Landor and his team Sir'

'It certainly is. Oh by the way we've heard back from Elizabeth and she thinks they've come up with a solution. She'll be down in the next couple of days to have it fitted. Time for home and a well-earned drink don't you think?'

Oliver admired Elizabeth's solution but was sceptical that they could be sure that the signal had set the timer, 'We can only guarantee a delay of between six to ten minutes' she explained, 'the light we'll install on the conning tower will flash once when the timer activates'

'That's the bit that bothers me Elizabeth, don't forget I'll be looking through the periscope and depending what time they choose to move T102 it could be directly into the sun so I could well miss the light flashing just the once'

'The thing is Oliver you can transmit the code as many times as you like it's bound to pick one of them up'

'And of course' the Commodore added, 'once she's on the move we're in the lap of the Gods anyway.'

Oliver couldn't argue with that, 'What if they don't take her in for a while Sir?'

'If you feel they're taking too long just let us know and I'll arrange for some aircraft to go over and put a few bombs close by which I think should get their arses into gear.'

'Okay Sir. Anything from the Engineers about T102 bumping into us Sir?'

'Not yet no but I'm going over this afternoon to chivvy

them along if you'd like to join me.'

Rodney Gillespie a tall lanky clean shaven bald man of fifty years. As the newly appointed Workshop Foreman he was more than pleased to demonstrate their latest creation, 'The water version of air brakes' he said proudly, 'hydraulic of course.' He pulled the lever and with an ear shattering hiss both five foot left and right sections swung out,

'And that's going to stop a few thousand ton of submarine is it?'

'Dead in the water Commodore'

'When can it be fitted?'

'Later today as soon as we can get the boat over here'

'You can't do it at Dolphin?'

'Good God no it's quite an undertaking to get it in. I guess you wouldn't want it to leak?'

'We'd prefer not Rodney. You guarantee it'll be completed by tomorrow?'

'I can't guarantee anything but we'll make every effort to have it completed by then.'

As they walked back through the Dockyard the Commodore removed an envelope from his pocket and passed it to Oliver, 'The code and frequency' he said, 'so don't lose it.'

Oliver stuffed it into his pocket, 'I'll stow it in my cabin before I meet Pam'

'Are you home tonight?'

'I would think so yes Sir.'

Operation Trojan Submarine commences

The remaining weeks passed in a flash and it was time for Oliver to say goodbye to Pam, 'You make sure you come back' she said tearfully, 'if anything happens to you I'll kill you myself'

'There's no need for you to worry I'll be fine and back before you know it.'

317

With a final lingering kiss he went down Kings Stairs and onto the launch to ship him over to Dolphin. Pam kept waving until they disappeared behind the many ships moored in the Harbour.

Although they'd been parted on several occasions Oliver had always returned largely unscathed but suddenly she sensed a dreadful premonition that this time it would be different and end badly. Whatever she did or thought for the remainder of the day it wouldn't go away, permanently nagging at her mind. She confided in her Mother as soon as she got home, 'Don't be silly dear' she said, 'he'll be home right as rain in just a few days' time you just wait and see.'

As soon as dusk fell Oliver navigated Troy out of the narrow Harbour mouth and waited for the Tug to bring T102 out to them with her deadly cargo of explosives and thirty corpses now dressed in naval clothing and stored in the forward torpedo space.

The weather was perfect with little breeze and a slight swell so with T102 attached they dived and crept the speed up to twenty knots dropping back almost immediately as their tow rose up above them lifting Troy's stern making it almost impossible to keep to depth, 'Problem Roger?' Oliver called over the Intercom

'The planes operators are finding life a bit difficult Oliver they say they're not used to them any more what with Troy being all poshed up with single man operation. But not to worry we'll get the hang of it I'm sure.'

Fifteen knots seemed to be the optimum speed so they stuck to it for the next eight hours before encountering their first test when they had to traverse the straits of Dover. Within the hour they were clear and into the North Sea, 'Ready to try twenty knots again Roger?'

'Give it a go Oliver I'll shout if we get a problem.'

They surged ahead with an estimated arrival time off Dorfhaven at eighteen-hundred remaining submerged overnight then beach T102 at zero-five-hundred.

'I'm having difficulty holding course Sir' the Helmsman shouted urgently, 'the stern's being dragged again.'

Before Oliver had chance to use the Intercom it burst into life and Roger's voice boomed out, 'We've got a massive Hydraulic leak Oliver we'll have to stop and surface to try and fix it.'

Oliver slowed and guided them to periscope depth, 'Give a sweep on Radar Sumner.'

A few seconds past, 'Nothing within twenty miles Sir.'

'Surface.'

Oliver went in the dinghy with two Engineers over to T102. It was the first time he'd seen her in the light for quite some time and was rather amused to see that a large white ensign had been painted on the conning tower. He climbed down the after hatch the stench of hot Hydraulic oil was heavy in the air. He was greeted by Roger who was looking grave, 'We've found the leak but can't do bugger all about it. Come I'll show you.'

He led them aft to the plant room flat opened up a hatch and pointed, 'Down there just forward of the Bulkhead.'

Oliver squinted down, 'I see it yes but I'm sure one of the Engineers will be able to crawl in to repair it'

'I don't think that would be wise Oliver. Use the torch and take another good look.'

Oliver squatted down and shone the torch around the space, 'Ah I see the problem' he said handing the torch back to Roger,

'It's everywhere' Roger muttered, 'God only knows how many tons they've packed in even the Wardroom cupboards are stuffed full with it. It's going to make one hell of a bang that's for sure.'

Both Engineers were chatting quietly to each other, 'That should work Chief'

'I don't see why it shouldn't but it'll take a while'

'Have you got something Chief?'

'We have Sir. Crawly and I think that as the After

319

Torpedo rams aren't needed we should be able to use the tube to bypass the leak completely'

'How long will it take?'

'A good five or six hours.' Oliver drew in his breath, 'I'm sorry Sir but with all the explosives packed round we've got to take our time'

'Okay Chief you'd better get on with it. Roger we'll stay on the surface but push forward at five or so knots otherwise it's going to be pretty tight. I'll get a signal off to let them know what's going on.'

The work was completed and tested in just a mite over four and a half hours not a moment too soon as multiple contacts closing fast had been detected and reported by Sumner.

The remainder of the voyage was quiet, the weather kind and a complete absence of the enemy so with some relief they arrived off the coast of Dorfhaven at twenty-three-fifty just six hours behind schedule.

Oliver and Steven went through the beaching procedure for what must have been the hundredth time, 'I'm wondering if we will be able to make twenty-five knots Sir'

'I've had the same thought Steven so we'll make it twenty; we know that's achievable,'

Troy surfaced at zero-three-fifty and moved to two miles out from the beach, 'Everything ready Roger?'

'All raring to go Oliver.'

They surged forward managing twenty-three knots. The only guide they had was the waves breaking against the rocks either side of the Beach, 'Standby. Standby. Port thirty. Release the cable.' They all had to hang on for dear life as Troy spun round slamming into T102 with a deafening squeal of tortured metal before being dragged violently backwards coming to rest on the very sandbank Oliver had been so desperate to avoid,

'The bloody cable didn't release on time Sir' Rogers shouted above the creaking of the hull wedged securely in the sand.

Oliver ordered first fifty then seventy-five and in desperation one hundred percent power, 'We can't go on like that Sir we're down to twenty-percent battery life'

'Then start up the generator Chief' Oliver snapped.

Troy shook, shuddered and bumped but remained firmly wedged. The sky was gradually getting lighter as the sun made its way towards the horizon. Oliver decided to launch the dinghy to take the anchor out to deeper water in the desperate hope they could winch themselves clear. Twice it turned over with the weight but third time lucky managed to drop it at a hundred yards. The winch took up the strain but at first frustratingly started to drag the anchor but at last when all seemed to be lost it finally bit into the seabed and slowly but surely inched Troy forward, 'Ten percent power' Oliver called down, 'Twenty percent.' They almost lost their footing as Troy shot forward into deep water free at last.

Oliver looked at his watch, five-thirty-five, 'Get a party over to T102 and help them get everything organised.'

The sun finally peeped over the horizon bathing the cliff top in an orange hue. A mist quickly formed over the water T102's conning tower poked above it like a monster about to strike, 'How's it going?' Oliver asked over the Intercom acutely aware they were running out of time,

'We've just finished placing the bodies. Not pleasant'

'Okay but we've got to be away in the next few minutes so can you release anyone you don't need and send them back in the Dinghy.'

With the last body placed half in and half out of the forward hatch Roger ran back along the casing and dropped down into the after hatch reappearing a few minutes later coughing and spluttering. He leapt into the dinghy as the seaman paddled like fury to get back to Troy. Oliver got underway as soon as their feet touched the casing and dived the moment the dinghy was stowed and its crew safely below.

'I opened a sea cock and let water into the battery

space' Roger said, 'near choked me to death but it should add to the effect.'

In Portsmouth Commodore Warwick who'd stayed at his desk all night breathed a sigh of relief as the signal was handed to him to say that the beaching had been completed.

With a quick knock at the door the Dockyard Manager and one of the Engineers rushed in.

'Is there a fire or something' the Commodore joked, 'sit down and relax.'

They both sat on the edge of the seats worried looks on their faces, 'We think there may be a problem Commodore'

'Go on.' The Manager hesitated, 'spit it out man it can't be that bad'

'I'm afraid it is. We believe that the detonator boxes that the Irish chap left with us could've been mixed up when they were fitted'

'Mixed up? What do you mean mixed up?' The Commodore raised his voice, 'I hope you're not telling me that Troy may have the one meant for T102'

'And T102 have Troy's yes Commodore that's exactly what we're saying'

'Good God man how the bloody hell did that happen?'

'We don't know. We don't even know for sure that it did.'

The Commodore got up and went into the outer Office finding it empty, 'Where the hell is everybody' then grabbing the telephone, 'thank God somebody's still around' he bellowed as an operator answered, 'put me through to Southwick urgently.'

Oliver was in his cabin making up the Log when the Radio Operator put his head around the curtain, 'We've just had a weird signal Sir. Decrypted it twice but it's still the same.' He handed it over:

Possible mix-up urgent you check the Irishman's box of tricks. Yours must repeat must have the letter I on the case. If it has the letter P then use code INK and frequency 12.6 Megacycles to detonate T102 not PEN and frequency 8.4 Megacycles as in your envelope. Acknowledge.

'Does it make sense to you Sir?'

'It does yes. Will you ask the First Lieutenant to come to my cabin immediately?'

'Problem Sir?' Steven asked squeezing in behind the small table

'Certainly is' he passed the signal to Steven, 'one huge one.'

'Bloody hell Sir. Where is the box?'

'I've no idea but it's got to be connected to an aerial somewhere so we'll start in the Wireless office.'

They turned the Wireless office upside down and apart from unearthing a pint flask half filled with Rum that the operators had bottled to drink at a later date or more likely sell to the Dockyard workers when back in Harbour they found nothing.

After they'd left the Killick Sparky turned to his oppo, 'Christ the old man must be in a panic to ignore our stash'

'Must be that signal we got in'

'Didn't make much sense to me but the words mix-up and detonate is a bit of a worry.'

Oliver rushed back into the Wireless Office, 'Encrypt and get this sent off immediately.'

Please advise urgently where the Irishman's box of tricks has been fitted. We can't find it.

Friedrich Bauer pushed his bike up the hill towards Dorfhaven as he always did every single morning six days a week to collect the mail. He was a large twenty-four year old man and despite his daily cycling extremely unfit. Excused active service because of his mental disability he was renowned for his wild stories especially following his favourite leisure activity, drinking beer and plenty of it.

Finally reaching the top puffing and wheezing like an old steam engine he threw his bike down and sat on a low wall to rest before the much welcomed downhill run where he could just hold his feet out and cruise all the way down to Dorfhaven.

The autumn sun had lost much of its heat and a chilly off-shore breeze moved the morning mist around like a blanket being rolled back towards the sea. His bladder was still filling from his last night's visit to the local Bier Keller so he swung his legs over the wall unbuttoned his flies and peed as far out over the cliff as he could. The breeze picked up a little more and cleared the mist away from the beach. Friedrich scratched his head and stared for a moment at the Submarine below before the mist cleared enough for him to see the white ensign painted on the side, 'The British' he gulped, 'they're here, they're here.' He stepped back over the wall grabbed the bike and sped down the hill screeching to a halt outside Johann's Bar. Throwing his bike down he rushed in, 'The British are here' he shouted, 'on the beach with a Submarine'

'Of course they are Friedrich' Johann said laughing 'of course they are,'

Otto and Dieter wandered in, 'Two Coffees please Johann'

'You'll need more than coffee; Friedrich has just seen the British having a beach party'

'A submarine' Friedrich whined, 'stranded on the Beach'

'Only one Friedrich? I would've thought you normally see things in twos' Dieter said collecting the coffees, 'submarine my arse,'

'I don't know how you think them up' Otto added, 'it'll get you into trouble one day'

'I'm not making it up honestly come and I'll show you'

'What Beach?' Johann asked dryly

'Weststrand'

'Well if you think I'm going to climb up that bloody

hill for one of your stories Friedrich you've got another think coming'

'It isn't a story' Friedrich protested, 'I saw it with my very own eyes.'

Johann huffed and disappeared behind the bar,

'You believe me don't you?' He asked Otto and Dieter.

They looked at each other, 'You're always telling some story or other aren't you Friedrich?'

'It's true' he persisted, 'the British are on Weststrand. You go and have a look'

'Alright Friedrich but if you're lying they'll be trouble okay?'

'Why the hell are we doing this?' Dieter asked as they marched up the hill together,

'One day Friedrich is going to be telling the truth'

'It's not likely to be today. Submarine on the beach? I don't think......' They stared in amazement over the cliff, 'bloody hell he's right, the drunken bastard's bloody well right,'

'I think we'd better tell someone at the base don't you?'

'I reckon Lieutenant Berger is our best bet.'

In Portsmouth the Commodore swore as the engineer's telephone remained unanswered, 'For crying out bloody loud where the hell is everybody today?' He slammed the receiver down and stormed out of his Office, 'I'm going over to Engineering if anyone wants me' he said to his secretary as he rushed by.

The Engineers office was empty except for a young lad filing down a hunk of metal, 'Where have they all gone?'

The lad shrugged his shoulders, 'Dunno they all went off about half an hour ago'

'And they didn't say where?'

'Nope' the lad replied before getting back to his task of filing the metal down.

As he hurried out the Telephone extension bell clanged.

He looked back through the glass partition; the lad never moved but continued to file away at the metal. He went back in and grabbed the receiver, it as he suspected was for him, 'We've just had a signal Sir to say that the Germans have found T102 and small boats are landing troops onto her.'

He replaced the receiver deeply concerned that if he can't find the Engineers before they start moving T102 then what? He knew the onus would be upon him and him alone to abort the mission or take the chance that the boxes weren't mixed. So deep in thought he very nearly missed the Workshop Foreman walking the other side of the road. He called over to him 'Rodney isn't it?'

'Yes Commodore, Rodney Gillespie'

'Did you have anything to do with installing a radio controlled detonator box in Troy?'

He shook his head, 'I don't even know what you mean Commodore I've never heard of such a thing. Have you thought of contacting Elizabeth Hardy it's more her department for radio and electrical?'

The Commodore cursed himself for not thinking of contacting her before now. Of course she'd know.

'*To be honest Commodore I'm afraid I don't know where it was located. Professor Landor used his engineers to do it*'

'Couldn't you at least guess Elizabeth' he asked desperately, 'we're running out of time'

'*Well I know that the one in T102 is fitted in the conning tower*'

'You're sure?'

'*Well that's where it was when we fitted the timer*'

'I know it's a long shot but do you remember what letter was marked on it?'

'*Afraid not sorry*'

'Okay thank you Elizabeth. Goodbye.'

Petty Officer Helmut Brandt gingerly walked along T102's casing towards the forward hatch. He knelt by the lifeless body hanging through and gently shook it, 'Dead' he shouted to his men who were following. He indicated for the hatch to be opened falling back as the distinct smell of chlorine wafted through, 'Poor Bastards' he muttered, 'a real shitty way of dying.'

With both the forward and after hatches wide open the gas quickly cleared allowing the men access. Helmut respectfully dragged the body out through the hatch and carefully laid it on the casing before climbing down the ladder into the crew's messdeck. With his men behind him and MP34 machine gun at the ready he moved slowly along the narrow passageway lit only by the bulkhead emergency lanterns. He swept the curtain aside and peered into the Wardroom, 'Empty' he whispered back to his men, 'Empty in here as well' he called quietly looking into the Captain's cabin. They moved forward stealthily expecting any minute to be cut down by a volley of shots from the surviving crew. In a heart stopping moment they all threw themselves to the deck as a huge clatter sounded from the Galley. Helmut slowly crawled to the door and looked through, 'All clear' he called getting to his feet, 'another dead one'

'So what was the noise?' A young seaman asked still shaking nervously,

'The boat's settling into the sand so the pans must've tipped over that's all.'

They entered the control room where most of the bodies had been placed. Helmut lowered his MP34 and indicated for the rest to follow suite, 'I don't think anyone's left alive here'

'Can we leave then Sir I really don't feel comfortable here?'

'We can yes. There's nothing more for us to do.'

Oliver poked his head into the wireless office for what must've been the tenth time, 'Sorry Sir still nothing' the Killick Sparky said removing his earphones, 'I'll shout loud enough when there is.'

He returned to the control room, 'Periscope depth number one.'

'Heaps of surface contacts Sir' the Hydrophone operator called out, 'mostly small stuff.'

Oliver gingerly swung the scope round for a three-sixty sweep, 'Half the population of Dorfhaven must be out in their boats to gawp'

'That's going to be a bit of a problem Sir'

'It is Steven but with luck they may be cleared out of the way when they pull T102 off'

'Not much we can do if we don't know which code to use though is it Sir' he whispered,

'Not really no but we've still got a bit of time left.'

'Your reply Sir' the Killick Sparky shouted loudly

'Don't get too smart Leading Hand I've not forgotten the Rum' Oliver replied taking it from him,

Believe Irishman's box of tricks located in the conning tower. Acknowledge

A thorough search revealed nothing, 'What now Sir?'

'Well I guess it's a fifty fifty chance of getting it right'

'Excuse me Sir' Sumner chipped in, 'what exactly is it you're looking for?'

'A box Sumner with a small lamp on top'

'Like this one under my seat Sir?'

'Yes exactly like the one under your seat Sumner' Oliver replied gleefully.

They squatted down and attempted to see how it was marked but however much they tried they couldn't make out the letter, 'Cut the chair away from the deck' Oliver ordered.

Within minutes Sumner's chair was removed and thrown aside. 'I' Oliver shouted aloud 'They weren't mixed after all.'

'I suppose in future I'll just have to stand up to man the Radar then Sir' Sumner complained,

'I guess you will yes.'

Oliver poked his head into the Wireless Office and had them send off in plain language,

I found. Everything okay now. Nothing moved so far.

Gradually the fleet of small boats lost interest and by noon scuttled back into Harbour.

'Perhaps they'll wait until dark to move her'

'I don't see what they'd gain from that it'd be a damn sight more difficult. We'll wait until fourteen-hundred and let the Commodore know if nothing has happened.'

At fourteen-fifteen the Commodore put an urgent call into Air Commodore Hamish Dewar's Office, 'Hamish I need a squadron to pop over to Dorfhaven for us to chivvy Jerry up to move S102.'

Wing Commander Robert Thorpe most unusually walked into the briefing room at the same time as the crews of the Mosquito squadron, 'Right Gentlemen we've been called in to help the Navy.' He ignored the boos and jeers and carried on, 'They've beached a submarine off of Dorfhaven' an audible groan came from the crews, 'I know we've been over there a few times now but this is different'

'How different Sir?' Flying Officer John Wright asked,

'Much better for you John because the Navy doesn't want us to hit the target but bomb close enough for Jerry to panic and take the Submarine away into the Pens.' He looked at each of them in turn proud of every last one, 'Take off in half an hour; Navigators check with Nigel for the Target's position. And of course needless to say good luck and for God's sake don't forget to miss the bloody thing.'

Oliver watched as the Mosquito's swooped down one after the other and released their bombs sending columns of sand and water high into the sky. One bomb fell extremely close to T102 Oliver was convinced that she must be damaged by the shrapnel, 'God that was close'

'Too close and the thing could go up in a cloud of smoke where it stands' Steven muttered

'ME109's buzzing about now. Looks as though our chaps have shot off home'

'Well let's hope that it's done the trick'

'We'll find out in an hour or so' Oliver replied, 'High tide's up then.'

In Berlin Admirals Hans Klusmeyer, Manfred Tanenbaum, and Wolfgang Heidemann were in a huddle around the table. Manfred was first to speak, 'So Hans' he shouted holding up the signal, 'there's no doubt at all now. I have the feeling your Loch Ness Monster you dismissed so quickly has popped up on our beach in the form of the huge British Submarine that according to you couldn't exist'

'Okay' Hans replied 'I admit I was wrong it does exist but at least thank God I didn't promise to eat my hat if it did'

'Wolfgang you may as well let the Führer know all about it but certainly not' he wagged his finger, 'until I get to Dorfhaven or he'll try to take over and make a complete mess of it as usual.'

'You're going to Dorfhaven then Manfred?'

'Too bloody right I am. This my friend is a gift from heaven.'

Oliver stared through the periscope at T102 still silent and wedged on the beach, 'They still don't seem inclined to shift her. What the hell's wrong with them?'

'I thought the bombing would've stirred them up'

'So did I Steven but they're certainly taking their time.'

'Surface noise pretty heavy stuff Sir, red' Rogers reported then paused for a second before continuing, 'red one-seven-five.'

Oliver swung the periscope round, 'Well I'll be damned' he shouted, ' it's Nürnberg. My God how I'd love to put a couple of torpedoes into her. I can hear Commander Harvey shouting at the top of his voice from above, sink the Bastard, I couldn't you can. Now do it lad do it!'

In truth Oliver knew that there was no chance whatsoever of launching a torpedo because if the Germans even had an inkling of their presence they'd never move T102 in fear of her being destroyed.

'She's closing Sir'

'I think we'll have to make a move' Oliver said sending the scope down into the well, 'she's moving in far too close for comfort'

'Now or never Sir' Steven declared, 'high tide is just about now and we'll barely and I do really mean barely have enough depth to pass under Nürnberg.'

'What depth have we?'

'One-hundred and four feet Sir.'

Troy silently moved forward just a few feet above the sea bed and even less below Nürnberg's hull. The Chief Engineer rushed into the control room. 'We're shipping water Sir' he whispered

'Where?'

'After Torpedo space and Buffers store room Sir.'

'Must've been the collision with T102 Sir'

Oliver exhaled, 'That's the last thing we need at the moment Steven. What next?'

As if specially arranged to thwart their efforts the Killick Sparky poked his head into the control room, 'The HF Transmitter's on the blink Sir I think the ATU's knackered'

'Well get a spare from the...' Oliver paused for a second, 'Oh hell don't tell me the store's flooded?' He turned to Steven, 'What the dickens can we do now?'

Burt Entwhistle the Killick Sparky smiled. 'I know where we can get the spare from Sir'

'Go on'

'T102'

'Oh brilliant Entwhistle Perhaps we can ask the

Germans to bring it over to us'

'Well excuse me Sir but we're definitely not going to be able to transmit any codes if we can't fix it are we?'

'He's got a point Oliver'

'I know he has but how can we pull it off?'

Fred Sumner who'd heard the conversation dropped down from his position in the conning tower into the control room, 'If Burt's happy about it Sir I can row him over in the Dinghy and bring back the replacement.'

Oliver rubbed his chin unsure if he should sanction such a perilous operation, 'I don't think it'll be a good idea' he finally said shaking his head

'So have you got anything better Sir?'

'No I haven't Steven. But good God that's one hell of a risk they'd be taking'

'We're quite happy with that Sir' Sumner said looking at Burt who nodded his agreement.

Oliver took Troy two miles out before surfacing; the noise of the tanks blowing would've certainly alerted the watch keepers on the Cruiser. At twenty percent power they moved silently to less than a hundred yards of Nürnberg. The sky was overcast with no chance of the moon breaking through. They quickly unshipped the Dinghy and Sumner and Entwhistle dressed in black with faces boot polished climbed in and started to paddle away.

Oliver stood on the Bridge still worried about their safety, 'I still don't like the idea Steven'

'I don't think we had any other choice Sir I really don't.'

Sumner paddled as quietly as he could as they passed the Cruiser between the bow and anchor cable. They could clearly hear the conversations of the watch keepers on the deck above them. A few minutes later they bumped up against T102's hull. Entwhistle clambered up immediately flattening himself against the deck as a beam of light from Nürnberg's search light swept over the area. Sumner pulled the dinghy into the hull as close as he could and stretched out in the bottom. With the search light extinguished Entwhistle ran over the casing and down into the after hatch. It was eerie; most emergency lamps had gone out completely or provided such a low light that he permanently needed his torch to find his way around. Entering the Wireless Office he was shocked to find that the two corpses were still there slumped into the chairs. Pulling one away from the desk he managed to undo the thumb screws from the front of the HF Transmitter and extract the ATU. Holding onto it tightly he carefully picked his way along the dark companionway and back up the after hatch ducking down immediately as the searchlight beam cut through the darkness highlighting the area in a huge pool of light. To Sumner it'd seemed an age before Entwhistle reappeared with the ATU in his hand just managing to slide down into the dinghy before the next blinding beam shone across the area. The moment it was extinguished Sumner paddled as quickly and silently as possible back towards Troy passing once again between Nürnberg's bow and anchor cable. A shout went up from directly above chilling their blood but was quickly followed by raucous laughter. Somewhat relieved they pushed on until thankfully bumped against Troy's hull.

'How long will it take to fit?' Oliver asked much happier as both clambered unscathed through the hatch into the control room,

'Just a few minutes Sir' Entwhistle said waving it above his head, 'I knew we could pull it off Sir.' with that he disappeared into the Wireless Office.

Admiral Manfred Tanenbaum was furious, 'Why the bloody hell is the damn thing still on the beach?' He bellowed, 'And for God's sake get that Cruiser out of the way it's a bloody magnet for the British to attack.'

Lieutenant Berger who was unfortunate to be the Senior Officer on site attempted to justify his actions, 'I wasn't sure what to do Sir so I contacted our Commanding Officer'

'Who is?'

'Admiral Oskar Schröder Sir'

'So where the hell is he then?'

'I'm not sure Sir he went off with Miss Eva two days ago and said he'd be back next week'

'Miss Eva? Miss Eva who?'

'Maas Sir Eva Maas'

'His whore?'

'I'm afraid I can't comment on that Sir.'

Manfred scowled, 'On tomorrow mornings tide Lieutenant I want that boat pulled off the beach and towed into the Pens. You understand?'

'But Admiral Schröder said…'

'I don't give a damn what Schröder said or didn't say' Manfred shouted, 'The man is obviously an idiot. In the meantime get that bloody Cruiser out of here.'

'Sounds as if Nürnberg's on the move Sir' Rogers reported,

'Stand bye to dive. Twenty degree down bubble, two hundred feet. Dive.'

Troy glided down into the depths as Nürnberg passed overhead her screws pounding the water into froth, 'I feel pretty bad about having to let them go. Where ever Commander Harvey's ended up after crossing the bar he surely must be bawling out as loud as he can'

'We'll have another chance Sir that I'm sure of'

'I hope you're right Steven, I really do.'

The Chief Engineer rushed into the control room, 'Water's bucketing in now Sir we can't maintain this depth the pressure's too high'

'Can't the pumps cope?'

'Not a chance Sir no'

'We'll wait until Nürnberg's out of the way then we should be able to surface'

'If nothing seems to be happening with T102 Sir do you think we'll be able to go out a fair distance to assess the damage to the outer hull?'

Confident that T102 was staying put for the night Oliver took Troy thirty miles out. The Dinghy was launched and the Chief Engineer with the aid of two Seamen and half a dozen torches carried out the assessment he'd requested.

'I'm afraid it isn't good news Sir' he said clambering up to the bridge, 'there's a large gash about fifteen, twenty feet long just above the waterline Port side stern. The inner hull is less damaged but obviously much weakened. Too much pressure and' he drew in a breath, 'pop.'

'Large contact green four-five fifteen miles closing Sir' Sumner shouted down then cursing loudly fell off his chair which had only been temporarily replaced,

'That could be Nürnberg' Oliver said hopefully, 'if it is we should be able to take a crack at her out here.'

Oliver took Troy down and laid in wait at Periscope depth. Thirty minutes past before he was able to identify the contact, 'It is Nürnberg' he said happily, 'thank you Commander Harvey.'

At two thousand yards Oliver called off the range course and speed. Sub Lieutenant Jordan still tackling the Trigonometry using only his slide rule ordered his settings to be made, 'How many Sir?'

'Four' Oliver replied knowing full well that two would be quite sufficient,

'Four it is then Sir' Jordan replied more than a little surprise showing in his voice.

His stopwatch ticked the seconds down, 'Now!' He shouted as they felt the impact of four explosions one after the other.

Oliver looked through the periscope, 'No doubt about it on this occasion' he lowered the scope, 'they aren't going to be able to repair it this time that's for sure.'

'She's breaking up Sir' Rogers reported sliding one of his earphones away. Another enormous explosion reverberated through the water, 'Boilers have gone now Sir.'

'Okay job done let's get back to Dorfhaven' Oliver said

jubilant that he'd been able to destroy Nürnberg somehow squaring Commander Harvey's unsuccessful encounter.

At dawn four tugs left the port sailed round the headland and laid off of the beach. Two smaller craft moved in and attached four cables to S102's stern. The tugs took up the slack then with their powerful engines at full throttle stirring up tons of mud and sand from the seabed S102 shook and shuddered as if knowing her fate before reluctantly sliding astern into deep water.

An encrypted signal was immediately sent off to Fort Southwick,

T102 on the move. Troy standing by.

Oliver watched as two tugs moved positions and their cables reattached to the bow. He was surprised at the speed they moved and struggled to get into the best position to transmit the code, 'Steven give this to Leading Telegraphist Entwhistle and have him stand by.'

Entwhistle had already tuned the transmitter to 8.4 Megacycles as ordered and sat quietly contemplating that this simple three letter code in front of him he was soon to transmit would possibly kill tens if not hundreds of people.

Dieter and Otto rose early and walked down into the Village to witness the British Submarine being brought in. The morning was chilly with a strong northerly breeze, 'Wish I'd put my thick coat on now' Dieter moaned, 'I'm bloody freezing'

'Never mind Dieter we'll go in for a Coffee later. I don't think it'll take long for it to pass by.'

Luckily they found a good spot on the old pier before most of the residents turned out to watch giving a real carnival atmosphere to an otherwise ordinary dull working day.

A shout went up from those standing on the headland, 'I guess it must be on its way then'

'I bloody well hope so Otto' Dieter replied stamping

his feet.

With great ceremony S102 was slowly towed past. An Orchestra set up on the stern thumped out Handel's water music, Admiral Manfred Tanenbaum stood on the Bridge waving as the crowd started to applaud. A bugle sounded as the Kriegsmarine Ensign was unfurled which cracked like a whip as the breeze caught it streaming it out in a shimmering red, white and black towards the crowd who clapped and cheered even louder.

Oliver squinted through the periscope into the morning sun as the tugs rounded the headland and slowly moved towards the Pens, 'Send the code now Entwhistle and keep sending it.'

His hand shaking a little he tapped out PEN PEN PEN. Repeating it over and over again in sets of three until Oliver shouted through for him to stop.

'Well that's it Steven there isn't much else we can do but wait and hope there's a big bang in a few minutes.'

Otto and Dieter walked the short distance to the bar, 'Helga not with you today Otto?'

'No all the roads and transport shut down for this Submarine business'

'You saw it go by then?'

'We did indeed' Dieter answered for him, 'and it even winked at us'

'It what?' Otto scoffed, 'Sounds a bit like one of Friedrich's tales'

'A light flashed from the Bridge didn't you see it?'

Before Otto had chance to answer the bottles on the bar clanked loudly together then tables and chairs shook before a deafening blast tore through the crowded streets. People screamed out as hunks of concrete bricks and earth crashed down. The bar windows shattered throwing shards of glass into the bar as an enormous slab smashed straight through the canvas cover onto the outside tables reducing them to scrap, 'Into the cellar quickly' Johann shouted above the sound of debris falling onto the roof, 'I didn't hear the siren did you?'

Fifteen minutes later they emerged from the cellar still convinced that there had been an air raid, 'Good God what type of bombs are the British using these days?' Johann asked looking at what remained of his pristine bar, 'What a mess.' All the bottles were smashed on the floor, beer was still oozing out of a damaged barrel, 'All ruined' he said shaking his head, 'and I'll bet you anything you like that it was in revenge for the Kriegsmarine bringing that British Submarine in. Why the bloody hell they didn't just leave it there for the English to bomb it like they wanted too I don't know.'

Friedrich Bauer rushed in through what used to be a door blood trickling down his cheek from a deep cut on the top of his head, 'The Submarine Pens have been smashed to bits' he shouted still breathless, 'The base you two work at has fallen right down inside and there's nothing left up there, nothing. And before you shout at me I'm telling the truth come see for yourselves.'

Oliver was ecstatic as he watched the hill above the Pens almost visibly swell and lift up before disappearing into the void below. Clouds of dust enveloped the Village but dispersed quite quickly with the northerly breeze, 'Well Gentlemen I don't think they'll be repairing U-Boats at Dorfhaven any time soon.' The men cheered, 'so let's be off home and bugger the rules Chief splice the mainbrace' wild cheers came from every quarter of the boat, 'and please make sure that Leading Telegraphist Entwhistle and his mates not only drink this Tot but share out their stash with the rest of the men but not before he sends this off. Plain language will be fine.'

Operation Trojan Submarine completed successfully. God save the King.

'Aye aye Sir I'll get to it right away.'

'I think the Officers could do with a drink as well Steven'

The Chief Engineer put his head through the open hatch, 'Don't forget Sir much deeper than a hundred and twenty feet and we'll leak like a sieve.'

Helga sat on her bed in the Woman's Dormitory at Fort Kruger tears pouring down her cheeks. They'd all heard the massive explosion from Dorfhaven and saw the huge pall of black smoke shoot high into the air even temporarily blotting out the sun. Rumours were rife that the whole village had been wiped out by a new bomb developed by the Americans and dropped by the British to test it for them.

She dabbed her eyes dry with a white lace handkerchief monogramed in pink at the corner; one of a pair bought for her by Otto. She squeezed it tight against her lips and started to sob again.

Klara Engel rushed in and came straight to her. Sitting next to her on the bed she put her arm around her, 'Don't worry too much Helga, Otto will be fine you wait and see'

'But they say the whole place has been destroyed by a huge bomb'

'When we're back on shift ask old starchy knickers what happened she always knows what's going on'

'That's not for another four hours'

'Trust me Helga Otto will be fine.'

'Good God Gerber have you messed the bed or what? Early for your shift for once. Look everyone Gerber isn't even out of breath today, no rushing in at the very last minute, it must be a miracle.'

Helga ignored her Supervisor Oda Hahn's taunts and still tearful went along to take over from her opposite number, 'Everything all right Helga?' she asked

Helga shook her head, 'I think Otto might've been killed in Dorfhaven'

'I'm sure he'll be okay but ask Oda if you can take the shift off I'll cover for you.'

Helga smiled, 'That's sweet of you but I think it'll be better with something for me to do'

'Okay but if you change your mind then send for me.'

Helga was desperate to try and contact Otto but Oda seemed to be constantly at her shoulder, 'You seem worried about something Gerber. Lover boy given you the push has he?' Oda snarled still cruelly taunting her

'I think he may have been killed at Dorfhaven' Helga replied her eyes welling up.

Oda leant right down and whispered in her ear, 'Then try and contact him'

'You know?' Helga completely surprised whispered back

'Of course I do Helga I'm not stupid. I have someone I love and miss so desperately and would do the same if I could. Now get on with it but still keep it from the others okay?'

Oda grinned moved away and got on with some other work. Helga pulled out her piece of paper. Seeing Otto's lovely clear writing she prayed that he would be alive to write out the next set.

She turned the dial to 12.6 Megacycles, tuned the aerial to maximum power and sent her code.

INK INK INK

On Troy Sumner hung down through the hatch, 'This bloody box keeps flashing Sir.'

THE END

TIME CURE:

NORWEGIAN KEY:

TROJAN SUBMARINE

Lightning Source UK Ltd.
Milton Keynes UK
UKOW02f0016100316

269944UK00004BA/124/P